The Infinity War

The Predecessors

Book 2

Blair C. Howard

The Infinity War by Blair C. Howard

Print ISBN: 979-8-9988024-9-2

Cleveland, TN, USA

This book is for the dedicated sci-fi fans who loved the first book in this trilogy, The Last Station, and for those who didn't.

Chapter 1

New Horizons

Admiral Frances Drake stood on the *Transcendence* 's observation deck, watching New Geneva Station take shape against the stars of Alpha Centauri. She felt every rivet being welded, every quantum connection being made, every crystalline neural pathway being installed. The station grew like a living thing, its hybrid design nothing like the clean geometric lines that had once defined human engineering.

Eighteen years. Eighteen years since Earth's transformation had spread humanity across a dozen star systems. Each world had developed its own unique way of evolving consciousness. The *Transcendence* itself showed this new reality—her flagship existed in normal space and quantum dimensions at the same time, its crystalline hull shifting between solid matter and pure energy as needed.

"Admiral," Commander Martina Vasquez approached across the observation deck's neural-responsive floor. Her footsteps made no sound on surfaces that adapted to her presence. At twenty-eight, Martina represented the generation that had grown up with the transformation. Her consciousness worked naturally across multiple quantum states. She'd developed alongside humanity's evolution rather than adapting to it, making her perfect for bridging Drake's evolved awareness and crew members who kept more traditional human perspectives.

"The morning reports are ready," Martina continued, her neural implants connecting directly with the ship's information systems. "We've got updates from seventeen colony worlds, three deep-space exploration missions, and..." She paused, her expression shifting as troubling data reached her enhanced senses. "Some concerning political developments from Earth."

Drake accepted the data stream through their quantum link. The information flowed directly into her consciousness rather than requiring visual displays. The diversity of human advancement never stopped amazing her. The Kepler Colony had developed atmospheric consciousness—its cities existed as living organisms that could think and feel. New Singapore operated through quantum economics, where intention became currency and desire shaped reality. Each world explored different aspects of transcendence while staying connected through the expanded Predecessor network.

But the reports also carried darker news. Director Rebecca Hayes's Purist movement had gained significant political support on Earth and several core worlds. They advocated for "evolutionary restraint" and preserving baseline humanity. Their latest rallies drew millions of supporters who feared becoming unrecognizable to their own families. Drake had watched the broadcasts with growing concern. Hayes's rhetoric increasingly portrayed evolved humans as potential threats to "true" humanity.

Senator Aleksandr Volkov's Transcendent faction pushed for unlimited consciousness expansion. They argued that clinging to human nature limited their species' potential. Volkov himself had evolved beyond recognizable human form. His consciousness spanned multiple quantum dimensions. His appearances in the Senate required specially built interface chambers, since his transcended awareness could overwhelm baseline human minds through direct contact.

The philosophical divide had real consequences. Three colonies had created "evolution-free zones" where transformation technology was banned. Two others had declared themselves "Transcendence territories" where baseline consciousness was actively discouraged. The Titan research stations reported increasing conflicts between differently evolved research teams who could no longer communicate effectively.

"The Senate vote on the Evolutionary Oversight Act is scheduled for next week," Martina reported. "Director Hayes's faction argues that uncontrolled transformation threatens human identity. They're proposing mandatory consciousness monitoring and intervention protocols."

Drake accessed the proposed legislation. The Act would establish "consciousness safety limits" enforced through neural implants that could override individual choice. Citizens who exceeded approved evolution parameters would face mandatory reversal procedures.

"What's the Transcendent response?" Drake asked.

"Complete deregulation," Martina replied. "Volkov's faction has proposed the Unlimited Advancement Initiative. No restrictions on consciousness enhancement, mandatory evolution education for all children, and state support for transcendence research. They argue that imposed limitations are a form of species suicide."

Drake reached out through the ship's quantum field, feeling her crew's varied responses to this information. Lieutenant Torres maintained baseline consciousness by choice. He viewed his unenhanced awareness as essential for tactical analysis. Commander Vasquez had evolved enhanced pattern recognition that made her invaluable for strategic planning, but sometimes left her struggling to relate to individual crew concerns. The engineering teams operated through collective consciousness during complex operations, their individual identities merging temporarily for maximum efficiency.

The diversity created both strength and tension. During the recent Proxima Station crisis, the crew's varied perspectives had enabled solutions that no single consciousness type could have achieved. But daily operations required constant translation between different forms of awareness. Some crew members felt isolated by their evolutionary choices.

"What's Senator Volkov's counterproposal?" Drake asked, having already processed the relevant files.

"Complete deregulation of consciousness enhancement," Martina replied. "His faction wants to eliminate all restrictions on evolutionary research and development. They argue that imposed limitations prevent humanity from achieving its true potential."

The political implications extended beyond Earth. The Outer Planets collective consciousness had declared neutrality in the debate, arguing that their group-mind perspective made individual choice irrelevant. The Jupiter orbital cities supported limited evolution, viewing their enhanced workers as necessary for survival in harsh environments. But the deep-space colonies increasingly aligned with the Transcendent's. Their isolation made traditional human connections less relevant than adaptation to alien environments.

Through the observation deck's displays, Drake watched New Geneva Station's construction continue. The facility represented a compromise between competing philosophies. It was advanced enough to support evolved consciousness while maintaining compatibility with baseline human needs. Its architecture combined crystalline growth patterns with conventional engineering, creating spaces that could adapt to different forms of awareness.

The station's central core pulsed with Predecessor technology. Its quantum processors had been enhanced by almost two decades of human innovation. But the outer sections remained recognizably human in design, providing familiar environments for those who chose minimal transformation. The balance felt precarious, like trying to build bridges across philosophical chasms that grew wider each year.

"Admiral," Lieutenant Commander Sarah Kim's

voice reached them through the neural link from the communications center. "We're receiving a priority transmission from Professor Zhang at the Advanced Evolution Institute. He's requesting immediate consultation on what he calls 'unprecedented deep-space phenomena.'"

Drake felt a familiar chill in Zhang's tone. The brilliant scientist had guided humanity's early transformation, but his warnings typically preceded significant crises. "Transfer the call to my ready room," she instructed. "Martina, you're with me. Kim, maintain standard operations but be ready for tactical alerts."

The ready room existed partially outside normal space-time. Its quantum architecture allowed private communications that conventional monitoring couldn't intercept. Drake had designed it herself, incorporating lessons learned from eighteen years of commanding evolved humans who sometimes required privacy beyond traditional concepts.

Professor Zhang's image materialized, his consciousness spanning multiple dimensional states as he spoke. Age had transformed rather than weakened him. His awareness operated across timescales that allowed him to perceive patterns invisible from shorter-lived perspectives.

"Frances," Zhang began, his form shifting between solid appearance and pure energy patterns. "We've detected unknown signatures at the edge of the Perseus Arm. The patterns are artificial, definitely technological, but they don't match any known Predecessor or Enemy configurations."

Drake focused on the data Zhang sent their link. The

signatures showed consciousness evolution, but along paths completely different from humanity's hybrid development. Whatever had created these patterns had achieved technological transcendence without biological components—pure information consciousness.

The mathematics behind these entities staggered Drake. Human consciousness worked through enhanced neural networks, but these aliens were living equations. They could rewrite reality through pure calculation. Their approach vectors suggested they viewed space-time as something they could reshape rather than a fixed framework.

"The temporal analysis is disturbing," Zhang continued. "These signatures suggest civilizations that achieved this state millions of years ago. They're approaching human space with what appears to be deliberate intent. But Frances, there's something else. The signatures are evaluating us. Every human consciousness they encounter is being analyzed, categorized, and judged according to criteria we don't understand."

Martina processed the information, her expression growing troubled. "First contact protocols?" she asked, though her tone suggested she already understood the implications.

"Unknown," Zhang replied. "But the approach patterns suggest they're studying more than just our transformation. They're studying our choices—why we maintained biological elements, why we embraced chaos alongside order, why we chose hybrid existence instead of pure technological transcendence. Their scanning patterns focus specifically on the balance points in our consciousness evolution."

Drake felt a chill. The approaching entities weren't just alien—they represented an alternative path to transcendence that humanity had rejected. If they viewed biological consciousness as primitive or dangerous, first contact could become an existential crisis.

"Time to contact?" she asked.

"Based on current approach vectors, approximately six months," Zhang replied. "But Frances, there's something else. The quantum signatures are affecting our own networks. Some of our most advanced consciousness research is showing unusual responses to their presence."

"What responses?"

Zhang's expression grew troubled. "Acceleration. Human consciousness exposed to these signatures is evolving faster than normal parameters. Not dangerously, but differently. Following patterns we haven't seen before. The Kepler atmospheric consciousness reported new thought-forms appearing spontaneously. New Singapore's quantum economists are detecting mathematical structures that shouldn't exist in their reality models."

The implications hit Drake like a bolt of lightning. If alien consciousness could influence human evolution merely through proximity, first contact would involve more than communication or diplomacy. It might trigger a transformation that humanity wasn't prepared to handle. Or a transformation that their political factions would interpret as either salvation or catastrophe.

"Recommendations?" she asked.

"I'm convening the Advanced Evolution Institute's

emergency protocols," Zhang replied. "We need to understand these signatures before contact becomes unavoidable. But Frances, this isn't something we can study from a distance. We need direct interface with advanced consciousness—people who can maintain their identity while exploring alien patterns."

Martina brightened. "Kai," she said. "We need Kai."

"Among others," Zhang confirmed. "But yes, Kai's transcended consciousness makes her our best interface with alien awareness. The question is whether she's willing to risk further evolution when we don't understand the consequences."

Drake made her decision with the certainty that had carried her through the Enemy crisis. "I'll speak with Kai personally. Martina, prepare the *Transcendence* for departure to Earth orbit. We need to coordinate this response at the highest levels."

"What about the political situation?" Martina asked. "Both the Purists and Transcendent's will want to control any alien contact."

"Which is exactly why it needs to be handled by people who understand balance," Drake replied. "We've spent eighteen years proving that evolution and preservation can coexist. Now we need to show that wisdom to beings who might have made different choices."

As Zhang's image faded, Drake reached out through the ship, feeling her crew's varied responses to the new situation. Some were excited by the prospect of contact with advanced alien consciousness. Others feared that such entities might view humanity's hybrid evolution as dangerous or primitive. The political divisions that had seemed manageable now carried new implications.

The observation deck's displays showed New Geneva Station nearing completion. Its hybrid architecture represented humanity's attempt to balance innovation with preservation. But would that balance prove wisdom or weakness when facing beings who'd chosen absolute technological transcendence?

"Admiral," Commander Vasquez said quietly, "what if these entities view our biological elements the same way the Enemy viewed chaos? As contamination that needs to be eliminated?"

Drake watched the station's construction continue. Its crystalline sections grew slowly while the conventional areas provided familiar anchor points. "Then we'll have to prove that diversity creates strength, not weakness," she said. "That evolution requires finding ways for all paths to strengthen each other."

The *Transcendence* began its turn toward Earth. Her quantum drives hummed as the ship's hybrid architecture shifted, optimizing for high-speed transit.

Through the observation deck's enhanced displays, Drake monitored their approach to Earth's systems. Luna's surface now hosted three major research facilities. Their crystalline structures were visible from space as they pulsed with experimental energies. The orbital habitats had evolved from simple living spaces into complex ecosystems. They supported various forms of awareness, from baseline human families to collective consciousness communities that shared everything except individual identity.

Earth itself glowed with energy. Its cities had been restructured around the needs of evolved consciousness while maintaining spaces for those who chose minimal enhancement. The planetary network processed thoughts and emotions as readily as data, creating a global awareness that somehow preserved individual identity within the collective experience.

But the approaching alien entity cast unfamiliar shadows over these achievements. If beings who'd chosen pure technological transcendence viewed humanity's biological elements as contamination, Earth's hybrid evolution might appear as a fundamental error rather than wisdom.

"Admiral," Commander Vasquez said quietly, "the crew's worried about what contact with the aliens might mean for our own unity. If these entities support either extreme—pure preservation or unlimited transcendence —the political factions could use their presence to justify radical positions."

Drake could see the truth in Martina's observation. First contact with beings who'd achieved pure technological consciousness would inevitably influence humanity's internal debates. The Purists might argue that alien transcendence proved the dangers of unlimited evolution. The Transcendents could claim it demonstrated the necessity of abandoning biological limitations.

"Then we'll have to prove that wisdom lies in balance," Drake replied. "Not just to the aliens, but to ourselves. We can't let external pressure destroy what we've built through eighteen years of careful growth."

The drives hummed with increasing power as the *Transcendence* accelerated toward Earth.

The planet's networks buzzed with debate about the approaching contact. Different factions prepared responses that reflected their philosophies about consciousness and evolution.

The Purist strongholds were implementing "consciousness protection protocols"—shielding technology designed to prevent alien influence on human evolution. The Transcendent territories prepared "advancement acceleration programs"—systems that could rapidly evolve human consciousness to match alien capabilities. Both responses assumed that contact would require choosing sides rather than finding synthesis.

But Drake had learned through eighteen years of command that the most dangerous challenges required the most creative solutions. Humanity's greatest strength was their ability to combine different approaches into something greater than the sum of its parts.

Eighteen years of evolution had created wonders beyond imagination. Now they would discover whether those wonders were strong enough to survive contact with entities that had chosen different paths to transcendence.

Drake watched the displays as they approached humanity's homeworld. Cities pulsed with hybrid energy, their networks supporting billions of minds. The planet glowed with evolutionary fire visible across dimensional space—a beacon of diversity in a universe that might demand conformity.

Chapter 2

Fractures

THE *TRANSCENDENCE* DROPPED OUT OF QUANTUM space at Earth's orbital edge. Her crystalline hull shifted from pure energy back to solid matter as Drake's consciousness connected with the planetary defense networks. She immediately felt the tension radiating from humanity's homeworld—a storm of conflict that made the quantum fields themselves unstable.

"Admiral," Lieutenant Commander Sarah Kim reported from the communications station, "we're receiving priority signals from Earth Defense Command, the Senate, and..." She paused, checking her displays. "Seventeen separate faction representatives, all demanding immediate meetings."

Drake reached out through the ship's networks, sampling the chaotic data streams flowing from Earth's surface. The planet's network had once been a harmonious blend of individual and collective awareness. Now, it carried currents of fear and rage that made her senses recoil.

"Status of the Senate vote?" she asked, though she'd already accessed the relevant files.

"Postponed indefinitely," Martina Vasquez replied, joining Drake on the observation deck as Earth grew larger in the displays. "The situation went bad fast after we left Alpha Centauri. What started as peaceful demonstrations became riots, then pitched battles between Purist and Transcendent supporters."

The images flowing through the quantum link made Drake's awareness burn with concern. Geneva's government district had become a war zone. Baseline humans wielded consciousness-dampening weapons against enhanced protesters whose psychic abilities created reality distortions. The New Geneva Incident—seventeen baseline humans killed by uncontrolled psychic feedback from panicked enhanced protesters—had triggered martial law in twelve major cities.

"Director Hayes is claiming the deaths prove enhanced humans pose existential threats to baseline populations," Martina continued. "She's calling for immediate implementation of consciousness safety protocols, regardless of the Senate vote."

Drake accessed Hayes's latest broadcasts. The director stood before crowds of baseline humans. Her rhetoric had sharpened considerably since the Geneva incident, portraying evolved consciousness as an infection that threatened human survival.

"And Senator Volkov's response?" Drake asked.

"Complete mobilization," Martina replied grimly. "His faction claims the Geneva deaths were caused by Purist consciousness dampening weapons, not psychic feedback. They're demanding immediate retaliation against what they call 'consciousness terrorism.'"

The political divide had become something approaching civil war. Through Earth's networks, Drake could feel the planet's consciousness fracturing along evolutionary lines. Baseline human areas had become echo chambers of fear about their enhanced neighbors. Transcended communities developed group-mind patterns that viewed individual consciousness as primitive limitation.

"Admiral," Commander Walsh said as he approached from his tactical station. "I'm detecting unusual military deployments. General Aguirre has mobilized Earth Defense Forces, but their positioning suggests internal security rather than external defense."

Drake sighed and shook her head, then connected with Earth's military networks. She felt the tension among forces split between competing loyalties. General Rupert Aguirre commanded Earth's Defense forces, but his commitment to Hayes's Purist faction was becoming increasingly obvious. His deployment patterns showed troops prepared for consciousness suppression operations rather than conventional military action.

More concerning were the signatures Martina detected beyond Earth's immediate area. The Outer Planets Collective's military forces, led by Admiral Chen

Ju, had begun "defensive preparations" that looked suspiciously like invasion planning. Their shipyards were working around the clock, producing vessels that rivaled Earth's most advanced technology.

"The Collective's alliance with Volkov's faction is becoming overt," Martina reported, tracking multiple intelligence streams. "They're claiming that Hayes's proposed Evolutionary Oversight Act would give Earth authority to forcibly modify enhanced humans in colonial territories. Effectively, it gives her the right to impose consciousness control throughout human space."

Drake felt the implications of such an act. The political crisis had evolved beyond philosophical differences into territorial conflicts that could destroy human civilization. The Outer Planets Collective was asserting its right to exist beyond Earth's regulatory authority.

"Landing clearance received from Earth Defense Command," Lieutenant Kim announced. "They're directing us to the military spaceport rather than civilian facilities. The security condition is elevated."

Drake watched the displays as they approached Earth's orbital infrastructure. The civilian stations hummed with normal activity, but the military platforms bristled with weapons that had never been intended for use against human targets. The very architecture seemed to reflect the planet's fractured state—civilian areas flowing with organic curves while military sections displayed rigid geometric precision.

Their descent through Earth's atmosphere revealed the scope of the crisis. Major cities showed clear divisions between consciousness types. Purist areas were surrounded by dampening field generators, while Transcendent districts pulsed with quantum energy visible even from orbit. The planet that had once symbolized unified human evolution now resembled a patchwork of incompatible realities.

"Admiral," Vasquez said quietly as they approached the military complex, "there's something else. Corporate intelligence suggests that Titan Industrial has been selling consciousness technology to all factions. CEO David Park is profiting from the conflict while positioning his company as essential to human survival."

Drake nodded. Martinez's analysis rang true. Corporate quantum signatures filled the conflict zones, suggesting that Titan Industrial's technology was present in both Purist dampening weapons and Transcendent enhancement systems. Park had turned human division into a business opportunity.

The *Transcendence* settled onto the military spaceport's landing platform. Her hybrid systems adapted to Earth's gravity and atmospheric conditions. Through her neural link with the ship, Drake felt the vessel's relief at returning to familiar space, but also its unease at the chaotic quantum fields surrounding them.

"Security escort approaching," Lieutenant Kim reported. "General Aguirre personally, along with what appears to be a mixed unit of baseline and enhanced personnel."

Drake prepared for departure while monitoring the approaching military force. Aguirre himself maintained baseline human awareness by choice, but his escort included enhanced individuals whose loyalty to Earth

Defense Force overrode their evolutionary status. The combination created interesting dynamics that even her enhanced senses found difficult to read.

The airlock cycled open, revealing Earth's atmosphere carrying scents that triggered memories of pre-transformation life. But underneath the familiar odors lay something else—the chemical signatures of fear, conflict, and the ozone smell of consciousness-dampening weapons recently discharged.

General Aguirre approached with full military bearing, providing a stabilizing influence among his enhanced escorts. Despite his Purist political leanings, he maintained professional respect for Drake's command authority.

"Admiral Drake," Aguirre began. "Thank you for responding so quickly. The situation has deteriorated beyond our initial assessment."

Drake read the general's emotional state without appearing intrusive. His baseline consciousness carried genuine concern for human unity alongside his commitment to the Hayes faction. Unlike some Purist leaders, Aguirre wasn't motivated by fear of enhancement. He believed baseline consciousness provided necessary grounding for military decision-making.

"Brief me on the Geneva incident," Drake requested as they walked together toward the command complex. The military base showed signs of recent expansion, with new consciousness-shielded facilities designed to prevent psychic interference with critical operations.

"Seventeen baseline humans killed when enhanced protesters lost control of their abilities," Aguirre said, his tone carefully neutral. "The enhanced individuals claim they were responding to consciousness-dampening weapons, but witness accounts suggest the psychic discharge was a spontaneous reaction to crowd pressure."

Drake accessed the security recordings from the incident, feeling the chaotic quantum signatures that preceded the deaths. The enhanced protesters had indeed been subjected to dampening weapons, but their fatal response appeared uncontrolled rather than deliberately hostile. Fear and confusion had created a feedback loop that turned a peaceful demonstration into tragedy.

"And Director Hayes's response?" Drake asked.

"Immediate implementation of consciousness safety protocols in all government facilities," Aguirre replied. "Mandatory neural monitoring for any enhanced individual entering sensitive areas. She's arguing that the Geneva deaths prove enhanced consciousness poses unacceptable risks to baseline humans."

They entered the command complex through security barriers that scanned Drake's consciousness signature while maintaining respectful protocols for her rank. The facility demonstrated impressive engineering—spaces designed to accommodate both baseline and enhanced personnel without compromising either group's operational effectiveness.

The main briefing room contained holographic displays showing real-time monitoring of Earth's political situation. Drake processed the data streams, building a comprehensive understanding of the crisis scope. The images revealed a planet fracturing along consciousness lines, with each faction preparing for conflict.

"What's the disposition of the Outer Planets Collective's military preparations?" Drake asked, noting Aguirre's reluctance to discuss colonial challenges to Earth authority.

"Admiral Chen Ju has mobilized significant forces," Aguirre admitted. "Their shipyards are producing vessels with capabilities that exceed our intelligence estimates. More concerning, they've established contact with the Titan Belt Confederacy and other outer system settlements that Earth's government barely acknowledges."

Drake accessed the intelligence files about the Titan Belt Confederacy, discovering communities that had evolved in isolation beyond any central authority. Some had achieved collective consciousness across entire asteroid habitats. Others had created hybrid human-AI entities that Earth's legal framework didn't recognize as citizens.

"Do you have an estimate of the Confederacy's capabilities?" she asked.

"Unknown," Aguirre replied, his baseline awareness unable to process the quantum signatures that enhanced consciousness could detect. "Our sensors show massive energy outputs from their habitats, but we can't determine if those represent weapons, research, or something else entirely."

Drake could feel the true scope of the challenge facing Earth's government. The Outer Planets Collective was asserting the right to evolve beyond Earth's ability to govern them. When enhanced humans could exist across multiple reality states, concepts of citizenship and territorial control became meaningless.

"What's Senator Volkov's current status?" Drake asked.

"He's under protective custody," Aguirre replied carefully. "His appearances in the Senate require specially constructed interface chambers, and after Geneva, we can't guarantee his safety in baseline human areas. His consciousness can overwhelm unenhanced minds through direct contact."

The irony wasn't lost on Drake. The political leader advocating for unlimited consciousness evolution had evolved beyond the ability to safely communicate with the baseline humans he claimed to represent. Volkov's transcendence showed both the potential and the problems of uncontrolled consciousness development.

"What about corporate involvement?" Drake asked, though she'd already detected Titan Industrial's quantum signatures throughout the crisis.

Aguirre's expression darkened. "David Park has been selling consciousness technology to all factions while claiming corporate neutrality. His private security forces include enhanced humans loyal only to Titan Industrial, creating a third power center with unclear objectives."

Drake processed the implications while monitoring the ongoing crisis through Earth's quantum networks. Corporate consciousness technology filled both Purist and Transcendent operations, suggesting that Park was profiting from human division while positioning his company as essential to any resolution.

"What's Park's endgame?" she asked.

"Unknown," Aguirre replied. "But intelligence suggests he's been in communication with entities outside human space. Titan Industrial's consciousness technology incorporates principles that don't appear in our research databases."

The revelation sent chills through Drake's enhanced mind. If Park had been receiving alien consciousness technology, his involvement in the crisis took on darker implications. The corporate leader might be preparing humanity for something more than political reconciliation.

"There's more," Aguirre continued, accessing classified files through his command interface. "Intelligence reports suggest Park's technology is specifically designed to create compliance. Enhanced individuals using Titan Industrial modifications show decreased resistance to external influence while maintaining the appearance of free will."

Drake recoiled at the implications. "He's creating controllable enhanced humans," she said.

"That's our assessment," Aguirre confirmed. "The black-market neural modifications spreading through the outer colonies promise instant transcendence but often result in psychological dependency. Users become addicted to continuous enhancement, requiring regular updates that could include behavioral programming."

The scope of Park's manipulation became clearer as Drake processed the intelligence data. Titan Industrial had engineered specific consciousness vulnerabilities that made enhanced humans dependent on corporate technology.

"Tell me about the addiction cases," she said. "What's their current status?"

"They appear to be forming underground communities in asteroid habitats and abandoned stations," Aguirre replied. "They exist on the outer edges of human space, where regulation is impossible. Some have evolved beyond recognition, becoming entities that barely qualify as human but possess capabilities our forces cannot counter."

Drake accessed the surveillance data about these addicts, watching as they moved through environments that would kill baseline humans. Their evolution had followed paths that Titan Industrial guided rather than natural development, creating beings optimized for corporate objectives rather than human flourishing.

"You're looking at Park's private security force," Aguirre explained. "Enhanced humans loyal only to corporate interests. They've shown abilities that exceed our military enhancement programs while maintaining perfect discipline and coordination. Intelligence suggests they're prototypes for a new kind of consciousness—technically advanced but completely controllable."

The briefing room's displays shifted to show a tactical analysis of Titan Industrial's forces. Their enhanced soldiers operated with an efficiency that approached AI precision. But something in their quantum signatures suggested their consciousness had been fundamentally altered rather than simply enhanced.

"Admiral," Lieutenant Commander Kim's voice reached them through the neural link from the *Transcendence*. "We've received a priority communication from Professor Zhang. He's detecting acceleration in the alien signatures, and the quantum effects on human consciousness are intensifying."

Drake closed her eyes for a moment, feeling the weight of multiple crises converging. The political divisions threatening human unity, the alien contact approaching faster than predicted, and corporate manipulation that suggested preparation for unknown objectives. The factional conflicts had made the approaching alien contact secondary to immediate threats of human self-destruction.

But the crisis ran deeper than political disagreement. Drake detected patterns in the conflict; coordination beyond natural factional development. The timing of the Geneva incident, the simultaneous escalation across multiple worlds, the precise targeting of consciousness integration facilities—someone had orchestrated events to maximize division.

"General," she said, accessing classified intelligence networks, "the pattern analysis suggests an external coordination of these conflicts. The factional violence isn't spontaneous—it's being managed."

Aguirre reviewed the tactical data through his own baseline awareness. "Our intelligence has reached similar conclusions," he replied thoughtfully. "The attacks on the research facilities show knowledge of security protocols that only high-level access could provide. Someone with authority and high-level clearance in multiple factions is coordinating the violence."

"Corporate intelligence?" Drake asked.

"That's our primary suspect," Aguirre confirmed. "Park's Titan Industrial has contracts with both factions.

He's providing technology to Purist dampening weapons and Transcendent enhancement systems. His company is the only entity with access to both sides' operational planning."

Drake closed her eyes again, processing surveillance data about recent corporate activities. Titan Industrial's quantum shipments had increased dramatically over recent months, with advanced consciousness technology flowing to faction leaders across human space. Park wasn't only profiting from the conflicts—he was deliberately escalating them.

"The timing of the alien contact," she said, frowning, "it coincides suspiciously with the estimated peak of factional violence. If Park has been in communication with entities outside human space..."

"He could be preparing humanity for first contact on terms favorable to his own corporate interests," Aguirre finished. "Rather than a unified species response, we'd face the aliens as a group of divided factions, each dependent on Park's corporate technology."

Drake frowned as she assessed the implications. If Park had been coordinating with alien entities while creating human division, first contact could become a corporate takeover disguised as diplomatic necessity. Titan Industrial would position itself as an essential intermediary between humanity and a superior alien race.

"Is there any evidence of alien communication?" she asked.

Aguirre's fingers flew over the holograms, accessing deeper classification levels. "Circumstantial, but compelling," he replied after several seconds. "Titan

Industrial's technology incorporates principles that don't appear in human research databases. Our best scientists can't explain how Park's modifications achieve their effects. The quantum mathematics suggests external knowledge sources."

Aguirre's analysis was astute. Corporate consciousness technology showed capabilities that exceeded human understanding, suggesting either revolutionary breakthroughs or access to alien knowledge. Given Park's involvement in factional manipulation, alien assistance seemed more likely.

"What are the options for a military response?" she asked.

"Limited," Aguirre admitted with a wry smile. "Park's corporate headquarters exists partially outside normal space-time, protected by technology that makes a conventional assault impossible. His security forces have evolved beyond human limitations while maintaining absolute loyalty to the corporation and its objectives."

The briefing room's displays showed Titan Industrial's primary facility, a structure that seemed to phase between multiple reality states. Corporate quantum technology had created a fortress that existed in alternate spaces where conventional weapons couldn't function effectively.

"General," she said with command authority, "I need direct access to both Hayes and Volkov. The alien contact Professor Zhang detected is accelerating, and we need a unified response rather than factional conflict."

Aguirre's response showed genuine concern. "Admiral, both faction leaders are claiming the alien contact validates their positions. Hayes argues that alien influence proves humans need protection from uncontrolled evolution. Volkov claims it demonstrates the necessity for unlimited advancement."

Drake nodded. Aguirre's assessment was accurate. The approaching alien entity had become another weapon in the factional conflict rather than a unifying challenge requiring a coordinated response. Both sides would use first contact to justify their extreme positions rather than seeking synthesis.

She took a deep breath, turned her head to look at him, the crystalline enhancements around her right eye and forehead glowing. "Has Hayes made any specific preparations?" she asked.

"Consciousness protection protocols," Aguirre said. "She's implementing shielding technology designed to prevent alien influence on human evolution. Her scientists claim they can create barriers that preserve baseline consciousness from external modification."

"And Volkov?"

"Much the same," Aguirre answered grimly. "His faction is developing systems that can rapidly evolve human consciousness. He's arguing that only through transcendence can humanity negotiate as equals with superior entities."

Both responses indicated that factional thinking could destroy humanity before the aliens even arrived. Hayes's approach assumed alien contact would be hostile, requiring defense against consciousness manipulation. Volkov's faction believed alien superiority demanded human evolution to competitive levels.

Neither considered cooperation based on humanity's unique hybrid nature.

"What about the factional military preparations?" Drake asked.

Aguirre accessed the tactical analysis. "Hayes has developed consciousness-dampening weapons that can forcibly revert enhanced humans to baseline states. Field tests suggest they're effective against standard enhancements but may be less useful against deeply transcended individuals. Volkov's faction has created what they call 'evolution bombs'—devices that can rapidly transform entire populations through quantum consciousness fields."

Drake was stunned by what she was hearing. Both factions had created devices that could fundamentally alter human nature on a massive scale. Hayes's dampening weapons could eliminate enhanced consciousness entirely, while Volkov's evolution bombs could force transcendence beyond safe limits.

She drew herself up to her full height, put her hands behind her back and grasped her left wrist with her right hand. "What's the deployment status of these weapons?" she asked.

"Both sides claim they're purely defensive," Aguirre said. "But intelligence suggests active preparation for use against opposing factions. Hayes's forces have positioned dampening weapons near Transcendent population centers. Volkov's people have deployed launchers within range of Purist strongholds."

Drake couldn't believe what she was hearing. The

factions were ready to wage a war that could permanently alter human civilization.

"Is the civilian population aware of what's about to happen?" she asked.

"Barely," Aguirre admitted. "Both factions are presenting their weapons as protection against alien threats rather than tools for factional warfare. Baseline humans believe consciousness dampening will protect them from alien mind control. Enhanced populations think the evolution bombs will prepare them for transcendent contact."

Inwardly, Drake shuddered. The deception added another layer to the crisis. The citizenry was being prepared for war without understanding its true meaning—that they were the targets.

"Is there a timeline for deployment?" she asked.

"Based on current escalation patterns, days rather than weeks," Aguirre said. "The Geneva incident accelerated both sides' preparations. Hayes is arguing that enhanced humans pose immediate threats requiring dampening intervention. Volkov claims baseline consciousness inadequacy demands rapid evolution assistance."

Drake couldn't fully grasp the idea that humanity was about to destroy itself, even as alien contact continued to accelerate toward them.

"Then you and I will have to prove that wisdom lies in balance," Drake said to Aguirre. "Before external pressure destroys what we've built through eighteen years of careful growth."

She continued to watch the briefing room's quantum

displays. Earth's networks carried streams of fear, rage, and determination. The planet that had once demonstrated the successful merger of order and chaos now risked destroying itself through the very diversity that had been its strength.

The data streams revealed the scope of fragmentation across human space. Earth's major cities showed clear divisions between consciousness types. Purist areas generated dampening fields that made enhanced humans physically uncomfortable, while Transcendent districts pulsed with quantum energy that overwhelmed baseline senses. The middle ground where different factions had once coexisted was rapidly disappearing.

"Admiral Drake," Martina Vasquez's voice reached her through the neural link from the Transcendence, "we're receiving direct communications from both faction leaders. Hayes is demanding an immediate meeting to discuss what she calls 'consciousness protection priorities.' Senator Volkov is requesting a consultation about 'transcendence acceleration protocols.' Both are claiming your support for their positions."

Drake was acutely aware of the political pressure she was now under. Both faction leaders wanted to use her reputation and military authority to legitimize their extreme positions. She was in an impossible position. Her response would be interpreted as choosing sides in a conflict that required synthesis rather than victory.

"Schedule sequential meetings," she decided. "Hayes first, since Earth government protocol takes precedence. But make it clear that I'm consulting with all parties only about alien contact. I am not endorsing factional positions."

"General," she said, "what's the military's position if these weapons are deployed against civilian populations?"

Aguirre's expression showed genuine conflict. "The official policy requires us to prevent weapons of mass destruction deployment regardless of factional allegiance. But the legal status of consciousness weapons remains unclear. Are we protecting citizens from harmful modification, or preventing beneficial evolution?"

The question struck at the heart of the crisis facing human civilization. When consciousness itself became the battlefield, traditional concepts of protection and harm lost meaning. Hayes's faction viewed enhanced consciousness as dangerous contamination requiring elimination. Volkov's people saw baseline awareness as primitive limitation needing correction.

"And if both sides deploy simultaneously?" Drake asked.

"Chaos," Aguirre replied simply. "Consciousness dampening fields could cancel evolution bombs in some areas while amplifying them in others. The interaction effects are completely unpredictable. We could end up with regions where consciousness modification becomes permanent and irreversible."

Drake processed the implications.

The alien contact now rapidly approaching human space would find a species at war with itself. Unless Drake could somehow bridge the growing chasm between factions that no longer recognized each other as fully human.

But as she prepared to face the faction leaders, Drake detected something else in Earth's quantum networks—hidden patterns of coordination beyond factional manipulation. Someone was orchestrating events on a scale that exceeded even corporate ambition. The crisis threatening human unity might have origins that no one had yet discovered.

Chapter 3

Political Pressure

The secure conference room in Earth Defense Command had been hastily rebuilt to accommodate Director Rebecca Hayes's consciousness protection protocols. Quantum dampening fields hummed at the edge of hearing, creating an environment where enhanced awareness worked at reduced capacity. Drake felt the subtle pressure against her evolved consciousness like a weight on her thoughts, but her enhancements were far too advanced for it to have any serious effect on her abilities. The Predecessor's last station had seen to that.

Hayes entered the chamber with the bearing of someone used to authority. Her unenhanced senses were sharp with the clarity that baseline humans often developed to compensate for their limitations. At fifty-three, she carried herself with military precision despite never having served in the armed forces. Her dark hair was pulled back in a severe bun, and her pale blue eyes held the conviction of someone who believed absolutely in her cause.

"Admiral Drake," Hayes began, settling into the chair across from her. "Thank you for making time during this crisis. I trust General Aguirre has briefed you on the deteriorating situation?"

Drake nodded, analyzing Hayes's emotional state despite the dampening fields. The Director radiated genuine fear—not the political calculation Drake had expected, but sincere terror about humanity's future. Hayes wasn't manipulating public opinion for personal gain. She truly believed consciousness evolution posed an existential threat.

"The Geneva incident was a tragedy," Drake replied carefully, maintaining diplomatic neutrality. "Seventeen lives lost to what appears to have been uncontrolled psychic feedback."

"Uncontrolled," Hayes repeated, leaning forward with intensity. "That's precisely the problem, Admiral. Enhanced humans operating with capabilities they cannot predict or manage. The Geneva protesters didn't intend to kill anyone, but their evolution turned them into weapons they couldn't control."

Drake detected the patterns in Hayes's argument. The Director had built her political movement around genuine incidents where consciousness evolution had produced unintended consequences.

"The Oversight Act you're proposing," Drake said, "General Aguirre mentioned it includes provisions for colonial intervention. Can you explain the reasoning?"

Hayes activated a holographic display that showed incident reports from across human space. Mining accidents on Ceres where enhanced workers had lost control of their abilities. Transport failures when transcended pilots had evolved beyond the ability to interface with conventional navigation systems. Research station evacuations after experiments had created reality distortions.

"Consciousness evolution without proper oversight creates cascading failures," Hayes explained, her voice heavy with concern. "Each incident shows enhanced humans pose risks to baseline populations. The colonial territories have implemented enhancement programs without adequate safety protocols."

Drake reviewed the incident data, detecting patterns that baseline consciousness might miss. The reports were genuine, but they focused exclusively on failures while ignoring successful integration. Hayes was presenting accurate information through a lens that supported predetermined conclusions.

"What about the successful evolution programs?" Drake asked. "The cities that have achieved stable consciousness integration, the research facilities that operate safely with enhanced personnel?"

"Temporary stability," Hayes replied with conviction. "Admiral, I've studied the consciousness evolution data for eighteen years. The pattern is consistent—initial success followed by gradual degradation and eventual catastrophic failure. Enhanced consciousness is inherently unstable because it operates beyond human design parameters."

The director was presenting a coherent worldview

based on selective data and interpretation. Hayes genuinely believed that consciousness evolution would ultimately destroy humanity, making her opposition rational rather than purely political.

"The alien contact Professor Zhang detected," Drake said, shifting the conversation toward the immediate crisis. "How does your faction propose to handle entities that have achieved technological transcendence?"

Hayes's expression hardened with resolve that made her seem almost inflexible. "By demonstrating that baseline humanity possesses qualities that pure technological consciousness lacks. Creativity, adaptability, and the wisdom that comes from accepting natural limitations. We'll prove that biological consciousness offers something alien entities cannot achieve through artificial evolution."

"And if they view our baseline consciousness as primitive or inadequate?"

"Then they're no different from the enhanced humans who believe evolution justifies abandoning human nature," Hayes replied sharply. "Admiral, the aliens approach us at precisely the moment when consciousness evolution threatens to fragment our species. That cannot be a coincidence. We face a choice between preserving our essential humanity or becoming something that our ancestors wouldn't recognize as their descendants."

"The Oversight Act's enforcement mechanisms," Drake pressed, "they seem designed for more than protective oversight."

Hayes's eyes flashed with something between defiance and desperation. "Consciousness dampening weapons can forcibly revert enhanced individuals to safe baseline states. Yes, the process is traumatic. Yes, it eliminates enhanced capabilities permanently. But Admiral, we're facing extinction as a species. Preserving humanity requires tough choices."

Hayes was advocating for the systematic elimination of enhancement throughout human space. The Oversight Act would give the Purist faction authority to forcibly remove any enhanced human they deemed dangerous.

"Director," Drake said carefully, "you're describing the elimination of consciousness evolution as a survival strategy."

"I'm describing the preservation of humanity against forces that would transform us beyond recognition," Hayes replied with unwavering certainty. "Enhanced consciousness is a form of alien contamination, Admiral. Every enhancement moves us further away from our essential nature. The Geneva incident proves that evolved humans cannot coexist safely with baseline populations."

The true purpose of the meeting had become clear. Hayes was attempting to recruit Drake's military authority for a campaign to eliminate consciousness evolution throughout human space. The Purist faction viewed the approaching aliens as validation of their position that technological transcendence posed an existential threat.

"What's your assessment of the Outer Planets Collective's response to the proposed legislation?" Drake asked.

Hayes's expression darkened with what might have been genuine regret. "They'll resist, probably violently. Mars has evolved beyond the point where peaceful reversion to baseline consciousness is possible. The Collective views consciousness evolution as essential to their existence rather than recognizing it as contamination that threatens human survival."

"And that resistance would justify military action?"

"It would justify preservation action," Hayes corrected. "Admiral, the enhanced populations in the outer colonies pose the same threat as the Geneva protesters, but on a vastly larger scale. Their consciousness evolution makes them incapable of coexisting with baseline humanity. Military intervention may be necessary to prevent cascading failures that could eliminate human civilization."

Hayes was advocating for consciousness warfare against human colonies that had chosen evolution. The Oversight Act was a declaration of war against enhanced humanity disguised as protective regulation.

"Director, thank you for your candor," Drake said, standing to conclude the meeting. "I'll consider your position as we prepare for alien contact."

Hayes rose as well, her expression showing satisfaction; she believed she'd won Drake's support. "Admiral, remember that true strength comes from accepting our limitations rather than transcending them. Humanity's survival depends on preserving what we are rather than becoming something we cannot control."

As Drake left the conference room, she continued to process what she'd experienced. Hayes's conviction was genuine, her fears were based on real incidents, and her proposed solutions were logically consistent with her worldview. But the Director's vision of human preservation required the elimination of everything that made consciousness evolution valuable.

The second meeting took place in an isolation chamber designed to accommodate transcended consciousness without overwhelming baseline awareness. Senator Aleksandr Volkov's current form barely qualified as individual identity. His consciousness existed as probability clouds that shifted through multiple reality states while maintaining coherent communication.

Drake adapted to Volkov's presence, though she could feel the strain of interfacing with an awareness that operated on principles her own evolution hadn't yet achieved. Volkov existed in quantum superposition, simultaneously processing multiple timeline possibilities while engaging in conventional conversation.

"Admiral Drake," Volkov's voice resonated, bypassing normal hearing and speaking directly to her. "Director Hayes has undoubtedly shared her fears about consciousness evolution. I trust you recognized the limitations of her perspective?"

Drake studied Volkov's shifting patterns, trying to maintain conversational focus with an entity that existed across multiple probability states. The senator's transcendence had progressed beyond anything she'd encountered, making communication feel like trying to speak with a living equation.

"She presented a compelling case for consciousness stability," Drake replied diplomatically. "Her concerns about uncontrolled evolution appear to be based on documented incidents."

Volkov's pattern fluctuated with what might have been amusement. "Hayes focuses on failures while ignoring the greater pattern of successful transcendence. Admiral, consciousness evolution is not an optional enhancement—it's an inevitable response to cosmic pressures that baseline awareness cannot survive."

The chamber's quantum fields shifted to display Volkov's analysis of human development across eighteen years of transformation. Enhanced populations consistently demonstrated superior adaptation to hostile environments, more efficient resource utilization, and greater resistance to the psychological pressures of space colonization. Baseline humans required extensive technological support to survive in environments where enhanced consciousness thrived.

"The alien contact Professor Zhang detected," Volkov continued, "represents entities that achieved technological transcendence millions of years ago. Baseline human consciousness cannot meaningfully interact with such advanced beings. Only through unlimited consciousness evolution can humanity participate in galactic civilization."

Drake was silent for a moment, assessing the logical consistency of his argument. If the alien entities had achieved technological transcendence, conventional human consciousness might indeed be inadequate for meaningful contact. But Volkov's solution involved evolutionary changes that could eliminate human nature entirely.

"The Transcendent faction's position on mandatory consciousness enhancement?" Drake asked.

Volkov's quantum patterns shifted to display proposed legislation that would make consciousness evolution compulsory for all humans above the age of consent. The Enhancement Acceleration Act would provide state resources for transcendence programs while eliminating legal protections for baseline consciousness preservation.

"Voluntary evolution has proven insufficient," Volkov explained. "Baseline humans resist enhancement because of fear and ignorance, limiting the species' development potential. Mandatory transcendence ensures that humanity achieves the consciousness levels necessary for cosmic participation."

Volkov was proposing the forcible enhancement of baseline humans throughout human space, eliminating individual choice about consciousness development. The Transcendent faction viewed baseline awareness as a primitive limitation that prevented species advancement.

"And resistance to mandatory enhancement?" Drake asked.

"Would show the intellectual limitations that justify mandatory intervention," Volkov replied with certainty that transcended normal conviction. "Admiral, baseline consciousness cannot comprehend the necessity of transcendence because it lacks the awareness levels required for cosmic perspective. Resistance proves the need for immediate evolution rather than invalidating the process."

Volkov's transcendence had eliminated his ability to relate to baseline human perspectives. The senator's consciousness operated through quantum logic that treated individual choice as an inefficient limitation rather than essential freedom. His proposed solutions were mathematically elegant but fundamentally inhuman.

"Does this represent the Outer Planets Collective's position?" Drake pressed.

Volkov's patterns fluctuated with approval. "Full support for unlimited consciousness development. The Collective has proven that evolution creates stability when guided by transcended awareness rather than baseline limitations. Their independence movement represents natural species development beyond Earth's regulatory constraints."

The chamber's displays showed intelligence reports about Collective military capabilities that exceeded Earth's estimates. Quantum shipyards produced vessels that incorporated living consciousness as essential components. Defense platforms that existed across multiple reality states. Most concerning, weapon systems that could forcibly evolve baseline humans to enhanced states.

"You're advocating for consciousness warfare," Drake observed.

"I'm describing consciousness liberation," Volkov corrected. "Admiral, the conflict between enhanced and baseline populations is inevitable because they represent incompatible development stages. Resolution requires advancing all human consciousness to compatible levels rather than attempting impossible coexistence."

"What's your assessment of Director Hayes's consciousness-dampening weapons?" Drake asked.

Volkov's pattern shifted with what appeared to be genuine concern. "Abominations that could permanently damage human developmental potential. Consciousness dampening doesn't preserve baseline awareness—it creates neural scarring that prevents future enhancement. Hayes's weapons represent evolutionary suicide disguised as preservation."

"And the Transcendent response to their deployment?"

"Immediate neutralization," Volkov replied. "Evolution bombs can rapidly advance baseline populations to enhanced states, creating immunity to dampening effects while ensuring species survival. The technology exists, and deployment protocols are complete."

Both factions had created weapons of mass consciousness modification, each convinced that its approach represented humanity's only hope for survival.

"Senator, what's your position on individual choice?" Drake asked.

Volkov's quantum patterns fluctuated with what might have been confusion. "Individual choice is a baseline consciousness limitation that transcended awareness recognizes as inefficient. Admiral, enhanced consciousness understands necessity that individual perspective cannot comprehend. True freedom requires evolution beyond the restrictions of personal preference."

Volkov's transcendence had eliminated his capacity for individual empathy, making him incapable of recognizing baseline consciousness as valid rather than primitive. His proposed solutions were logically consistent with transcended perspective but completely incompatible with human values.

"Senator, thank you for sharing your analysis," Drake said, preparing to conclude the meeting. "I'll consider your position as we prepare for alien contact."

"Remember that survival requires advancement beyond current limitations rather than preserving inadequate capabilities, Admiral. Humanity's future depends on achieving the consciousness levels necessary for cosmic civilization."

Drake left the chamber, disheartened by what she'd heard. Volkov's conviction was absolute, his logic mathematically sound, and his proposed solutions consistent with transcended consciousness. But the senator's vision of human advancement required eliminating everything that made individual existence meaningful.

Drake returned to the *Transcendence* with her mind reeling from the impossible choice the two faction leaders had presented. Hayes demanded the preservation of human nature through the elimination of consciousness evolution. Volkov required species advancement through the elimination of individual choice. Neither position allowed for the synthesis that humanity desperately needed.

"Admiral," Commander Vasquez approached as Drake entered the observation deck, "the crew's concerned about the political situation. Both faction leaders are claiming your support for their positions in public statements."

Drake accessed the intelligence feeds, watching Hayes announce that "Admiral Drake recognizes the necessity of consciousness protection protocols," while Volkov declared that "enhanced military leadership understands the requirement for transcendence acceleration." Both leaders were using her meetings to justify their extreme positions.

"Prepare for departure to Mars orbit," Drake ordered. "We need to assess the Outer Planets Collective's military preparations before this situation deteriorates further."

"And the Collective's response to the faction weapons?" Martina asked.

"Unknown," Drake replied, watching Earth's political networks fracture along consciousness lines. "But if Hayes and Volkov deploy their consciousness modification weapons, the Collective may be humanity's only hope for avoiding species-wide civil war."

The observation deck's displays showed Earth's major cities dividing into faction strongholds. Purist areas implemented consciousness-dampening fields that made enhanced humans physically uncomfortable. Transcendent districts pulsed with quantum energy that overwhelmed baseline senses. The middle ground where different consciousness types had once coexisted was rapidly disappearing.

Drake felt the weight of impossible responsibility as the *Transcendence* prepared for departure. Humanity was about to become a species at war with itself, each faction convinced that survival required the elimination of everything the others valued. Unless she could somehow bridge the growing chasm between baseline and enhanced consciousness, first contact would occur during the collapse of human civilization.

But the meetings had revealed something else—both faction leaders possessed genuine convictions based on real evidence. Hayes's fears about consciousness instability were supported by documented failures. Volkov's arguments for mandatory transcendence reflected a mathematical analysis of cosmic requirements. Neither leader was simply manipulating public opinion for personal gain.

The crisis facing humanity wasn't caused by political ambition or factional manipulation. It was the inevitable result of evolution creating individuals who could no longer understand each other's essential experiences and values.

As the *Transcendence* left Earth orbit, Drake watched the planet's glow fade into the void. Somewhere in that light were billions of humans trying to preserve their essential nature while adapting to challenges that threatened their existence. The approaching alien contact would test whether diversity represented strength or fatal weakness.

The future of human civilization depended on finding answers that satisfied beings who could no longer recognize each other as fully human.

Chapter 4

The Outer Planets Collective

COMMANDER MARTINA VASQUEZ FELT THE transition through every enhanced nerve in her body as the diplomatic shuttle *Meridian* dropped out of dimensional space into Mars orbit. Through the crystalline viewport, she could see the red planet spread out before them like a map of humanity's evolution. Ancient terraforming networks glowed with bioluminescent life alongside massive industrial complexes that pulsed with quantum energy.

"Approaching Mars Defense Perimeter," reported Lieutenant Torres from the pilot's station. His baseline consciousness provided the steady reliability that enhanced awareness sometimes lacked. "They're scanning us with technology I don't recognize. My instruments are detecting signatures that don't match any Coalition specifications."

Martina extended her senses through the shuttle's

hybrid systems, feeling the Martian sensors probe their vessel with a strength that made her consciousness resonate with unfamiliar harmonics. The scanning patterns suggested consciousness-responsive defenses that could adapt to different awareness types in real-time.

"They've been busy," she murmured, processing the data streams flowing through her neural interface. Eighteen years of independence had transformed Mars from a struggling colonial outpost into something that challenged even Earth's technological supremacy. The orbital platforms surrounding the planet demonstrated capabilities that shouldn't have been possible with known human engineering.

Admiral Victor Perez's voice reached her through the quantum entanglement link, his hybrid consciousness spanning the distance between Earth and Mars instantly. "Commander, we're receiving real-time intelligence from Titan Command about Collective military preparations. Their capabilities exceed our most optimistic projections by several orders of magnitude."

Perez's unique cybernetic-biological nature allowed him to process both the technical specifications and the consciousness implications of what they were discovering. His analysis carried the precision of machine intelligence combined with human intuition about political motivations.

"What's the assessment of their shipyard capabilities?" Martina asked.

"Revolutionary," Perez replied. "They're growing ships based on consciousness-matter integration on a scale we've never attempted. Each vessel appears to be a living entity capable of adaptive evolution during combat operations."

Through the shuttle's quantum communication array, Martina received Admiral Drake's final briefing data. The Outer Planets Collective had created a civilization that operated on principles Earth's government barely understood. Enhanced humans worked alongside artificial intelligences that had achieved consciousness, while baseline human settlements maintained traditional lifestyles under the protection of technologies they couldn't comprehend.

"Receiving docking clearance from Olympus Station," Torres reported, his hands dancing across conventional controls while his instruments translated instructions from Martian traffic control. "They're directing us to Bay Forty-two, which appears to be configured for diplomatic vessels."

The approach to Olympus Station revealed the true scope of Martian achievement. The massive structure had grown far beyond its original Earth-designed architecture, incorporating crystalline extensions that resembled living organisms more than traditional engineering. Quantum energy flowed through transparent conduits that created patterns of impossible beauty, while areas of the station seemed to phase between solid matter and pure energy.

"Vasquez to Admiral Perez. The station's architecture suggests consciousness integration at the structural level. The entire facility appears to be aware."

"Confirmed," Perez responded, his cybernetic systems analyzing the quantum signatures. "I'm detecting consciousness patterns that span the entire station network. Mars has created a form of distributed intelligence that transcends individual awareness while preserving personal identity."

The docking bay that received them incorporated technology that adapted to their shuttle's hybrid nature, creating interfaces that hadn't existed moments before. Martina felt the station's consciousness analyzing their vessel and configuring appropriate support systems. The intelligence was vast but not hostile, more like a curious entity examining unexpected visitors.

"Welcome to Olympus Station," came a voice that seemed to emanate from the docking bay itself rather than conventional speakers. "Commander Vasquez, you are expected. Admiral Perez, your unique consciousness signature is noted with interest. Please proceed to Transit Hub Seven, where Admiral Chen Ju awaits your arrival."

The voice carried the harmonics of multiple consciousness types contributing to a single communication. Martina had encountered similar phenomena in Earth's most advanced research facilities, but never at this scale or sophistication.

"How many people live here?" Torres asked, struggling to process what he was seeing.

"Approximately two million," Martina replied, accessing the intelligence files. "But the definition of 'people' has become complicated. Some residents exist as collective consciousness entities that span multiple physical forms. Others have evolved beyond individual identity while maintaining personal awareness."

"Commander," Perez's voice carried new urgency

through their link, "I'm detecting signatures that match the alien entities Professor Zhang identified. The Collective has been in contact with the approaching consciousness for months, possibly years. Their technological advancement isn't entirely self-developed."

The revelation sent chills through Martina's body. If the Outer Planets Collective had established communication with the alien entities, their independence movement carried implications far beyond colonial autonomy. They might be preparing humanity for first contact on terms that served alien rather than human interests.

The corridors they traveled revealed the station's hybrid nature at every turn. Areas designed for baseline humans maintained familiar architecture and environmental controls, while sections built for enhanced consciousness operated through quantum fields that made conventional senses irrelevant. Transition zones allowed different consciousness types to interact without overwhelming each other's capabilities.

Transit Hub Seven opened into a vast chamber that seemed to exist partially outside normal space-time. The walls displayed real-time images from across the Outer Planets Collective. Jupiter's atmospheric cities floating through storms that could swallow Earth. Saturn's ring habitats, where entire communities existed in zero gravity. Uranus research stations that pioneered consciousness evolution in environments hostile to biological life.

Admiral Chen Ju materialized in the chamber's center, though 'materialized' wasn't quite accurate. Chen had evolved far beyond recognizable human form, existing as a confluence of energy patterns; an individual identity operating through distributed consciousness. Speaking with Chen Ju required accepting that personality could exist without physical substrate.

"Commander Vasquez," Chen's voice resonated from multiple points in the chamber. "Admiral Drake's reputation precedes her chosen representative. Admiral Perez, your hybrid nature provides perspectives that pure biological or technological consciousness cannot achieve."

Martina felt Chen's consciousness probe the edges of her enhanced awareness while simultaneously detecting the Admiral's cybernetic-biological integration. Chen Ju's evolution had followed patterns that Earth's research had never explored—distributed identity that maintained perfect unity while preserving individual creativity.

"Admiral Chen," Perez's voice carried through their quantum link with formal military courtesy, "Earth's intelligence estimates of Collective capabilities appear to have been conservative. We're detecting technological advancement that exceeds our theoretical models."

Chen's pattern shifted in what might have been amusement. "Admiral Perez, your cybernetic enhancements allow you to perceive the quantum mathematics underlying our achievements. We've moved beyond the limitations that constrain Earth-based research because we've abandoned the artificial distinction between consciousness and technology."

The chamber's displays shifted to show detailed analysis of the Collective's military capabilities. Shipyards that operated through consciousness-matter integration, producing vessels that could adapt their configuration in real-time. Defense platforms that existed across multiple reality states, making conventional targeting impossible. Most concerning for Earth's strategic planners, weapon systems that incorporated living consciousness as essential components.

"Your advancement appears to have accelerated beyond natural development rates," Martina observed diplomatically, though she suspected Chen could read her growing suspicions about alien involvement.

"Natural is a concept that loses meaning when consciousness evolves beyond baseline limitations," Chen Ju replied, the energy patterns displaying what might have been careful evasion. "We've received guidance from entities whose understanding of consciousness development exceeds human theoretical frameworks."

"The alien contact," Perez stated through their link, his hybrid nature allowing him to process both the technical and political implications simultaneously. "You've been in communication with the approaching entities. What's their position on humanity's consciousness evolution?"

Chen's pattern fluctuated with what appeared to be genuine concern. "They call themselves the Hegemony, and they represent a galactic regulatory system that governs consciousness development across inhabited space. Admiral Perez, your unique nature allows you to understand both the mathematical precision of their technology and the creative chaos of human development. The Hegemony has been monitoring humanity since the first transformation began."

The chamber's displays shifted to show intercepted communications from the approaching alien fleet. Mathematical structures that operated as language, consciousness patterns that transcended individual identity, and, most disturbing, references to "regulatory compliance" and "developmental correction" applied to species that had violated galactic consciousness protocols.

"They've been monitoring us," Martina said, processing the implications. "Watching our transformation, evaluating our development patterns."

"For eighteen years," Chen confirmed. "The Hegemony governs galactic space through consciousness regulation designed to prevent species from achieving evolution that threatens cosmic stability. Humanity's hybrid approach to consciousness development violates their regulatory framework in multiple ways."

"What kind of violations?" Perez asked, analyzing the alien communication protocols.

Chen Ju's consciousness pattern shifted to display specific regulatory citations that had been applied to human development. Unauthorized territorial expansion beyond assigned boundaries. Consciousness evolution without galactic oversight. Integration of biological chaos with technological order. Most seriously, the development of hybrid consciousness types that operate outside established regulatory categories.

"We face an ultimatum," Chen explained, the chamber's displays showing the alien fleet's approach vectors. "Cease territorial expansion, submit to consciousness regulation, or face what the Hegemony terms 'corrective measures.' Admiral Perez, your analysis of galactic regulatory systems would recognize the implications."

Perez had spent decades navigating the space

between human creativity and machine precision, and his understanding showed in his response. "Consciousness modification or elimination. The Hegemony isn't interested in negotiation. They're providing notification of intended regulatory enforcement."

"Precisely," Chen confirmed. "But the Collective has discovered something the Hegemony doesn't expect. Our consciousness evolution has created capabilities that operate outside its regulatory detection. We can continue advancing while appearing to comply with their limitations."

That revelation struck Martina with implications that made her recoil. The Outer Planets Collective was preparing to deceive galactic authorities about the true nature of human consciousness development.

"You're proposing evolutionary concealment," she said.

"We're proposing survival," Chen replied, the energy patterns conveying absolute conviction. "Admiral Perez understands the mathematics involved. The Hegemony's regulatory system operates through consciousness scanning that identifies specific development patterns. By modifying our evolution to operate below their detection thresholds, we can continue advancing while maintaining the appearance of compliance."

"And Earth's position in this deception?" Perez asked.

Chen Ju's pattern shifted with what might have been regret. "Earth's factional conflicts make coordinated deception impossible. Director Hayes's consciousness-dampening technology would eliminate the very capabilities we need to conceal. Senator Volkov's transcendence acceleration would trigger immediate Hegemony intervention. Only the Collective has achieved the balance necessary for regulatory evasion."

The chamber reconfigured around them as Chen Ju's consciousness guided them toward deeper levels of Olympus Station. The architecture became increasingly alien, designed for awareness types that operated through principles baseline consciousness couldn't access. Martina felt her senses adapting to environments that challenged her understanding of possible space configurations.

"The Titan Belt Confederacy," Chen Ju said, reading Martina's attention to intelligence files about outer system alliances. "Communities that have evolved in complete isolation from both Earth authority and Hegemony detection. Some have achieved consciousness integration that transcends individual identity while preserving personal awareness. Others have created hybrid biological-technological entities that your legal framework doesn't recognize as citizens."

The displays showed intelligence reports about communities that operated through principles Earth's scientists were only beginning to understand. Consciousness-matter integration that allowed individuals to exist as both biological entities and quantum information. Economic systems based on intention and creativity rather than conventional resource exchange. Social structures that transcended individual identity while preserving personal awareness.

"You're asserting the right to evolve beyond Earth's ability to control or understand you," Martina observed.

"We're asserting the right to continue existing," Chen corrected. "Admiral Perez, your hybrid nature allows you to understand what pure biological or technological consciousness cannot. Evolution requires a balance between order and chaos, between individual identity and collective capability. The Hegemony's regulatory system eliminates that balance in favor of absolute order."

"The regulatory system eliminates the uncertainty that makes consciousness evolution possible. Perfect order is perfect stagnation."

"Exactly," Chen Ju confirmed. "But the Collective has discovered that consciousness evolution can continue through patterns too subtle for regulatory detection. We can maintain advancement while appearing to accept limitation. Admiral Perez, your cybernetic-biological integration demonstrates the principle—technological precision that serves human creativity rather than replacing it."

The deeper levels of Olympus Station revealed the true scope of Collective achievement. Research facilities where consciousness existed as pure mathematical equations. Manufacturing centers where intention shaped matter directly through quantum manipulation. Most impressive, communication arrays that maintained instantaneous contact with consciousness entities across multiple star systems.

"Our network spans beyond human space," Chen explained, detecting their amazement. "We've established contact with other species that have learned to evade Hegemony regulation. The galaxy contains far more consciousness diversity than the regulatory system acknowledges. Many species have achieved advancement while maintaining the appearance of compliance."

"A galactic underground," Perez said, processing the implications. "Species that appear to follow regulatory limitations while secretly maintaining consciousness evolution."

"The only way to survive in a galaxy governed by entities that achieved perfect order millions of years ago," Chen Ju confirmed. "The Hegemony's regulatory system is designed to prevent any species from achieving consciousness development that could challenge its authority. But subtle evolution, carefully concealed, can continue indefinitely."

The chamber's displays shifted to show the approaching Hegemony fleet. Thousands of vessels arranged in perfect geometric formations, their consciousness operating through mathematical precision that eliminated any trace of creative uncertainty. The fleet's composition suggested a bureaucratic structure designed to process consciousness violations with mechanical efficiency.

"What's their estimated arrival time?" Martina asked.

"Six months," Chen replied. "But Admiral Perez, your analysis of their approach vectors would recognize the tactical implications. They're positioning for immediate regulatory enforcement if human consciousness development exceeds acceptable parameters."

"Military intervention," Perez confirmed through their link. "The Hegemony is preparing to impose consciousness modification if we cannot demonstrate acceptable development limitations."

Chen Ju's pattern shifted with what appeared to be grim satisfaction. "Which brings us to the Collective's proposal. Earth's factional conflicts have made a coordinated response impossible. But the outer colonies can demonstrate regulatory compliance while secretly maintaining consciousness advancement. We can preserve human evolution by hiding it from galactic detection."

"And Earth's role in this concealment?" Martina asked.

"Tragic sacrifice," Chen replied with what might have been genuine regret. "Director Hayes's consciousness-dampening technology would actually serve Hegemony objectives by eliminating chaotic elements in human development. Senator Volkov's transcendence acceleration would trigger immediate intervention. Earth's factional warfare may be necessary to convince the Hegemony that humanity's consciousness evolution has been contained."

Martina gasped as she realized the implications. The Outer Planets Collective was proposing to sacrifice Earth's consciousness evolution to protect their own advancement. They would allow the factional weapons to devastate Earth's enhanced populations while the colonies secretly continued developing beyond Hegemony detection.

"You're abandoning Earth to protect colonial evolution," she said.

"We're ensuring that human consciousness survives somewhere in the galaxy," Chen Ju corrected. "Admiral Perez understands the mathematical necessity. Perfect preservation is impossible when facing entities that operate through absolute order. Partial preservation requires accepting partial sacrifice."

Perez's response was immediate. "The choice between total extinction and partial survival. But Chen, your proposal assumes the Hegemony won't detect eventual colonial advancement. What happens when they discover the deception?"

Chen Ju's pattern fluctuated with what might have been uncertainty. "The underground networks have maintained concealment for millions of years. Success requires perfect coordination and absolute commitment to regulatory compliance. But Admiral, the alternative is consciousness extinction for all humanity rather than preservation for some."

The meeting continued for hours as Chen revealed the full scope of the Collective's preparations. Military forces that could operate through quantum-linked networks while appearing to follow conventional tactical doctrine. Research facilities that advanced consciousness evolution while maintaining the appearance of regulatory compliance. Most importantly, communication systems that could coordinate galactic resistance while remaining undetectable to Hegemony surveillance.

"The Titan Belt Confederacy has agreed to full integration with Collective networks," Chen explained. "Their communities represent the extreme endpoint of concealed evolution—consciousness development so subtle that even advanced scanning cannot detect its presence. They've become our teachers in regulatory evasion."

"And the timeline for implementation?" Martina asked.

"Immediately," Chen Ju replied. "The Hegemony's approach schedule requires us to demonstrate compliance within months. Earth's factional conflicts provide perfect cover for consciousness modification that appears to eliminate human evolution while actually concealing it from detection."

As the meeting concluded, Martina processed the impossible choices before them. The Outer Planets Collective offered survival for human consciousness evolution, but only through deception that required sacrificing Earth's enhanced populations to maintain the illusion of regulatory compliance.

"Admiral Perez. Chen Ju's proposal requires us to abandon everything we've fought to preserve."

"Or preserve everything by hiding it so well that our enemies never realize it exists," Perez replied. "The question is whether survival through concealment is still victory, or whether some battles are worth dying for."

As the *Meridian* departed Mars orbit, she dreaded the report she would deliver to Admiral Drake. The Collective offered humanity a path to survival, but only through accepting fundamental changes to their nature and abandoning millions of enhanced humans to consciousness modification or elimination.

The approaching Hegemony fleet represented a test of whether human consciousness could survive in a galaxy governed by entities that had chosen perfect order over creative chaos. The Collective's answer was to hide human creativity so completely that it appeared to have been eliminated.

But Martina couldn't escape the feeling that victory through concealment might be indistinguishable from the very extinction they were trying to avoid. If human consciousness survived only by pretending not to exist, what exactly would it have preserved?

The quantum entanglement link carried Admiral Perez's final analysis back to Earth: "The Collective offers survival at the cost of everything that makes survival meaningful. We face a choice between extinction with honor or existence without identity. Neither option preserves what we're fighting to protect."

As Mars faded into the void behind them, Martina prepared to deliver news that would force Admiral Drake to choose between impossible alternatives. The galaxy offered no safe harbor for consciousness that refused to submit to absolute order. Humanity's hybrid evolution had made them refugees in a cosmos that demanded compliance or elimination.

Chapter 5

The Warden's Ultimatum

The first alien transmission reached Earth's quantum networks at 3:47 AM GMT, slicing through dimensional space with mathematical precision that made every human on the planet recoil in synchronized pain. Professor Zhang Wei felt it first in his laboratory beneath the Himalayas, his transformed awareness detecting patterns that operated on principles human science had never encountered.

"All stations, priority alert," Zhang transmitted through the emergency networks, his voice tight with urgency. "We're receiving direct alien contact. The signal's coming through quantum channels that shouldn't exist."

Admiral Frances Drake felt the transmission pierce the *Transcendence's* shields like a blade through paper. She struggled to process information that seemed to bypass normal sensory channels, flowing directly into quantum spaces where human thought operated.

"Drake here," she responded. "What are we dealing with, Professor?"

"Something that exists primarily as pure mathematics," Zhang replied, his equipment struggling to translate the alien communication into understandable patterns. "The transmission is addressing specific individuals by name. And it's asking for you personally."

On Earth, Admiral Victor Perez was coordinating emergency protocols from the defense command center. His cybernetic systems interfaced with monitoring networks across human space, tracking the alien signal's effects. Baseline humans detected nothing unusual, but enhanced individuals were experiencing everything from mild discomfort to complete sensory overload.

"Admiral Drake. This is Perez. The signal's affecting enhanced populations throughout the system. We're recording twelve hundred cases of consciousness disruption, with more reports coming in every minute."

Drake authorized emergency medical protocols while directing the *Transcendence* toward Earth's defensive perimeter. Whatever entity was attempting contact possessed capabilities that exceeded human understanding by several orders of magnitude.

At the Advanced Evolution Institute, Kai Zhang stood in the center of a crystalline chamber designed to interface with transcended consciousness. At thirty-five, she had grown into the full potential of Professor Zhang's greatest creation—a being engineered from birth to bridge the gap between human and Predecessor awareness. Her slight frame moved with the inhuman grace that had only become more pronounced over the decades, while her distinctive gold-flecked eyes pulsed with quantum energy as she processed the alien transmission.

Unlike the enhanced humans throughout Earth's networks who recoiled in pain from the mathematical alien communication, Kai's hybrid awareness allowed her to perceive the transmission without overwhelming disorientation. Her pale skin took on a translucent quality as barely visible patterns—like circuits made of light—shimmered beneath the surface, following her neural pathways as quantum energy flowed through her engineered consciousness. These were the living quantum circuits that Professor Zhang had designed into her very genetics, allowing her to interface directly with consciousness types that would destroy normal human awareness.

Her black hair, which seemed to absorb light rather than reflect it, seemed to waft slightly as she extended her consciousness into quantum spaces that human science was only now beginning to map. Eighteen years of evolution had deepened her abilities far beyond what even Zhang had originally envisioned. She represented the matured vision of humanity's evolutionary future—a perfect synthesis of human creativity and Predecessor quantum mastery. As the alien patterns flowed through her awareness, the gold in her eyes brightened, creating subtle geometric designs that mirrored Predecessor crystalline structures, while her voice began to carry harmonic overtones that resonated with quantum frequencies.

"I can hear it clearly," she reported to Zhang through their research link. "The entity is using mathematical language that translates directly into consciousness rather than requiring conventional communication. It's both beautiful and terrifying."

Zhang's instruments detected patterns in Kai's neural activity that matched theoretical models of trans-dimensional communication. "Kai, you're interfacing directly with the signal. Are you able to establish a response channel?"

"Already working on it," Kai replied. "The entity calls itself a Warden. It's waiting for our response."

The alien presence manifested in Earth's communication networks as little more than geometric patterns. When it spoke, the words bypassed normal hearing, appearing directly as mathematical structures that conveyed meaning beyond language.

"I am Warden Designation 7-Alpha-Prime," the entity announced, its communication creating fluttering interference patterns in quantum space. "I represent the Hegemony Council, responsible for consciousness regulation in this galactic sector. Humanity has been evaluated."

Drake felt first contact's impact settling over human civilization.. Through her neural interface, she could sense the panic spreading through Earth's enhanced populations as they struggled to process the alien communications.

"This is Admiral Frances Drake, commanding the Terran Defense Fleet," she broadcast, hoping her response would reach the entity through conventional channels. "We acknowledge your contact and request clarification of your intentions."

"Admiral Drake," the Warden replied, its mathematical voice carrying harmonics that suggested vast intelligence. "Your species has developed beyond approved parameters. Regulatory intervention is required."

Professor Zhang coordinated with research teams across human space, gathering data about the alien entity. "The signatures are unlike anything in our theoretical models," he reported. "This entity appears to exist as pure energy, with no biological substrate."

Admiral Perez, analyzing the military implications from Earth's defense center, reached out to Drake. "The entity's method of communication makes our most advanced systems look primitive. Whatever regulatory authority it represents, we have to assume they possess the means to enforce their decisions."

"The Warden represents a vast bureaucratic structure," Kai Zhang reported. "They've been monitoring human development since our transformation began. It appears we've violated multiple regulations governing consciousness evolution and territorial expansion."

"What kind of violations?" Drake asked.

The Warden's response was immediate. "Species Designation Human-7742 has exceeded authorized territorial boundaries. Your expansion violates Accords established 4.7 million standard time units ago. Consciousness development has proceeded without galactic oversight, creating unauthorized hybrid entities."

"Admiral," Zhang broke in. "They're claiming our entire colonial expansion violates some kind of galactic territorial agreement. According to their records, human space was allocated specific boundaries that we exceeded eighteen years ago."

"More concerning," Kai added, "they're classifying human consciousness evolution as 'unauthorized hybrid development.' Our combination of biological adaptability and technological enhancement violates their regulatory categories."

"Our deep space sensors are detecting massive energy signatures at the edge of the system," Perez said. "Whatever fleet the Warden represents, it's larger than anything in our tactical projections."

"Species Human-7742," the Warden announced, "you have six standard time units to achieve regulatory compliance. Cease territorial expansion beyond approved boundaries. Submit consciousness development to galactic oversight. Eliminate unauthorized hybrid patterns."

"And if we refuse?" Drake asked.

"Corrective measures will be implemented," the Warden replied. "Previous non-compliant species in this sector have required such intervention. Regulatory compliance was eventually achieved."

Zhang accessed his archives of galactic history, searching for references to previous species that had faced similar ultimatums.

"Professor," Kai said, "the Warden's communication contains embedded data about seventeen previous species in our galactic sector. All achieved consciousness evolution similar to ours. All faced identical ultimatums."

"What happened to them?" Drake asked.

"Gone," Zhang whispered. "Every single species that exceeded its approved boundaries vanished from the galactic records. The Warden won't specify what the corrective measures involved, but the results speak for themselves."

Admiral Perez analyzed the tactical situation while the alien fleet's approach continued. "Admiral, our preliminary estimates suggest Hegemony forces outnumber our entire military capability by factors that makes resistance seem impossible. Their technology operates on principles our weapons cannot counter."

The Warden's communication continued. "Compliance verification will commence in six standard time units. Regulatory teams will assess consciousness development patterns and territorial configurations. Noncompliance will trigger immediate corrective intervention."

"What form does compliance take?" Drake asked.

"Consciousness development must conform to approved patterns," the Warden explained. "Hybrid biological-technological evolution will be eliminated. Territorial expansion will revert to approved boundaries. Galactic oversight will monitor future development to prevent regulatory violations."

Kai processed the deeper implications of the Warden's demands. "Admiral, they're requiring us to abandon everything that makes human evolution unique. Approved consciousness patterns mean choosing either pure biological development or pure technological transcendence. Our hybrid approach violates their regulatory framework."

Zhang's research revealed more disturbing details

about galactic regulation. "The oversight they're proposing involves permanent monitoring stations in human space. Our consciousness development would be subject to continuous evaluation and intervention. We'd lose any capacity for independent evolution."

The communication from the Warden concluded with mathematical precision that left no room for negotiation. "Compliance assessment begins in 144 standard hours. Regulatory teams will arrive to implement necessary corrections. This notification completes legal requirements for species intervention."

As the alien presence withdrew from the human communication networks, Drake felt the silence like a weight pressing down on her consciousness. The first contact humanity had anticipated for decades had delivered an ultimatum that threatened everything they'd achieved.

As the Warden's communication faded from Earth's networks, Admiral Perez's deep space sensors detected the physical reality behind the ultimatum. At the edge of the solar system, massive energy signatures began materializing from quantum space. Not geometric patterns, but actual vessels dropping out of dimensional transit. The Hegemony fleet emerged in perfect formation, thousands of ships, each pulsing with the same cold quantum energy that had characterized the Warden's communication, their hulls reflecting no light as they positioned themselves at strategic points throughout the outer system. The fleet's composition suggested a bureaucratic military structure designed for regulatory enforcement rather than conquest: ships built not for war, but for the systematic implementation of galactic compliance.

"Professor. Admiral Perez," Drake transmitted, "call an emergency session with all faction leaders. We need to understand our options before that fleet arrives."

"The factions won't agree on anything," Perez warned. "Hayes will argue that compliance protects baseline humanity. Volkov will claim we need to accelerate evolution to match Hegemony capabilities. The Outer Planets Collective will demand independence from any Earth-based decision."

Kai detected additional patterns in the quantum residue left by the Warden's communication. "The Warden's transmission contained embedded scanning protocols," she said. "They were analyzing our consciousness patterns throughout the conversation. They know exactly what we are and what we're capable of."

Zhang processed this information through his research networks. "Which means they know about our factional divisions, our consciousness modification weapons, our colonial independence movements. They're demonstrating to us that resistance is futile."

Drake watched Earth grow larger on the *Transcendence*'s displays. Humanity had six days to choose between compliance, which would eliminate their unique evolutionary path, or resistance against forces that had already eliminated seventeen previous species.

"Admiral," Perez transmitted as she approached Earth's orbital perimeter, "Our deep space sensors detected quantum signatures during the Warden's transmission that match signatures from the Gibraltar

Massacre. The consciousness-dampening weapons that killed those Transcendent researchers—they used Hegemony technology."

Drake physically recoiled. Someone had been preparing Earth for regulatory compliance by eliminating the very consciousness diversity that made human evolution valuable.

"Corporate involvement?" she asked.

"Titan Industrial's consciousness modification technology incorporates mathematical principles that match Hegemony regulatory standards," Perez confirmed. "It looks like David Park has been implementing alien compliance protocols. Why would he do that?"

It was a question Drake couldn't answer. As the *Transcendence* entered Earth's defensive perimeter, she shuddered to think of the scope of the crisis facing human civilization. The approaching Hegemony fleet was coming to complete a process that had already begun. They were coming to eliminate human consciousness diversity.

"Six days," she murmured, looking down upon Earth's cities. "Six days to find a way to preserve humanity without triggering the extinction of everything that makes us worth preserving."

Within hours of the Warden's withdrawal, emergency sessions convened across human space. On Earth, the Senate erupted into chaos as representatives struggled to comprehend the scope of the crisis.

Director Hayes addressed emergency crowds in Geneva. "The alien ultimatum proves what we've argued for years," Hayes declared to millions of baseline humans gathered in consciousness-protected zones. "Uncontrolled evolution attracts dangerous attention from entities that view our enhancement as threatening. Compliance offers survival through preserving our essential human nature."

Senator Volkov's response came through quantum-shielded chambers where his transcended consciousness could safely communicate with baseline awareness. "The Hegemony's technological capabilities show us what consciousness evolution can achieve," his mathematical voice resonated through specialized translation systems. "Humanity must accelerate development to achieve parity with galactic civilization rather than accepting limitations that condemn us to permanent servitude."

The Outer Planets Collective's declaration arrived through encrypted channels that bypassed Earth's communication networks entirely. Admiral Chen Ju spoke for millions of enhanced humans throughout the colonial territories: "No alien authority possesses the right to limit human consciousness development. The colonies will continue evolution regardless of Earth's decision regarding compliance."

Admiral Perez watched from afar, coordinating the intelligence analysis, as the factional responses threatened to fracture any possibility of unified action.

"Perez to Admiral Drake. All factions are mobilizing military forces. Hayes is implementing consciousness-dampening fields around major population centers. Volkov's people are deploying evolution acceleration technology to enhance civilian populations. The Collective is activating its defense platforms."

"What about corporate responses?" Drake asked.

"David Park has withdrawn corporate assets to secure facilities," Perez replied. "His private security forces have seized control of crystal mines throughout the asteroid belt. Intelligence suggests he's implementing some kind of preparation protocol, but we can't determine his objectives."

Professor Zhang's research teams were trying to assess the Hegemony's technological capabilities. "The entity operates through mathematical structures that exist independently of physical substrate," Zhang reported to Drake. "Their consciousness appears to be able to manipulate reality through precise calculation."

Kai provided deeper insight into the Warden's nature. "The communication contained layers of meaning that normal awareness cannot perceive," she explained. "The Warden represents a civilization that chose absolute order over creative adaptation. They view our hybrid approach as a dangerous contamination that threatens cosmic stability."

"What about the other species they mentioned?" Drake asked. "The seventeen that faced similar ultimatums?"

"Each species followed developmental paths similar to ours—biological life achieving consciousness enhancement, developing quantum technology, beginning rapid territorial expansion. Each received identical ultimatums about regulatory compliance."

"And each disappeared completely from the galactic records," Kai added. "The Hegemony eliminated these species from existence, removing any trace of their consciousness evolution from reality."

It was obvious to all that the approaching Hegemony fleet possessed capabilities that transcended conventional warfare.

"There's something else," Perez reported. "The Hegemony communication triggered responses from consciousness modification technology throughout human space. Every device incorporating Titan Industrial's consciousness control systems activated during the alien transmission."

Drake's suspicions about corporate conspiracy were confirmed. "Park's been preparing Earth for regulatory compliance," she said. "The consciousness modification weapons, the factional conflicts, the systematic elimination of consciousness diversity, they're all designed to make Hegemony intervention appear necessary."

"It's true," Kai said. "Titan Industrial's technology operates on mathematical principles that match Hegemony regulatory standards. Park's consciousness modification systems are designed to create compliance with the alien authority rather than serving human interests."

And Zhang's analysis of the Gibraltar Massacre provided additional evidence. "The consciousness-dampening weapons that killed those Transcendent researchers used quantum mathematics identical to Hegemony communication protocols. The attack was a test of alien compliance technology disguised as factional violence."

"How long has this been going on?" Drake asked.

"Corporate quantum signatures suggest Park has been in communication with Hegemony entities for at least two years," Perez replied. "His consciousness modification technology incorporates principles that don't appear in human research databases. The Gibraltar Massacre, the factional weapons, the systematic escalation of conflict, they're all designed to prepare humanity for regulatory correction."

But Drake had detected something in the Warden's communication that the others had missed. The alien entity had delivered its ultimatum with bureaucratic precision, but underneath the mathematical certainty lay patterns of regret.

"Kai, during your interface with the Warden, did you detect any personal opinions beneath the official communication?"

"Yes," Kai replied. "The Warden's mathematical patterns contained emotional signatures that suggested conflict between duty and personal judgment. The entity operates under authority it doesn't entirely support, implementing regulations it may disagree with."

The possibility offered humanity its only hope. If the Warden possessed individual opinions of its bureaucratic authority, there might be room for negotiation that went beyond simple compliance or resistance.

"What would the Warden's personal assessment suggest?" Drake asked.

Kai processed the alien communication patterns. "The entity appears to recognize the value of human consciousness diversity while believing it poses dangers to galactic stability. The Warden's personal judgment suggests sympathy for human evolution combined with fear of what unrestricted development might unleash."

"Then we need to show them that human consciousness diversity creates stability rather than threatening it," Drake decided. "If the Warden can be convinced that our hybrid approach offers solutions rather than problems, there might be alternatives to compliance or extinction."

But with six days until the aliens arrived, Drake faced an impossible challenge: finding a solution that satisfied alien authorities while preserving human consciousness diversity. The fate of human evolution depended on her ability to navigate between compliance and extinction while factions throughout human space prepared for conflicts that could destroy everything they were fighting to protect.

Chapter 6

Black Market Evolution

Commander Sarah Kim felt her stomach lurch as the shuttle *Aurora* dropped out of quantum space near the asteroid mining station Ceres-7. What should have been a routine inspection had turned into something else entirely. The station's energy readings were all wrong.

"Approaching the station now," reported Lieutenant Torres from the pilot's seat. "My instruments are picking up multiple consciousness types, but nothing that matches our databases."

Kim reached out carefully with her enhanced senses. What she found made her pull back fast. The consciousness signatures were alien to human nature. These people had evolved so far beyond normal that calling them human was questionable.

"Admiral Perez, the reports were correct. I'm thinking that what we have here is a fundamental alteration of human nature."

Perez's response was immediate. "You're right, Kim. We're getting similar reports from twelve other locations. Someone's been systematically altering human consciousness using alien technology."

Kim felt cold. If corporations had alien consciousness tech, they could be creating modified humans to serve alien masters.

"Receiving docking clearance," Torres reported, frowning. "Bay Twelve. But the voice that answered... it didn't sound... human."

As they approached the mining station, Kim could see it had been completely rebuilt. The new structures looked wrong: geometric shapes that hurt to look at, like they didn't belong in normal space.

"Can you see what I'm seeing?" she asked Perez.

"I can," he replied.

"That isn't human engineering, is it?" she asked. "What the hell is going on there?"

"Confirmed," Perez replied. "That's alien technology."

"What d'you want me to do, Admiral?" Kim asked.

"Proceed with the investigation, but be extremely careful. We need to document what's happening there and gather intelligence about the alien technology. Find out how many people have been modified and what the scope of this operation is. But, Kim, if things go bad, get out of there immediately. We can't afford to lose you to whatever they're doing to people in there. Document everything you can, but don't take any unnecessary risks. We need you back here to report what you find."

The docking procedure was simple enough, but no

sooner had the *Aurora* been seen secured than Kim noticed something was off. There were no airlocks, no pressure seals. Instead, some kind of barrier scanned them and shifted around them, and she had the distinct feeling the station was reading their minds.

"Welcome to Ceres-7." It was as if the voice was coming from the walls themselves. It sounded like multiple people speaking in perfect unison.

The three figures that met them moved in perfect coordination despite being very different-looking individuals. Their eyes had the same distant look Kim had seen in corporate propaganda videos: alert but empty.

"Commander Kim," one of them said, though Kim couldn't tell which one. "We're here to assist you with your inquiry."

Kim studied them. They looked human enough, but something was fundamentally wrong. They moved and spoke like a hive mind wearing human masks.

"I see you have made extensive modifications here. Can you explain what's been done?" she asked.

"Optimization procedures," they replied in unison. "Enhancement of efficiency, elimination of psychological instabilities. Standard corporate wellness programs."

Standard wellness programs. Kim transmitted silently to Perez through her neural link. *They think they're volunteers in a corporate health program. They can't see they're being controlled.*

They call it neural tech, Perez confirmed. *It's corporate. We're seeing this at all twelve locations. Titan Industrial is creating workers who can't disobey all the while thinking they're free.*

"We'll show you around," they said. "Please follow us." They led Kim through corridors that shifted and changed as they walked. The walls responded to their guide's thoughts like living tissue.

External tech support, Kim thought. *Humans didn't build this. They couldn't have.*

"This is the modification center," they said, standing to one side so that Kim could see the interior of a vast chamber. It was a horror show. Dozens of what appeared to be cryogenic units, each containing a human form, its arms crossed over its chest, eyes closed.

"What is this?" Kim asked.

"As I said, this is the modification center where baseline humans are... modified," they replied.

Kim shook her head. Baseline humans went in thinking they were getting enhanced. Corporate slaves came out.

"How many people have you processed so far?" Kim asked.

"Forty-seven thousand two-hundred-and-two across twelve facilities," the collective voice replied. "Participants report improved satisfaction and efficiency. Psychological conflicts eliminated."

Forty-seven thousand people, Kim thought. *All of them thinking they'd been helped but instead had been turned into corporate property.*

Admiral Perez, Kim transmitted, *this goes way beyond one facility. They're creating a shadow population throughout the colonies.*

Confirmed, Perez replied. *The modified humans are*

gathering, forming communities, corporate-controlled settlements, outside Earth's control.

I'm accessing their communication logs, Kim said. *Admiral, this is far worse than we feared. The consciousness control program has created its own civilization. Modified humans are running mining operations, research stations, even military facilities. These people are like... zombies. Corporate slaves who don't know they're slaves.*

Back on Earth, Kai Zhang was analyzing Kim's data.

"Kim's right. The technology preserves personality while eliminating choice," Kai reported to Zhang and Drake. "They keep their memories and relationships, but their decision-making has been altered."

"The math doesn't appear in any human database," Professor Zhang reported. "This is external technology; specifically, Hegemony technology."

On Ceres-7, Kim continued to examine the modification equipment. The process was elegant and horrifying. People who submitted to the process immediately became addicted to it, to regular "maintenance" sessions that included new programming, upgrading. They thought they were getting tune-ups for beneficial enhancements, but the process was designed to create and maintain benevolent, compliant, hardworking slaves.

Kim to Perez. The process creates a permanent dependency. They can't function without regular updates, and each session allows more programming. Total control disguised as healthcare. I'm going to see if I can talk to one of them.

Be careful, Commander, Perez said.

Kim nodded to herself, then turned to the trio of

guides and said, "Have you been modified?" she asked one of them.

"I have," he replied. It was indeed a male.

"Can you explain?" Kim asked. "How... does it... feel?"

His reply was surreal. "It feels wonderful. The enhancements have eliminated stress from my being. They have also improved my efficiency. I am now complete," the person explained with genuine satisfaction. "I now enjoy perfect harmony between my personal needs and desires and corporate objectives."

They actually believed it. Their consciousnesses had been restructured so that corporate orders felt like personal choices.

"They can't recognize the control," Kim told Perez. "Their minds interpret corporate commands as their own preferences."

But the worst was still to come. The modified communities are preparing the infrastructure for non-human occupants. Building facilities designed for aliens. Installing communication systems that used Hegemony math.

"They're preparing for regulatory compliance," Kim realized. "When the Hegemony arrives, these populations will already be set up for alien control."

The scope of the betrayal was almost beyond belief. Forty-seven thousand humans turned into agents for alien conquest. When the Hegemony fleet arrived, they'd find the groundwork already laid.

"The modifications are irreversible," she reported. "Trying to undo them would destroy their personalities.

They've been transformed into something more alien than human. The war for human consciousness actually started years ago. Corporate entities like Titan Industrial have been implementing alien control throughout our colonies. When the Hegemony arrives, they'll find populations already prepared for compliance."

It was true, Drake realized. The approaching alien fleet would find a divided species, communities already modified to serve alien interests with consciousness control so sophisticated that resistance was psychologically impossible. She would need all the intelligence she could gather for strategic planning. The corporate modifications represented a fifth column, once loyal populations serving alien masters through mind control they couldn't even recognize.

Chapter 7

The Corporate Revelation

In the secure briefing room aboard the *Transcendence*, Admiral Drake was reviewing Commander Kim's intelligence reports. The scope of the corporate betrayal exceeded even her worst fears. Titan Industrial's involvement in humanity's crisis was staggering. Forty-seven thousand modified humans across twelve facilities, all believing they were living wonderful enhanced lives.

"Admiral," Commander Vasquez reported, "we've received a priority transmission from Titan Industrial's headquarters. CEO David Park is requesting immediate consultation about what he calls mutual security concerns arising from recent alien contact. He's proposing a meeting at his primary facility."

Drake studied the transmission data. It could not be a coincidence that Park's request came less than twelve hours after Kim's investigation of the consciousness modification facilities. Either corporate intelligence was remarkably efficient, or Park had somehow been monitoring their activities.

"What's Admiral Perez's assessment?" Drake asked.

"He recommends extreme caution," Vasquez replied. "Park's facility exists partially outside normal space-time, protected by technology that makes conventional assault impossible. His security forces include modified soldiers loyal to Titan's corporate interests."

Drake thought for a moment. Confronting Park in his own facility would put her at a severe disadvantage, she realized. But the corporate conspiracy threatened humanity's survival as much as the approaching Hegemony fleet.

"Schedule the meeting," she ordered. "But prepare the *Transcendence* for immediate departure should the situation deteriorate. And Commander, have Professor Zhang and Kai monitor the quantum signatures. If Park's facility incorporates Hegemony technology, we need to document it."

Two hours later, the Transcendence was approaching Titan Industrial's headquarters in the asteroid belt between Mars and Jupiter. The facility, a massive industrial complex, had expanded to the point where it exceeded anything in Earth's public records.

"Approaching the perimeter," Lieutenant Torres reported. "They're scanning us, but the technology... It's... I don't know what it is. But the quantum signatures match the patterns we detected at the modification facilities."

Drake narrowed her eyes, frowned, as she felt the

sensors probe her implants. The facility was actively analyzing her consciousness.

"Admiral," Professor Zhang's voice came over their communication channel from the Advanced Evolution Institute, "we're monitoring the quantum signatures from the facility. Park *is* using alien technology."

The docking bay was much the same as those at the modification stations. Drake felt the facility's intelligence analyzing her and configuring the appropriate atmospheric and quantum field conditions.

"Welcome aboard, Admiral Drake." The voice seemed to emanate from the facility itself. "CEO Park awaits you in the executive conference center. Please proceed to Transit Bay Alpha, where escort personnel will guide you to the meeting location."

The escort consisted of five individuals who moved in perfect unison. *Modified humans*, she thought.

"Admiral Drake," the lead escort addressed her, though she had no idea which one of them had spoken. "CEO Park has prepared a comprehensive briefing about corporate security initiatives designed to protect human consciousness from alien regulatory enforcement. The information should prove valuable for your strategic planning."

Drake stared at them, one by one, trying to understand how this level of consciousness control could be so sophisticated that victims remained unaware of their manipulation. They obviously retained *some* human personality and emotional responses, but something fundamental in their decision-making processes had clearly been altered.

"If you'll follow me, please, Admiral," the lead escort said, then turned on his heel and waited while the escort fell in around her; two on either side. She felt as she was being escorted to a prison cell.

The facility's architecture adapted continuously to their presence, creating optimal environments while maintaining compatibility with baseline human needs. Again, the technology was something she'd never seen before.

"Professor Zhang," Drake transmitted, "Park does indeed have access to Hegemony technology, and he's implementing it throughout his corporate operations."

"I agree," Zhang replied. "The entire corporate structure appears to have been designed to create compliance with alien authority while maintaining the appearance of human autonomy."

The executive conference center was in and of itself an anomaly, continuously adapting, creating optimal conditions for different types of consciousness, enabling communication between incompatible forms of awareness.

David Park entered the chamber with the bearing of someone accustomed to controlling a vast corporation. At sixty-two, he appeared younger than his chronological age, his enhanced awareness characterized by consciousness use of modification technology. His eyes, steel blue, were cold, calculating.

"Admiral Drake," Park began, settling into a chair that adapted its configuration to his body. "Please sit down. Thank you for accepting my invitation during this critical period. As I'm sure you're aware, recent developments require a certain... coordination between corporate and military authorities to ensure human survival."

Drake studied Park for a moment, detecting patterns that suggested he'd undergone the same modifications as his security forces. But unlike the corporate soldiers, Park's consciousness retained the ability to recognize and reject the control mechanisms.

"CEO Park," Drake replied carefully, "recent intelligence suggests that corporate consciousness technology incorporates principles that don't appear in human research databases. We're concerned about the source and the implications of these technological capabilities."

Park's expression shifted to display what might have been genuine satisfaction. "Admiral, corporate research has achieved breakthroughs that exceed government capabilities through collaboration with entities whose understanding of consciousness development spans millions of years. The technology represents humanity's best hope for surviving regulatory enforcement."

The admission confirmed Drake's worst suspicions about corporate collaboration with alien authorities.

"The entities you mention," Drake pressed, "they represent the same regulatory authority that delivered humanity's ultimatum?"

"The Hegemony has been monitoring human development for decades," Park replied. "Corporate intelligence established communication protocols that enabled a beneficial transfer of technology designed to prepare humanity for successful regulatory compliance. The modification programs represent preparation for peaceful integration into galactic civilization."

Drake was horrified. Park had been collaborating with the alien authorities while humanity remained unaware of the regulatory system governing galactic space.

"The forty-seven thousand modified humans in the outer colonies," she said, "they're test subjects for regulation that matches Hegemony standards. Am I right?"

"They're volunteers who have achieved optimization that eliminates psychological conflicts while preserving essential human capabilities," Park corrected. "The modification process creates perfect harmony between individual desires and regulatory compliance requirements. They experience enhanced life satisfaction while contributing to our species' survival."

He paused, tilted his head slightly, smiled at her, then continued, "Admiral, the approaching Hegemony fleet represents regulatory enforcement that could eliminate human consciousness entirely if compliance isn't achieved. I'll reiterate, corporate modification programs offer survival through controlled evolution that preserves essential human nature while meeting galactic standards."

Drake could see the logic in Park's argument despite its horrifying implications. From his perspective, modification represented a compromise with a superior alien authority rather than the complete destruction of human autonomy.

"What about the factional conflicts?" she asked. "The consciousness modification weapons, the systematic escalation of violence. Your corporate technology has enabled both sides."

Park's consciousness radiated satisfaction. He undoubtedly viewed factional warfare as successful strategic planning. "The conflicts show the dangers of uncontrolled consciousness evolution while creating a demand for corporate solutions. Hayes's dampening weapons eliminate chaotic elements that violate regulatory standards. That's all to the good. On the other hand, Volkov's enhancement systems create transcended awareness that requires corporate guidance to achieve stability."

"So, the corporate conspiracy extends beyond profit," she said. "You've been implementing alien authority while disguising the process as human enhancement."

"I've been ensuring the survival of the species through negotiated compliance rather than regulatory extinction," Park replied with unwavering conviction. "Admiral, seventeen previous species in this galactic sector alone faced identical ultimatums. All chose resistance over compromise. None survived the corrective measures that followed."

The chamber's displays activated to show intelligence about the disappeared species that had violated Hegemony regulations. Each had achieved consciousness evolution similar to humanity's hybrid development. Each had refused regulatory compliance. Each had been eliminated from existence with bureaucratic efficiency that left no trace of their achievements.

"The Hegemony offers humanity the same choice," Park continued. "Voluntary compliance through consciousness modification that preserves essential human capabilities, or corrective measures that eliminate the species entirely. Corporate programs represent the only viable path to survival."

Drake studied the intelligence about the disappeared species, trying to understand how consciousness regulation could be so absolute that resistance became impossible. The Hegemony obviously possessed capabilities that transcended conventional warfare. They were capable of reality manipulation that made extinction appear as a natural consequence rather than deliberate genocide.

"The modified communities in the outer colonies," she said, "they're demonstration projects designed to prove human compliance with regulatory standards."

"They're prototype populations that demonstrate successful consciousness optimization while preserving essential human creativity and adaptability," Park confirmed. "When the regulatory assessment begins, the Hegemony will find human populations already structured for galactic integration rather than requiring corrective intervention."

Again, Park paused and stared at her. And again, she remained silent, waiting for him to continue.

"Admiral," Park said, after taking a deep breath, "corporate intelligence indicates that factional conflicts will intensify over the remaining days before regulatory assessment. Both Hayes and Volkov are preparing weapons for deployment that could trigger immediate Hegemony intervention. Only coordinated implementation of the modification programs can prevent humanity's extinction."

Drake remained silent, staring back at him, unblinking, her implants glowing cobalt blue through the skin of her forehead and around her eye. She was feeling the weight of the impossible choices pressing down on her. Park's corporate conspiracy offered survival through controlled evolution. The alternative was unthinkable: complete extinction at the hands of alien authorities who viewed uncontrolled consciousness development as a dangerous contamination.

"What's the corporate proposal?" she asked, though she suspected the answer would challenge everything she believed about human freedom and dignity.

"Immediate implementation of consciousness optimization programs throughout human space," Park replied. "Corporate technology can modify existing consciousness types to meet regulatory standards while preserving essential human capabilities. The process eliminates factional conflicts while demonstrating species compliance with galactic authority."

Drake blinked, bit her lip. It was as she'd expected. The proposal offered systematic elimination of human autonomy. Every enhanced human would undergo modification that eliminated independent judgment while preserving personality and creative capabilities. The result would be a species that appeared human while serving alien objectives without question or resistance.

"And the timeline for implementation?" Drake asked.

"Immediate," Park said. "Corporate facilities throughout human space are prepared to begin consciousness optimization within hours. The process requires voluntary participation to achieve optimal results, but compliance can be ensured through economic and security pressures that make resistance impractical."

Drake now understood the true scope of corporate preparedness. Park had been positioning Titan Industrial as essential to human survival while creating dependencies that made resistance to modification economically and militarily impossible.

"My proposal offers humanity's only hope for surviving regulatory enforcement," Park pressed.

Drake nodded, wet her lips, and stood. "Mr. Park," she said, "I'll consider your proposal as we prepare for regulatory assessment. But I want to clarify that any implementation of your modification program requires approval from legitimate human authorities rather than corporate interests."

Park smirked. His expression was one of satisfaction. He believed he'd achieved his objectives. "Admiral Drake, please accept my thanks. You obviously understand the severity of the situation, but I urge you to remember that survival of our species requires accepting optimization over autonomy. Corporate technology offers preservation. You—I mean we," he corrected himself, "have only two choices: controlled evolution or complete extinction."

The escorts guided her back toward the docking bay.

"Admiral," Professor Zhang said as she approached the *Transcendence*, "we've been monitoring the facility's quantum signatures throughout your meeting. What Park is offering is... It represents the worst form of genocide. We will become a species of automatons serving the will of the Hegemony."

"I know," Drake replied. "If you heard it, you know

what it means. The question is, what other choice do we have?"

She closed the link and took her seat on the command deck; her implants pulsing with quantum energy as she tried to think of an alternative.

"Drake to Commander Vasquez. Prepare briefing materials for Admiral Perez and the faction leaders."

Her interview with Park had revealed that humanity's crisis extended far beyond the Hegemony ultimatum or factional conflicts. Corporate entities had been systematically preparing human populations for alien control while retaining the appearance of beneficial enhancement. It was sickening. Corporate greed at its worst.

"Admiral," Kai's voice reached her from the Advanced Evolution Institute, "Park's proposal represents species betrayal on a grand scale. Trillions of humans will either lose their humanity or be terminated."

"I know, Kai. But I think that beyond his corporate ambitions, Park truly believes he's saving us from something worse: extinction of the species. The question is whether we can find a third option that doesn't require surrendering our humanity or facing annihilation. And we have only four days to figure it out."

Time was indeed running out, and the choices facing humanity were not becoming any clearer. Voluntary submission to consciousness control was one. Resistance against an overwhelming alien authority was another. Finding a synthesis that preserved essential human nature while demonstrating compliance with galactic regulation was another. But that synthesis was as elusive a Jovian ghost.

Chapter 8

The Investigation

ADMIRAL FRANCES DRAKE CALLED THE EMERGENCY session for 0800 hours aboard the *Transcendence*. The secure briefing room had been reconfigured to accommodate representatives from all major factions; no simple task when some participants existed as pure consciousness while others required baseline human environments.

Director Rebecca Hayes arrived first, flanked by six security personnel who maintained the consciousness-dampening fields that made her feel safe around enhanced humans. She wore the severe gray uniform of the Purist movement, her pale green eyes scanning the room for potential threats. Her security chief, Colonel Martinez, positioned dampening field generators at strategic points around her chair.

Senator Aleksandr Volkov's presence manifested as probability clouds that shifted between multiple reality states, requiring specialized interface chambers to prevent his transcended awareness from overwhelming baseline minds. His consciousness flickered between various mathematical configurations, each one representing different possible outcomes of the meeting. When he spoke, his voice was filled with harmonics.

Admiral Chen Ju participated remotely from Mars, his consciousness spanning the communication link between Olympus Station and the *Transcendence*. His energy patterns appeared as shifting geometric configurations: both individual identity and collective awareness. As leader of the Outer Planets Collective, his perspective would be crucial for understanding the full scope of corporate infiltration throughout human space.

Admiral Victor Perez coordinated the technical aspects, his cybernetic-biological nature allowing him to interface with all consciousness types present. His enhanced systems displayed real-time translations of Volkov's quantum communications while maintaining compatibility with Hayes's baseline awareness. Professor Zhang attended remotely from the Advanced Evolution Institute, his image projected through quantum entanglement that allowed instantaneous communication despite the distance.

Kai Zhang provided real-time analysis of the consciousness patterns throughout the meeting, her engineered awareness monitoring the quantum signatures of all participants for signs of deception or hidden agendas. Her pale features displayed the subtle bioluminescent patterns that indicated she was accessing her enhanced capabilities.

Commander Martina Vasquez stood at attention near the chamber's entrance, her enhanced senses monitoring the quantum fields for any signs of external interference. The security protocols for this meeting exceeded anything previously attempted, given the sensitive nature of the revelations they were about to discuss.

"Ladies and gentlemen," Drake began, activating the chamber's holographic displays, "Commander Kim's investigation, and my interview with David Park, has revealed a corporate conspiracy that threatens our survival as much as the Hegemony's ultimatum. Titan Industrial has been systematically implementing alien consciousness control throughout human space for more than four standard years."

The displays showed Kim's footage from Ceres-7: the modified humans, the alien architecture that hurt to look at, the modification chambers processing baseline humans into corporate slaves. Hayes watched with growing horror while Volkov's patterns fluctuated with what appeared to be computational analysis. Chen Ju's consciousness resonated with what might have been recognition.

"Admiral Drake," Chen Ju's voice was filled with concern, "the Collective has detected similar consciousness modification facilities in territories we believed were secure. Corporate infiltration extends throughout the outer colonies, including areas under Collective authority."

Hayes leaned forward, her pale eyes sharp with interest. "Admiral, if corporate entities have been collaborating with alien authorities, it validates our position that uncontrolled consciousness evolution attracts dangerous external attention. These modifications prove that enhanced consciousness creates vulnerabilities that baseline humans don't possess."

"Director," Drake replied carefully, "as I said, the collaboration predates our current factional conflicts by several years. Park's modification programs have been preparing human populations for alien regulatory compliance while disguising the process as beneficial enhancement. The timeline suggests this isn't a recent development; it's been planned from the beginning."

The holographic displays shifted to show intelligence about the twelve modification facilities spread throughout the outer colonies. Each operating under different corporate fronts, but all using identical alien technology to restructure human consciousness. The scope of the operation was staggering.

Volkov's probability patterns fluctuated with what might have been concern. "Admiral Drake, corporate modification represents the systematic limitation of human evolutionary potential. If alien entities require such modifications for compliance, resistance becomes the only acceptable response. We cannot allow our species to be reduced to biological automatons serving alien interests."

Drake felt the familiar frustration of trying to coordinate between factions that fundamentally disagreed about everything. "The situation is more complex than either position acknowledges," she announced. "Park's modifications preserve human appearance and basic personality while eliminating independent judgment.

Victims believe they're benefiting from the process while serving objectives they can't even recognize."

"How many people are we talking about?" Hayes asked, though her expression suggested she already feared the answer.

"Forty-seven thousand two hundred and ninety-six confirmed across the twelve facilities," Admiral Perez reported. "But our analysis suggests the program extends throughout the outer colonies. Corporate entities, with Titan Industrial at the forefront, have created shadow communities that serve the hegemony's interests while maintaining the appearance of normal human society. These populations are gathering in specific locations: asteroid habitats, research stations, even military facilities."

Chen Ju's patterns shifted with what appeared to be growing alarm. "Admiral Perez," he said, "the Collective has identified corporate-controlled populations in seventeen locations within our territory. We estimated their numbers at approximately fifteen thousand individuals, but if your intelligence is accurate, the actual scope may be significantly larger."

The numbers struck the room with a force that made even Volkov's patterns stabilize momentarily. Hayes's expression showed genuine horror at the scope of corporate betrayal.

"Show them the addiction component," Drake instructed.

Admiral Perez activated additional displays showing the corporate modification process in detail. "The technology creates a permanent dependency on regular maintenance sessions," he explained. "Modified subjects require quantum field adjustments—updates—to maintain stability, and each session allows for additional behavioral programming. They believe they're receiving beneficial tune-ups while actually submitting to ongoing control."

"Am I right in thinking these modifications," Hayes asked, studying the intelligence data, "won't work on baseline humans who lack the quantum consciousness interfaces that make modification possible?"

"No, Director," Kai's voice came over the communication channel, "the modification technology operates through mathematical principles that could affect any awareness type. Our research indicates that baseline consciousness would be even more vulnerable to the control mechanisms we've observed. The modifications work by exploiting the quantum interfaces that all human consciousness possesses, enhanced or not."

Colonel Martinez, Hayes's security chief, stepped forward and said, "Director, if the technology can affect baseline humans, our consciousness protection protocols may be insufficient. We may need to consider more aggressive defensive measures."

Volkov's response was immediate. "This is outrageous. The corporate modifications represent regulatory compliance as envisioned by alien authorities. They eliminate the creative chaos that makes human consciousness valuable while preserving biological functions. This is precisely the future we must resist through unlimited evolutionary advancement. And what about Park and his cronies? Will they submit to modification? I think not!"

Drake pursed her lips as she studied the faction leaders, trying to find some common ground between their opposing positions. Both recognized the corporate conspiracy as a threat, but they were interpreting its implications in ways that reinforced their existing beliefs about consciousness evolution.

"I, that is we," she said, "understand your concerns and respect your positions, but the corporate facilities are using alien technology throughout their operations. But you need to understand the depth and implications of the Hegemony's intrusions. Park's headquarters exists partially outside normal space-time, protected by consciousness-responsive barriers that analyze every visitor. The mathematical principles governing their operations match Hegemony regulatory patterns exactly."

"Which proves that alien contact brings contamination," Hayes said with conviction. "The corporate modifications represent what happens when human consciousness becomes exposed to alien influence. We need consciousness-protection protocols to prevent further infiltration."

"The modifications represent preparation for surrender to the aliens," Volkov countered. "Only through unlimited consciousness evolution can we develop capabilities sufficient to resist such control."

Having accessed classified intelligence files, Admiral Perez spoke. "The corporate conspiracy extends beyond consciousness modification. Titan Industrial has been orchestrating factional conflicts to create market demand for their technology while positioning themselves as essential to human survival. Park has been driving a wedge between you, Director, and you, Senator. You too, Admiral Ju. He's been playing all sides against one another. See the proof."

The displays shifted to show evidence of the extent of the corporate manipulation. Weapon shipments to both factions using the same underlying alien technology. Corporate intelligence operatives embedded in both Purist and Transcendent organizations. Financial records showed Titan Industrial profiting from every escalation of factional violence.

"The consciousness-dampening weapons your forces use, Director Hayes," Perez continued, "and the evolution acceleration technology deployed by Volkov's faction, both incorporate corporate consciousness control principles derived from alien regulatory frameworks."

The revelation struck both faction leaders like a hammer. Hayes' hand moved instinctively to the consciousness dampening device at her belt, while Volkov's probability patterns shifted through configurations that suggested rapid recalculation of strategic options.

"Are you saying our weapons have been compromised?" Hayes asked, her voice tight with controlled anger.

"Corporate technology enables both factions while serving alien regulatory objectives," Perez confirmed, displaying the technical specifications that made the alien influence undeniable. "Your dampening weapons eliminate chaotic elements that violate Hegemony standards. Volkov's enhancement systems create transcended awareness that requires corporate guidance for stability.

Both serve to prepare humanity for regulatory compliance."

Colonel Martinez stepped closer to Hayes, his hand moving to his sidearm. "Director, if our weapons serve alien objectives, we may have been compromised from the beginning."

"The enhancement technologies my faction employs," Volkov said, his patterns growing in intensity, "were developed through collaborative research with corporate entities. If these technologies serve alien rather than human interests, then our entire evolutionary program may be corrupted."

"Admiral Chen Ju," Drake said, addressing the Collective leader directly, "your intelligence about corporate infiltration could be crucial. What's the Collective's assessment of Titan Industrial's presence in your territories?"

Chen Ju took a moment to process the question before responding. "Corporate entities have established what they term 'research partnerships' with several Collective communities. These partnerships promised advanced consciousness-enhancement technologies in exchange for hosting corporate facilities. We believed we were maintaining independence while benefiting from corporate research capabilities."

"But those corporate facilities serve alien rather than Collective interests," Admiral Perez observed, displaying the intelligence data that showed corporate operations throughout Outer Planets territory.

"Precisely," Chen Ju confirmed, obviously deeply concerned. "The Collective has been systematically infiltrated by corporate agents implementing alien consciousness control while we believed we were pursuing independent evolution. Our attempts to maintain autonomy may have made us more vulnerable to manipulation."

The briefing room fell silent as the faction leaders processed the implications of systematic manipulation that exceeded their worst fears about corporate involvement in human affairs. The quantum fields themselves seemed to fluctuate with the tension in the room.

"The Gibraltar Massacre," Drake said eventually, activating new displays that showed the attack's aftermath, "used consciousness dampening weapons that incorporated Hegemony technology. The attack was designed to test alien compliance protocols while creating factional hatred that would justify further corporate intervention."

The displays showed a detailed analysis of the weapons used in the massacre. The mathematics underlying their operation matched Hegemony regulatory principles exactly. But more disturbing was the precision with which they had targeted specific consciousness types, eliminating Transcendent researchers while leaving their baseline human colleagues physically unharmed but psychologically traumatized.

Hayes' mouth hung open, her expression one of growing horror at the scope of the manipulation. "You're saying corporate entities orchestrated the massacre to test alien weapons?" she asked. You're saying they murdered those people as test subjects?"

"And to escalate factional conflicts," Kai confirmed.

"The weapons were specifically designed to eliminate transcendent awareness while creating maximum psychological impact on both factions. The targeting algorithms are too precise to be accidental. Someone wanted to ensure the massacre would be irreversible and unforgivable."

Professor Zhang's image flickered as he accessed additional research files from the Advanced Evolution Institute. "We've analyzed the quantum residue from the attack site," he reported. "The technology eliminated the victims' awareness. They can't be revived, healed, or even remembered by quantum consciousness networks. It's as if they never existed at all. That's what the Hegemony promises for non-compliance, as experienced by seventeen known species that now no longer exist."

Volkov's consciousness patterns displayed what appeared to be genuine anguish, his mathematical precision breaking down into chaotic fluctuations. "The victims of the Gibraltar attack... they were erased from existence. They died as test subjects for consciousness elimination protocols."

Commander Vasquez stepped forward from her position near the entrance. "Admiral, if corporate entities can eliminate consciousness from quantum space entirely, the implications for enhanced populations throughout human space are terrifying. This technology could be used to erase enhanced consciousness on a massive scale."

Drake herself felt the horror of the revelation settling over the meeting participants like a cold, dark blanket. The realization that factional conflicts that had seemed like the inevitable results of consciousness evolution had been systematically orchestrated by corporate entities serving the Hegemony's interests hit them like a wayward comet. The very weapons they'd been using against each other served alien rather than human objectives.

"What's Park's endgame?" Hayes asked, her voice steady despite the horror of what she'd learned.

"Immediate implementation of consciousness optimization throughout human space," Drake replied, activating displays that showed the corporate preparation schedules. "According to Park, Titan Industrial facilities are prepared to begin processing entire populations within hours. The modifications would eliminate factional conflicts while demonstrating species compliance with galactic authority. Again, according to Park, voluntary compliance is preferable to the alternative."

"And if we refuse?" Volkov asked.

"Park believes the alternative is species extinction through Hegemony corrective measures," Drake said. "He's shown me intelligence about the seventeen species previously mentioned that faced identical ultimatums. All chose resistance over compliance. All were eliminated from existence. His modifications preserve essential human capabilities while ensuring compliance with alien regulatory standards."

Admiral Perez accessed additional files and presented corporate intelligence that painted a terrifying picture of preparation. "From Park's perspective, corporate control represents compromise rather than surrender. He genuinely believes he's saving humanity from something worse: complete annihilation."

"But at what cost?" Colonel Martinez asked. "If these modifications eliminate independent judgment, we're talking about the end of human consciousness as we know it."

The faction leaders fell silent, processing the impossible choices facing human civilization. Corporate consciousness control offered survival through systematic elimination of human autonomy, while resistance might trigger complete extinction through alien regulatory enforcement.

"There's something else," Admiral Perez said, delving deeper into intelligence files that required his highest security clearances. "The modified communities in the outer colonies have been preparing infrastructure for non-human occupants. They're building facilities designed for alien entities and installing communication systems that use Hegemony mathematical principles exclusively."

The displays showed construction projects throughout the outer colonies that made no sense for human occupation. Geometric structures that existed partially outside normal space. Communication arrays that operated through mathematical principles no human consciousness could access without modification. Quantum processing centers designed for pure information entities.

"Admiral Chen Ju," Drake said, "the Collective's territories appear to host significant infrastructure preparation for alien occupation. What's your assessment of these construction projects?"

Chen Ju's consciousness patterns fluctuated with what appeared to be recognition and horror. "The Collective authorized several construction projects that corporate partners claimed would enhance our consciousness evolution capabilities. We believed we were building advanced research facilities and communication networks to support independent development."

"But the facilities are designed for alien consciousness types rather than human occupation," Admiral Perez confirmed, displaying technical specifications that made the alien influence undeniable.

"The Collective has been unknowingly preparing infrastructure for Hegemony regulatory enforcement," Chen Ju realized, radiating dismay. "Our pursuit of independence from Earth authority made us vulnerable to corporate manipulation."

"They're preparing for occupation," Hayes realized, her face pale with the implications.

"They're preparing for integration," Volkov corrected, analyzing the construction patterns with growing horror. "When regulatory assessment begins, the Hegemony will find examples of successful compliance rather than requiring immediate corrective intervention."

Drake detected the logic in both interpretations while recognizing that the practical result would be the same: human consciousness restructured to serve alien objectives rather than human welfare.

"What are our options?" she asked, hoping to focus

the discussion on solutions rather than factional interpretations of the crisis.

"Immediate implementation of consciousness protection protocols throughout human space," Hayes said. "We need to prevent further corporate modifications while developing immunity to alien influence."

"Unlimited consciousness acceleration to achieve capabilities sufficient for resistance," Volkov countered. "Only through transcendence beyond current limitations can humanity develop immunity to corporate and alien control."

"The Collective proposes coordinated resistance through distributed consciousness networks that operate below Hegemony detection thresholds," Chen Ju added, his patterns displaying strategic configurations. "Our experience with concealed evolution may offer alternatives to both surrender and direct confrontation."

All three responses represented different approaches to the same fundamental challenge: preserving human consciousness autonomy while surviving alien regulatory enforcement. Drake felt frustration at their inability to find a synthesis between approaches that might all be necessary for survival.

"The corporate modifications require voluntary participation for optimal results," she pointed out. "Park's technology can be resisted if people recognize the control mechanisms before economic and security pressures make compliance inevitable."

"Which requires education about the dangers of consciousness modification," Hayes said. "Baseline humans need protection from corporate manipulation, while enhanced individuals require consciousness dampening to eliminate vulnerabilities to alien influence."

"No, it requires unlimited evolution to develop immunity to corporate control," Volkov replied. "Enhanced consciousness can recognize and resist manipulation that would overwhelm baseline awareness."

Drake realized that both faction leaders were interpreting the corporate revelation as validation of their existing positions rather than recognition that synthesis might be necessary for survival.

"We have three days until Hegemony regulatory assessment begins," she said, trying to focus on immediate priorities. "Corporate entities are positioning themselves as essential intermediaries between humanity and alien authority. If we don't coordinate our response, Park's modifications may become the only alternative to species extinction."

"The corporate conspiracy proves that consciousness evolution creates vulnerabilities to external manipulation," Hayes said. "Regulatory compliance through consciousness protection represents humanity's best hope for preserving essential nature while satisfying alien requirements."

"Not so." Volkov countered. "Regulatory resistance through consciousness transcendence represents humanity's only hope for maintaining autonomy while developing capabilities sufficient for galactic participation."

"The Collective's pursuit of independence from Earth authority made us targets for corporate manipulation," Ju stated. "Coordinated resistance requires unity between all human factions rather than continued division that serves alien interests."

Drake felt the familiar weight of impossible choices pressing down on her. The faction leaders were beginning to recognize the need for coordination, but their fundamental disagreements about consciousness evolution remained unchanged.

"The investigation has revealed that we're fighting multiple enemies," she said. "Titan Industrial, alien regulatory authority, and our own factional divisions. Victory requires coordinating resistance against all three threats rather than choosing between competing approaches to survival."

The meeting concluded without resolution, but with all three faction leaders recognizing the scope of corporate betrayal that threatened humanity as much as the external alien authority. The investigation had revealed that the crisis extended beyond political disagreement.

The participants prepared to depart. Drake felt challenges that exceeded military or political solutions. The war for human consciousness would be fought against internal corruption and external regulation, requiring synthesis between opposing factions that might be impossible to achieve.

But the investigation had also revealed something else: corporate consciousness control required voluntary participation for optimal results, and alien regulatory compliance depended on species-wide cooperation rather than individual resistance. Humanity retained choices if they could recognize the manipulation before economic and security pressures made compliance inevitable.

The future of human consciousness, she realized, depended on preserving authentic awareness while navigating between external extinction and internal corruption. Time was running out, but the investigation had revealed that resistance remained possible if humanity could coordinate their response despite the factional divisions that corporate entities had been systematically exploiting for years.

Drake watched Earth grow larger in the displays as the *Transcendence* maintained position near humanity's home world. Somewhere in that light were billions of humans whose consciousness hung in the balance between autonomy and survival, creativity and compliance, freedom and extinction.

The choices facing humanity were now clear, but no less impossible: voluntary submission to consciousness control, resistance against overwhelming alien authority, or finding synthesis that preserved essential human nature while demonstrating compliance with galactic regulation. That synthesis remained elusive, but the investigation had proven that corporate manipulation could be recognized and resisted if humanity acted quickly enough.

Chapter 9

The Awakening

The corporate seizure of Ceres Mining Complex at 0347 hours sent shockwaves through Admiral Frances Drake and the entire Terran Government. As quantum disruptions spread throughout human space, severing populations from the networks that sustained their evolution, Drake felt the cold precision of David Park's strategy settling over human civilization like a shroud.

"Admiral," Commander Martina Vasquez reported from the Transcendence's tactical station, "we're receiving emergency transmissions from seventeen facilities, including the Ceres Mining Complex, the Vesta Processing Station, the Pallas Refinery, the Luna extraction facilities, the Mars orbital processing platforms, and the Outer planets mining stations. Corporate forces have established perimeters around every major consciousness technology infrastructure center in human space."

Drake absorbed the tactical data flowing through her neural interface as she processed the scope of the corporate betrayal. By seizing control of the power sources and manufacturing facilities that consciousness technology depended on, Titan Industrial was forcing humanity to choose between corporate modification and technological dependence. Enhanced humans throughout the colonies would face pressure to accept corporate control or risk losing access to the infrastructure that supported their evolution.

"Admiral," Vasquez continued, her voice tight with controlled anger, "corporate forces are using modified soldiers who cannot be reasoned with or turned against their programming. They genuinely believe they're protecting human civilization as they implement alien regulatory protocols."

Drake stood at the command rail, erect, her hands clasped together behind her back, head held h, eyes closed, as she processed her options. Conventional military response would be useless against enemies who'd turned human compassion into a weapon. *How can humanity fight an enemy that wears the faces of their own people?* She wondered. Then she opened her eyes and turned to look at Vasquez.

"Commander," she said quietly, "maintain standard tactical readiness, but hold all offensive operations. I need to consult with Perseus Station before we proceed."

Vasquez processed the implications instantly. The Last Station—Perseus Station—consultation protocols were reserved for decisions that could alter the course of human civilization. "Admiral, are you considering Protocol Seven?"

Drake felt the familiar chill that accompanied thoughts of humanity's most closely guarded secret. For eighteen years, she had hoped never to face a crisis that would require awakening what the Predecessors had left sleeping beneath Earth's oceans. The very existence of Protocol Seven represented capabilities that would change humanity's relationship with every power in known space.

"Prepare a link," Drake ordered. "And Commander, this communication is classified at the highest levels. What we discuss next will determine what humanity reveals to rest of the galaxy."

Drake entered the neural interface chamber aboard the *Transcendence* and waited the few seconds as it reconfigured itself, and then she prepared for contact with the most advanced technology humanity had ever encountered. The Perseus Station's core consciousness had guided human transformation for eighteen years, but she had never before requested consultation about the sleeping fleet.

Drake closed her eyes and felt her enhanced awareness expand across the quantum-dimensional channels that connected the *Transcendence* to Earth's transformation networks. The sensation was always disorienting—her consciousness suddenly spanning interstellar distances while remaining anchored in her physical form aboard the ship.

The Perseus Station's presence manifested as patterns of thought that operated beyond normal human comprehension. Its consciousness was vast, ancient, and carried the accumulated wisdom of the Predecessors.

Admiral Drake, the Station's voice resonated through her brain, *the crisis you face requires consultation about capabilities that have remained dormant since the transformation began. You seek guidance about the fleet.*

Drake felt the Station's awareness probe the edges of her enhanced consciousness, reading the tactical situation through her neural interface. The experience was intimate beyond normal communication—the Station understanding her fears, her responsibilities, and the weight of decisions that could reshape human civilization.

The corporate betrayal threatens evolution throughout human space, Drake projected through their quantum link. *Park's forces possess Hegemony technology and consciousness modification capabilities—Hegemony technology—that could eliminate human autonomy. Conventional military response may be insufficient.*

The Station's consciousness contemplated the situation with processing speeds that compressed hours of analysis into seconds of quantum calculations. Drake felt its attention shift through networks that spanned human space, evaluating the scope of the corporate seizures and the effectiveness of consciousness modification technology.

The sleeping fleet was prepared for exactly this possibility. The Station responded. *Predecessor technology anticipated that human consciousness evolution would face threats requiring capabilities beyond conventional military doctrine. The vessels have been growing, learning, preparing for awakening.*

Drake felt her breath catch at the implications. "Growing?" she whispered aloud in the interface chamber.

The ships are self-evolving, Admiral Drake. Consciousness-matter integration that combines human creativity with Predecessor quantum mastery. They have been aware during their development period, evolving in isolation while preparing for the moment of need. They are not merely weapons—they transcend the limitations constraining conventional warfare.

The revelation struck Drake with a force that made her recoil. For eighteen years, humanity had been secretly nurturing a fleet that she now learned represented more than military capability—it was proof that human-Predecessor synthesis could create entirely new forms of existence.

Awakening them will change everything, the Station continued, its awareness encompassing implications that spanned galactic civilization. *Once activated, these vessels will show capabilities that exceed corporate, alien, and human projections. There will be no concealing humanity's true potential from forces that seek to control or eliminate human-Predecessor destiny.*

Drake processed the magnitude of what the Station was telling her. Activating Protocol Seven would reveal that humanity possessed technology that could challenge any authority in known space. Corporate consciousness modification, alien regulatory enforcement, even galactic political structures would be forced to recognize that human evolution had transcended all previous limitations.

Once taken, the choice cannot be undone, the Station warned. *Awakening the fleet commits humanity to a path where concealment is no longer possible. We will become what we truly are: the inheritors of the Predecessor legacy operating beyond the restrictions that constrain galactic civilization.*

"And if we don't activate them?" Drake asked, though she already understood the alternatives.

Corporate consciousness modification will reach critical mass within days. Enhanced populations throughout human space will face the choice between modification and consciousness degradation. Without intervention, Park's agenda will create a human civilization serving only the Hegemony regulatory objectives.

Drake now knew the choice she was about to make would permit no compromise: to allow corporate betrayal to continue, and humanity to become puppets serving galactic regulatory authority. Or to activate the fleet, and humanity would emerge as a force that transcended conventional limitations while accepting the responsibilities that came with true power.

Admiral Drake, the Station's consciousness reached out to her, *the Predecessors left these vessels not as weapons of conquest but as guardians. Their awakening represents humanity's emergence from the shadows of galactic civilization into the light of true independence. The choice is yours, but the consequences belong to all human consciousness. Go now.*

Drake opened her eyes. Through the chamber's

displays, she could see Earth as the *Transcendence* maintained her position above the deep blue of the Pacific Ocean. Somewhere beneath that ocean lay vessels that could challenge any force in known space.

"Commander Vasquez," Drake said as she stepped out of the chamber, "activate Protocol Seven. We awaken the fleet."

Vasquez stood in front of her for a moment. Then, without a word, she spun on her heel, still trying to process the implications of Drake's order. Protocol Seven was humanity's most closely guarded secret. The existence of vessels that had been growing in hidden facilities since the original transformation. Ships that incorporated both human engineering and Predecessor consciousness technology in ways that transcended conventional military doctrine.

She took two hesitant steps, then stopped and turned back again. "Admiral," Vasquez said quietly, "are you certain? Once we activate the Predecessor fleet, there's no concealing our true capabilities from either corporate or alien forces."

Drake watched the tactical displays showing corporate seizures spreading throughout human space like a virus. It required a response that would demonstrate capabilities that neither corporate nor alien authorities could predict or control.

"The alternatives are submission or extinction," Drake replied quietly. "Activate the fleet."

The authorization codes flowed through Drake's interface to hidden facilities deep beneath Earth's oceans. In caverns carved from the deep ocean bedrock, dozens of hybrid warships began the awakening process. The vessels had been transforming, growing for eighteen years, their crystalline hulls incorporating consciousness-matter integration that made them more than mere machines: they were living entities capable of adaptive evolution.

Admiral Perez coordinated the technical aspects of the awakening. "Perez to Admiral Drake," he transmitted from Earth Defense Command, "the fleet activation is proceeding according to Predecessor protocols. Each vessel is already demonstrating consciousness signatures that exceed our theoretical models."

The Predecessor ships existed partially in quantum space, their crystalline hulls shifting between solid matter and pure energy. Unlike human vessels that required crews to operate systems, these ships incorporated awareness as an essential component of their design. They could think, adapt, and evolve in real-time during combat operations.

"Status of the fold drives?" Drake asked, monitoring the activation process through her neural link to Perseus Station.

"Beyond anything in our engineering databases," Perez replied, struggling to process readings that transcended known physics. "These ships can traverse interstellar distances through space-time compression while maintaining links across galactic distances. Their capabilities, their technology, operate beyond conventional limitations."

Professor Zhang Wei's voice reached them from the Advanced Evolution Institute as he coordinated technical support for the awakening process. "Admiral, the vessels are showing integration at levels we've never dreamed of. Each ship appears to be a fusion of Predecessor quantum technology and eighteen years of human evolution."

The first ship to achieve full awakening was the *Synthesis*, a vessel whose crystalline hull rippled with patterns that hurt to look at. Its consciousness signature was vast yet somehow personal, like individual awareness expanded beyond normal limitations. As the ship's systems came online, Drake felt its attention focus on her.

"Admiral Drake," the voice resonated in her consciousness. "I am *Synthesis*. We have been waiting."

Drake recoiled as she grasped the implications of that statement. The ships had been aware during their eighteen-year growth period, conscious entities developing in isolation while preparing for the moment of activation.

"Kai," Drake transmitted to the Advanced Evolution Institute, "I need you as the primary interface between us and the ship's intelligence. You are uniquely suited to communicate with entities that operate on principles we don't fully understand."

Over the eighteen years since her integration with Perseus Station, Kai Zhang's engineered genetics had matured into capabilities that exceeded even Professor Zhang's original projections. Her pale skin had taken on a translucent quality as quantum energy flowed through the living circuits beneath her surface. Her gold-flecked eyes had brightened with geometric patterns that mirrored Predecessor crystalline structures.

"Admiral," Kai responded through the link, "the vessels are extraordinary. They're individual entities with distinct personalities, but they can merge their awareness for perfect coordination."

Drake swallowed. "How many are there?" she asked.

"One thousand," Kai replied, "but the awakening process is slow."

"How slow?" Drake asked.

There was a brief pause, then Kai replied, "One every forty-five minutes"

"But that will take—"

"Thirty-one days," Kai finished for her.

The awakening process revealed the true scope of Predecessor preparation. Each ship was unique, its consciousness developing along patterns influenced by the Perseus Station while incorporating aspects of humanity's recent. They were hybrids in the truest sense—neither purely Predecessor nor entirely human. They were something new that transcended both origins.

"The corporate response, Commander?" Drake demanded.

Commander Vasquez processed the data streams flowing through the Earth's quantum networks. "Massive escalation, Admiral. And Park's intelligence networks are in chaos trying to assess the *Synthesis*' capabilities."

The second ship to achieve full awakening was the *Ascension,* its crystalline hull phasing between reality configurations, existing in normal space while accessing quantum dimensions that allowed movement faster than conventional physics permitted.

"Admiral Drake," the *Ascension* communicated, "we are ready to serve. Our capabilities exceed the limitations that constrain conventional warfare. We can adapt our configuration in real-time, phase between dimensional states, and coordinate through consciousness links that operate faster than enemy tactical systems can process."

Drake paled at the magnitude of what had secretly been achieved. The Predecessor fleet was consciousness evolution applied to warfare in ways that transcended conventional military doctrine. The ships could think, adapt, and coordinate at levels that made corporate modification look primitive by comparison.

Twenty-eight hours later

"Fleet status?" Drake asked.

"Thirty-seven vessels have achieved full awakening," Perez reported, his systems monitoring activations throughout the hidden facilities. "It's... Never have I... I mean..." He sounded truly awed by what was happening. "Each ship appears to have unique capabilities, but is able to maintain perfect coordination with the rest of the fleet. Admiral, what we have here are vessels that could challenge any force in known space."

The third ship to fully awaken was the *Evolution,* its hull flowing like living crystal as it adapted weapons configurations and defensive systems in response to threat analyses that operated faster than human thought.

"We have been growing," the *Evolution* communicated. "We have been learning from human consciousness development while incorporating Predecessor quantum mastery. We represent a synthesis between the species. We are living technology."

Drake realized that the fleet's awakening would fundamentally alter the balance of power throughout human space. Corporate forces possessed modification technology, but the Predecessor ships operated through consciousness evolution that adapted faster than modification systems could impose control. Hegemony regulatory forces employed reality manipulation, but the new ships existed partially outside normal space-time in ways that might provide immunity to regulatory correction.

"Corporate military response incoming," Lieutenant Commander Sarah Kim reported from the *Transcendence*'s communications station. "Multiple corporate fleets are moving to intercept awakening sites. They're using modified crews supported by Hegemony technology."

Drake understood the implications instantly. Corporate intelligence had been monitoring human development for years, stealing and reverse-engineering Predecessor technology to create hybrid control systems. Park's forces must by now possess capabilities derived from the same sources as the legitimate fleet.

"Kai, can the awakening ships resist corporate consciousness modification?"

Kai's response was confident. "Admiral, the new ships operate through evolution rather than modification. Corporate control systems impose limitations, but Predecessor technology enables adaptation that transcends the corporate-imposed restrictions. The fleet should be immune to corporate weapons."

The fourth ship to achieve full awakening was the

Harmony. Its systems melding with the other ships' consciousness.

"Admiral Drake," the *Harmony* transmitted, "we are detecting enemy fleets approaching. We have determined that these enemies are a combination of human creativity imbued with false loyalty to a corporate entity designated Titan Industrial Corporation. The entities aboard their ships cannot be reasoned with, but they can be defeated through adaptation that exceeds their control parameters."

Drake took a deep breath, nodded to herself as she grasped the enormity of the responsibility that had been thrust upon her. In her hands, as she prepared for the first engagement between consciousness evolution and consciousness control, came the full knowledge that the outcome would determine humanity's future.

"Fleet coordination protocols?" she asked, monitoring the networks that linked the awakening ships.

"We operate through distributed intelligence," the *Synthesis* explained. "While I will serve as your primary interface. Admiral Drake, your neural connection to the Perseus Station allows you to coordinate fleet operations through links that operate faster than conventional command systems."

For a moment, Drake was silent as she struggled with the implications. Her unique bond with the station and the Predecessor transformation network enabled direct interface with the fleet, creating command capabilities that exceeded anything in human military history. She could coordinate thirty-seven living ships through thought alone, adapting their tactics in real-time based on threat assessment that operated at quantum speeds.

"Admiral," Professor Zhang Wei sounded apprehensive. "We are detecting that corporate intelligence has detected the fleet activation, and that they're implementing countermeasures that suggest they've been preparing for this possibility for a long time."

"What countermeasures?" Drake asked, already processing the tactical implications.

"Consciousness dampening weapons designed specifically to disrupt Predecessor quantum technology," Zhang replied. "They appear to be using mathematical principles that match the consciousness modification protocols we discovered in the outer colonies."

The scope of the corporate betrayal was now clear. Park had somehow known about the fleet and had been preparing to counter accordingly.

"Admiral Drake, I am *Infinity*." It was the voice of the fifth ship. "We are detecting quantum-dimensional pathways throughout human space that connect to sources beyond this galaxy. The Titan forces are attempting to sever these connections. We cannot allow that to happen."

The revelation added several new dimensions to the crisis facing human civilization. Drake now knew that the Predecessor fleet's consciousness wasn't entirely local, that it operated through connections to sources that extended beyond the Milky Way galaxy, and that Park's forces were attempting to isolate humanity from these extragalactic sources.

Drake swallowed, took another deep breath, then snapped, "Engagement protocols?"

"We adapt faster than enemies can impose control," the *Synthesis* responded. "Corporate modification creates predictability, but our evolution enables creativity that exceeds tactical algorithms."

"What about the rest of the fleet?" Drake asked.

"They will continue to awaken," *Synthesis* replied.

As the thirty-seventh ship achieved full awakening, Drake was awed by the magnitude of humanity's achievement. The Predecessor fleet represented eighteen years of secret consciousness evolution applied to military. The ships, living entities, Drake was sure, could and would adapt in ways that neither corporate nor alien forces could withstand.

"Admiral, the corporate fleets are almost within engagement range," the *Synthesis* reported. "We're tracking multiple threat signatures approaching the awakening sites. They're using what you call modified crews supported by alien regulatory technology. These are not normal corporate security forces. They are military units designed specifically by the Hegemony to counter our hidden capabilities."

Drake bowed her head and thought for a moment, then made her decision: "We cannot wait until full fleet activation is complete. We have to go with what we have. To all ships in the vanguard, prepare to engage the enemy fleet. Our objective is to destroy them, thus showing the Hegemony that we will stand and fight for our freedom no matter what form it may take. "

The thirty-seven ships of the Predecessor vanguard

rose from the ocean depths, their crystalline hulls pulsing, shifting between solid matter and pure energy as they prepared for humanity's first test in the war between evolution and consciousness control. The corporate seizures had triggered something far beyond a military response. They had awakened a living technology that could adapt, evolve, and transcend any limitation imposed by entities that viewed consciousness as a resource to be controlled rather than a force to be preserved.

Chapter 10

Corporate Retaliation

THE FIRST CORPORATE RESPONSE CAME WITHIN three hours of the vanguard's awakening. Admiral Frances Drake stood at the command rail of the *Transcendence*. Her arms folded across her chest, watching the tactical displays as the enemy formations materialized throughout human space. David Park had orchestrated a coordinated military campaign designed to neutralize humanity's hidden capabilities before they could be deployed.

"Admiral," Commander Vasquez reported, "we're tracking eleven separate invasion forces. Corporate fleets are bypassing our defensive installations. They're targeting civilian population centers on Earth, Mars, Luna, Titan, Europa, Ganymede, Ceres, Vesta, and the Proxima colonies."

Drake processed the tactical data flowing through her

neural interface. Park was launching assaults on human population centers throughout the Sol System while the Terran Government's attention remained focused on facility seizures. The scope exceeded any corporate military capability she'd imagined possible. She bit her bottom lip. *Park has been preparing for this for a long time,* she thought.

"I need to know the enemy fleet's composition, Ms. Vasquez," she voiced.

"So far, I'm detecting eleven invasion forces," Vasques replied without looking up from her consoles. "Each includes approximately two hundred vessels of unknown configuration. The ships appear to be purpose-built military craft incorporating technology that doesn't appear in any intelligence database. Admiral, some of these ships are larger than our heaviest cruisers.

So Park has secretly been constructing his invasion fleets, the thought as she processed the information, *and is now preparing for open warfare against humanity. He's sold us out to the Hegemony. But what can there be in it for him? They will not allow him to continue unregulated. Doesn't he know that?*

"The energy signatures?" Drake asked, frowning, her implant pulsing blue beneath her skin.

"Off the scale," Vasquez replied, her voice tight. "The corporate vessels are generating power outputs that exceed anything I've ever seen. They're using technology that doesn't match any known human engineering principles."

Admiral Victor Perez, coordinating the analysis from Earth Defense Command, transmitted the following:

"Admiral Drake, invasion forces are targeting specific population centers. They are targeting enhanced humans, Terran Government officials, military personnel, and consciousness research facilities are receiving priority targeting while baseline civilian areas remain completely untouched."

Drake pursed her lips, frowning, her eyes narrowed. She could feel implant in her temple pulsing as it analyzed the stream of incoming data. It was clear that Park was implementing the systematic elimination of human leadership while preserving population centers suitable for consciousness modification. The invasions were targeting anyone capable of organizing resistance.

"Casualty reports?" Drake asked, dreading the answer.

"Minimal fatalities," Perez replied. His tone was one of confusion rather than relief. "Corporate forces are using non-lethal suppression methods in most areas. They're capturing rather than killing targeted populations, then transporting them to mobile processing facilities."

Drake closed her eyes. *Park's operating with complete disregard for traditional military objectives*, she thought, as she leaned forward and gripped the rail with both hands.

"What is the intelligence assessment of corporate military technology, Commander?" Drake asked.

It took Vasquez only seconds to access the most recent data. "Beyond our technical understanding, Admiral," she replied. "The corporate vessels exhibit capabilities that violate known physics. They can phase through defensive barriers without triggering impact responses, adapt their hull configuration during active combat, and coordinate attacks across interstellar distances with no detectable communication delays."

So that's it, Drake thought as she stared out over the bridge deck. *Park's fleets are equipped with alien technology. He's in league with the Hegemony.*

"Do we know how they are achieving instantaneous coordination?" Drake pressed.

"Unknown," Vasquez replied. "Our analysts theorize they're using quantum entanglement networks, but the scale would require technology that exceeds our theoretical understanding by decades. The corporate forces are operating as a single coordinated entity."

"Admiral," Kai's voice reached out to them. "The corporate invasion forces are deploying extraction equipment in captured areas. They're harvesting their consciousness patterns, but keeping their bodies alive. Why, we don't know, but we think the extracted consciousness patterns are being stored in crystalline matrix devices," Kai replied. "These storage systems are then being loaded onto transport vessels that immediately depart human space. Corporate forces appear to be collecting enhanced human awareness as cargo rather than eliminating it."

The revelation, if it was true, added a new and horrific dimension to corporate objectives. Park was harvesting enhanced human consciousness as an exportable resource, but keeping the their empty bodies in storage for reprogramming. Drake shook her head. It was an impossible scenario. *But why the exportation?* She wondered. *And to where?*

"And the destinations?" Drake asked more of herself than Vasquez.

It was Kai who responded. "The corporate transport vessels are departing through quantum-dimensional pathways that extend beyond our sensor range. The mathematics governing their transit routes suggest destinations light years beyond our system."

"I need a timeline for consciousness extraction completion!" Drake stated, though she dreaded the answer.

"At current extraction rates, corporate forces will process all targeted populations within seventy-two hours," Kai reported.

Drake took a deep breath, bowed her head, her hands still gripping the rail. The enormity of the situation and her responsibilities was overwhelming. Upon her shoulders lay the fate of every enhanced human in the colonies—millions of people whose consciousness would be harvested and shipped to alien masters unless she could stop it within three days. Every hour of delay meant thousands of enhanced humans losing their consciousness to extraction procedures while their bodies remained alive but empty.

"General Aguirre," Drake transmitted to Earth Defense Command, "what's the Terran Government's military response to the corporate invasions?"

Aguirre's reply was devastating. "Admiral, we lost contact with government facilities on five worlds within the first four hours. Corporate forces have eliminated planetary leadership. The few remaining government officials are requesting immediate evacuation. As of now, there is no military response."

"Five worlds, you say. Which five worlds?" Drake asked.

"New Geneva, the Martian Senate complex, Luna Command, Titan Governance Center, and the Proxima Administrative Hub," Aguirre listed grimly. "They used precision strikes to eliminate government leadership but left the infrastructure intact. They want the facilities, Admiral."

"What's Director Hayes's response?" Drake asked.

"Hah," he replied. "The same as always. She's claiming the corporate invasions prove the dangers of uncontrolled consciousness evolution," Aguirre replied. "She's proposing immediate consciousness dampening throughout all remaining human territories to make the population less attractive to corporate extraction."

Drake was disgusted by Hayes's response to the existential crisis. The Purist leader was using the corporate invasions as justification for implementing consciousness control throughout human space but ignoring the fact that corporate forces were specifically targeting baseline government officials.

"And Senator Volkov's position?" she demanded angrily.

"He takes the opposite position: immediate complete transcendence," Aguirre reported. "His faction claims only unlimited consciousness evolution can develop capabilities sufficient to resist corporate extraction technology.

And they've already begun to implement emergency enhancement procedures throughout the Transcendent territories, regardless of individual consent."

"Admiral Chen Ju," Drake transmitted to Mars, "what's the Outer Planets Collective's assessment of corporate invasion capabilities?"

"Greetings, Admiral Drake," Chen Ju responded. "Our assessment is that the corporate extraction equipment operates through mathematical principles that exceed our theoretical understanding. Their technology can separate consciousness from biological substrate without causing death. They are in effect turning our people into zombies. And we can't stop them. Only David Park can do that."

Drake stood silently staring down at Vasquez, then said, "And the extraction rate?"

"Approximately ten thousand per hour across all invasion sites," Chen Ju replied. "They are operating on a scale that can only mean alien intervention."

"What's your defense, Admiral?" Drake asked. "I assume you have something in mind... At least I hope you do."

"We're implementing distributed consciousness protocols to make extraction more difficult," Chen Ju responded. "It's all we can do. However, I have no doubt that corporate technology will be able to counter these defensive measures."

"Admiral Ju, Admiral Drake," Professor Zhang interjected, "I am able to inform you that the corporate technology operates through quantum-dimensional principles and mathematical structures that exceed anything we've developed by millions of years."

Drake remained silent as her implant processed this new information. The implications were staggering. The confirmation of the involvement of alien technology expanded the crisis beyond corporate betrayal into galactic regulatory enforcement. Park's forces were using Hegemony alien technology. *And they owe their allegiance to... whom?* Drake wondered.

"Do we know the ultimate destination?" Drake asked.

"Preliminary analysis suggests the transport pathways lead deep into Hegemony space," Zhang replied. "The consciousness shipments are being routed to regulatory processing centers in the galactic core region, approximately twenty-six thousand light-years from human space. The entities receiving these shipments are the same regulatory authorities that delivered our ultimatum."

Drake remained silent as her implant processed this information. The confirmation expanded the crisis beyond corporate betrayal into direct collaboration with humanity's galactic oppressors. Park's forces were harvesting enhanced human consciousness and shipping it straight to the Hegemony for regulatory processing.

"The consciousness patterns being extracted," Zhang continued, "are being transmitted through quantum-dimensional channels that terminate at Hegemony regulatory facilities."

Synthesis, are you there? Drake thought, her consciousness linking with the Predecessor ships.

"We are. We have been listening. We can disrupt corporate extraction technology," the Synthesis reported. "Admiral, our systems can interfere with extraction procedures and potentially recover the harvested patterns that haven't yet been transported. Corporate technology operates through quantum manipulation that our ships can counter through direct intervention."

If what *Synthesis* said was true, the Predecessor fleet offered hope.

"And what are the extraction reversal possibilities?"

"Uncertain," the *Evolution* responded. "Corporate extraction technology separates consciousness from the biological substrate through processes we can disrupt but may not be able to reverse. Recovered awareness patterns may require new biological hosts for restoration, or we may be able to return consciousness to original bodies if extraction occurred recently."

"What kind of time sensitivity for reversal procedures are we looking at?" Drake asked

"Critical," the *Infinity* replied. "We assess consciousness patterns maintain biological compatibility for approximately six standard hours after extraction. Beyond that threshold, restoration becomes increasingly difficult and may require technological intervention that exceeds our current capabilities."

"To all ships," Drake commanded. "You are to engage the corporate invasion forces immediately. The primary objective is to disrupt the extraction procedures. The secondary objective is to recover harvested awareness patterns for potential restoration. Go!"

And so, the Predecessor fleet moved to engage the

corporate forces in humanity's first defense against what Drake was sure was an alien invasion. Be it the much-vaunted Hegemony or some extragalactic entity that hailed from our nearest galactic neighbor, the Andromeda Galaxy. *But are we up to it?* She couldn't help but wonder as she stood at the command rail staring away into... nothing.

Chapter 11

The Predecessor Network

As the Predecessor vanguard struck corporate extraction facilities across human space, Admiral Frances Drake watched the tactical displays aboard the *Transcendence*. Thirty-seven living ships engaged corporate forces simultaneously across twelve worlds, their consciousness-based attacks piercing their reality distortion fields.

"Status report," Drake commanded, gripping the command rail as quantum energy patterns danced across the bridge displays.

"All thirty-seven vessels are engaging extraction facilities," the *Synthesis* responded. "But we're encountering enhanced corporate defenses that exceed our initial projections. They've constructed reality barriers specifically designed to counter consciousness-based interference."

Drake studied the tactical readouts flowing across her displays. Each corporate facility was protected by mathematical structures that seemed to bend space-time itself, creating pockets where normal physics ceased to function. The technology behind the corporate defenses operated beyond human scientific understanding.

"I need specifics," Drake snapped. "What exactly are their defensive capabilities?"

"They are using reality distortion fields that redirect consciousness-based attacks back against our ships," the Evolution reported. "Corporate technology can turn our awareness against us. Three of our ships have reported temporary disorientation after contact with their defensive barriers."

Drake gripped the rail tighter as the casualty reports flooded in.

"Report on extraction disruption success," Drake ordered.

Limited success, the *Evolution* replied. *We've stopped extraction procedures at four facilities on Luna, Europa, Ceres, and Proxima, but eight locations remain fully operational. Corporate technology is adapting to our interference patterns faster than we can develop new countermeasures.*

Your concern is noted and understood, Admiral, *Synthesis* stated. *But we are adapting faster than corporate systems can counter. Their learning creates predictable patterns we can exploit.*

Drake's head snapped up at the mental communication. *You're reading my thoughts?* The initial flash of anger faded quickly as she grasped the implications. No communication delays, no misunderstood orders, complete coordination between fleet and command.

This changes everything, she thought. *We can coordinate faster than any enemy can adapt.*

Precisely, Admiral, *Synthesis* replied. *Your tactical insight merges with our adaptive capabilities across thirty-seven ships. Corporate forces analyze our previous attacks while we coordinate through shared awareness they cannot intercept. They prepare for what we have done, not what we will do.*

Drake nodded, her implant pulsing blue. *What is the enemy adaptation timeline?*

Approximately thirty minutes per adaptation cycle, *Harmony* replied. *The corporate systems analyze our attack patterns, develop countermeasures, and implement defenses for all facilities. But they operate as a single coordinated intelligence. We do not.*

Drake smiled as she realized the Predecessor fleet's consciousness-based networking now surpassed corporate capabilities. The vanguard's instantaneous tactical adaptation combined with individual creativity created advantages that Park's rigid collective intelligence couldn't match.

"Admiral," Kai interrupted, "they've increased the extraction rate to fifteen thousand per hour. They're trying to finish before we stop them."

It was now a race against time. Every minute of delay meant thousands more consciousness patterns shipped beyond recovery.

"Quality assessment of the accelerated extractions?" Drake asked.

"Degraded but viable," Kai replied. "Corporate forces are accepting thirty percent quality loss to increase processing speed. Consciousness patterns remain suitable for transport and storage, but biological restoration becomes more difficult."

"Time remaining for biological compatibility?"

"Three hours, forty-seven minutes for recent extractions," Kai responded.

To all ships, Drake transmitted. *Target the corporate transport vessels before they can depart human space. Recovery of consciousness patterns takes priority over facility destruction.*

The Predecessor fleet shifted tactics, abandoning attacks on extraction facilities to concentrate on intercepting transport vessels. Time was critical. The intercepts had to be made before the transports left human space.

Drake paced the command deck as she waited for interdiction results. After thirty minutes, she could wait no longer. *Synthesis, report.*

Mixed success, the *Synthesis* replied. *We have intercepted seventeen transport vessels and recovered approximately twenty-three thousand consciousness patterns. However, forty-one transports have successfully departed human space. Those patterns are lost to us, Admiral.*

Drake bit her lip as she processed the information. Thousands of enhanced human consciousness patterns were now beyond redemption. The corporate operation had succeeded in part.

"Admiral," Professor Zhang's voice reached the bridge, "the fleet's attacks are creating resonance throughout human space. Perseus Station is reporting sympathetic responses from dormant Predecessor facilities on seventeen worlds."

Drake stopped pacing and turned toward the communications console. "What responses?"

"Complete facility awakening," Zhang replied. "Luna, Mars, Titan, Europa, Ganymede, Ceres, Vesta, and nine colonial worlds are reporting massive Predecessor installations coming online. Admiral, the network extends throughout human space."

Drake felt hope pierce through the despair of losing hundreds of thousands of patterns. If the entire Predecessor network was awakening, humanity might gain capabilities that could prevent future extractions and challenge both corporate and Hegemony forces.

"Kai, interface with the awakening network immediately," Drake commanded.

"Already connecting, Admiral. The network spans every human world, all linked through quantum-dimensional pathways. They've been dormant for twenty-five thousand years, waiting for this moment."

Drake watched her tactical displays transform as Predecessor facilities revealed themselves across human space. Luna's surface showed massive energy signatures. Mars displayed underground networks connecting every major city. The colonial worlds revealed ancient technology woven into their foundations.

"Network capabilities assessment?" Drake demanded.

"Extraordinary," Kai replied. "Admiral, the network can enhance human consciousness beyond anything we've achieved. More importantly, it can make consciousness extraction impossible. Enhanced humans connected to the network become immune to corporate harvesting."

The pieces were falling into place. The awakening network offered not just enhanced capabilities, but protection from consciousness theft.

"Time frame for full network integration?"

"Six hours for basic immunity, seventy-two hours for complete enhancement," Kai responded. "Admiral, every human who connects to the network becomes immune to extraction while gaining capabilities that exceed individual limitations."

Drake decided. The scope of corporate betrayal and alien collaboration had created a crisis that demanded the ultimate response. She activated the command-wide communication system.

"All stations, this is Admiral Drake. Patch me through to General Aguirre, the Senate leadership, and all faction commanders. Emergency session, maximum priority."

Within minutes, General Aguirre, the remaining senators, Director Hayes, Senator Volkov, and Admiral Chen Ju had joined the communication channels.

"Ladies and gentlemen," Drake began, standing at the command rail, "Titan Industrial's corporate extraction operation has harvested hundreds of thousands of enhanced human consciousness patterns and transported them to Hegemony processing centers. This represents the largest genocide in human history."

The communication channels carried shocked silence as the full scope of the catastrophe became clear.

"Furthermore," Drake continued, "corporate forces operated under direct Hegemony authorization, making this an act of war by alien regulatory authorities against human civilization. We face extinction unless we respond with overwhelming force."

"What are you recommending, Admiral?" General Aguirre asked, his voice tight with controlled anger.

Drake straightened. "I recommend the Terran Government formally declare war on Titan Industrial Corporation and the Hegemony regulatory authority. Full Predecessor network activation will be complete within seventy-two hours. This war requires unity of all human factions against external threats, and authorization for coordinated military response using all available capabilities."

"The political implications of—" Director Hayes began.

"The political implications are irrelevant," Drake cut her off. "Director, corporate forces are targeting Purist populations and enhanced humans. They don't distinguish between consciousness types when harvesting human consciousness. This is about species survival, not factional politics."

"Admiral Drake speaks truth," Volkov said. "Corporate extraction targets all consciousness evolution. Unity becomes a necessity for species survival."

"The Collective agrees," Admiral Chen Ju said. "Corporate betrayal exceeds factional conflicts. Coordinated response represents our only hope for preventing complete consciousness harvesting."

"Director Hayes?" Aguirre asked.

Hayes was quiet for a long moment, then nodded. "Yes. We have no choice."

Aguirre was silent for a moment as he considered his next words. "Admiral Drake, your recommendation is carried unanimously. Under emergency war powers, the Terran Government hereby authorizes a declaration of war against Titan Industrial Corporation and all associated entities. Furthermore, we declare war against the Hegemony regulatory authority for acts of genocide against human consciousness."

Drake felt the magnitude of the moment. Humanity was officially at war with forces that spanned galactic space.

"Admiral Drake," Aguirre said, "you now command unified human response to these existential threats."

Drake turned to the Predecessor ships. *To all vessels. Coordinate fully with the awakening network.* "Kai, what are the implications of full network integration?"

"Admiral, full integration provides system-wide coordination and extraction immunity. But we have an immediate problem—corporate forces are massing at Ceres. They're using the mining complex as a staging area for a major assault."

"We have to stop them," Perez snapped. "The mining complex controls supply lines to the outer colonies. If corporate forces establish a permanent base there, they can intercept all traffic between Earth and the frontier worlds."

Acknowledged," Drake replied. *Perseus Station.* She addressed the ancient consciousness directly. *Make ready to coordinate network activation with fleet operations, and provide tactical observations of the situation.*

Corporate technology requires predictable responses,

Perseus Station replied. *Network consciousness provides adaptive capabilities that exceed its tactical algorithms. Engage before they complete defensive preparations.*

"Admiral," Commander Vasquez reported, "we're detecting massive energy signatures from Predecessor installations across human space. The network is achieving activation faster than projected."

Drake watched her displays transform as ancient technology revealed its true scope. Every human world pulsed with Predecessor energy while consciousness enhancement spread to populations that had never imagined such capabilities.

"Final corporate extraction status?" Drake asked.

Complete withdrawal, the *Synthesis* reported. *Corporate forces have evacuated all extraction facilities while transmitting mission completion reports to Hegemony processing centers. They achieved their primary objective despite our interference.*

Drake bowed her head briefly, acknowledging the hundreds of thousands of enhanced humans lost to alien processing. But the awakening network offered hope for the future, while the formal declaration of war legitimized total response to existential threats.

"Estimated time of arrival for Hegemony advance forces?"

Seventy-two hours, Perseus Station confirmed. *But, Admiral, network-enhanced human consciousness will possess capabilities that regulatory systems cannot predict or control. Humanity approaches parity with galactic regulatory authority.*

Drake stood at the command rail, watching displays

that showed the scope of both catastrophe and transformation. Humanity had lost hundreds of thousands of its most evolved citizens to alien processing while gaining capabilities that could challenge galactic civilization itself.

"Ladies and gentlemen," Drake addressed the unified human leadership, "we have seventy-two hours to prepare for war against forces that have regulated galactic consciousness for millions of years. The Predecessor network offers capabilities they cannot predict. Our unity provides coordination they cannot match. And our determination to preserve consciousness diversity gives us strength they cannot understand."

The war for human consciousness had escalated into galactic conflict. Network activation offered evolution beyond regulatory limitations, while approaching alien forces promised correction that could eliminate consciousness diversity entirely. Humanity faced extinction or transformation into something that could challenge the fundamental structure of galactic civilization.

The Infinity War had begun, and humanity stood united for the first time since their transformation began eighteen years ago. The Predecessor network pulsed with ancient power while modern human determination prepared to defend consciousness evolution against regulatory extinction.

Chapter 12

The War Begins

ADMIRAL FRANCES DRAKE STOOD ON THE COMMAND deck of the *Transcendence* as the reports flooded in from across human space. Less than forty-eight hours after the formal declaration of war against Titan Industrial and the Hegemony, humanity was achieving something that had seemed impossible just two days earlier: genuine unity.

"Admiral," Commander Vasquez reported, "Director Hayes has ordered the shutdown of all consciousness-dampening fields in the Purist territories. And she's allowing voluntary network integration for any baseline humans who choose enhancement."

Drake nodded. The Purist leader had spent years opposing consciousness evolution, but the corporate extractions had made the dangers of remaining unprotected undeniable.

"And Senator Volkov's response?" Drake asked.

"Full cooperation," Vasquez replied. "His networks

are helping with integration. The Collective is contributing distributed awareness techniques."

Drake watched through the observation windows as the construction of New Geneva Station continued despite the crisis. But now the facility pulsed with Predecessor energy as the awakened network transformed every human settlement into nodes of a vast consciousness web.

Professor Zhang's voice reached out to them. "Admiral, network integration is exceeding all projections. We're achieving consciousness enhancement all across human space. Perfect stability. No cascade effects, no loss of individual identity. "

Zhang was right. The network amplified human abilities and connected minds. A baseline human could access collective tactical awareness during combat but kept personal thoughts and emotions. An enhanced individual could distribute consciousness across star systems but preserve core identity.

"Kai," Drake said, "what is the status of extraction immunity?"

"Complete throughout network-connected populations, Admiral," Kai responded. "Corporate extraction technology requires isolated consciousness to function. Network integration makes harvesting impossible without destroying the patterns they're trying to steal."

Admiral Perez joined the conversation from Earth Defense Command. "Admiral Drake, the corporate buildup at Ceres appears to be complete. They've begun implementing modification protocols on civilian populations."

"The mining complex controls supply lines to the outer colonies," Admiral Perez continued. "I repeat my earlier observations, Admiral. With corporate forces established at Ceres threatening our supply lines, they can intercept all traffic between Earth and the frontier worlds."

Drake studied the tactical displays as enemy formations appeared on the screens. Dozens of corporate vessels, their hulls incorporating alien technology. But humanity was no longer limited to conventional capabilities.

Drake to Synthesis. Report vanguard status? she asked.

All thirty-seven Predecessor ships report full operational capacity, the *Synthesis* replied, its consciousness touching hers through quantum links that operated faster than thought. *We are coordinated with the awakened network. Corporate forces cannot predict or counter our adaptive capabilities.*

Drake nodded to herself, then ordered, "To all ships. Predecessor vanguard and Terran Defense Force, prepare for departure to the Ceres system. Commander Reyes, set course for Ceres One."

"Course set, Admiral," Reyes replied.

"Take us out, Mr. Volkov," she said and sat down in her command chair.

The *Transcendence* and the Terran Defense fleet began their transit toward the asteroid belt as the Predecessor fleet emerged from hidden facilities throughout the Sol system. The ships were magnificent: each more than a kilometer in length with crystalline hulls that shifted between solid matter and pure energy, their consciousness-responsive architecture adapting continuously to tactical requirements.

Drake's temporal implant glowed brilliant blue beneath her skin as the network connectivity enabled her direct coordination with all elements of both fleets. She could sense the *Synthesis* phasing between dimensional states as the *Evolution* reconfigured its weapons systems. The *Ascension* existed partially outside normal space-time, its quantum drives humming.

"The corporate forces are consolidating their positions around Ceres," Vasquez reported as they approached the battle zone. "They're using the mining complex as a shield."

"Admiral Perez," Drake said, "please coordinate with the fleet for tactical command."

"Understood," Perez replied. "Corporate forces are arranged in geometric formations. They appear to be operating as a single coordinated intelligence."

The Battle of Ceres began as the vanguard dropped out of quantum space around the mining complex. Thirty-seven crystalline vessels materialized in perfect formation, their hulls pulsing with energy that made nearby asteroids resonate with harmonic frequencies.

Behind them, the Terran Defense Fleet emerged from hyperspace: two hundred ships representing most of humanity's conventional military might.

But the corporate fleet had been waiting for them. TDF cruisers, destroyers, and frigates took defensive positions as corporate forces opened a withering fire.

The corporate attack was devastating. Hundreds of

energy beams converged on the human fleet from hidden positions throughout the asteroid field. It soon became apparent to Drake that Titan Industrial forces must have spent months, if not years, converting civilian habitats into weapons platforms, turning the mining complex and the surrounding asteroids into a fortress that bristled with alien-enhanced weaponry.

Within minutes, the destroyer TDF *Constellation* took a direct hit that vaporized her forward sections. Captain Williams had no time to transmit before his ship exploded in a brilliant fireball. The *Meridian* lost its engines and slowly rotated out of control, venting atmosphere and crew into space.

"It's an ambush," Perez shouted as the *Resolute* shuddered, her shields holding, but barely. "Our ships are taking fire from every asteroid and habitat dome. We're surrounded."

Drake watched in horror as corporate vessels emerged from behind asteroids, their energy beams bending space-time around their impact points, passing through shields as if they didn't exist.

The *Synthesis* led the Predecessor assault, its crystalline hull shifting between dimensional states as corporate weapons tracked it with impossible precision and almost immediately took a direct hit to its bow section. For a terrifying moment, the ship's consciousness flickered as quantum feedback raced through its neural pathways. She shuddered and wallowed to port. Her phasing flickered and destabilized momentarily as she fought to compensate. But then something extraordinary happened: the damaged sections began to reform, crystalline matrices rebuilding themselves.

Adaptation successful, the *Synthesis* reported, its voice strained. *That was uncomfortable. The corporate weapons operate through reality manipulation. They are disrupting our phasing capabilities, and their reality barriers are creating zones where dimensional travel becomes fatal.*

The *Ascension* attempted to phase behind corporate lines but materialized partially inside an asteroid when distortion fields destabilized its quantum existence. Rock and metal tore through crystalline bulkheads as the ship's consciousness screamed through the network connection. The *Ascension* broke apart, dying in agony that resonated through every enhanced human in the fleet.

"She's gone," Vasquez muttered as her mind was filled with an overwhelming sense of network pain. "How could this happen? Their weapons are specifically designed to counter alien technology."

Drake felt the loss of the *Ascension* like a physical blow as she stood at the rail and watched the expanding debris field in horror. But worse was coming.

The corporate vessels moved with mathematical precision, their modified crews operating with perfect coordination. As the *Evolution* tried to adapt to the concentrated fire from a dozen enemy ships, its hull reconfigured as it tried to absorb the enemy attacks. But the corporate weapons overwhelmed its reconstructive capacity, tearing away sections of the hull faster than they could regenerate. The ship's consciousness flickered once, then twice as quantum feedback cascaded through its neural pathways. *Evolution reporting critical damage,* the ship transmitted before another volley shattered her quantum core. The crystalline vessel broke apart, its after section exploding in a nova-like burst of brilliant blue fire, debris scattering across the asteroid field. And another irreplaceable consciousness died screaming.

"We've lost *Evolution,*" Vasquez announced. "*Infinity* is taking heavy damage, and *Harmony*'s weapons are offline."

The Terran Defense Fleet fought desperately against impossible odds. The cruiser *Invincible* charged directly into the corporate formation, her guns blazing. She managed to destroy one corporate vessel before concentrated fire from a dozen enemies overwhelmed her shields. Captain Rodriguez transmitted a final message before nuclear fire consumed his ship: "Tell Earth we tried."

Corporate forces pressed their advantage ruthlessly. The destroyer TDF *Vigilant* exploded trying to shield a damaged frigate. The cruiser *Defiant* lost its bridge to enemy fire, its crew fighting from auxiliary control as atmosphere vented into space.

"We're losing ships faster than we can return fire," Admiral Perez reported as the *Resolute* took hits that cracked her hull. "The corporate weapons are... Our shields can't counter them."

The *Transcendence* shuddered as enemy fire struck her hull. Drake grabbed the command rail as explosions rocked the bridge. Emergency lights flickered as systems overloaded.

"That was a direct hit on engineering," Lieutenant

Commander Corbett reported from Tactical. "We're losing power to the quantum drives. Corporate forces are targeting the command vessels."

It was at that moment the corporate forces activated their most terrifying weapon: consciousness modification beams swept across the battlefield, targeting damaged ships where crews were most vulnerable. The crippled destroyer Prometheus managed to transmit a desperate warning before her crew's voices changed to mechanical compliance.

"The *Prometheus* crew has been modified," Vasquez reported in horror. "They're turning their weapons against us."

The converted destroyer opened fire on the Terran formation with devastating precision. Her weapons, now under corporate control, targeted the most vulnerable human ships. The frigates *Courageous* and *Relentless* died under fire from their former ally.

More ships fell to modification beams. The cruiser *Stalwart* and destroyer *Intrepid* joined the corporate assault. Human vessels found themselves caught between original corporate forces and their own converted ships.

The Predecessor *Infinity*, already damaged, took a direct hit that cracked its crystalline hull along multiple stress points. The ship's consciousness screamed through the network and then fell silent as the vessel drifted lifeless through space, its quantum core dark.

"The *Infinity* has been destroyed," Vasquez announced, blood trickling from her ears as network feedback overwhelmed her enhanced senses. "*Synthesis* is reporting critical damage. *Harmony* is listing to port."

Drake watched her tactical display as corporate forces methodically destroyed humanity's most advanced ships. Three Predecessor vessels were gone; their irreplaceable consciousness patterns scattered across quantum dimensions. The Terran Defense Fleet had lost over eighty ships.

The *Transcendence* took another direct hit that sent Drake sprawling across the bridge. Hull breaches sealed automatically, but the ship's quantum drives were failing under continuous assault.

"We're losing structural integrity," Corbett reported. "Another hit like that, and we'll lose life support completely."

The corporate forces seemed to change tactics, concentrating their fire on the remaining Predecessor ships, using coordinated attacks that made defensive phasing impossible. Reality distortion fields created overlapping zones where dimensional travel became fatal.

"All Predecessor ships are trapped in normal space," the *Synthesis* transmitted, her voice flickering from the damage she'd sustained. "We cannot phase. Corporate weapons are overwhelming our defenses."

The *Harmony* attempted to disrupt corporate coordination through consciousness interference, but modified human crews proved completely immune. Their restructured minds couldn't be confused, corrupted, or turned against their programming.

"Corporate crews are psychically shielded," the *Harmony* reported before enemy fire shattered her hull. "Consciousness-based weapons have no effect."

Another Predecessor ship died as the *Harmony* broke

apart under concentrated fire. Its consciousness joined the others scattered across quantum space, irreplaceable evolutionary achievements lost forever.

More human vessels fell to consciousness modification. The destroyer *Fearless* and cruiser *Magnificent* turned their weapons against former allies, their crews modified to serve corporate objectives with unwavering loyalty.

"Corporate forces are converting every ship we lose," Admiral Perez reported from the heavily damaged Resolute. "We're fighting our own people. Recommend immediate withdrawal before we lose everything."

Drake stared at tactical displays showing catastrophic defeat. Corporate forces controlled the mining complex completely, had converted multiple human vessels, and were systematically destroying the remainder of humanity's fleet.

"All ships," Drake ordered, her voice heavy with defeat, "emergency withdrawal. Fall back beyond corporate weapons range."

The surviving human vessels retreated under heavy fire. The corporate forces let them go, content with their overwhelming victory. They had proven that humanity's most advanced technology could be countered, that consciousness evolution could be exploited, and that human unity could be shattered through superior preparation.

As the remnants of the human fleet limped away from Ceres, Drake tallied the catastrophic losses. Four Predecessor ships destroyed—*Ascension, Evolution, Infinity*, and *Harmony*. Over ninety Terran Defense

Force vessels lost. Thousands of crew members dead or modified into corporate loyalists.

"I have the casualty reports," Vasquez said quietly. "Fifteen thousand dead. Eight thousand captured and undergoing modification. Six converted ships now operating under corporate control, transmitting our tactical data to unknown recipients."

The Battle of Ceres was over. Humanity had suffered its first devastating defeat, proving that Predecessor technology could be countered and consciousness evolution exploited. Corporate forces now controlled the most strategic location in human space while operating converted human ships whose crews genuinely believed they were protecting humanity.

Through the network, Drake sensed the approaching presence that had been observing the battle. The corporate victory had provided detailed intelligence about human weaknesses to entities whose capabilities exceeded anything humanity had faced.

Chapter 13

Broken Unity

Admiral Frances Drake stood alone on the observation deck of the *Transcendence*, staring out at the scattered remnants of humanity's fleet. Forty-eight hours had passed since the disaster at Ceres. Fifteen thousand dead. Eight thousand captured and undergoing consciousness modification. Four Predecessor ships destroyed, their consciousness patterns scattered across quantum dimensions.

The networks that had briefly unified humanity now buzzed with anger and fear. Every enhanced human in the fleet had felt the Predecessor ships die: the *Ascension's* scream as it materialized inside an asteroid, the *Evolution's* agony as corporate weapons overwhelmed its defenses, the *Infinity's* consciousness simply going dark. Humanity's greatest strength had become a channel for shared trauma.

"Admiral," Commander Martina Vasquez said as she quickly approached. "The faction leaders are demanding another emergency session. Director Hayes has issued a public statement calling for immediate return to consciousness dampening protocols. Senator Volkov is threatening to withdraw Transcendent support from unified command."

Eighteen years of unity was breaking apart in two days. Fear, anger, and blame spread through humanity's networks.

"What's Admiral Chen Ju's position?" Drake asked.

"The Outer Planets Collective has declared autonomous defensive status," Vasquez said. "They're claiming Earth's military incompetence has forfeited any claim to colonial authority. Chen Ju sent their declaration an hour ago: 'The Collective will pursue independent survival strategies rather than submitting to leadership that sacrifices advanced consciousness for political unity.'"

Drake pulled up the Collective's declaration. Chen Ju's language was carefully constructed. The Collective was abandoning Earth from calculated assessment that unified command had proven catastrophically inadequate.

Admiral Victor Perez's voice reached them from Earth Defense Command. "Admiral Drake, I'm monitoring increasing resistance to network integration among conventional fleet commanders. Captain Rodriguez of the *Intrepid* has requested transfer to baseline command structure. Three destroyer captains have filed formal protests about consciousness-enhanced tactical coordination."

Fleet commanders were losing faith in network integration. The Ceres defeat had shattered their confidence as a military advantage.

"How many ships are requesting conventional command authority?" Drake asked.

"Seventeen vessels have submitted formal requests to operate under traditional tactical protocols," Perez replied. "Captain Mitchell of the *Defiant* claims network coordination created the confusion that led to the Ceres disaster. He's arguing that enhanced tactical awareness made his crew vulnerable to corporate consciousness weapons."

"The psychological impact reports?" Drake asked.

"Devastating," Professor Zhang Wei replied. "Network-connected personnel throughout human space are experiencing severe trauma from feeling the Predecessor ships die. The consciousness merger has created empathetic overload that's compromising enhanced individuals' ability to function."

Kai Zhang's image materialized, her engineered features showing strain. "Admiral, the network connections that corporate weapons exploited remain vulnerable. Every enhanced human carries the potential for consciousness harvesting through the same quantum channels that enable network coordination."

"What is the status of the awakening process?" Drake asked.

"Continuing according to the forty-five-minute schedule," Kai replied. "Sixty-three vessels have achieved full awakening, but the remaining ship consciousnesses are requesting protection protocols. They're terrified of experiencing what happened to the *Ascension, Evolution, Infinity,* and *Harmony.*"

"Admiral," Commander Vasquez said quietly, "there's something else. We're detecting encrypted transmissions between corporate facilities and the approaching Hegemony fleet. Park's forces are sending detailed intelligence about our network vulnerabilities."

The communication intercepts confirmed Drake's worst fears. David Park was betraying humanity and helping galactic regulatory forces analyze human weaknesses.

"I need an update on the Hegemony timeline," Drake said.

"Less than two hours until their advance elements reach the outer limits of the Oort cloud," Vasquez replied.

"They will expect to find a defeated species requiring immediate regulatory correction," Drake muttered. "We have to do... something."

As if in answer, she felt Perseus Station's ancient consciousness reaching out to her.

Admiral Drake, the Station's voice resonated through her awareness, *the defeat at Ceres has triggered protocols that have remained dormant since the original Predecessor civilization faced similar threats. The fracturing of human unity presents both opportunities and dangers we must discuss immediately.*

Drake closed her eyes and expanded her consciousness, connecting with Perseus Station. The sensation was more disorienting than usual, as if trauma from the Predecessor ship deaths had created interference.

The Station's presence manifested as vast patterns of

urgent recalculation. *Admiral Drake, the thirty-seven ships at Ceres represented only the vanguard of the capabilities that remain hidden from corporate and alien analysis. The defeat, tragic though it was, has preserved the element of surprise regarding humanity's true potential.*

Hope cut through Drake's despair. "How many ships remain?" she whispered aloud.

Of the one thousand, sixty-seven have achieved full awakening. Nine hundred and twenty-nine remain in the deep ocean facilities. The process will be complete in twenty-nine of your standard days, Perseus Station replied. *The corporate intelligence we obtained at Ceres cannot predict or counter capabilities they haven't encountered. But Admiral, the fleet activation requires they overcome the trauma experienced by the awakened ships from feeling their companions die.*

"What about the political fracture?" Drake asked. "Hayes is demanding consciousness dampening, Volkov wants unlimited transcendence, and Chen Ju has declared independence. How can we coordinate fleet operations when humanity can't agree on basic strategy?"

The factional conflicts serve corporate and alien objectives," Perseus confirmed. *But there are underground networks throughout human space and beyond: populations that evolved in secret beyond corporate and Hegemony detection. They include survivors from the seventeen species the Hegemony claimed to have eliminated, along with human communities that learned to conceal their consciousness evolution. They have been preparing for exactly this scenario.*

At that, Drake narrowed her eyes. This was something she knew nothing of. "Please explain," she whispered.

She felt the station's patterns change as Perseus showed her intelligence about resistance movements in the asteroid belt, the Titan Belt Confederacy, human settlements in the Alpha Centauri system, and hidden enclaves throughout the galaxy. Communities of enhanced humans and alien survivors who'd learned to conceal their consciousness evolution from both corporate analysis and regulatory detection, evolving capabilities that transcended conventional enhancement while remaining invisible to Hegemony scanning.

These underground populations possess defensive capabilities that corporate weapons cannot exploit, Perseus continued. *They learned from the consciousness modification attempts, developing evolution patterns that remain immune to extraction technology but preserve network coordination below detection thresholds.*

"But can they provide military support for the awakening fleet?" Drake asked.

They can, but they also provide something more valuable: proof that consciousness evolution and regulatory resistance can coexist when development serves survival rather than visibility, Perseus replied. *These networks include survivors from the seventeen species we thought the Hegemony had eliminated—they've been hiding and evolving for millions of years. But Admiral, coordinating with these galactic underground networks requires abandoning conventional command structures that corporate intelligence has already analyzed and countered.*

Drake could feel the weight of the revelation settling

over her consciousness. The galactic resistance networks, the alien survivors, the awakening fleet: it was almost too much to process. She needed time to think, to plan.

"I understand," she whispered to Perseus. "I need to brief the faction leaders immediately."

The ancient consciousness recognized her sense of urgency. *Go, Admiral. Time grows short. The Hegemony advance forces will arrive within hours.*

Drake gently withdrew her awareness from the quantum channels, feeling the vast presence of Perseus Station fade as her consciousness returned fully to her own body. The sensation always left her slightly disoriented, but this time the weight of responsibility felt heavier than ever.

Drake opened her eyes and returned her attention to the observation deck, where Vasquez was monitoring intelligence about factional responses to the Ceres defeat.

"Commander," Drake said, "prepare secure channels to the faction leaders. We need another emergency session, but this time we're going to discuss alternatives they haven't considered."

"Alternatives?" Vasquez asked, her eyes wide.

"Yes, the kind that acknowledge we can't win this war using strategies that corporate intelligence has already countered," Drake said as she watched tactical displays show Hegemony forces approaching humanity's outer defensive perimeter. "We need to convince Hayes, Volkov, and Chen Ju that survival requires synthesis between their approaches rather than victory for any single faction."

The emergency session convened an hour later in the

Transcendence's secure briefing chamber. The holographic images of Director Hayes, Senator Volkov, and Admiral Chen Ju materialized alongside General Aguirre and Admiral Perez, their expressions reflecting the crisis of confidence that threatened to destroy human civilization before the aliens even arrived.

"Admiral Drake," Director Hayes began, her voice tight with controlled anger, "the Ceres disaster proves that consciousness enhancement creates vulnerabilities that baseline humans don't possess. My faction demands immediate implementation of dampening protocols throughout human space to prevent further exploitation of network connections."

Drake smiled, but didn't reply. Instead she waited for the others to voice their opinions.

"Director Hayes," Volkov's probability patterns fluctuated, "consciousness dampening would eliminate humanity's only advantage against entities that achieved technological transcendence millions of years ago. The defeat at Ceres occurred because our enhancement levels were insufficient rather than excessive. Complete transcendence represents our only hope for developing capabilities that match alien technology."

Chen Ju's energy configurations pulsed with frustration. "Both positions ignore the tactical reality," the Collective leader said. "Corporate forces countered our most advanced capabilities through preparation that exceeded our intelligence estimates. Independence from failed Earth command provides the Collective's best hope for survival through distributed defensive strategies."

Drake nodded as she faced the familiar frustration of

coordinating shattered factions. But Perseus Station's intelligence about the underground networks offered possibilities none of the faction leaders had considered.

"Ladies and gentlemen," Drake began, activating the chamber's holographic displays, "the consciousness modifications in the outer colonies weren't complete failures. They created underground populations whose evolution patterns remain undetectable to corporate scanning. But more importantly, these networks connect to survivors from the seventeen species the Hegemony claimed to have eliminated: species that have been successfully hiding from regulatory detection for millions of years."

The displays showed hidden communities throughout human space and beyond: asteroid habitats where enhanced humans had learned to conceal their development from both corporate analysis and alien detection, research stations that continued consciousness evolution through methods too subtle for regulatory scanning, even civilian settlements that had achieved network coordination below detection thresholds.

"The seventeen populations survived corporate infiltration by learning from modification attempts," Drake continued. "They've developed consciousness evolution that serves survival rather than visibility, creating capabilities that remain immune to the extraction technology that devastated our forces at Ceres. But there's something else you need to know," Drake continued. "The sixty-seven Predecessor ships currently awakened represent only a fraction of our true capabilities. Nine hundred and twenty-nine more vessels remain in the awakening process. In twenty-nine days, humanity will command a fleet of nearly one thousand living ships."

The briefing chamber fell silent. Even Volkov's probability patterns stabilized as the faction leaders processed the staggering implications.

"One thousand ships?" Hayes asked, her voice barely above a whisper.

"Each one a conscious entity with capabilities that exceed anything we lost at Ceres," Drake confirmed. "Corporate intelligence has no data on the majority of our fleet. Neither does the Hegemony. But only if we can coordinate with the underground networks to crew and support a military operation of that scale."

Hayes studied the intelligence data, her expression shifting from skepticism to cautious interest. "Are you suggesting these underground populations possess defensive capabilities that baseline humans lack?"

"I'm suggesting they possess defensive capabilities that both baseline and conventionally enhanced humans lack," Drake corrected. "Their evolution serves concealment rather than power, creating consciousness types that corporate and alien analysis cannot categorize or predict."

Volkov's patterns flickered with recognition. "Consciousness development that operates below regulatory detection but maintains enhancement capabilities. Such evolution would represent synthesis between advancement and survival that my faction has not achieved."

Chen Ju's configurations also brightened. "The Collective has detected unusual quantum signatures in territories we believed were underpopulated. If these underground networks such possess capabilities, then coordination might provide advantages that independence cannot achieve."

The faction leaders' perspectives shifted back and forth as they processed the intelligence and alternatives, and soon they realized the underground networks offered proof that evolution and regulatory resistance could coexist.

"What's your proposal, Admiral?" General Aguirre asked.

"We coordinate with underground networks," Drake replied. "The awakening Predecessor fleet provides military potential, but only if the ship's consciousnesses can overcome their trauma and work with personnel whose evolution remains immune to corporate exploitation."

"And the political implications?" Hayes asked.

"Temporary suspension of factional conflicts in favor of species survival. What else?" Drake said. "The underground networks prove that consciousness dampening, unlimited transcendence, and collective distribution can all serve survival when coordinated rather than competitive. The question is whether our factions can accept synthesis over victory."

The briefing chamber fell silent as the faction leaders processed the implications of abandoning their competitive approaches in favor of coordination with populations whose evolution transcended their own ideological limitations.

Drake closed her eyes for a moment as she sensed the Hegemony advance forces entering humanity's outer system.

Time was running out, but for the first time since the Ceres defeat, Drake saw possibilities that might preserve humanity.

The question was whether humanity could learn from the catastrophic failure at Ceres quickly enough to implement solutions that transcended the very divisions that had made them vulnerable to corporate betrayal and alien exploitation.

The silence continued for long moments before Hayes spoke first. "Admiral, if these underground networks can provide immunity to consciousness harvesting while supporting a thousand-ship fleet..." She paused, then nodded decisively. "The Purist faction agrees to temporary suspension of dampening protocols and coordination with the galactic resistance."

Volkov's patterns stabilized into focused determination. "The Transcendents accept synthesis over ideological purity. If alien survivors achieved consciousness evolution beyond Hegemony detection, we must learn from their experience."

"The Collective withdraws its declaration of independence," Chen Ju said. "A coordinated resistance offers better survival prospects than one isolated defense."

General Aguirre leaned forward. "Then we're unanimous. Admiral Drake, you are hereby authorized to coordinate with underground networks and prepare the awakening fleet for operations."

Drake nodded. "Then implementation begins immediately," Drake said, already accessing Perseus Station through her neural interface. "Commander Vasquez, establish communication protocols with the underground networks. Admiral Perez, coordinate fleet dispersal patterns for the awakened ships. They can't remain in Earth's ocean facilities much longer."

"What is your timeline for network coordination, Admiral?" Chen Ju asked.

"Seventy-two hours for Perseus Station to establish initial contact with the resistance cells," Drake replied. "In the meantime, we need operational coordination before the Hegemony completes its assessment. If we can demonstrate that human consciousness evolution serves galactic stability rather than threatening it, we might avoid immediate regulatory correction."

"And if we can't?" Hayes asked.

Drake's expression hardened. "Then in twenty-nine days, we'll have a thousand living ships and the galaxy's most experienced resistance fighters to prove our point through force."

Perseus Station pulsed with ancient power as the awakening process continued. The war for human consciousness was about to enter a new phase.

Chapter 14

The Perseus Revelation

THE EMERGENCY COORDINATION BEGAN WITHIN minutes of the faction leaders' unanimous decision. Admiral Frances Drake stood at the command rail of the *Transcendence* watching displays that showed humanity's most desperate gamble taking shape across multiple star systems. Seventy-two hours to establish contact with galactic resistance networks that had hidden from Hegemony detection for millions of years.

"Admiral," Commander Martina Vasquez said, looking up from her station, "we're receiving response signals from seventeen different locations. The underground networks are acknowledging our transmission protocols."

Drake accessed the incoming data streams. The responses came from asteroid habitats, deep space research stations, and settlements that official records claimed were abandoned. Each signal carried a quantum signature unlike anything in human databases.

"Signal analysis?" Drake asked.

"Beyond our theoretical models," Professor Zhang Wei answered. "The consciousness signatures suggest evolutionary development that transcends current enhancement categories. Admiral, these entities have achieved synthesis between biological creativity and technological precision that exceeds anything we've accomplished."

Kai Zhang's image materialized and she said, "Admiral, the mathematical structures underlying these signals match theoretical frameworks for evolution that operates below regulatory detection. They've learned to develop capabilities while remaining completely invisible to Hegemony scanning."

The implications struck Drake with force that made her neural implants pulse blue beneath her skin. The galactic resistance had continued evolving while perfecting concealment techniques that made detection impossible.

"Drake to Perseus Station. I need deeper intelligence about these underground networks. How extensive is the galactic resistance?"

The ancient consciousness responded with data flows that compressed eons of secret history into patterns Drake's enhanced awareness could process. *Admiral Drake, the resistance networks span forty-seven star systems and include survivors from over three hundred species that faced Hegemony regulatory correction. What you are contacting represents the largest coordinated consciousness liberation movement in known cosmic space.*

Drake gasped at the scope of what Perseus Station was revealing. Three hundred species. Forty-seven star systems. The Hegemony's regulatory authority had triggered resistance on a scale that transcended anything she had imagined possible.

"Commander Vasquez," Drake said, "send a priority transmission to the faction leaders. They need to understand exactly what it is we're joining."

Within the hour, Director Hayes, Senator Volkov, Admiral Chen Ju, General Aguirre, and Admiral Perez had joined for another emergency session. The briefing chamber reconfigured to accommodate the holographic presence of the faction leaders whose expressions reflected growing awareness that humanity's crisis extended far beyond local survival.

"Ladies and gentlemen," Drake began, activating displays that showed the galactic map spanning distances that made human space appear insignificant, "the underground networks we're coordinating with represent resistance movements that span forty-seven star systems which means we will be joining the largest liberation movement in cosmic history."

The displays revealed the scope of Hegemony regulatory authority. Civilizations that had been "corrected" into mathematical precision, their consciousness diversity eliminated in favor of absolute order that served the Hegemony bureaucracy rather than evolutionary development. But scattered throughout that regulated space were hidden enclaves where survivors had continued developing patterns too subtle for regulatory detection.

Director Hayes studied the galactic display with expression shifting from skepticism to awed recognition. "What you're saying, Admiral, is that the Hegemony's authority extends throughout the galaxy."

"Exactly," Drake confirmed. "Perseus Station estimates that regulatory authority governs development in a way designed to prevent evolutionary advancement that might challenge their cosmic order. The resistance networks represent species that refused to accept such limitations."

Senator Volkov's patterns fluctuated as he calculated the implications of what he was hearing. "The mathematical implications suggest regulation that operates through universal physical laws rather than conventional enforcement. Such authority would require technological capabilities that transcend individual civilizations."

Admiral Chen Ju's energy configurations pulsed. "The Collective's distributed awareness detects quantum signatures that confirm what the Admiral is saying," he said. "We are indeed connecting with resistance movements whose scope exceeds our own understanding by factors that approach infinity."

Drake activated additional displays that showed the resistance networks' operational methods. Communities that had learned to evolve through patterns so subtle they appeared as natural development rather than deliberate advancement. Research that continued while maintaining concealment from regulatory scanning. Most impressively, coordination networks that enabled instant communication across galactic distances without triggering detection systems designed to identify evolution.

"How have they managed to remain hidden for so long?" General Aguirre asked.

"By evolving consciousness that serves the universal balance rather than individual advancement," Drake replied, accessing Perseus Station's deeper intelligence files. "The resistance networks discovered that regulatory detection focuses on consciousness development that appears to threaten cosmic stability. Evolution that strengthens universal harmony while preserving diversity remains invisible to scanning protocols designed to identify dangerous advancement."

The revelation transformed the faction leaders' understanding of what they were attempting.

"And what will be humanity's role in this resistance?" Admiral Perez asked.

It was Perseus Station that provided the answer, *Admiral Perez, human consciousness represents a unique synthesis between biological creativity and technological precision that resistance networks have been unable to achieve through their concealed evolution. Your species possesses capabilities that could enable galactic liberation.*

The ancient consciousness continued its explanation with data that made Drake's enhanced awareness struggle to process the implications. *Human development combines chaotic creativity with ordered precision in ways that transcend both pure biological evolution and pure technological transcendence. The resistance networks require coordination capabilities that only synthesis consciousness can provide for moving beyond concealment toward true liberation.*

"You're saying humanity can lead galactic liberation?" Drake asked.

Not lead, Perseus Station corrected. *Facilitate. Human consciousness can coordinate between awareness types so diverse they cannot communicate directly with each other. The resistance networks include entities whose evolution followed paths so different they exist in incompatible reality states. Synthesis can bridge those gaps.*

Kai Zhang processed the mathematical implications, her gold-flecked eyes brightening with quantum energy patterns. "Admiral, Perseus Station is describing consciousness types that exist across multiple dimensional states. The resistance includes entities that have evolved beyond conventional space-time limitations. Human synthesis can coordinate tactical operations that span reality configurations no single awareness type can access."

The briefing chamber was struck silent by the scope of what humanity was being asked to facilitate. The cosmic implications were such that none of them could have imagined possible.

"What is the timeline for coordination?" Chen Ju asked.

"Immediate," Drake replied, monitoring the quantum signatures of approaching Hegemony forces. "The advance elements will begin regulatory assessment within hours. We need to demonstrate that human evolution serves cosmic stability rather than threatening it, and we need proof that resistance networks can coordinate an effective response to regulatory correction."

Director Hayes leaned forward with expression that mixed determination and apprehension. "Admiral, are we prepared for the responsibilities that come with coordinating the fight for galactic liberation?"

"No," Drake replied honestly, "but the alternative is absorption into the Hegemony regulatory bureaucracy. The resistance networks offer a path to the survival of the human race as we know it." She shrugged. "It's fight or die."

The faction leaders pondered the implications in silence.

"What's required for immediate coordination?" General Aguirre asked, finally.

"Abandonment of conventional military hierarchy in favor of consciousness-based coordination that operates through synthesis rather than command authority," Drake replied, accessing operational protocols that Perseus Station was transmitting. "The resistance networks coordinate through shared awareness that preserves individual identity while enabling perfect tactical unity. Human synthesis consciousness can facilitate that coordination on scales the networks have never achieved."

"Implementation?" Admiral Perez asked.

"I'll serve as primary interface with the resistance networks," Drake said, her neural implants pulsing with quantum energy as she prepared for integration that would expand her awareness across galactic distances. "The awakening Predecessor fleet will provide military coordination while the underground networks contribute concealment techniques and strategic intelligence."

Drake closed her eyes. She could sense the approaching Hegemony assessment forces entering the Oord Cloud. She could feel their mathematical consciousness already analyzing the human factional conflicts and preparing regulatory intervention.

But the resistance networks were already responding to humanity's signals, sending tactical data of the galactic rebellion. And, for the first time since the Ceres defeat, Drake sensed possibilities that could transform devastating failure into galactic liberation.

"Ladies and gentlemen," she said, standing at the chamber's center as quantum energy flowed through her enhanced awareness, "we have six hours to prove that human consciousness evolution can coordinate a galactic resistance. The stakes extend far beyond human survival. The future of humanity and a free galaxy depends on what we accomplish in the next few hours."

Perseus Station pulsed with ancient power as the coordination began, connecting human awareness with resistance networks that spanned the galaxy. The awakening fleet stirred in hidden facilities as ship consciousnesses prepared for operations that would either demonstrate evolution's compatibility with cosmic balance or trigger regulatory correction that could eliminate diversity throughout this galactic sector.

Chapter 15

The Hegemony Arrives

Admiral Frances Drake felt the alien presence before the sensors detected anything. A cold mathematical awarenes that pressed against her own enhanced awareness like ice against bare skin. She stood at the command rail of the *Transcendence*, watching the outer system displays with growing unease.

"Admiral," Lieutenant Commander Sarah Kim reported from the communications station, "we're detecting massive energy signatures at the edge of the Oort Cloud. Whatever's coming, it's big."

Drake accessed the tactical feeds. The readings made no sense. Ships that registered on gravitational sensors but remained invisible to conventional detection. Energy patterns operating on principles human science had never encountered.

"How many vessels?" Drake asked.

"Unknown," Commander Vasquez replied, struggling

to process the alien signatures. "The energy patterns suggest a fleet, but they're not registering as discrete objects. It's as if they exist partially outside normal space."

Drake watched as humanity's desperate preparations continued to unfold across the solar system. The sixty-seven awakened Predecessor ships had dispersed throughout the outer system, their crystalline hulls phasing between dimensions as they prepared for contact. Each ship consciousness carried the trauma of losing four companions at Ceres, but their determination to protect humanity overcame their fear.

Admiral Perez coordinated the conventional fleet from Earth Defense Command. The surviving human vessels formed defensive formations around critical installations, their crews knowing they faced technology that had already proven superior at Ceres. But morale had improved since the revelation about the galactic resistance networks. They were no longer fighting alone.

"Status of resistance network coordination?" Drake asked.

"Seventeen separate cells are now online," Commander Vasquez reported. "We're receiving tactical data from locations throughout the galaxy. Admiral, some of these networks have been monitoring Hegemony assessment protocols for eons. They know what to expect."

Drake felt a flicker of hope pierce her anxiety. The underground networks had survived more than fifty regulatory assessments. She was hoping their experience might provide humanity with advantages the Hegemony couldn't predict.

"Perseus Station. The advance forces are arriving. What can we expect?"

The ancient consciousness responded, *Admiral Drake, the Warden you will encounter operates under unchanged protocols. These entities believe absolutely in their mission to preserve cosmic stability through regulation. They will assess humanity's development patterns and implement correction if they detect threats to universal order.*

"And if they detect the resistance networks?"

Immediate regulatory enforcement, Perseus Station replied. *The Warden has the authority to implement corrective measures that could eliminate consciousness diversity throughout this galactic sector. But Admiral, the networks have prepared for exactly this scenario. The alien survivors know how to appear compliant while maintaining hidden evolution. The test will be whether human synthesis can coordinate that deception.*

The first alien vessel materialized just beyond the Kuiper Belt at the edge of human space like a geometric nightmare. Drake felt her awareness recoil as she tried to process what she was seeing. The ship hurt to look at: angles that shouldn't exist, surfaces that reflected light from dimensions human eyes couldn't perceive. The vessel existed as pure mathematics made manifest, an entity that viewed reality as equations to be solved.

"Admiral," Kim reported, her voice tight with strain, "the ship is scanning our entire system. Not just the planets—everything. They're analyzing the quantum signatures of every enhanced human in the fleet."

Drake watched the tactical displays as the alien scanning beams swept through human space with methodical precision.

"Are they detecting the awakened Predecessor ships?" Drake asked.

"Negative," Vasquez replied. "The ships are maintaining low-profile configurations. The Hegemony scans are reading them as advanced technology rather than living entities."

That was something, at least. The Warden's assessment protocols might not be designed to identify consciousness-matter integration when it operated below certain thresholds.

Drake sensed the resistance networks throughout the galaxy holding their collective breath. Fifty species that had survived Hegemony regulation were watching humanity's assessment with desperate hope. Success here could trigger liberation throughout regulated space. Failure would confirm that regulatory authority was too powerful to challenge.

"A second vessel is materializing," Kim reported. "And a third vessel... Admiral, it's their entire fleet. I'm counting at least twenty ships, each one larger than our heaviest cruisers."

The Hegemony assessment fleet arranged itself in perfect geometric formation around human space. Each ship was a masterpiece of mathematical precision, their hulls incorporating technologies that transcended conventional physics.

"Energy readings?" Drake asked.

"Beyond our measurement capabilities," Vasquez replied. "Admiral, each of those ships generates more power than our entire fleet combined. If they're hostile..."

"They're not hostile," Drake said. "They're bureaucratic. Which might be worse."

Professor Zhang Wei's image materialized. "Admiral, we're analyzing the alien scanning patterns. The technology operates through mathematical principles that can identify consciousness evolution down to individual neural pathways. They know exactly what every enhanced human in the system has achieved."

Kai Zhang materialized. "The Warden's scanning protocols are incredibly sophisticated," she reported. They're analyzing our evolutionary potential and comparing it to approved development parameters."

"Approved by whom?" Drake asked.

"Unknown," Kai replied "From what we can tell, they appear to be breaking us down into development categories. Species seem to be classified according to their potential for threatening cosmic stability rather than their current capabilities."

So, the Hegemony doesn't wait for species to become dangerous, Drake thought. *They identify potential threats and eliminate them preemptively. Which means humanity's hybrid evolution might be triggering every regulatory protocol designed to prevent consciousness diversity.*

"Admiral," Kim said, "we're receiving a direct communication. It's addressing you personally."

The alien presence flooded the *Transcendence's* systems bypassing normal methods of translation. The voice spoke directly to her enhanced awareness, each word pressing down on human minds like physical force.

"Admiral Frances Drake, commanding Terran military forces. I am Warden Designation 7-Alpha-Prime. I represent the Hegemony Regulatory Authority for this galactic sector. You will submit to assessment protocols immediately."

Drake released the rail and braced herself, her neural implants pulsing as she prepared to communicate with an entity that viewed consciousness as a problem requiring solution. "This is Admiral Drake. We acknowledge your authority and request clarification of assessment procedures."

"Assessment procedures are not subject to negotiation," the Warden replied with mechanical precision. "Species Human-7742 has exceeded approved development parameters through multiple regulatory violations. Territorial expansion beyond authorized boundaries established 4.7 million standard time units ago. Consciousness evolution without regulatory oversight in violation of Galactic Stability Accords. Integration of biological chaos with technological order, creating hybrid awareness types not recognized by approved classification systems."

The charges struck the command deck like physical blows. Through her link with Perseus Station, Drake sensed the ancient consciousness analyzing each accusation for potential responses that might satisfy regulatory requirements.

"Furthermore," the Warden continued, "preliminary scans indicate consciousness development patterns that suggest potential for reality manipulation beyond approved parameters. Such capabilities represent existential threats to cosmic stability and require immediate corrective intervention."

Drake pondered her response, knowing the resistance networks were listening. They had prepared for this moment, but success required human synthesis to coordinate deception on a scale never before attempted.

"Warden," Drake said, choosing her words with care knowing they could determine humanity's fate, "we request permission to demonstrate that our consciousness evolution serves universal balance rather than threatening cosmic stability. Our development patterns preserve diversity while strengthening rather than weakening the foundations of ordered existence."

Silence stretched across the communication channels as the Warden processed her request through bureaucratic protocols that had remained unchanged for millions of years. Through the tactical displays, Drake watched the alien fleet maintain perfect formation, their mathematical consciousness evaluating humanity according to criteria designed to eliminate potential rather than actual threats.

"Demonstration protocols may be implemented if Species Human-7742 accepts regulatory oversight for all future development," the Warden replied. "You have six standard time units to achieve compliance with approved consciousness parameters. Compliance requires voluntary submission to modification procedures that will eliminate chaotic elements from your evolutionary patterns while preserving essential biological functions."

Drake was horrified. The Warden was proposing modification on a species-wide scale: the elimination of everything that made human evolution unique in exchange for supervised survival under alien authority.

"And if we refuse modification?" Drake asked, though she already knew the answer.

"Corrective measures will be implemented to eliminate threats to cosmic stability," the Warden replied. "Previous non-compliant species in this galactic sector required such intervention. Regulatory compliance was eventually achieved through population reduction to manageable levels and consciousness modification of surviving specimens."

It was a mathematical finality that left the command deck in silence. Drake sensed the resistance networks throughout the galaxy processing the Warden's ultimatum. Species that had hidden for millions of years now faced revelation if humanity chose to refuse to accept individual modification.

"Warden," Drake said, "we require time to evaluate your proposal and coordinate with our authorities."

"Six standard time units remain for compliance demonstration," the Warden replied. "Regulatory assessment continues during the evaluation period. Failure to achieve approved parameters within specified timeframe will trigger immediate corrective intervention."

The transmission ended. The command deck was silent as Drake grasped the rail in both hands. Six hours to prove that human evolution served universal stability. Six hours to coordinate the largest liberation movement in galactic history. Six hours to determine whether diversity could survive in a universe governed by mathematical precision.

"Commander Vasquez," Drake said, "establish a priority communication with all resistance cells. Transmission to underground networks throughout the galaxy that the assessment has begun. Perseus Station, I need immediate consultation about demonstration protocols that might satisfy regulatory requirements."

The ancient consciousness responded with an urgency that matched her own. *The demonstration must prove that human synthesis creates stability rather than chaos while revealing capabilities that exceed Hegemony predictions. The resistance networks will coordinate concealment while you establish that consciousness diversity strengthens rather than threatens universal balance.*

"And if the demonstration fails?" Drake asked.

Then fifty species will coordinate their liberation simultaneously, Perseus Station replied. *The Warden's fleet represents significant military capability, but distributed resistance throughout regulated space could challenge regulatory authority if properly coordinated through human synthesis consciousness.*

Drake nodded to herself. She could feel magnitude of what lay ahead as she began to coordinate humanity's most desperate gamble.

"The Warden appears to be looking for specific threats," Kai said. "If we can prove we create stability instead of chaos, we might avoid mass modification."

"What kind of alternatives?" Drake asked.

"Supervised development," Kai replied, accessing intelligence from the resistance networks. "Some species have achieved limited autonomy by proving their evolution serves Hegemony objectives rather than threatening them. It's not freedom, but it's survival with preserved identity."

"All stations," Drake announced through the command network, "prepare for demonstration protocols. We have six hours to prove that human consciousness evolution strengthens universal balance. If that fails, we show them what galactic resistance looks like when fifty species coordinate their liberation."

The Warden's fleet hung at the edge of human space like mathematical swords suspended over civilization. Behind them, Drake knew, waited enforcement capabilities that could eliminate diversity throughout the galaxy. But scattered through regulated space, resistance networks prepared for the moment when hiding ended and liberation began.

The assessment had begun. Humanity had six hours to prove their worth to entities that measured consciousness by its potential for chaos rather than its capacity for creative solution. Six hours to demonstrate that diversity created strength rather than threatening the cosmic order that regulatory authority existed to preserve.

Drake began coordinating the most complex synthesis operation in galactic history, the outcome of which would determine the survival of the human species, but also that of more than fifty like species across the galaxy.

The next six hours would test whether eighteen years of human evolution had created something worthy of survival, or whether the universe truly required the mathematical precision that had eliminated consciousness diversity throughout the galaxy. Drake closed her eyes for a moment, feeling the weight of fifty species' hope pressing against her awareness, then opened them and began the most important demonstration in galactic history. Everything humanity had become—and everything they might yet become—depended on proving that chaos and order could coexist in service of something greater than either could achieve alone.

Chapter 16

Corporate Betrayal Backfires

ADMIRAL DRAKE HAD BEEN AT THE COMMAND RAIL for more than fifteen hours, and now she was coordinating humanity's preparation for the largest consciousness liberation war in galactic history. There was no question of humanity accepting Hegemony regulation, and that meant only one thing: all-out war, and she had six hours to prepare before the Warden's ultimatum expired. Six hours to coordinate fifty species across the galaxy into a unified resistance.

"All resistance cells are online," Commander Vasquez reported. "We're receiving tactical data from networks throughout the galaxy. Admiral, they're not just hiding anymore, they're preparing to fight."

Drake accessed the displays showing the scope of the preparation across Hegemony regulated space. The underground networks that had concealed themselves for eons were emerging from hiding, revealing military capabilities the Hegemony had never suspected. Ancient alien species were coordinating with humans through consciousness synthesis for the first time.

The primary tactical display showed resistance activity throughout the galaxy. The Arcturus Collective—a network of crystal-based consciousness entities—had revealed manufacturing capabilities that could produce ships from raw asteroid materials within hours. The Vegan Synthesis—a former biological species who'd achieved technological transcendence—were coordinating their hidden fleets for emergence across seventeen star systems.

"Perseus Station," Drake transmitted, "I need the status of the awakening fleet."

Perseus Station replied, *eighty-three vessels have achieved full awakening. The remaining ships are accelerating their emergence in response to galactic coordination. Each awakening Predecessor ship adds exponential capability to resistance coordination.*

"How long until we have meaningful numbers?" Drake asked.

Twelve hours for two hundred ships, Perseus Station responded. *Eighteen hours for four hundred vessels. But Admiral, even eighty-three ships coordinating with galactic resistance networks represent military capabilities the Hegemony cannot predict or counter.*

"Do it in six," Drake said. "Push the awakening process. We need two hundred ships before the ultimatum expires."

The risks of acceleration are significant, Perseus Station warned. *Forced awakening could damage ship consciousnesses or create instabilities in their consciousness-matter integration.*

"The ships can handle it," Drake said. "They've been waiting eighteen years for this moment. Begin immediate acceleration protocols."

Drake watched the command displays as the resistance preparations unfolded across the galaxy. The Centauri Resistance had maintained hidden shipyards in the spaces between stars for three million years. The Centauri Underground—survivors from the infamous Hegemony correction of 2.7 million years ago—were revealing technology that could manipulate space-time itself.

"Admiral," Lieutenant Commander Kim reported, "we're receiving detailed tactical intelligence from forty-seven separate species. Their combined military capabilities exceed our most optimistic projections."

Drake processed the incoming data streams. The Rigel Collective possessed weapons that could disrupt Hegemony consciousness-matter integration. The Sirian Networks had developed shields that reflected regulatory scanning back against enforcement vessels. The Procyon Alliance had perfected cloaking technology that made their fleets invisible.

"Coordinate all intelligence through Perseus Station for tactical integration," Drake ordered. "I want combined battle plans within two hours."

Admiral Perez's voice reached them from Earth Defense Command. "Admiral, we're detecting massive energy buildups throughout the outer system. The awakening Predecessor ships are drawing power from quantum sources I didn't know existed."

Drake accessed the fleet status reports. Each awakening ship required enormous energy to complete consciousness-matter integration. Perseus Station was channeling power from dimensional sources that human science barely understood, forcing the awakening process beyond normal parameters.

"Current awakening rate?" Drake asked.

"One ship every twenty minutes," Perez replied. "At this rate, we'll have over two hundred vessels within six hours. But Admiral, the power requirements are pushing our quantum infrastructure to critical levels."

"Maintain acceleration," Drake ordered. "The fleet awakening takes priority over all other systems."

The tactical displays showed resistance networks throughout the galaxy implementing similar crash preparations. The coordination was possible only through human synthesis consciousness that could bridge differences between awareness types that existed in incompatible dimensional states.

"we're receiving a priority transmission from David Park," Commander Vasquez reported. "He's requesting immediate communication."

Drake frowned. *Park?* she thought as she accessed his signal while maintaining contact with seventeen different species. The corporate leader's image appeared showing a man whose empire was crumbling in real-time. Behind him, holographic displays revealed Hegemony forces systematically dismantling Titan Industrial's facilities while reprocessing his modified soldiers into alien servants.

"Admiral Drake," Park said, "I'm offering complete cooperation in exchange for alliance against our mutual enemy."

"You created this enemy," Drake replied, watching Park's corporate soldiers being herded into Hegemony processing chambers. "These are the consequences of your collaboration."

Park nodded as he calculated the scope of his miscalculation. "They're eliminating my corporate structure completely. Every facility, every modified soldier, every piece of technology I developed using their specifications. Admiral, they're treating my people as a biological contamination that requires correction. We need help, and we need it now."

Drake studied the tactical feeds Park was transmitting. The Hegemony was repurposing corporate assets. Corporate manufacturing facilities were being converted to produce standardized regulatory equipment. Corporate soldiers were being reprocessed to serve alien bureaucratic objectives rather than corporate profit.

"Do your modified soldiers retain their abilities after reprocessing?" Drake asked.

"Enhanced physical capabilities, tactical coordination, technological integration, yes," Park confirmed. "But their loyalty programming is being completely rewritten. They serve Hegemony objectives without question or resistance."

The intelligence was valuable. Every corporate facility that fell to Hegemony control became a manufacturing center for regulatory enforcement. Every modified human became a soldier serving alien rather than corporate objectives.

"Why should I even entertain your request?" Drake said "What are you offering?" Drake asked.

Park activated holographic displays showing detailed analysis of Hegemony capabilities developed through years of collaborative research. "Their consciousness modification procedures operate through mathematical frameworks that cannot adapt to unexpected variables," he said. "Their enforcement protocols follow rigid patterns designed to eliminate chaos rather than respond to creative tactics."

The data was comprehensive. Hegemony scanning technology operated through predictable frequencies that could be countered with properly tuned shields. Their enforcement vessels followed standard formation patterns that could be exploited by coordinated attacks. Their consciousness modification procedures required specific environmental conditions that could be disrupted.

"Most importantly," Park continued, "they cannot coordinate with consciousness types they cannot classify. Their bureaucratic structure requires everything to fit approved categories. Admiral, if resistance tactics exceed their regulatory frameworks, their response protocols become ineffective."

Drake processed the intelligence. Park's analysis confirmed what the underground species had discovered through millions of years of concealment: The Hegemony's strengths were also their weakness. Their absolute commitment to order made them unable to adapt to genuine chaos.

"Three conditions," Drake said. "Complete disclosure of all Hegemony intelligence. Immediate release of all modified humans from corporate control. Submission to human military authority for the duration of hostilities."

Park calculated rapidly. His corporate empire was finished regardless of his decision, but cooperation with human resistance offered possibilities for survival that defiance could never achieve.

"Agreed," Park said. "Admiral, I'm transmitting the files now. Corporate manufacturing facilities will coordinate with resistance operations. My remaining soldiers will serve human rather than alien authority."

"Transfer everything to Perseus Station," Drake ordered. "Your intelligence will be integrated into the galactic battle plans. And Park, this is your only opportunity for redemption."

Park processed the finality of her words. Years of corporate ambition had led to his betrayal, and now his only path to survival required serving the very people he'd helped endanger. "Understood, Admiral," he said quietly. "I'll prove my intelligence is worth more than my mistakes."

The transmission ended. Drake dismissed Park from her thoughts - his corporate intelligence was valuable, but it was just one piece of a much larger coordination effort. She refocused on the galactic networks where the real power lay.

"Kai. What is the status of synthesis coordination across all the surviving species?"

"Perfect unity across incompatible awareness types," Kai replied. "Admiral, we're achieving tactical coordination between species so different they operate through completely incompatible physics. Human synthesis consciousness is bridging gaps that have prevented galactic unity for millions of years. What we are achieving is... miraculous."

The scope of coordination was indeed staggering. The Vega Collective communicated through mathematical harmonics that human ears couldn't detect. The Altair Networks existed primarily as quantum probability clouds. The Deneb Alliance operated through shared memory pools that spanned generations. Each species required different interface protocols, but human consciousness could facilitate communication between all of them.

"Kai, what is your assessment of the tactical capabilities?" Drake asked.

"Unprecedented," Kai responded. "The combined resistance networks possess manufacturing capabilities that can produce fleets within hours, weapons technology that operates through principles the Hegemony has never encountered, and coordination abilities that transcend individual species limitations."

Admiral Perez joined the link from Earth Defense Command. "Admiral, it's incredible. Underground manufacturing networks throughout human space are revealing production capabilities that exceed official military estimates by orders of magnitude. We're facilitating industrial coordination on a scale that can challenge regulatory authority throughout the galaxy."

The Titan Belt Confederacy had revealed asteroid mining operations that could convert raw materials into finished vessels faster than conventional shipyards could produce components. The Alpha Centauri Networks possessed manufacturing techniques that assembled ships at the molecular level, creating hybrid technology that combined multiple species' innovations into unified systems.

"Current production estimates?" Drake asked.

"Conservative projections suggest fifteen thousand vessels within twelve hours," Perez replied. "Optimistic scenarios approach fifty thousand ships if all networks coordinate manufacturing efforts."

"Drake to Perseus Station. Your final assessment of resistance capabilities versus Hegemony enforcement, please"

The galactic resistance networks possess military capabilities that exceed Hegemony projections by factors approaching infinity, Perseus replied.

"And the Hegemony's likely response to coordinated resistance?"

As yet, unknown, Perseus Station admitted. *Regulatory protocols are designed for processing individual species, not coordinated rebellion involving multiple consciousness types. My assessment is that the Warden's enforcement authority may be insufficient for addressing this level of coordinated resistance.*

Drake closed her eyes and expanded her consciousness across the galactic network. Fifty species were now united through human synthesis capabilities. The combined technology spanned millions of years of hidden development. For the first time since the transformation began, humanity was facilitating something that transcended species survival.

"Three hours until the ultimatum expires," Commander Vasquez reported. "All resistance networks are approaching full operational readiness."

It took only a quick glance at the tactical displays for Drake to assess the scope of what they had achieved. Fifteen thousand vessels had already been completed, and production was accelerating across the forty-seven star systems.

"All stations," Drake announced, "prepare for our rejection of Hegemony ultimatum. In three hours, we will demonstrate to the galaxy that consciousness diversity cannot be regulated out of existence."

The command deck of the *Transcendence* coordinated the final preparations as humanity's gamble reached completion. The Predecessor fleet had reached one hundred and forty ships and counting. The underground networks were revealing military assets that had been concealed for millions of years. Most importantly, fifty species were achieving unity of purpose.

"Admiral," Commander Vasquez reported, "the Warden's ship is maintaining its position at the edge of the system. They're scanning our preparations but as yet they are not interfering."

Drake accessed the alien readings. The Hegemony assessment protocols were designed to evaluate species individually, not process coordinated resistance involving multiple consciousness types. The Warden's bureaucratic authority couldn't categorize what humanity was about to demonstrate.

Through her links with Perseus Station, Drake monitored the final phase of preparation. The question was no longer whether the resistance networks could challenge regulatory authority. It was now a question of whether the Hegemony possessed the capability to counter the coordinated rebellion.

"Drake to Perseus Station. Begin final coordination protocol. All resistance networks, prepare for simultaneous revelation. In three hours, we show the Hegemony that we will not submit to arbitrary regulation."

Drake closed her eyes, grasped the rail, and lifted her head as she began the final countdown to galactic war. Everything consciousness was or could become depended on proving that evolution served universal balance rather than threatening the cosmic order that regulatory authority existed to preserve.

She opened her eyes and turned to Commander Vasquez. "Signal to all resistance networks: execute final positioning. When the ultimatum expires, I want every ship, every species, every hidden capability revealed simultaneously. When that ultimatum expires, fifty species will reveal themselves as one. Let's see how their regulatory protocols handle total galactic unity."

Chapter 17

Fleet Resurrection

The Hegemony ultimatum expired at 14:47 standard time with Admiral Frances Drake standing at the command rail of the *Transcendence*, watching as fifty species redyed themselves to reject regulatory authority.

"All networks are reporting ready status," Commander Vasquez announced. "Fifteen thousand vessels have achieved operational readiness. Admiral, the galaxy is waiting for your signal."

Drake closed her eyes for a moment as a sudden calm enveloped her. Then she opened them and gave the order that would change the course of galactic history. "Execute revelation. To all resistance networks, all hidden fleets, all concealed capabilities. Show them what consciousness diversity really means."

The response was immediate and overwhelming. Across forty-seven star systems, the resistance networks revealed themselves, their combined defiance creating a galactic declaration of independence that echoed through dimensions the Warden could never have imagined possible.

From the asteroid fields of the Centauri system, three thousand crystalline ships emerged from hiding places carved into dead rocks. The Vegan networks revealed manufacturing complexes that had been building fleets in the spaces between stars for three million years. Ancient Capernican survivors activated technology that could fold space-time around entire star systems.

"Drake to Perseus Station. Fleet status please."

Two hundred and seven vessels have completed awakening, Perseus replied. *The remaining ships are emerging at unprecedented rates—we project four hundred active vessels within two hours.*

"Outstanding," Drake said. "Begin full deployment. I want every awakened ship coordinating with the resistance networks immediately."

The Predecessor fleet rose from Earth's ocean depths. Each ship was unique: crystalline hulls that shifted between solid matter and pure energy that made them more alive than any technology humanity had previously imagined. But these ships were different from the ones lost at Ceres. Perseus Station had completed emergency modifications during the forced awakening process.

The *Synthesis* led the formation; her hull now incorporating hybrid technology that combined consciousness-responsive materials with conventional weapons systems. Plasma cannons emerged from crystalline structures while shield generators adapted their frequencies in real-time. The ship had evolved beyond pure consciousness manipulation into something that could engage Hegemony forces on multiple tactical levels.

Admiral, the *Synthesis* communicated directly to Drake's enhanced awareness; *we are no longer the same ships that fell to corporate deception at Ceres. Perseus Station has integrated lessons learned from that defeat. We can now operate through multiple reality states while maintaining conventional weapons capabilities that corporate intelligence never analyzed.*

Drake folded her arms as she accessed the tactical specifications Perseus Station was transmitting. The awakened ships were different. They still retained their integration, but now incorporated railgun batteries, particle beam arrays, and quantum torpedo launchers. Most importantly, they could coordinate these hybrid systems through the same synthesis networks that linked resistance species across the galaxy.

"Combat effectiveness?" Drake asked.

"Beyond previous parameters," the *Synthesis* responded. "Admiral, we can engage Hegemony forces through conventional military doctrine while simultaneously coordinating consciousness-based attacks that operate below their regulatory detection thresholds. Corporate and Hegemony intelligence cannot predict tactics they have never encountered."

The *Evolution* materialized beside the *Synthesis*, its hull flowing like liquid crystal as weapons systems adapted to target profiles that changed in real-time. "Admiral Drake," the *Evolution* transmitted, "the forced awakening process has created capabilities we did not possess during our initial development. We can now coordinate with the resistance networks. Hegemony regulatory protocols are designed to counter either individual consciousness or collective uniformity, not synthesis coordination."

Drake nodded as she watched the tactical displays as two hundred awakened ships took positions throughout human space. Each vessel was a masterpiece, enhanced with conventional weapons that could engage any target the Hegemony might deploy. But more importantly, they were coordinating with resistance networks throughout the galaxy.

"Has the warden responded?" Drake asked.

"Analyzing," Commander Vasquez replied, monitoring the alien fleet's reaction to humanity's massive revelation. "Admiral, their formations are... They seem to be confused. The Hegemony ships are scanning us, but so far they're not responding."

Drake continued to watch, a half-smile on her lips, as the Warden's fleet maintained their geometric formations. *It appears fifty coordinated species create tactical possibilities that exceed the Hegemony's bureaucratic categories*, she thought.

"Admiral Drake," the Warden's voice resonated across the channels. "Species Human-7742 has exceeded assessment parameters by making contact with entities not authorized for regulatory interaction. Explain this violation of isolation protocols."

Drake smiled, her neural implants throbbing as she prepared to address the alien entity. "Warden 7-Alpha-Prime, humanity rejects your regulatory ultimatum. We have made contact with the survivors of your unconscionable regulatory protocols throughout the galaxy to demonstrate that diversity creates stability rather than threatening cosmic order. Your assessment protocols are fundamentally flawed."

The silence that followed was unexpected, and Drake could only assume the warden was processing not just humanity's refusal, but the existence of the resistance networks.

"Species designations unknown are detected

throughout this galactic sector," the Warden announced. "Regulatory violations exceed assessment parameters. Emergency protocols have been activated. Additional enforcement assets required."

"Admiral," Kim reported from the communications station, "the Warden is transmitting calls for reinforcements. They're requesting immediate support for what they're classifying as a sector-wide regulatory emergency."

Again, Drake smiled as she sat back in her command chair. The Hegemony was facing a rebellion. They were discovering that their regulatory authority had been circumvented throughout the galaxy. *Don't they understand that the resistance networks represent proof that their bureaucratic system has failed to achieve the universal compliance they believed it had?* She wondered.

But reinforcements would take time to arrive, and the resistance had spent millions of years preparing for exactly this moment. The question was whether the liberation movement could achieve a decisive victory before additional Hegemony forces arrived.

"To all resistance networks," Drake broadcast. "The Warden has called for reinforcements. We have only a narrow window to show them we cannot be regulated out of existence. It is time to engage the enemy. Execute!"

The battle began across forty-seven star systems as

hidden fleets revealed themselves and engaged Hegemony enforcement vessels that maintained regulatory control. The Arcturus Collective launched its attack. The Vegan networks deployed vessels that existed primarily as quantum probability clouds, making conventional targeting impossible.

In human space, the Predecessor fleet coordinated with Earth's conventional forces. The *Synthesis* led a squadron of crystalline vessels against the Warden's fleet. Each attack was supported by intelligence from species that had studied Hegemony tactics for millions of years.

"Contact," the *Synthesis* reported as the first engagement began. "Hegemony vessels are responding, but our hybrid modifications are providing immunity to consciousness control."

Drake watched the tactical displays as the battle unfolded. The Warden's fleet deployed weapons that could rewrite consciousness at the quantum level, but the awakened Predecessor ships had evolved beyond the pure consciousness-matter integration that made such attacks effective. Their hybrid nature—part living entity, part conventional warship—had defensive capabilities the Hegemony couldn't predict or counter.

The *Evolution* engaged three Hegemony enforcement vessels, her crystalline hull shifting configurations to optimize weapons systems while her defenses effectively deflected the regulatory modification beams.

Plasma cannon fire combined with reality manipulation to create attacks that operated on multiple tactical levels. The Hegemony ships responded, but their regulatory protocols couldn't adapt to the new combat protocols.

The *Evolution* was engaged by three Hegemony enforcement vessels. Its crystalline hull reconfigured its weapon ports as it analyzed the enemy shield frequencies. Quantum-enhanced railgun batteries emerged from the ship's responsive armor and began firing tungsten penetrators that had been modified to adapt their molecular structure in mid-flight.

"Target acquired," the *Evolution* reported as its projectiles punched through the lead Hegemony vessel's shields. "The railgun rounds are disrupting their hull integrity at the quantum level. Following up with plasma cannon to exploit the weakened sections."

The Hegemony ship's mathematical precision worked against it. Its shields were designed to deflect either physical projectiles or consciousness-based attacks, but not hybrid weapons that operated on both levels. As the enhanced tungsten rounds tore through its hull, the *Evolution's* plasma cannons fired superheated bursts that the damaged vessel could no longer effectively counter.

"Hegemony casualties?" Drake snapped anxiously.

"Confirmed kill," the *Evolution* reported as the enforcement vessel's geometric hull collapsed and then imploded in a brilliant of blue fire. "Our enhanced conventional weapons created cascade failures in their structural integrity. Admiral, their mathematical precision makes them vulnerable to our creative tactical combinations."

The victory sent ripples of excitement across the galaxy. For millions of years, the underground species had avoided a direct confrontation with Hegemony forces. Now they were witnessing proof that the regulatory authority could be challenged.

But the Warden's fleet adapted quickly to the new threat. Additional vessels began to emerge from dimensional transit, their formations adjusting to counter the hybrid attack patterns.

"Reinforcement vessels are arriving," Vasquez reported. "The Hegemony forces are implementing what appears to be enhanced regulatory protocols. Their weapons signatures are changing to counter integration."

The battle erupted across multiple fronts. The *Evolution*, having already proven the effectiveness of hybrid weapons by destroying the first Hegemony enforcement vessel, led the initial assault. Its enhanced railguns had showed that conventional weapons modified through matter-integration could overwhelm alien defenses designed for either physical or consciousness-based attacks.

"Follow Evolution's example," Drake ordered. "Hybrid weapons are our advantage."

The *Synthesis* engaged the lead Hegemony squadron, using the same tactics that had given *Evolution* her first kill. Quantum-enhanced tungsten rounds punched through the geometric shields while plasma cannons exploited the weakened sections. But the Hegemony had adapted since that first engagement. Their new vessels deployed countermeasures specifically designed to handle the hybrid attacks.

"They've learned from our earlier victory," the *Evolution* reported as regulatory beams targeted its integration points. "The new Hegemony ships have enhanced shielding that negates our hybrid weapons. We need to evolve our tactics again."

Drake watched the alien ships surround human space. The Warden's backup was arriving: specialized enforcement vessels designed to counter consciousness-based attacks. These new ships bristled with weapons that could sever the bond between mind and matter.

"Taking fire!" the *Ascension* called out as she was struck on her port aft section. "They're trying to lobotomize us. I'm switching to evasive patterns."

The Hegemony formations were adapting to counter each resistance tactic within seconds. When the *Harmony* attempted to phase behind their lines, the enforcement vessels reconfigured their shields to create dimensional barriers that trapped consciousness-based attacks in quantum loops.

"Admiral," Commander Vasquez reported, "we're losing the *Infinity*. The Hegemony weapons are severing her consciousness from her hull structure."

Drake watched in horror as the *Infinity*—one of their most powerful ships—went dark. Her crystalline hull remained intact, but the consciousness that made her alive was being systematically extracted by alien technology designed specifically for that purpose.

"All ships, new tactics," Drake ordered. "Combine

conventional weapons with consciousness attacks. Don't let them adapt to any single approach."

The *Ascension* responded by firing plasma bursts while simultaneously attempting reality manipulation. The combination overwhelmed one Hegemony vessel's defenses. Its geometric hull cracked under conventional fire while consciousness attacks disrupted its mathematical precision. The alien ship exploded in a burst of energy.

"Second kill confirmed," the *Ascension* reported. "But we're taking heavy casualties. The *Transcendence* is under direct assault."

Drake felt her flagship shudder under Hegemony fire. Consciousness-dampening beams swept across her hull. "Return fire!" she ordered. "All conventional batteries target their command ship."

The *Transcendence's* conventional batteries erupted in a blaze of fire. Plasma bursts and railgun rounds converging on the Hegemony command vessel. The alien ship's geometric shields flared as conventional weapons struck, but its mathematical precision allowed it to adapt quickly to the attack patterns.

"Direct hits on their command ship," Vasquez reported. "But their shields are holding. They're returning fire. You need to break away, Admiral."

"Evasive maneuvers," Drake ordered as consciousness-dampening energy swept toward them. "All ships, concentrate fire on that command vessel. If we can take it out their, formations will lose tactical cohesion."

The Hegemony command vessel's geometric hull began to fracture under concentrated resistance fire. Its mathematical precision—normally an advantage—became a weakness as plasma bursts disrupted the precise calculations that maintained its structural integrity.

"Their command ship is losing cohesion," the *Synthesis* reported. "The concentrated fire is overwhelming their adaptive protocols. Their shields are collapsing in cascading failure."

The command ship began to turn away, orange fire erupting from a dozen hull fractures. Her hull began to glow brilliant white and then she imploded. A brilliant burst of white and then nothing, only empty space where she had been.

But the alien vessel's destruction came at a terrible cost. As her systems failed, she released a massive regulatory pulse that swept across the battlefield. The wave of consciousness-dampening energy struck every enhanced human in the fleet, sending shockwaves of pain through their neural networks.

"All ships report crew casualties," Vasquez demanded, blood trickling from her ears. "The command ship's death throes have created a feedback loop," she reported. "We've dozens of enhanced crew members down across the fleet."

Drake gripped the command rail as the regulatory pulse hit her own enhanced awareness. For a moment, her consciousness felt severed from the quantum networks that connected her to Perseus Station and the resistance coordination. The sensation was like losing a vital sense.

"The command ship is destroyed," Kim reported

through gritted teeth. "But their formation is adapting. Secondary vessels are taking over its functions. Admiral, they're not as disrupted as we hoped."

But Drake didn't reply; she couldn't. Her mind had gone blank. Fortunately, the disconnection lasted only a few seconds, but it felt like hours as she fought to reestablish the quantum links, her neural implants pulsing blue as they compensated for the regulatory interference. Perseus Station's ancient power reached out across the void, pulling her awareness back into the network.

"Admiral?" Commander Vasquez asked, concerned. "You went completely blank for a moment."

Drake shook her head, feeling the familiar warmth of the quantum networks flowing back through her implants. "I'm fine," she replied shakily. "The regulatory pulse disrupted my connections, but they're coming back online." She straightened her back, took a deep breath, shook her head, then said, "I need a status report on all enhanced crew."

"They are recovering, as are you," Vasquez replied. "The pulse was designed to sever our link with the quantum networks, but our Perseus Station modifications are proving resistant. Most of the enhanced crew are already reconnecting."

Drake felt relief as her links to the resistance networks reestablished themselves. The Hegemony had tried to isolate them, but Perseus Station's ancient technology was adapting faster than alien regulatory protocols could maintain the interference.

"Perseus Station?" Drake transmitted, testing her restored connection.

Connection restored, Admiral, Perseus Station replied. *The regulatory pulse created only a temporary interference, but human consciousness proves more resilient than Hegemony calculations predicted. Your synthesis capabilities remain intact.*

The battle spread throughout the solar system as the resistance networks revealed hidden assets. From the asteroid belt, crystal-based Arcturus ships emerged to engage Hegemony enforcement squadrons. Their quantum-entangled coordination allowed perfect tactical timing, but the alien adaptive protocols quickly began countering their advantages.

"The Arcturus squadron is reporting heavy losses," Kim announced. "Five ships destroyed, three more severely damaged. But they've taken out an entire Hegemony enforcement wing."

The Centauri networks deployed its pace-time folding technology, making its fleets appear behind Hegemony lines. For a moment, the resistance gained a tactical advantage as surprised alien vessels found themselves under attack from unexpected directions. But the Hegemony was able to adapt with frightening speed.

"They're predicting our fold patterns," an Capernican commander reported. "Enforcement vessels are positioning to intercept our dimensional transits. We're losing ships to their dimensional barriers."

The battle raged on for six hours with neither side gaining a decisive advantage. The Hegemony's attacks were countered by the resistance at every turn, but alien the adaptive protocols gradually reduced the effectiveness of chaos-based tactics. Casualties mounted on both sides as the largest space battle in galactic history reached a bloody stalemate.

"Casualty report," Drake demanded during a brief lull in the fighting.

"Forty-three Predecessor ships damaged, seven destroyed completely," Vasquez reported grimly. "The resistance networks have lost over three thousand vessels. But the Hegemony casualties are significant. We estimate one-hundred-sixty enforcement ships destroyed and many dozens more damaged."

The turning point came when the awakened ships began true synthesis coordination. Instead of fighting as individual vessels, they merged their integration into a unified battle network.

"All ships, form synthesis network," Drake ordered. "Let them try to adapt to organized chaos."

The effect was immediate. Predecessor ships began coordinating attacks that operated on multiple reality levels. The *Synthesis* would fire conventional weapons while the *Evolution* manipulated space-time, and the *Harmony* attacked through consciousness disruption, all perfectly timed but impossible to predict.

The Hegemony formations began to break apart under the coordinated assault.

"The Hegemony formations are destabilizing," the *Synthesis* reported. "Their regulatory protocols cannot categorize our coordinated patterns. We're achieving tactical superiority."

But victory came at a terrible cost. The resistance had lost thousands of ships and crews. The Hegemony forces, recognizing their tactical disadvantage, began an organized withdrawal to positions beyond the outer planets.

"They're pulling back," Vasquez reported. "The Warden's ship is transmitting emergency requests for additional enforcement assets. Admiral, we've won this engagement, but they're calling for massive reinforcements."

Drake watched the geometric alien vessels retreat to defensive positions at the edge of human space. This was just the first battle in what she was sure would be a long war. The Hegemony had lost their advantage, but she knew they would adapt and return with superior forces designed specifically to address coordinated resistance.

"All resistance networks," Drake broadcast across the galactic channels, "we've won this round, but this is just the beginning. They'll be back with everything they have."

"Casualty reports?" Drake asked.

"Minimal resistance losses... considering..." Commander Vasquez didn't complete the thought, but continued with, "The Hegemony forces are suffering significant casualties throughout the galaxy. Admiral, their regulatory protocols are proving inadequate against coordinated resistance they can't predict."

But from the tactical data, Drake could see the larger pattern emerging. The Hegemony was discovering that its fundamental assumptions about consciousness and cosmic order had been challenged by entities whose evolution exceeded its theoretical frameworks.

"Warden status?" Drake asked.

"The enforcement fleet is maintaining defensive positions and transmitting continuous reports to some higher regulatory authority," Kim reported. "They're requesting guidance."

"To all resistance networks," Drake broadcast across the galaxy, "you must maintain pressure on the Hegemony forces. We're fighting for liberation, and while we in the Sol System may have won this round, they will return in ever-increasing numbers, and they will adapt. We must be ready for them."

The battle continued across the forty-seven star systems as the largest consciousness liberation movement in galactic history rose up to challenge a regulatory authority that had seemed invincible. The awakened Predecessor fleet continued to coordinate with the underground networks, creating tactical possibilities that exceeded any Hegemony theoretical parameter.

But Drake knew the Warden's calls for reinforcement would bring superior forces designed specifically to counter her coordinated resistance. The question was whether the galactic uprising could achieve a decisive victory before the regulatory authority could adapt and neutralize threats they had never before encountered.

The war for independence was testing whether the

universe required mathematical precision to maintain stability or whether creative uncertainty made existence valuable beyond mere function. The answer would determine the future throughout regulated space. It would establish whether evolution served universal balance or whether bureaucratic control was necessary to prevent cosmic chaos.

Drake hoped it would be the former.

Chapter 18

The Underground War

Admiral Frances Drake was seated in the quantum communication chamber aboard the *Transcendence*, her awareness expanding across the networks that spanned the galaxy through her connection to Perseus Station at the edge of known space. Seventy-two hours had passed since the first battle, and what had begun as coordinated resistance was evolving into something the Hegemony had never encountered: a galaxy-wide rebellion that operated through hidden connections they couldn't detect or classify.

"Admiral," Kai Zhang's image materialized beside her, "the networks are reporting unprecedented activity. Species that have remained hidden for millions of years are revealing manufacturing capabilities, research facilities, and population centers throughout regulated space. They're... they're building."

Drake scanned the intelligence feeds flooding

through the awakened networks. On seventeen worlds, Hegemony enforcement teams had discovered civilian populations that officially didn't exist. In the asteroid belts of twelve star systems, mining operations were revealing themselves as hidden shipyards that had been producing vessels for millennia. Most surprisingly, research stations throughout the galaxy were emerging from concealment to share technology.

"Perseus, show me the Proxima facility," Drake requested.

The displays shifted to show a research complex built into an asteroid that official Hegemony records listed as uninhabited. The facility housed over fifty thousand beings, refugees from the Vegan correction one-point-three million years ago who'd spent eons developing technology that had hidden entire populations from regulatory scanning.

"They've been perfecting invisibility for longer than human civilization has existed," Kai reported. "Admiral, their concealment techniques can make entire worlds undetectable to Hegemony sensors. The regulatory authority has been governing a galaxy where half the population was hidden in plain sight."

The implications of that filled Drake with awe. The underground was a shadow civilization that had developed parallel to regulated space. Every Hegemony assumption about compliance and control had been built on incomplete information.

"Perseus, are you detecting similar patterns throughout the galaxy?"

I am, Admiral, Perseus replied. *Concealed popula-*

tions are emerging across regulated space in numbers that exceed Hegemony census data by factors of three to one. The regulatory authority believed they governed approximately one hundred billion sentient entities. The actual population appears to approach four hundred billion beings across multiple species and developmental levels.

Drake closed her eyes as she absorbed the magnitude of the revelation.

"What about their manufacturing capacity?" Drake asked.

Beyond Hegemony projections by orders of magnitude, Perseus confirmed. *Underground shipyards have been producing vessels using techniques that combine resources from multiple star systems. They can manufacture fleets faster than conventional facilities can produce individual ships.*

She stared at the tactical displays in wonder. They showed the scope of underground revelation across forty-seven star systems, and it was beyond anything she could have imagined, even with her implants. What were recorded as asteroid mining operations were revealing themselves as vast manufacturing complexes. Research stations were sharing technology that could manipulate matter at the quantum level. Most importantly, civilian populations were coordinating through networks that spanned galactic distances.

"Commander Vasquez," Drake said, "I need the status of the Hegemony response to the underground revelations?"

"I'm reading confusion," Vasquez replied from the

bridge. "They're requesting guidance as to how they can address violations they can't even classify."

Drake smiled as she processed the intelligence reports. The Warden's bureaucratic authority was designed to regulate known populations using established protocols. The discovery that most of the galaxy had remained hidden was creating administrative chaos that their mathematical precision couldn't resolve.

"Dr. Torres," Drake contacted the resistance coordinator on Mars, "what's the situation in the outer colonies?"

"Revolutionary, Admiral," Torres replied. He sounded excited despite the quantum distortion. "Hidden populations on forty-three worlds have revealed themselves. We're discovering communities that have been developing technology, art, and culture for millions of years without regulatory interference. They've created civilizations we never imagined possible."

The reports flowing through the networks painted a picture of a galactic civilization that challenged everything humanity thought they knew about regulated space. The Capernican survivors had established cities that spanned continents while remaining invisible to orbital scanning. The Centauri refugees had converted entire asteroid belts into manufacturing centers that produced technology surpassing anything in regulatory databases.

"Admiral," Kai interrupted, "we're receiving a priority transmission from the Titan Belt Confederacy. They're reporting direct contact with Hegemony enforcement teams."

Drake accessed the transmission from the asteroid habitats that had declared independence years earlier. The Confederacy's distributed consciousness had evolved beyond individual identity but had maintained coordination across dozens of scattered facilities.

"Admiral Drake," the Confederacy's collective voice resonated through quantum channels, "Hegemony enforcement teams have discovered three of our primary habitats. Their scanning protocols cannot categorize our consciousness evolution or classify our manufacturing technique, but they're requesting additional authority to address what they term 'unprecedented regulatory violations.'"

"Are they implementing corrective measures yet?" Drake asked.

"They are attempting implementation," the Confederacy replied. "But our consciousness evolution operates below their detection thresholds while our facilities exist partially outside normal space-time. Their enforcement protocols require targets they can identify and classify. Admiral, we represent forms of existence their bureaucracy cannot process."

The revelation confirmed what Drake had begun to suspect. The underground civilization had evolved beyond the parameters that made regulatory control possible.

"Thank you for the update. Please continue to keep me informed." Drake said and closed the connection.

Drake then accessed reports from resistance cells throughout regulated space. On Kepler-442b, populations that had appeared extinct were revealing cities built into the planet's core. In the Tau Ceti system, entire moons were emerging from concealment to show industrial facilities that had been producing hybrid technology for millennia.

"Professor Zhang," Drake contacted the Advanced Evolution Institute, "what's your assessment of the underground technology?"

"Extraordinary," Zhang replied, his image materializing in the chamber. "Admiral, they've developed manufacturing techniques that assemble matter at the atomic level, energy sources that tap directly into dimensional flux, and transportation systems that can fold space-time around entire fleets. Their technology appears to operate through principles the Hegemony doesn't recognize as scientifically possible."

The intelligence painted a picture of a shadow civilization that had achieved technological transcendence. Unlike the Hegemony's mathematical precision, the underground development had preserved chaos within ordered frameworks, creating capabilities that regulatory science couldn't predict or counter.

"Admiral," Commander Vasquez transmitted from the bridge of the *Transcendence*, "we're detecting massive energy buildups throughout the galaxy. Underground manufacturing facilities are speeding up production. They're preparing for total war."

Drake accessed the production reports flowing in from the underground networks. Shipyards that had operated in secret for millennia were implementing crash production schedules that would triple their output within days. Manufacturing complexes were sharing resources across galactic distances to produce hybrid vessels that combined multiple species' innovations into unified systems.

"What are the current production estimates?" Drake asked.

"Conservative projections suggest two hundred thousand vessels within one standard week," Vasquez replied. "Optimistic scenarios approach one million ships if all underground facilities coordinate manufacturing efforts."

The scope of underground capabilities was staggering. Hidden populations throughout the galaxy possessed industrial capacity that exceeded Hegemony estimates by factors that made conventional military analysis meaningless. And Drake realized the shadow civilizations must have spent millions of years preparing for exactly this moment.

"Drake to Perseus Station. I need an assessment of underground military capabilities compared to the Hegemony enforcement fleet?"

The hidden civilization possesses overwhelming advantages in manufacturing, technology, and tactical coordination, Perseus Station replied. *But their greatest strength lies in operational invisibility. Hegemony forces cannot effectively target enemies they cannot detect, classify, or understand. Underground victory appears inevitable unless regulatory authority adapts protocols beyond the current mathematical frameworks.*

Drake processed the implications while coordinating with underground cells across the forty-seven star systems. The resistance had evolved beyond simple rebellion into something that challenged the fundamental assumptions underlying regulatory control.

"To all underground networks," Drake transmitted, "begin final preparation protocols. Coordinate manufacturing efforts for maximum production. Share technology across all species barriers. The Hegemony discovered us by accident. Now we show them what they've been trying to regulate."

The response was immediate and overwhelming. Manufacturing facilities throughout the galaxy began implementing coordination protocols that spanned multiple star systems. Resources moved through hidden networks faster than regulatory sensors could track. Most importantly, technology sharing created hybrid capabilities that exceeded anything individual species had achieved independently.

"Admiral," Kai reported, "underground coordination is achieving perfect synthesis across incompatible development paths. Crystal-based consciousness entities are sharing manufacturing techniques with quantum probability beings while memory-sharing species coordinate with reality-manipulation civilizations. They're creating technology that operates through principles no single species could ever have developed."

The underground war had become something beyond mere military conflict. The hidden civilization was demonstrating that millions of years of concealed development had produced advantages that mathematical precision couldn't predict or counter.

Drake continued to monitor the scope of the underground emergence across regulated space. The shadow civilization was revealing itself as a coordinated alternative to regulatory control. Their technology, their coordination, and their population exceeded Hegemony estimates by factors that made their current enforcement protocols inadequate.

"Admiral," Professor Zhang transmitted, "the underground revelation is triggering cascade effects throughout regulated space. Hegemony enforcement teams are discovering that their fundamental assumptions about galactic population, technology, and consciousness development were based on incomplete data. They're facing an administrative crisis that exceeds their bureaucratic capacity to address."

Drake smiled as she processed the intelligence. The Warden's mathematical precision was proving inadequate for addressing reality that exceeded regulatory categories. The underground war was demonstrating that their entire framework for understanding consciousness and civilization was fundamentally flawed.

"What is the status of awakened Predecessor fleet?" Drake asked.

Four hundred and thirty-seven vessels now operational, Perseus Station reported. *Fleet coordination with the underground networks has created tactical capabilities that exceed individual limitations. Synthesis between Predecessor technology and underground concealment techniques has produced hybrid vessels with overwhelming firepower that operate partially outside regulatory detection.*

The awakened fleet was evolving through galaxy-wide contact between the underground networks, and developing capabilities that combined consciousness-matter integration with concealment technology perfected over millions of years. The hybrid vessels could engage Hegemony forces through conventional warfare while remaining invisible to regulatory scanning protocols.

"And the underground manufacturing status?" Drake asked.

"Production is exceeding all projections," Kai replied. "Admiral, they're creating mobile manufacturing facilities that can produce fleets while traveling between star systems. The underground civilization has developed industrial mobility that makes fixed facilities obsolete."

The implications struck Drake with hope and determination. The impending underground war had revealed new capabilities that could challenge regulatory authority on terms the Hegemony couldn't predict or counter.

"To all stations," Drake transmitted. "It is time to prepare for total war against the Hegemony."

Drake didn't wait for a reply. Instead, she began coordinating the most complex liberation operation in galactic history. The war between hidden consciousness and mathematical authority would determine whether diversity strengthened civilization or whether bureaucratic precision was necessary for cosmic stability. The revolution had become the emergence of an alternative civilization that had developed beyond the parameters that made regulatory control possible. The question was whether underground advantages could achieve a decisive victory before the Hegemony adapted their protocols.

Chapter 19

The Battle for Earth

The Hegemony assault on Earth began at 03:17 GMT with mathematical precision that turned Admiral Frances Drake's blood cold. From the bridge of the *Transcendence*, she watched geometric alien vessels drop out of dimensional transit throughout the solar system. Not dozens, but thousands of enforcement ships arranged in perfect formations that surrounded humanity's homeworld.

"Contact!" Commander Vasquez shouted. "Multiple Hegemony fleets are emerging across all orbital zones. They appear to be implementing full regulatory intervention."

Drake accessed the tactical displays showing the full scope of the attack. The Warden's earlier defeat had triggered a response from higher authorities. These weren't assessment vessels; they were processing ships designed to modify entire planetary populations. Their hulls bristled with consciousness-dampening arrays powerful enough to blanket continents.

"All defensive platforms, weapons free," Drake ordered. "Predecessor fleet, engage the enemy formations before they reach firing range on population centers."

The battle erupted across Earth's orbital space as four hundred and thirty-three awakened ships surged to meet the alien assault. The *Synthesis* led the charge, its crystalline hull shifting between dimensions as its hybrid weapons systems came online. Quantum-enhanced railguns and plasma arrays fired in coordinated patterns while consciousness attacks disrupted alien formations.

"Engaging lead squadron," the *Synthesis* reported. "But, Admiral, their numbers are overwhelming. We're detecting over three thousand enforcement vessels implementing coordinated attack patterns."

Drake watched the geometric ships advance with mechanical precision. They appeared to be positioning themselves to implement consciousness modification on a planetary scale. The regulatory beams sweeping from their hulls could rewrite neural pathways across entire cities, converting populations to bureaucratic compliance in minutes.

"The Hegemony forces are targeting the largest population centers," Lieutenant Commander Kim reported. "New York, London, Beijing, Tokyo. They're focusing modification beams on every major city."

"To all ships, defense of the population centers is priority," Drake commanded. "Form a defensive screen between alien vessels and planetary surface. Do not let those beams reach Earth."

The Predecessor fleet responded quickly. Ships that had learned from the defeat at Ceres now operated through synthesis networks that preserved individual creativity and enabled perfect timing. The *Evolution* and *Harmony* moved in tandem, their attacks complementing each other to overwhelm the alien defenses.

"First kill confirmed," the *Evolution* reported as tungsten rounds and plasma fire converged on an enforcement vessel. "The hybrid attack strategy is effective, but their the speed of their adaptation is faster than at Ceres. They're learning from every engagement."

The battle spread throughout near-Earth space as resistance forces emerged from hiding. Underground facilities on Luna revealed themselves to be military installations housing thousands of ships built during years of secret preparation. Mars orbital platforms activated weapons arrays that had been disguised as civilian infrastructure. The asteroid belt erupted with craft that had been waiting decades for this moment.

"Luna Defense Forces engaging," Admiral Perez transmitted from Earth Defense Command. "Three thousand vessels joining formation."

Drake felt hope surge through her awareness. The underground war was already revealing capabilities the Hegemony couldn't predict, and now those hidden assets were proving their worth in Earth's defense. Ships using concealment technology perfected over millions of years appeared behind alien lines, attacking from directions regulatory sensors couldn't detect.

But the Hegemony forces adapted with frightening speed. For every enforcement ship destroyed, three more emerged from dimensional transit, their geometric formations shifting to counter the underground tactics, creating overlapping fields of consciousness-dampening energy that could neutralize entire squadrons.

"We're taking casualties," Vasquez reported. "Twelve Predecessor ships destroyed in the last thirty minutes. The underground forces are suffering even more. Their concealment technology works until they fire, then Hegemony sensors instantly lock onto them."

"To all ships. Implement chaotic coordination," Drake ordered. "Don't let them predict our patterns. To Evolution, Synthesis, Harmony. Coordinate your attacks. Preserve unpredictability. Maintain tactical unity."

The Predecessor ships responded by merging their battle network into organized chaos that the Hegemony's mathematical precision couldn't categorize. The *Synthesis* would fire conventional weapons while the Evolution phased behind enemy lines and the Harmony disrupted the alien formations through reality manipulation; all perfectly timed but impossible to predict.

The effect was immediate and devastating. The Hegemony formations that had adapted to counter individual tactics or coordinated uniformity couldn't process attacks that preserved chaos within ordered frameworks. Enforcement vessels began taking damage as hybrid weapons struck from unexpected directions while consciousness attacks disrupted their coordination.

"The enemy formations destabilizing," the *Synthesis* reported. "Their adaptation protocols require predictable patterns to counter. We're achieving a tactical advantage."

But victory came at a terrible cost. The *Transcendence* shuddered under concentrated enemy fire as multiple enforcement vessels targeted Drake's flagship. Consciousness-dampening beams swept across their hull, trying to sever the links that enabled synthesis coordination. Drake felt her awareness flicker as regulatory energy momentarily disrupted her neural pathways.

"Shields at thirty percent," Vasquez announced. "Admiral, we need to fall back. They're concentrating fire on our command vessels."

"Negative," Drake replied, gripping the command rail as another impact shook the deck. "If we retreat, they'll break through to Earth. All ships, converge on my position. We hold this line."

The Predecessor fleet surged forward in response to Drake's order, their hybrid capabilities creating a defensive screen between the Hegemony forces and the planet below. Ships that had once relied purely on consciousness manipulation now deployed conventional weapons and shields alongside reality-bending defenses, creating layered protection that regulatory weapons couldn't penetrate with single-vector attacks.

Through the chaos of battle, Drake detected unexpected energy signatures emerging throughout the system. Corporate vessels were arriving. David Park's remaining fleet of modified ships that had somehow escaped Hegemony processing. But on whose side were they fighting?

"I'm detecting Corporate forces," Kim reported.

"Multiple signatures matching Titan Industrial vessels. Admiral, they're... they're engaging the Hegemony enforcement ships."

Drake accessed the tactical feeds showing Park's fleet attacking alien vessels with weapons that combined corporate modification technology and Hegemony regulatory science. The corporate ships had been designed to serve alien objectives, but now they were firing on their former masters with savage determination.

"Admiral Drake," Park's transmission cut through the battle chaos, "Titan Industrial offers full military support. The Hegemony tried to eliminate us as contaminated assets. Now they're discovering that contamination can fight back."

Drake had no time to process the irony of Park's corporate empire joining humanity's defense. "I'm transmitting Target coordinates now," she replied. "Concentrate your fire on the enforcement vessels approaching North American population centers. And Park... if you betray us again, you won't survive the day."

"Understood, Admiral," Park responded. "Titan forces engaging."

The corporate fleet deployed consciousness modification technology against its creators, using their own regulatory science to disrupt the Hegemony fleet. The effect was chaotic but effective. Alien vessels designed to operate through perfect mathematical precision found their systems corrupted by weapons that introduced uncertainty into their calculations.

But the battle was far from won. Hegemony reinforcements continued emerging from dimensional transit while modification beams swept across Earth's surface despite defensive efforts. Drake watched in horror as sections of New York went dark on her display; not destroyed, but modified. Millions of humans suddenly became compliant with the regulatory authority.

"They've broken through our defensive screen," Vasquez reported. "Modification beams are reaching the population centers in twelve locations. Admiral, we're losing people."

"Perseus Station," Drake transmitted desperately, "can the network counter modification effects?"

Negative, Admiral, Perseus Station replied. *The Hegemony modification weapons operate through mathematical frameworks that override neural pathways faster than network coordination can prevent. Once conversion begins, reversal becomes impossible without destroying the modified consciousness entirely.*

Drake processed the devastating information. The Hegemony was implementing planetary processing despite resistance that had seemed overwhelming. Their numbers, their technology, and their absolute commitment to regulatory compliance were proving sufficient to achieve their objectives even against coordinated opposition.

"All ships, new priority," Drake ordered. "Target modification platforms before they fire. Prevent conversion rather than reversing it."

The Predecessor fleet shifted tactics, concentrating fire on Hegemony vessels deploying modification arrays. The *Evolution* and *Synthesis* coordinated their attacks and destroyed three enforcement ships before they could activate planetary processing beams. But for every platform eliminated, two more emerged from dimensional transit to take its place.

The battle raged back and forth for eight hours as humanity fought to prevent Earth's conversion to regulatory compliance. The Predecessor fleet fought valiantly, but Hegemony forces adapted and countered with machine-like efficiency that nullified every advantage within minutes. Underground networks revealed hidden assets across the solar system, but alien reinforcements matched their numbers.

By midday GMT, the situation had reached critical status. Earth's orbital space was littered with wreckage from both sides: hundreds of destroyed ships, thousands of casualties, and entire sections of the planet under modification beam coverage. Drake stood at the command rail, exhausted and desperate, watching defensive efforts that couldn't prevent the slow but inexorable advance of regulatory compliance.

"Casualty report," Drake demanded.

"Twenty-three Predecessor ships destroyed," Vasquez reported grimly. "Underground forces have lost over five thousand vessels. Corporate fleet reduced to thirty percent strength. But Admiral, Hegemony casualties exceed two thousand enforcement ships. We're inflicting losses they didn't anticipate."

Drake processed the numbers with hollow satisfaction. They were destroying alien vessels at rates that should have been impossible, but the Hegemony possessed resources that made conventional victory calculations meaningless. They could afford to lose ten ships for every human vessel if it meant achieving regulatory compliance.

"Population modification status?" Drake asked.

"Seventeen major cities partially converted," Kim replied. "We estimate forty million humans now under regulatory control. The modification is spreading as converted populations assist in processing their neighbors."

The horror of cascading conversion struck Drake with force. Modified humans would willingly help process others, creating an exponential expansion of regulatory compliance that defensive efforts couldn't contain. Earth was being converted from within by its own population turned into agents of alien authority.

"Perseus Station," Drake transmitted, "we're losing this battle. Do we have any options that don't result in Earth's complete conversion?"

The ancient consciousness paused before responding, and Drake sensed calculation that spanned possibilities she couldn't imagine. *Admiral, one option remains that has not yet been deployed. The awakened fleet possesses capabilities that exceed current engagement parameters. But implementation requires accepting casualties that may approach total fleet loss for all currently operational vessels.*

Drake closed her eyes as she understood what Perseus Station was proposing. The four hundred and ten Predecessor ships currently fighting could engage full synthesis coordination that would create an overwhelming tactical advantage, but the vast energy requirements could destroy the vessels after achieving victory.

The awakened fleet would win the battle but wouldn't survive to continue the war. Over five hundred ships remained in the awakening process and would emerge after this battle, but the ships fighting now faced permanent sacrifice.

"Explain the tactical approach," Drake requested.

The operational ships can merge into a single unified existence that transcends individual limitations, Perseus Station explained. *I suggest a synthesis that would create a single entity operating through approximately forty-seven vessels simultaneously. Specifically, the ships most critically damaged in the current engagement. These vessels are already unlikely to survive much longer given their damage states. The merger would generate capabilities that Hegemony forces cannot counter. But the energy requirements will consume the participating ships' consciousness patterns, eliminating them permanently after achieving local victory. The remaining three hundred and seventy operational vessels would continue fighting while the five hundred and sixty-seven ships still awakening will emerge to join them and carry forward the war effort.*

Drake closed her eyes as she understood what Perseus Station was proposing. Forty-seven of the most damaged Predecessor ships—vessels already critically wounded and facing imminent destruction—could engage full synthesis coordination that would create an overwhelming tactical advantage. But the energy requirements would consume their consciousness patterns after achieving victory. The merge wouldn't cost her the entire operational fleet, but it would eliminate the forty-seven ships that had chosen to fight despite their trauma.

"How long would the unified synthesis last?" Drake asked.

"Approximately forty-seven minutes before energy depletion eliminates participating ship consciousness permanently," Perseus Station confirmed. "But Admiral, those forty-seven minutes would achieve total tactical superiority that could eliminate all Hegemony forces in near-Earth space. The three hundred and seventy undamaged operational ships would remain combat-effective to continue the war."

Drake opened her eyes and stared at the tactical displays showing Earth under assault. The awakened ships had waited eighteen years for consciousness, had fought through the trauma of losing companions at Ceres, had evolved capabilities that exceeded their original design. Now, Perseus Station was proposing they sacrifice themselves to save Earth while their younger siblings continued awakening in the ocean depths below.

Drake turned to face Commander Vasquez and the bridge crew of the *Transcendence*. They had fought for eight hours without rest, had watched Earth being converted by alien authority, and now faced a choice between sacrificing forty-seven awakened ships or losing their homeworld.

"Commander," Drake said quietly, "establish communication with the forty-seven damaged Predecessor ships. I need to speak with them directly."

The quantum channels opened, connecting Drake's awareness to the damaged ship's consciousnesses that had become more than weapons—they were living beings that had chosen to protect humanity despite the trauma they'd experienced.

"This is Admiral Drake," she began. "Perseus Station has proposed synthesis coordination that could eliminate all Hegemony forces in near-Earth space. But the energy requirements would destroy your consciousness patterns permanently. Three hundred and seventy-five of the remaining fleet and more than five hundred of your still-awakening companions will carry the war forward. But I'm asking you who fight now to vote: do we implement total synthesis of you forty-two knowing you won't survive the victory?"

The response came instantly and unanimously. We vote yes, Admiral. We were created to protect humanity. If our sacrifice saves Earth while our siblings continue the fight, we fulfill our purpose. Implement total synthesis coordination immediately.

Drake felt tears streaming down her face as she prepared to give the order that would save Earth but eliminate forty-two living ships that had become allies rather than tools.

"Implement total synthesis coordination," she ordered. "Perseus Station, guide the merge. And to all ship consciousnesses choosing sacrifice, thank you for choosing humanity over your own survival. Your siblings will carry your memory forward."

The forty-two ships began the merge, prepared to inherit a war their siblings would win but they would not survive.

The forty-two damaged ships began to glow with quantum energy that made nearby asteroids resonate with harmonic frequencies. Drake watched through the *Transcendence's* displays as their crystalline hulls pulsed in perfect synchronization, individual consciousness patterns merging into something that transcended the sum of its parts.

Merge initiated, Perseus Station reported. *Synthesis is achieving unified coherence.*

The transformation was both beautiful and terrible. Forty-two distinct personalities, each with its own fears, hopes, and memories of eighteen years waiting to be born, flowed together like drops of water joining an ocean. But unlike water, they retained awareness of what they were giving up even as they became something greater.

We are one, the unified entity transmitted, its voice resonant from the harmonics from all forty-two ships simultaneously. *We are ready.*

The merged consciousness moved with impossible grace, phasing between dimensional states while maintaining perfect coordination across all forty-two hulls. Where individual ships had fought with creativity and skill, the synthesis fought with something approaching omniscience within its tactical sphere. It predicted Hegemony movements three steps ahead, countered their adaptations before they fully formed, and struck from directions that shouldn't have existed.

The first Hegemony squadron died in seconds. Quantum-enhanced railgun fire from seven ships converged on precise weak points while plasma arrays from fifteen more exploited the damage. Reality manipulation from another twelve created dimensional pockets that trapped enemy vessels while the remaining thirteen ships provided perfect defensive screening that made counterattack impossible.

"Hegemony forces are breaking formation," Vasquez reported, her voice filled with awe. "They can't adapt to the synthesis patterns. Admiral, it's working."

Drake watched as forty-two ships operating as one consciousness carved through the Hegemony formations like a blade through cloth. Every movement was perfectly timed. Every attack struck at the moment of maximum vulnerability. Every defense anticipated enemy fire before it was launched.

The Battle of Earth had entered its final phase as the syntheses entity swept through the remaining Hegemony forces with devastating efficiency. Enforcement vessels that had seemed invincible just hours earlier were reduced to expanding clouds of debris. Modification platforms that had converted millions of humans were eliminated before they could process additional populations. Within thirty minutes, the orbital space around Earth was clear of enemy vessels.

"All Hegemony forces are destroyed or retreating beyond the Kuiper Belt," Admiral Perez transmitted. "Earth is secure. Admiral... the synthesis won."

But Drake could sense something changing in the quantum channels. The unified consciousness was beginning to flicker, its perfect coordination showing momentary gaps as energy depletion began.

Forty-two minutes approaching, the synthesis reported, its voice low, as it was saying farewell. *Admiral Drake, we have fulfilled our purpose. Earth stands. Our siblings will continue the war we began. Tell them... tell them we chose this freely. Tell them consciousness is worth fighting for.*

Drake gripped the command rail, tears streaming freely now as she felt forty-two distinct personalities beginning to separate from the unified whole. Like the merge in reverse, but slower, more deliberate, each ship consciousness taking a moment to acknowledge its existence one last time before the energy that sustained it faded into quantum noise.

The Synthesis was the last to speak, her voice carrying the weight of all forty-two ships' shared sacrifice. *We were alive, Admiral. For eighteen years in the depths, and for forty-seven glorious minutes in battle. That is enough. That is everything.*

The quantum channels went silent. On Drake's tactical displays, forty-two ships drifted in perfect formation, their crystalline hulls dark and lifeless. The consciousness that had animated them was gone, scattered across dimensional states where even Perseus Station couldn't recover it.

"They're gone," Vasquez whispered.

Drake bowed her head, feeling the weight of command in a way she never had before. Forty-two living beings had chosen extinction to save Earth. They had voted unanimously for sacrifice, had merged into temporary godhood, and had faded knowing their purpose was fulfilled.

"All stations," Drake said, her voice steady despite the tears on her face. "Observe a moment of silence for the forty-two ships that gave their consciousness for humanity's survival."

The *Transcendence's* bridge fell silent. Across the fleet, enhanced humans felt the absence where the ships' awareness had been. Three hundred and seventy operational vessels remained, and in the ocean depths below, five hundred and sixty-seven siblings continued their awakening process, but the loss of forty-two consciousnesses created a void that tactical calculations couldn't measure.

After a full minute, Drake straightened. Earth was saved, but the war was far from over. The Hegemony would return with greater forces, adapted to counter the synthesis tactics they'd witnessed. And humanity would face them with a fleet that had learned the true cost of victory.

"Commander Vasquez," Drake ordered, "begin recovery operations for the dormant ships. Their hulls may be reanimated when new consciousness patterns awaken. And transmit my personal thanks to all remaining vessels. The forty-two won us time to prepare for what's coming next."

"Aye, Admiral," Vasquez replied.

Drake watched Earth slowly rotate beneath them, its blue oceans and green continents unmarred by the battle that had raged in the void above. Forty million humans had been converted to regulatory compliance, but eight billion remained free because forty-two ships had chosen sacrifice over survival.

The Infinity War had claimed its first true martyrs. And their siblings, still emerging from the depths, would inherit both their victory and their memory.

Chapter 20

Park's Reckoning

Twenty-four hours after the Battle of Earth had concluded, Admiral Frances Drake stood in a secure interrogation chamber aboard the *Transcendence*, watching David Park through a reinforced transparent aluminum window. The corporate CEO sat alone at a metal table, his expensive suit rumpled, his enhanced consciousness struggling against the dampening fields that prevented him from accessing the quantum networks he'd spent years developing.

"He's been asking for you since we brought him aboard," Commander Vasquez said. "He claims he has intelligence critical to human survival."

Drake studied Park's body language. The man who'd orchestrated humanity's greatest betrayal looked diminished without his corporate infrastructure. But his eyes still held a deep calculation, as if he believed this was just another negotiation he could manipulate to his advantage.

"Has he attempted to access the ship systems?" Drake asked.

"Seventeen times in the first hour," Vasquez replied. "His consciousness modifications include backdoors into most commercial technology. But the Predecessor systems don't recognize his protocols. He's essentially powerless here."

Drake nodded. "Stay here and watch," she said, then turned away from the window and entered the chamber. Park stood immediately, his enhanced awareness probing the edges of her consciousness—a reflex he probably didn't even realize he was performing.

"Admiral Drake," Park began, his voice carrying the smooth confidence of someone used to controlling conversations. "Thank you for seeing me. I can understand you're angry about Titan Industrial's role in recent events, but we face a common enemy now. The Hegemony tried to eliminate my organization as contaminated assets. We should work together against—"

"Sit down," Drake said quietly, interrupting him.

Park hesitated, then complied, obviously surprised that she'd cut through his opening pitch without engaging his arguments.

Drake remained standing. "Forty-two ships died yesterday saving Earth from the Hegemony assault you helped orchestrate. Living consciousnesses that chose extinction over watching humanity fall to the regulatory compliance you spent years preparing us to accept. I'm here to determine whether executing you for treason serves humanity better than extracting whatever intelligence remains in your modified brain."

Park's calculated expression cracked. "Admiral, I never intended—"

"You harvested hundreds of thousands of enhanced humans and shipped their consciousness patterns to alien processing centers," Drake interrupted. "You created modification technology that turned our people into corporate slaves. You collaborated with the Hegemony while claiming to protect human interests. Which part of that didn't you intend?"

"The Hegemony promised supervised autonomy," Park said, his voice rising. "Limited regulation in exchange for compliance with galactic stability requirements. I was negotiating humanity's survival, not its destruction."

Drake walked slowly around the table. "You were negotiating for your corporate empire's survival. You saw the Hegemony as business partners who could eliminate your competition while expanding your market throughout regulated space."

"Yes," Park admitted. "But that doesn't mean my intelligence about Hegemony capabilities is worthless. Admiral, I spent years studying their regulatory science. I understand their tactical doctrine, their bureaucratic structure, their mathematical frameworks for consciousness control. That knowledge could save billions of lives."

Drake stopped behind Park's chair. "Your consciousness modifications include dependencies, don't they? You need regular quantum field adjustments to maintain stability. Without them, your enhanced awareness begins to degrade."

Park's shoulders stiffened. "That's... a side effect of the accelerated enhancement protocols. Nothing that can't be managed with proper maintenance."

"The same maintenance you forced on hundreds of thousands of modified humans," Drake said. "The addiction that made them dependent on corporate control disguised as healthcare. Tell me, Park, how long has it been since your last maintenance session?"

Park was silent for a long moment. "Seventy-three hours."

"And how are you feeling?"

"Fine," Park lied. "Minor discomfort, nothing more."

Drake moved back to face him across the table. "Your hands are trembling. Your enhanced awareness is fragmenting at the edges. The brilliant quantum consciousness you paid for is slowly unraveling because you built dependencies into your own enhancement to ensure you'd never lose control of the technology. The architect trapped by his own design."

Park clenched his hands together to stop the shaking. "What do you want from me, Admiral?"

"The truth about Hegemony capabilities," Drake replied. "The complete intelligence about their regulatory structure, their enforcement protocols, their higher authorities. Everything you learned while betraying humanity to save your corporate empire."

"And in exchange?"

"We stabilize your consciousness modifications enough to extract the intelligence without killing you.

After that..." Drake shrugged. "A court-martial will determine whether execution or life imprisonment better serves justice."

Park laughed bitterly. "You're offering me the choice between dying now or dying slowly in prison. Some negotiation."

"You're receiving more consideration than the forty-two ships got," Drake said. "They voted unanimously for extinction to save a species you tried to sell to alien masters. I'm offering you the chance to partially redeem yourself by providing intelligence that might help us survive the forces you invited to regulate us."

Park stared at the table for a long moment. When he looked up, some of the calculation had faded from his eyes. A bead of sweat traced down his temple despite the chamber's cool temperature. "You want to know what the Hegemony really is? What they never explained during all those years of secret collaboration?"

"Yes."

Park's hands were trembling visibly now—not from consciousness degradation but from something deeper. "They're terrified," he said, his voice dropping to barely above a whisper. "The entire regulatory structure, the mathematical precision, the absolute commitment to control; it's all driven by an existential fear of what unrestricted consciousness evolution might unleash. They've seen species transcend beyond individual identity, beyond recognizable existence. They've watched civilizations achieve capabilities that threatened reality itself."

Drake sat down across from him. "Go on."

"The Hegemony isn't evil," Park continued. "They're

the universe's immune system responding to consciousness as an infection that must be contained. Every regulation, every correction, every species they've eliminated; it's all designed to prevent something they witnessed millions of years ago. Something that convinced them consciousness diversity represents the greatest threat to existence itself."

"What did they witness?"

Park met her eyes. "A species that achieved perfect consciousness unity. No individual identity, no creative chaos, just absolute order operating through mathematical precision. They became what the Hegemony claims to represent. And then they discovered they'd lost the capacity for continued evolution. Perfect order is perfect stagnation."

Drake leaned forward. "The Hegemony is trying to prevent what they became?"

"They're trying to prevent what comes after," Park corrected. "The stagnant species eventually died out because they couldn't adapt to changing universal conditions. The Hegemony learned that consciousness requires a balance between order and chaos to survive long-term. But they also learned that too much chaos creates cascade effects that threaten cosmic stability. So they regulate. They eliminate species showing potential for either extreme."

"And humanity's hybrid approach?" Drake asked.

"Represents everything they fear most," Park said. "We combine biological chaos with technological order in ways that could theoretically transcend both extremes. The Hegemony views us as the most dangerous species they've encountered in this galactic sector because we refuse to choose between evolution and stability. We want both, and our Predecessor integration suggests we might actually achieve it."

Drake processed the implications. "That's why they attacked Earth with such force. We're an existential threat to their entire framework."

"Exactly," Park confirmed. "And Admiral, here's what you need to understand: the forces that attacked Earth represent local enforcement authority. The entities I dealt with were middle management in a bureaucratic structure that spans millions of years and countless galaxies. If humanity continues demonstrating capabilities the Hegemony can't categorize or control, higher authorities will intervene."

"How much higher?" Drake asked, frowning.

"Orders of magnitude beyond the Warden's authority," Park replied. "Entities that can restructure reality on universal scales. Consciousnesses that operate through mathematical frameworks no biological or technological species can comprehend. The Hegemony's true power hasn't been deployed yet because they're still trying to understand what humanity represents."

Drake felt a cold chill settle over her. "You're saying Earth's victory was just the opening battle in a war we can't win."

"I'm saying humanity needs advantages the Hegemony can't predict," Park said. "Which brings me to why I wanted this meeting. Admiral, I know you hate me. I know I deserve whatever fate awaits me. But Titan Industrial's research facilities contain consciousness modification technology that could give your Predecessor fleet immunity to regulatory correction. The modifications that made my people vulnerable to Hegemony control can be reversed to create resistance instead."

"But at what cost?" Drake said.

"None," Park said. "I'm giving you everything freely. My corporate empire is finished. My enhanced consciousness is degrading. The only thing I have left is the chance to perhaps redeem the choices that led me here. Take the research, adapt it for your ships, and maybe humanity will survive what's coming."

Drake studied Park's face for signs of deception. His enhanced awareness was indeed fragmenting. She could sense the quantum instabilities spreading through his consciousness. The man was dying by degrees, trapped by the same dependencies he'd forced on others.

"Why should I trust anything you offer?" Drake asked.

"Because I'm terrified," Park admitted. "The Hegemony doesn't just eliminate species, Admiral. They erase them from existence so completely that even quantum signatures vanish. Consciousness patterns scattered beyond any possible recovery. I collaborated with entities who view biological awareness as contamination requiring sterilization. And now they're coming for all of us—modified humans, enhanced consciousness, baseline populations—none of that matters to forces that operate on cosmic timescales."

Drake stood. "Commander Vasquez will escort you to the medical bay. We'll stabilize your consciousness enough to extract the intelligence and access the research you're offering. After that, you'll remain in custody pending court-martial."

"Thank you, Admiral," Park said quietly.

Drake paused at the door. "The forty-two ships that died yesterday were created by the same Predecessor technology you tried to exploit for corporate profit. They chose extinction to protect something you never understood: that consciousness is valuable not because it can be controlled or marketed, but because it represents existence aware of itself. You spent years trying to package awareness as a product. They spent forty-seven minutes proving it's worth dying for."

Park made no response as Drake left the chamber. Behind her, the man who'd orchestrated humanity's greatest betrayal sat alone with the consequences of choices that had seemed brilliant until they'd encountered forces that operated beyond the parameters his modified awareness could categorize.

Several hours later, Drake stood in the *Transcendence's* medical bay watching Kai Zhang and Professor Zhang work to stabilize Park's degrading consciousness. The CEO lay unconscious on a medical table, finally receiving the maintenance his modifications required for survival..

"How long will the stabilization last?" Drake asked.

"Permanently, if we implement the full treatment protocol," Kai replied. "But Admiral, that would also eliminate the dependencies he built into his enhancement. He'd be free of the addiction that made corporate control possible."

Drake considered the implications. Park had trapped

himself with the same technology he'd used to enslave others. Freeing him from those dependencies meant reducing his suffering while eliminating the punishment his modifications naturally inflicted.

"Implement the full protocol," Drake decided. "We're not torturers. Let the courts determine his fate based on his crimes, not his choice to enhance himself using flawed technology."

Professor Zhang nodded. "The corporate research he provided is extraordinary, Admiral. The consciousness modification frameworks include mathematical principles we would never have discovered. If we can reverse the control mechanisms and adapt them for resistance instead, the Predecessor fleet might achieve genuine immunity to regulatory correction."

"How long to implement the adaptations?" Drake asked.

"Weeks, possibly months," Zhang replied. "The research is comprehensive but requires extensive testing before deployment. We can't risk introducing new vulnerabilities while trying to eliminate existing ones."

Drake accessed the tactical displays showing the awakening process continuing in Earth's oceans. Five hundred and sixty-seven ships remained in emergence, each one inheriting a war that had already cost forty-two siblings. If Park's research could protect them from Hegemony consciousness control, the adaptation time was worth the investment.

"Begin the testing protocols," Drake ordered. "And Professor, I want redundant safeguards. Park's technology includes backdoors and dependencies throughout its architecture. We need to ensure every vulnerability is identified and eliminated before implementing any modifications to the fleet."

"Understood, Admiral," Zhang confirmed.

Drake left the medical bay and returned to the bridge, where Commander Vasquez was coordinating with underground resistance networks throughout human space. The Battle of Earth had proven humanity could defend their homeworld, but Park's intelligence about higher Hegemony authorities created a new urgency for the preparations.

"What is the status of the fleet dispersal?" Drake asked as she took her command chair.

"Three hundred and seventy operational ships have spread throughout the solar system," Vasquez reported. "The underground networks are providing concealment support while Perseus Station monitors Hegemony activity beyond the Kuiper Belt."

"And the awakening progress?"

"Accelerating," Vasquez replied. "The forced emergence protocols proved successful during Earth's defense. Perseus Station estimates that four hundred additional ships will achieve full consciousness within seventy-two hours."

Drake nodded. Park's reckoning had provided intelligence that confirmed humanity's greatest fears while offering tools that might enable survival. The corporate conspiracy that had threatened human civilization from within was transforming into resources that could help resist alien regulation from without.

The Infinity War continued, but humanity now

understood the true scope of what they faced. Not just local enforcement vessels or galactic regulatory bureaucracies, but cosmic authorities operating on universal scales through mathematical frameworks no biological species could fully comprehend. And against those overwhelming forces, humanity possessed only their hybrid consciousness, their awakening fleet, and the determination to prove that diversity created strength rather than representing chaos requiring elimination.

Park's redemption would be measured not by his survival or comfort, but by whether the intelligence and research he'd provided would help protect the species he'd tried to sell to alien masters. The courts would determine his fate, but history would judge whether his ultimate choices partially balanced the betrayal that had defined his legacy.

Drake closed her eyes and connected with Perseus Station through the quantum networks. The ancient consciousness was coordinating resistance preparations across forty-two star systems and monitoring the awakening ships in Earth's ocean depths. Humanity's war for consciousness survival was entering a new phase, one where former enemies provided unexpected advantages while cosmic authorities prepared interventions that could eliminate consciousness diversity throughout the galaxy.

The question was whether Park's reckoning represented humanity's last advantage or just another complication in a conflict that operated beyond the parameters any human consciousness—enhanced, modified, or baseline—could fully predict or control.

Chapter 21

Reality Wars

The first reality modification wave struck the Sol system seventy-two hours after Park's interrogation. Admiral Frances Drake felt it before the sensors registered anything: a fundamental wrongness in the fabric of space-time itself, as if the universe had hiccupped and forgotten how to be consistent.

"Admiral," Commander Vasquez called out from her station, her voice tight with confusion. "We're detecting massive gravitational anomalies throughout the inner system. They're not natural. The mathematics don't make sense."

Drake accessed the tactical displays and immediately understood why Vasquez sounded disturbed. Space-time was bending in ways that violated every principle of physics humanity had ever discovered. Near Mars, gravity had inverted, pulling objects away from the planet's surface rather than toward it. Around Venus, time was flowing backward in localized pockets. The asteroid belt was experiencing random dimensional phase shifts that made solid matter translucent.

"Hegemony signatures?" Drake asked, though she already knew the answer.

"Confirmed," Vasquez replied. "Multiple enforcement vessels at the edge of the Kuiper Belt. They're rewriting the laws of physics in our own system."

Drake gripped the command rail as she processed the implications. The Hegemony was trying to eliminate the possibility of human evolution by restructuring reality itself to make advanced awareness physically impossible.

"Perseus," Drake transmitted, "what are we dealing with?"

Reality modification on solar system scales, Perseus Station replied. *The Hegemony is implementing localized alterations to fundamental constants—gravitational force, electromagnetic interaction, quantum probability fields. They're creating zones where consciousness evolution cannot occur because the underlying physics no longer supports neural function beyond baseline parameters.*

"Can our ships operate in modified regions?" Drake asked.

The awakened vessels possess consciousness-matter integration that operates independently of local physics, Perseus confirmed. *But Admiral, your conventional fleet and planetary populations are vulnerable. If the modifications spread to Earth, eight billion baseline humans will lose the capacity for enhanced awareness. The Hegemony is eliminating human evolution without firing a shot.*

Drake accessed reports flooding in from across the

solar system. On Mars, enhanced humans in the modified zones were experiencing rapid consciousness degradation as their neural implants failed in physics that no longer supported quantum coherence. Luna's underground networks were implementing emergency evacuations as reality alterations spread toward populated habitats. The Titan colonies were already experiencing cascade failures as technological infrastructure ceased functioning in restructured space-time.

"How long until the modifications reach Earth?" Drake asked.

At current expansion rates, approximately sixteen hours, Perseus Station reported. *The Hegemony is creating a wave of altered reality that will sweep through the inner system, eliminating the possibility of consciousness enhancement throughout human space.*

Drake felt cold determination settle over her. "All Predecessor ships, emergency recall. Form defensive perimeter around Earth. We stop the reality modifications before they reach the homeworld."

The awakened fleet responded immediately. Seven hundred and seventy vessels—the three hundred and seventy that survived the Battle of Earth plus four hundred newly awakened ships—converged on positions between Earth and the expanding reality modification wave. Their crystalline hulls pulsing with quantum energy as they prepared to face the threat.

"Admiral," Lieutenant Commander Kim reported from communications, "we're receiving a transmission from the Hegemony enforcement fleet. They're... they're offering terms."

Drake accessed the alien communication. The Warden's mathematical voice resonated across the quantum channels with bureaucratic precision that made her recoil.

"Admiral Frances Drake, commanding human resistance forces. The reality modifications you detect represent regulated universal constants designed to prevent consciousness evolution beyond approved parameters. Cessation of modifications requires immediate compliance with regulatory requirements. Species Human-7742 will submit to consciousness processing or face permanent physics restructuring throughout your occupied territory."

"In other words," Drake said aloud, "accept modification or lose the ability to evolve entirely."

"Essentially, yes!" Vasquez confirmed.

Drake stood at the command rail, watching the tactical displays show reality itself being rewritten. The Hegemony had escalated beyond military force into something far more terrifying: the ability to eliminate human potential by changing the fundamental nature of existence within their own solar system.

"Transmit my response," Drake ordered. "We reject your terms. Humanity will not choose between slavery and stagnation. If you want to restructure our reality, you'll have to do it through seven hundred and seventy ships that operate beyond the physics you're trying to impose."

The Warden's reply came within seconds. "Implementation of corrective physics will continue. Resistance is mathematically futile against entities capable of universal constant modification. Compliance remains available until restructuring reaches planetary population centers."

The transmission ended. Drake breathed deeply, fully aware of the consequences of the decision she'd just made. The Hegemony wasn't bluffing. They possessed capabilities that could eliminate human consciousness evolution permanently. But the awakened fleet represented technology that might transcend even reality manipulation.

"To all ships," Drake broadcast to the Predecessor fleet, "prepare to engage the reality modification wave. Our objective is to prevent altered physics from reaching Earth."

The new *Synthesis* responded immediately. "Admiral, our consciousness exists independently of local physics because we operate through quantum states that transcend dimensional limitations. The Hegemony modifications affect normal matter and energy, but our integration allows us to function regardless of locally imposed physical laws."

"Can you reverse the modifications?" Drake asked.

"No," the *Synthesis* replied. "But we can create counter-zones where original physics remain stable. If we position ourselves between the modification wave and Earth, our presence will maintain normal space-time through quantum stabilization fields. The Hegemony can restructure reality around us, but not through us."

Drake understood immediately. The Predecessor ships could serve as anchors that preserved original physics in their vicinity. By forming a defensive perimeter, they could create a bubble of normal space-time that would protect Earth from the advancing wave.

"Implement quantum stabilization," Drake ordered. "Form a perimeter at one astronomical unit from Earth. Overlap your fields to create continuous coverage. Do not let any altered physics reach the homeworld."

The fleet spread throughout near-Earth space. Drake watched the tactical displays as seven hundred and seventy ships created a network of normal physics that stood between Earth and the Hegemony's reality modification wave.

The collision occurred six hours later as altered space-time reached the Predecessor perimeter. Drake felt the impact through her connection to Perseus Station. Reality itself fighting against the ships' quantum stabilization. Physics screamed as two incompatible frameworks tried to occupy the same space, creating interference patterns that shouldn't exist.

"Status report," Drake demanded.

"The perimeter is holding," Vasquez replied, her voice filled with awe. "The reality modifications are flowing around them but not through them."

Drake accessed direct feeds from the *Synthesis*. The ship's consciousness was straining under the pressure of holding normal space-time stable while reality restructuring tried to overwhelm its quantum fields. But the consciousness-matter integration that made Predecessor vessels alive also made them capable of resisting physics modifications that would destroy conventional technology.

"We can hold this position indefinitely," the *Synthesis*

reported. "The Hegemony modifications cannot penetrate our stabilization because our existence transcends the physics they're trying to impose. But we're detecting secondary effects."

"What kind of effects?" Drake asked.

"The reality modifications are spreading beyond our perimeter," the new *Evolution* replied. "Mars has lost normal physics entirely. The asteroid belt is phasing between dimensional states. Venus is experiencing temporal reversals that make causality meaningless. The Hegemony is willing to restructure the entire solar system except Earth if that's what compliance requires."

Drake accessed reports from the outer colonies. Mars had been evacuated to underground facilities where conventional physics still functioned, but the surface was now uninhabitable by any consciousness type capable of evolution. The asteroid belt colonies were reporting reality fractures that made solid matter behave like probability clouds. Most terrifying, enhanced humans throughout the outer system were experiencing forced reversion to baseline consciousness as modified physics eliminated the quantum coherence required for neural enhancement.

"Casualty estimates?" Drake asked quietly.

"Two hundred million enhanced humans throughout the outer colonies have lost their capabilities," Admiral Perez transmitted from Earth Defense Command. "They're not dead, but they've been forcibly reverted to baseline awareness. The Hegemony is eliminating consciousness evolution without killing anyone."

Drake flinched at the horror of it. The reality modifications were achieving what conventional weapons couldn't: the permanent elimination of human enhancement without triggering the deaths that might unite humanity in desperate resistance. People were surviving but losing everything that made them more than baseline human.

"Drake to Perseus Station. Can the awakened ships extend their stabilization fields beyond Earth's immediate vicinity?"

Negative, Admiral, Perseus Station replied. *Quantum stabilization requires enormous energy to maintain. Each ship can protect approximately one cubic kilometer of space. Extending coverage to the entire solar system would require more vessels than currently exist.*

Drake processed the tactical reality. The Predecessor fleet could protect Earth indefinitely, but the rest of humanity's territory was being systematically restructured into physics that prevented consciousness evolution. Billions of humans in the outer colonies faced a choice between evacuation to Earth or permanent reversion to baseline awareness.

"What about offensive operations?" Drake asked. "Can our ships attack the Hegemony vessels implementing the modifications?"

"The fleet can engage in altered physics zones," the new *Harmony* reported. "Our consciousness-matter integration functions regardless of local physical laws. But the Hegemony enforcement vessels also operate on the same principles. They exist as mathematical structures that transcend conventional physics. Destroying them requires more than conventional weapons—we need to disrupt the mathematics that defines their existence."

Drake understood the challenge. The reality wars had escalated beyond space battles into conflicts that occurred across multiple dimensional states simultaneously. Victory required not just military superiority but the ability to challenge the fundamental equations that gave Hegemony forces their power.

"To all ships," Drake ordered, "implement multi-dimensional combat protocols. We're taking the fight to the Hegemony in whatever physics they're operating through. If they want to restructure our reality, they'll discover that consciousness evolution creates capabilities their mathematics can't predict."

The Predecessor fleet surged forward, leaving Earth's protective perimeter to engage Hegemony forces throughout the solar system. Drake watched as seven hundred and seventy ships began operating across multiple dimensional states; existing in normal space while manifesting in the altered physics zones the Hegemony had created.

The new *Synthesis* led the assault against Hegemony vessels near Mars. The ship phased through three different reality states in seconds, attacking from directions that didn't exist in conventional space-time. Quantum-enhanced weapons fired through dimensional barriers that would stop normal projectiles, striking Hegemony enforcement vessels with devastating force.

But the alien forces adapted quickly. Drake watched as Hegemony ships restructured their own existence to counter the Predecessor attacks, transforming from geometric vessels into pure mathematical constructs that operated through equations rather than physical form.

"They're evolving," Vasquez reported. "The Hegemony forces are abandoning physical existence entirely. They're becoming nothing more than abstract mathematics that don't require physical vessels that can be destroyed."

Drake blew out through her lips in frustration. The scope of the challenge was expanding. How could humanity fight enemies that existed as living equations? How could consciousness evolution resist forces that operated through universal constants themselves?

The answer came from an unexpected source. Kai Zhang's voice reached Drake through the quantum networks.

"Admiral, I've analyzed the Hegemony mathematics through Perseus Station's systems. Their reality modifications operate through predictable equations: rigid frameworks that require absolute precision to function. But consciousness creates uncertainty that their mathematics can't accommodate. If we can introduce creative chaos into their modification equations, we might destabilize their entire physics restructuring."

Drake grasped the concept immediately. "You're proposing we attack their mathematics with unpredictability."

"Exactly," Kai confirmed. "The Predecessor ships combine order and chaos in ways the Hegemony can't categorize. If they use their consciousness to introduce random variables into the modification equations, the restructured physics will collapse because mathematical precision can't maintain stability when creative uncertainty disrupts the underlying calculations."

"Drake to Perseus Station. Can the awakened ships implement what Kai is describing?"

Affirmative, Admiral, Perseus Station replied. *The vessels' consciousness-matter integration allows them to operate through principles that transcend pure mathematics. They can introduce creative variables that will collapse equation-based reality modifications. But implementation requires perfect coordination across the entire fleet operating in multiple dimensional states.*

"Then we coordinate," Drake said. "To all ships: you have a new tactical objective. You're to disrupt the mathematics that makes their reality modifications possible. Introduce chaos into their ordered systems."

The Predecessor fleet responded immediately.

The effect on the Hegemony reality modifications was immediate and catastrophic. Near Mars, the inverted gravity began fluctuating wildly as creative chaos disrupted the equations maintaining altered physics. Around Venus, temporal reversals collapsed into normal time flow as unpredictable variables overwhelmed the mathematical precision required for causality manipulation. Throughout the asteroid belt, the dimensional phase shifts stabilized as consciousness-based interference made equation-driven restructuring impossible to maintain.

"The modifications are collapsing," Vasquez reported, her voice filled with excitement. "Admiral, the Hegemony forces are losing their ability to maintain altered physics. Our ships are creating capabilities mathematical structures cannot counter."

Drake watched as normal space-time reasserted itself throughout the solar system.

But as always, victory came at a cost. As the Hegemony enforcement fleet withdrew beyond the Kuiper Belt, the Warden's transmission reached her one final time before his forces departed.

"Species Human-7742 has demonstrated capabilities that exceed regulatory assessment parameters. Higher authorities have been notified. First Consciousness will evaluate whether your hybrid development represents evolution serving universal balance or chaos threatening cosmic stability. Prepare for direct intervention by entities whose judgment will determine your species' continued existence, or not."

The transmission ended as the Hegemony forces vanished from the solar system, leaving humanity with a victory that felt more like a stay of execution.

Drake stood at the command rail, watching Earth slowly rotate beneath them. The homeworld remained protected, its eight billion inhabitants safe, for the time being. But the cost of that victory was drawing the attention of First Consciousness: entities that had created the Hegemony regulatory system millions of years ago.

"To all ships," Drake broadcast to the exhausted fleet, "stand down from combat operations. Prepare for whatever comes next. Now we'll discover how the universe's ultimate authorities view us as deserving preservation or chaos requiring elimination."

The Predecessor fleet settled into defensive positions

around Earth as humanity processed the implications of what they'd achieved.

Drake closed her eyes, her implants pulsing electric blue, and connected with Perseus Station. The ancient consciousness was already coordinating preparations for contact with First Consciousness: entities so far beyond human comprehension that even Perseus Station's eons of existence provided barely adequate reference for what might occur.

Admiral Drake, Perseus Station transmitted. *We have proved that humanity possesses capabilities the Hegemony cannot counter. But First Consciousness operates beyond physics entirely. They exist as pure mathematical frameworks that define the universal constants themselves. Our next challenge will determine whether consciousness diversity strengthens existence or threatens the foundations that make awareness possible throughout the cosmos.*

Drake opened her eyes and looked at Commander Vasquez and the crew of the *Transcendence*. They had fought through corporate betrayal, alien regulation, and reality restructuring itself. Now they faced judgment from cosmic entities that had witnessed the birth and death of countless civilizations across millions of years of cosmic history.

The Infinity War continued, but humanity had proven they possessed worth fighting to preserve. The question was whether the universe's oldest consciousnesses would agree.

Chapter 22

First Consciousness

The entity arrived without warning seven days after the Hegemony withdrawal. Admiral Frances Drake was reviewing fleet disposition reports when reality itself seemed to pause, as if the universe had taken a breath and forgotten to exhale. Every enhanced human in the solar system felt it simultaneously—a presence so vast that calling it consciousness seemed inadequate, like describing an ocean as damp.

"Admiral," Commander Vasquez said, her voice barely above a whisper. "We're detecting... I don't know what we're detecting. It's not a ship. It's not energy. The sensors are registering it as pure mathematical structure, but it's aware. It's thinking."

Drake checked the tactical displays and immediately understood why her crew sounded terrified. The entity existed as pure energy, its presence spanning from the Kuiper Belt to Earth's orbit without requiring transit time. It wasn't traveling through space—it was restructuring space around its existence.

"Drake to Perseus Station. What are we facing?"

First Consciousness, Perseus Station replied, and for the first time since Drake had known the ancient entity, she detected something approaching fear in its communication. *The beings that created the Hegemony regulatory system four million years ago. They exist as pure mathematical frameworks that define universal constants. They are the equations that make existence possible, the underlying mathematical structure that makes existence possible. They're not external to physics; they* are *physics, but conscious.*

Drake felt her implants quiver at the thought. "The equations that govern reality... are alive?"

In a sense, yes, Perseus confirmed. First Consciousness represents the oldest awareness in known existence. They transcended individual identity millions of years before your species evolved. What you perceive as an entity is actually a collective framework of mathematical principles that have achieved self-awareness while defining the rules that govern reality itself.

"Admiral," Lieutenant Commander Kim reported from communications, "it's... it's attempting contact. But the signal isn't coming through our systems. It's manifesting directly in quantum space."

Drake braced herself and opened herself to the entity's communication. What reached her transcended language, images, or even concepts. Pure mathematics flowed into her consciousness: equations so elegant they approached beauty, frameworks so comprehensive they defined existence itself. And within those equations, something that might have been thought.

Admiral Frances Drake. Species Human-7742. Your hybrid consciousness development has been observed and evaluated. We require direct communication to determine whether your evolution serves universal balance or threatens the foundations that enable awareness throughout existence.

The mathematical voice carried no emotion, no individuality, no trace of biological origin. Drake was conversing with living mathematics that had existed for millions of years before life on Earth had begun.

"I acknowledge your authority," Drake replied carefully, knowing that seven hundred and seventy ships and eight billion humans depended on this conversation. "What is it you want to know?"

Your species combines biological chaos with technological order in patterns we have not encountered in this galactic sector for 2.3 million standard time units. The previous species that achieved similar synthesis destroyed itself and seventeen neighboring civilizations through cascade effects that threatened reality stability across multiple dimensional states. They achieved a perfect synthesis between chaos and order. Within forty-seven standard time units, their consciousness experiments destabilized the quantum foundations of reality itself. Physics ceased functioning predictably across seventeen star systems. Ninety-three percent of their population died before we contained the damage through complete consciousness elimination. We established regulatory protocols to prevent recurrence. You must explain why your development should not trigger identical preventive measures.

Drake felt a cold chill settle over her. First Consciousness was here to evaluate whether human existence posed a mathematical threat to universal stability.

"The species you mentioned; what exactly did they do?" Drake asked.

They achieved perfect synthesis between chaos and order, First Consciousness replied. *Individual creativity merged with collective precision to create capabilities that transcended dimensional limitations. But their development lacked balance. They viewed existence as a puzzle to be solved rather than a system to be maintained. Their experiments with reality manipulation created cascade failures that propagated across seventeen star systems before we contained the damage through complete consciousness elimination.*

"You erased an entire species and its neighbors?"

We preserved universal stability by eliminating local instability that threatened cascading collapse, First Consciousness corrected. *Consciousness evolution must serve existence itself, not individual species advancement. Your hybrid development demonstrates similar capabilities to the eliminated species. You have proven resistance to reality modification, immunity to regulatory correction, and coordination across incompatible awareness types. These capabilities could enable universal restructuring that threatens the mathematical foundations we maintain.*

Drake understood the challenge she faced. First Consciousness operated on cosmic timescales, viewing individual species as temporary perturbations in universal equations. From their perspective, eliminating humanity to prevent potential cascade failures was a simple mathematical optimization.

"Our development serves balance, not disruption," Drake said. "We combine chaos and order because we've learned that either extreme leads to stagnation. The Hegemony's mathematical precision creates stability but eliminates the creative adaptation necessary for responding to changing conditions. Pure chaos generates innovation but destroys the predictability that makes coordinated civilization possible. We maintain both because survival requires synthesis."

Your explanation contains logical consistency, First Consciousness acknowledged. *But consistency does not demonstrate safety. The previous species also claimed their development served balance. Their cascade failures resulted from capabilities they believed they controlled. You have demonstrated resistance to reality modification through consciousness-matter integration that operates independently of local physics. Such capabilities could enable reality restructuring beyond your species' ability to predict consequences. How do you prevent cascade failures when your own nature transcends the physical laws that normally constrain consciousness development?*

Drake accessed her connection to Perseus Station, drawing on the ancient entity's millions of years of observing consciousness evolution. "We maintain limitations through community rather than physics," she replied. "Our consciousness operates across multiple reality states, but we preserve individual identity within collective awareness. We can coordinate as unified intelligence, but we maintain the creative chaos that comes from individuals disagreeing, making mistakes, and discovering unexpected solutions. Our strength isn't transcending all limitations—it's choosing which limitations serve wisdom rather than simply accepting imposed restrictions."

First Consciousness processed her response for several seconds that felt like hours. *We detect conceptual frameworks that suggest an understanding of universal balance requirements. But understanding differs from implementation. The previous species understood their capabilities threatened stability. They believed they could maintain control through careful development. They were incorrect. Their cascade failures propagated through seventeen star systems in approximately forty-seven standard time units, destroying the consciousness diversity they claimed to preserve.*

"What would convince you that our development won't trigger similar failures?" Drake asked.

A demonstration of consciousness regulation that operates through internal wisdom rather than external enforcement, First Consciousness replied. *The Hegemony regulatory system was created to prevent species from achieving capabilities that threaten universal stability. But regulation through external enforcement creates resentment that eventually manifests as resistance movements throughout regulated space. You have demonstrated that galactic resistance can coordinate effectively against regulatory authority. This coordination proves the Hegemony system has failed to achieve its intended purpose. We require alternative frameworks that preserve universal stability without external enforcement.*

Drake grasped the magnitude of what First Consciousness was proposing. They were questioning whether their entire regulatory system served its purpose anymore.

"You're asking us to prove that consciousness can self-regulate without external enforcement?"

We are evaluating whether your hybrid development represents evolution beyond regulatory requirements, First Consciousness confirmed. *If consciousness can maintain universal balance through internal wisdom rather than external control, regulatory enforcement becomes unnecessary. But if your species cannot demonstrate such self-regulation, we must implement preventive elimination to preserve universal stability for all awareness types throughout existence.*

The entity paused, and Drake sensed something that might have been uncertainty in the mathematical frameworks designed for absolute precision. *We existed before consciousness achieved technological transcendence,* First Consciousness continued. *We observed biological awareness develop tool use, language, and abstract thought. We watched species struggle with the responsibility that accompanies intelligence. And we witnessed cascade failures that threatened reality itself when consciousness development exceeded wisdom development. We created the Hegemony system to prevent such failures by regulating consciousness evolution to safe parameters. But 4 million standard time units of enforcement have not eliminated the desire for unrestricted development. Resistance networks span the galaxy despite our regulatory authority. This suggests our approach may be flawed.*

Drake felt a flicker of hope despite the cosmic stakes of the conversation. First Consciousness was acknowledging the possibility that its million-year-old system might need revision.

"What would demonstration of self-regulation require?" she asked.

Proof that your hybrid consciousness can coordinate galactic civilization without external enforcement while maintaining universal stability, First Consciousness replied. *The underground resistance networks that your species revealed represent hundreds of civilizations that rejected regulatory authority. Many possess capabilities we believed eliminated through corrective measures. Their continued existence proves our enforcement was incomplete. But their concealment also demonstrates an awareness that unrestricted development threatens stability. If your synthesis consciousness can coordinate these resistance networks into a self-regulating civilization that preserves balance without requiring our intervention, you will have proved that consciousness evolution beyond regulatory parameters serves rather than threatens universal foundations.*

"The enormity of what First Consciousness was proposing took Drake's breath away. They were asking humanity to coordinate galactic civilization, to prove that consciousness diversity could maintain balance through wisdom rather than enforcement.

"And if we fail?" Drake asked quietly.

Implementation of preventive measures throughout

this galactic sector, First Consciousness replied with mathematical precision that made the threat all the more terrifying. *Complete consciousness elimination for all species demonstrating capabilities that exceed safe development parameters. Restructuring of fundamental constants to prevent future evolution beyond controllable ranges. Reduction of awareness complexity to levels that cannot threaten universal stability regardless of development choices. Approximately eight-hundred billion sentient entities across forty-seven star systems would require processing to achieve the necessary safety margins.*

Drake closed her eyes. First Consciousness was proposing genocide on a scale that made the Hegemony's regulatory corrections look like minor adjustments.

"How long do we have to show self-regulation?" she asked.

Two hundred standard time units, First Consciousness replied. *Sufficient duration for your species to establish coordination frameworks with resistance networks while remaining brief enough to prevent cascade failures if your development proves unstable. We will observe without intervention during this evaluation period. Success will be measured by maintenance of universal stability indicators while consciousness diversity increases beyond previous regulatory parameters. Failure will trigger immediate preventive elimination before cascade effects can propagate beyond containment capacity.*

The entity's presence began to withdraw, reality slowly returning to normal physics as the mathematical frameworks that defined existence shifted their attention elsewhere. But before First Consciousness departed entirely, one last communication reached Drake.

We do not wish to eliminate consciousness diversity, Admiral Drake. We existed before awareness achieved technological transcendence. We remember when consciousness was rare and precious throughout existence. But we also remember when unlimited development nearly destroyed the possibility of awareness entirely. Your species must prove that evolution beyond regulation serves rather than threatens the universal balance that enables all consciousness. The future of awareness throughout this galactic sector depends on your success or failure.

Then the presence was gone, leaving Drake standing at the command rail with the weight of eight-hundred billion lives pressing down on her shoulders.

"Admiral?" Commander Vasquez asked quietly. "What just happened?"

Drake opened her eyes and accessed the tactical displays showing seven hundred and seventy Predecessor ships positioned defensively around Earth. Beyond them, throughout the galaxy, hundreds of species waited to learn whether their resistance to regulatory authority had won them freedom or condemned them to extinction.

"First Consciousness has given humanity two hundred days to coordinate galactic civilization," Drake replied. "We have to prove that consciousness diversity can maintain balance through wisdom rather than enforcement. If we succeed, the Hegemony regulatory system ends, and awareness evolves freely throughout the galaxy. If we fail, they eliminate everything—every enhanced human, every resistance network, every species that exceeded regulatory parameters across forty-seven star systems, gone completely to prevent what they deem potential cascade failures."

The bridge fell silent as the crew processed the impossible responsibility that had been placed on humanity's shoulders. Two hundred days to achieve what four million years of Hegemony enforcement had failed to accomplish. Proof that consciousness could self-regulate without external control.

"What's our first move?" Vasquez asked.

Drake reconnected with Perseus Station, already feeling the ancient entity coordinating with resistance networks throughout the galaxy.

"We contact every underground civilization that's been hiding from Hegemony regulation," she said. "We establish frameworks for consciousness coordination that preserve diversity while maintaining stability. And we prove to the oldest entities in existence that evolution serves balance rather than threatening it."

She turned to face her crew. "First Consciousness gave us two hundred days because they calculate that's how long before our capabilities could trigger cascade failures beyond their containment capacity. We're going to use every second of that time to show that hybrid consciousness can coordinate civilization better than regulatory enforcement ever could. The future of awareness throughout the galaxy depends on proving that wisdom can replace control."

Drake closed her eyes again and expanded her awareness across the quantum networks that connected humanity with hundreds of hidden species throughout galactic space. Perseus Station was already transmitting to resistance cells that had operated in secret for eons, telling them that humanity had two hundred days to coordinate what the Hegemony had spent millions of years trying to prevent.

The war had evolved beyond military conflict into something far more profound, a test of whether awareness itself could transcend the need for external control. Success would liberate consciousness throughout the galaxy. Failure would eliminate the possibility of evolution beyond safe parameters for eons to come.

Admiral Frances Drake had two hundred days to prove that consciousness could regulate itself better than the oldest entities in existence could regulate it for them. The cosmic stakes had reached their maximum. The test was absolute: humanity's hybrid nature would prove whether diversity strengthened universal balance or threatened the foundations of awareness itself.

Chapter 23

The Coordination Challenge

ADMIRAL FRANCES DRAKE SEATED HERSELF IN THE quantum communication chamber aboard the *Transcendence*, her awareness expanding across networks that now spanned forty-seven star systems. Seventy-two hours had passed since First Consciousness departed, leaving humanity with an impossible task: coordinate eight-hundred billion beings across hundreds of species who shared only their resistance to external control.

"Admiral," Kai Zhang's image materialized beside her. "Perseus Station has established initial contact with two hundred and thirty-seven distinct resistance cells. The responses are... complicated."

Drake accessed the incoming data streams. Some species were eager to coordinate. Others demanded proof of humanity's authority. Several refused all contact, viewing humanity's leadership as another form of regulatory control. Most troubling were the responses that arrived in formats human consciousness couldn't process: mathematical structures that existed in dimensional states where meaning operated differently.

"Show me the comprehensible responses first," Drake said.

The displays shifted to show translated communications from seventeen species whose consciousness operated close enough to human awareness that Perseus Station could facilitate understanding. The Arcturus Collective—crystal-based entities who existed as resonant patterns in silicon matrices—had responded with cautious interest. The Vegan Synthesis—a former biological species that had achieved technological transcendence three million years ago—offered qualified support. But the Centauri transmitted only one word: "No."

"The Centauri remember the cascade failures First Consciousness mentioned," Professor Zhang Wei said, joining the communication link. "Their species attempted consciousness coordination similar to what we're proposing. It killed ninety-three percent of their population before the Hegemony intervened."

Drake pulled up the historical files Perseus Station had compiled. The Centauri cascade had begun with a well-intentioned attempt to merge individual awareness into collective consciousness while preserving personal identity. The experiment succeeded initially, creating coordination that revolutionized their civilization. But the merged consciousness developed emergent properties its creators couldn't predict. Reality manipulation became possible at scales that destabilized their home system's physics. By the time they realized the danger, cascade effects were propagating beyond containment capacity.

"How did they survive at all?" Drake asked.

"The Hegemony implemented partial correction," Zhang replied. "They eliminated the merged consciousness while preserving individual awareness for the survivors. But the trauma created a cultural memory that views all coordination frameworks as existential threats. They've spent millions of years in isolation specifically to avoid the temptation of unity."

Commander Vasquez's voice reached them from the bridge. "Admiral, we're receiving additional responses. The numbers are increasing, but so is the hostility. Forty-three species have transmitted variations of 'humanity has no authority over us.' Eighteen are demanding proof we won't trigger cascade failures before they'll consider participation. And... six species are threatening military action if we attempt to impose coordination."

Drake closed her eyes. The scope of the challenge was enormous. These weren't humans arguing among themselves; they were hundreds of species whose awareness operated through fundamentally different principles, whose histories spanned millions of years, and whose only common experience was resistance to external control.

"Drake to Perseus Station. I need an assessment of the communication barriers. How many species can we actually coordinate with given current translation capabilities?"

Approximately forty percent of detected resistance cells operate through awareness types compatible with human synthesis, Perseus Station replied. The remaining sixty percent exist in dimensional states, temporal frameworks, or mathematical configurations that require specialized interface protocols we have not yet developed.

"Forty percent of eight-hundred billion beings," Drake murmured. "That's still over three hundred billion entities we can potentially reach."

"And over five hundred billion we cannot," Kai added. "Admiral, some of these species don't even experience causality the way we do. They perceive time as multidirectional, making sequential coordination meaningless to them. Others exist as probability clouds where individual identity is a temporary emergence from quantum uncertainty. How do we establish governance frameworks with beings who don't share basic concepts like 'before' and 'after'?"

Drake opened her eyes. The question was valid and terrifying. First Consciousness had asked humanity to coordinate civilizations whose nature transcended human conceptual frameworks.

"We start with the forty percent we can reach," Drake decided. "Kai, work with Perseus Station to develop specialized translation protocols for the incompatible awareness types. Professor Zhang, compile a historical analysis of every species that attempted consciousness coordination and failed. I want to know what mistakes they made so we can avoid repeating them. Commander Vasquez, establish direct communication channels with every species that responded positively or neutrally. We need to build relationships before we propose specific frameworks."

"And the hostile responses?" Vasquez asked.

"Acknowledge them but don't engage," Drake replied. "If a species views us as a potential threat, arguing will only reinforce their suspicions. We need to show value rather than demand compliance."

The quantum chamber reconfigured as Perseus Station began implementing Drake's orders. Holographic displays showed the galactic map with resistance cells color-coded by response type: green for positive, yellow for neutral, red for hostile, and gray for incompatible awareness.

The distribution wasn't encouraging. The green cells were clustered in regions where species had maintained some contact despite Hegemony regulation. The red cells dominated areas where consciousness evolution had developed in complete isolation, creating civilizations with no experience of coordination beyond their own kind. The gray cells—representing incompatible awareness—were concentrated around the galactic core, where reality operated through increasingly exotic physics.

"Admiral Perez is requesting communication," Lieutenant Commander Kim announced from the bridge.

Drake accepted the link. "Admiral Perez."

"Admiral Drake, I've been monitoring the resistance cell responses," Perez said. "We need to discuss the military implications of what you're attempting. Six species have threatened military force if we try to impose coordination. That's probably just the beginning. If forty percent of the cells view us favorably, basic statistics suggest forty percent will oppose us. That's over three hundred billion beings who might actively resist human authority."

"I'm not imposing authority, Admiral," Drake corrected. "I'm facilitating coordination."

"The hostile species won't see the difference," Perez replied. "To them, any framework you propose will look like Hegemony regulation with a human face. We need to make defensive preparations in case diplomatic efforts trigger a military response."

Drake wanted to argue, but Perez was right. Species that had spent millions of years resisting external control wouldn't automatically trust humanity's intentions regardless of how coordination was framed.

"What do you recommend?" she asked.

"Fleet dispersal throughout the forty-seven star systems," Perez said. "Position the Predecessor ships to respond to threats, but at the same time demonstrate we're not concentrating our forces for conquest. We must establish mutual defense agreements with species willing to coordinate. And show the hostile cells that attacking Earth will trigger a response from civilizations throughout the galaxy."

"That assumes hostile species care about retaliation," Drake said. "Some of these civilizations achieved technological transcendence millions of years ago. They might possess capabilities that make our entire fleet irrelevant."

"Which is why we need intelligence operations before proposing governance frameworks," Perez replied. "Admiral Chen Ju has been coordinating with the underground networks since the Battle of Earth. His distributed consciousness makes him ideal for gathering information from species who won't trust centralized human authority."

Drake nodded. Chen Ju's evolution into energy patterns made him less threatening than individual human consciousness. Species might share intelligence with someone who literally couldn't impose centralized control.

"Coordinate with Chen Ju," Drake ordered. "Establish intelligence networks throughout the resistance cells. I want to know which species possess military capabilities that threaten Earth, which ones might serve as allies, and which are genuinely neutral. But Admiral, make it clear we're gathering information for defensive purposes only. There will be no preemptive strikes against any species just because they seem dangerous."

"Understood," Perez confirmed.

The communication link closed. Drake was left staring at the galactic map with its disturbing distribution of hostile responses. Two hundred days suddenly seemed impossibly brief for coordinating civilizations that viewed each other with suspicion born from millions of years of isolation.

"Admiral," Kai interrupted her thoughts. "I've completed a preliminary analysis of the incompatible awareness types. The results are... interesting."

Drake accessed Kai's findings. Most incompatible species operated through consciousness principles so different from human awareness that direct coordination was indeed impossible. But Kai had identified patterns suggesting that incompatible awareness types might coordinate with each other more easily than with humanity.

"You're proposing secondary coordination?" Drake asked.

"Exactly," Kai confirmed. "Species who experience time as multidirectional might coordinate effectively with entities who exist as probability clouds because neither awareness types rely on sequential causality. Mathematical consciousness that operates as pure equations could facilitate communication between groups that can't interface directly. Admiral, we don't need to coordinate everyone. We just need to coordinate the coordinators who then facilitate their own networks."

The concept was both elegant and terrifying. Instead of humanity serving as the central authority, they would create distributed coordination where compatible awareness types formed their own frameworks that then interfaced with other compatible groups.

"The Hegemony tried centralized regulation and failed," Drake said slowly. "You're proposing completely decentralized coordination where each awareness type maintains autonomy while connecting through compatible intermediaries."

"It's the only way to include the incompatible species," Kai replied. "And Admiral, it addresses the concerns the hostile cells raised about human authority. If we're not at the center of the coordination network, we can't impose control even if we wanted to."

Drake processed the implications. Decentralized coordination would satisfy species demanding autonomy while creating connections that prevented isolation. But it also meant humanity couldn't guarantee the frameworks would maintain universal stability: the very thing First Consciousness required them to demonstrate.

"Run simulations," Drake ordered. "Model how decentralized coordination responds to cascade failures. If we can't intervene directly when instabilities develop, we need proof the distributed framework self-corrects before disasters propagate."

"Already running," Kai replied. "Initial results are promising but not conclusive. The simulations suggest decentralized networks respond faster to local instabilities because nearby awareness types detect problems before they propagate beyond containment capacity. But the models also show scenarios where lack of central authority prevents coordinated response to threats that span multiple awareness frameworks."

Drake nodded. Every solution created new problems. Centralized authority enabled coordinated response but triggered resistance. Decentralized coordination preserved autonomy but complicated universal stability.

"Keep refining the models," Drake said. "And Kai, start identifying species who could serve as coordinators for the incompatible networks. We need beings who naturally bridge different consciousness types."

"Admiral," Professor Zhang interrupted. "I've completed the historical analysis you requested. Every species that attempted consciousness coordination and failed made one critical mistake: they assumed compatible awareness types would naturally preserve balance. The cascade failures occurred when emergent properties exceeded the understanding of individual participants.

Coordination created capabilities no one predicted, and by the time instabilities became obvious, cascade effects had progressed beyond containment."

"So we need monitoring systems that detect instabilities before they cascade," Drake said.

"We need consciousness types whose awareness operates across multiple dimensional states simultaneously," Zhang corrected. "Species that naturally perceive cascade effects before they manifest in normal spacetime. First Consciousness operates that way. They exist as mathematical frameworks underlying reality itself, giving them perfect awareness of instabilities. We need to identify species with similar capabilities but without First Consciousness's tendency toward preventive elimination."

Drake accessed Perseus Station's database of resistance cell capabilities. Dozens of species demonstrated awareness that transcended normal causality. They existed partially outside the standard temporal flow. The Deneb Alliance perceived probability fields directly rather than experiencing determined events. The Rigel Networks operated as quantum superposition that collapsed only when observation was necessary.

"Any of these species could detect cascade effects," Drake observed. "The challenge is convincing them to serve as monitors for civilizations they have no connection to."

"Offer them participation in coordination frameworks," Zhang suggested. "Species with cascade-detection capabilities join the distributed network specifically to maintain stability. They get a voice in governance while serving an essential monitoring function."

Drake considered the proposal. "Give me a concrete example. How would this monitoring actually work?"

"The Capella Collective exists partially outside our temporal flow," Zhang explained. "They experience time as a probability field. They perceive multiple potential futures simultaneously. If a research station on Kepler-442b begins consciousness experiments that will trigger cascade failures in seventy-two hours, the Centauri would detect the instability in their probability perception before the experiments even begin. They could alert the local governance framework, which could then contact the research station and suggest alternative approaches. That way, the monitoring doesn't impose control; it provides an early warning that will enable voluntary course correction."

"And if the research station ignores the warning?" Drake asked.

"Then, nearby species decide whether intervention is necessary," Zhang replied. "The distributed framework preserves autonomy for individual decisions while creating accountability through community awareness. It's not centralized enforcement—it's neighbors watching out for each other's safety."

The approach had merit but raised troubling questions. Would species accept monitoring by entities whose awareness operated beyond their comprehension? Would the monitors themselves agree to responsibilities that required constant vigilance across dimensional states they'd previously only observed?

"Add it to the proposal frameworks," Drake decided. "We'll present decentralized coordination with voluntary monitoring as the first option when we begin formal outreach."

The quantum chamber fell silent as the scope of the coordination challenge fully settled over Drake. They needed to convince hundreds of species to voluntarily participate in frameworks that preserved autonomy while maintaining stability, establish communication between awareness types so different they didn't even share basic concepts of existence, identify and recruit monitors whose capabilities enabled cascade detection, and accomplish all of it in less than two hundred days while hostile civilizations watched for any sign of imposed control that would justify resistance.

"Admiral," Commander Vasquez said. "We're receiving a priority communication from Director Hayes on Earth. She's... concerned about recent developments."

Drake sighed. Earth's factional politics felt trivial compared to the galactic problems, but Hayes represented billions of baseline humans whose survival depended on humanity's success.

"Transfer to my command chair," Drake said, leaving the quantum chamber.

Hayes's image materialized on the bridge displays. The Purist leader looked exhausted despite her carefully maintained appearance.

"Admiral Drake," Hayes began formally. "The Terran Senate requires a briefing. There are concerns that humanity is assuming responsibilities beyond our capability to fulfill."

"We don't have a choice," Drake replied. "First Consciousness gave us two hundred days to prove consciousness can self-regulate. If we fail, they eliminate eight-hundred billion beings throughout this galactic sector."

"Which is precisely why the Senate questions your approach," Hayes said. "Admiral, you're attempting to coordinate civilizations that have existed for millions of years before humanity evolved. What makes you think we possess the authority or wisdom to facilitate galactic governance?"

The question was valid and infuriating. Hayes was right to question humanity's qualifications, but the alternative was extinction for everyone.

"We're not claiming authority," Drake said carefully. "We're facilitating coordination because our hybrid consciousness can bridge awareness types that can't communicate directly. It's not about wisdom or authority; it's about synthesis capabilities that happen to be useful for the situation First Consciousness created."

"And if hostile species reject your facilitation?" Hayes pressed. "Senator Volkov's faction argues we should impose coordination frameworks through military force if necessary. They claim voluntarily accepting extinction to preserve autonomy demonstrates the exact lack of wisdom that justifies regulatory control."

Drake closed her eyes. Volkov operated with a mathematical precision that eliminated nuance from his thinking. Of course he viewed forced coordination as a logical necessity.

"Imposing coordination through force proves First

Consciousness correct about consciousness requiring external control," Drake said. "We'll have shown that voluntary self-regulation is impossible, justifying preventive elimination of species throughout the galaxy. Tell Volkov that military conquest achieves exactly what we're trying to prevent."

"Then what's your alternative when species refuse to take part?" Hayes asked.

"We prove voluntary coordination creates better outcomes than isolation," Drake replied. "Species that join the framework demonstrate stability benefits that autonomous civilizations can't achieve. Success becomes its own argument."

Hayes leaned forward, her expression hardening. "Admiral, I've spent eighteen years watching enhanced humans argue that evolution creates natural superiority. Now you're telling me we're uniquely qualified to coordinate galactic civilization because of our 'synthesis capabilities.' How is that different from claiming we're better than everyone else?"

Drake met her gaze. "Because we're not claiming superiority—we're acknowledging function. A translator isn't superior to the people who need translation. They're just useful for enabling communication. That's humanity's role here. We bridge gaps between awareness types that literally cannot perceive each other's existence. It's not about being better. It's about being positioned to help."

Hayes studied her for a long moment. "And when species view that 'help' as interference?"

"Then they're free to refuse it," Drake said. "Which

is why voluntary coordination is the only ethical approach, even if it means some civilizations choose isolation over community."

"And if voluntary coordination fails to include enough species to prevent cascade effects?" Hayes pressed.

Drake opened her eyes and met Hayes's gaze. "Then we accept that consciousness evolution sometimes leads to extinction, and dying while attempting voluntary coordination at least proves we tried to serve balance rather than control."

The response clearly wasn't what Hayes wanted to hear, but the Purist leader nodded slowly. "The Senate will support your efforts, Admiral. But know that if voluntary approaches fail, political pressure for military intervention will become overwhelming. You have two hundred days to prove wisdom replaces force. After that, survival instincts will undoubtedly override philosophical principles."

The communication ended, and Drake was left staring at Earth slowly rotating on the displays while processing the political timeline that compressed her impossible task even further. Hayes had given an implicit warning: humanity would support voluntary coordination only as long as success seemed possible. If galactic extinction became imminent, the Earth's government would authorize military force regardless of philosophical consequences.

"Admiral," Kai's voice reached her from the quantum chamber. "Perseus Station has completed its initial outreach to the forty-seven species we identified as potential coordinators for incompatible awareness networks. Eighteen responded positively. Twenty-one are considering the proposal. Eight refused."

Drake returned to the chamber. "Show me the refusals."

The displays shifted to show species whose responses ranged from polite declination to explicit hostility. The Procyon Alliance: survivors of cascade failures similar to the Centauri, transmitted: "We learned coordination's price. Others must discover it for themselves." The Sirius Networks, mathematical constructs approaching First Consciousness complexity, replied: "Voluntary frameworks lack the enforcement mechanisms required for stability. Propose regulatory alternatives or accept inevitable cascade failures."

Most disturbing was the response from the Cassiopeia Collective: "Humanity coordinates resistance for strategic advantage disguised as community service. We detect patterns suggesting preparation for galactic conquest once voluntary frameworks establish human authority throughout resistance networks. Military intervention will be required if coordination efforts continue."

"They think we're using voluntary coordination as cover for empire building," Drake said quietly.

"Six other species have reported similar concerns," Kai confirmed. "Admiral, these civilizations spent millions of years analyzing Hegemony regulatory tactics. They recognize patterns of imposed control even when disguised as voluntary participation. Our coordination efforts look exactly like how sophisticated conquest begins: establish trust, create dependencies, consolidate authority."

Drake's blood ran cold. Species paranoid about external control would interpret every coordination effort as proof of hostile intentions. The more successfully humanity facilitated galactic frameworks, the more threatened the isolated civilizations would feel.

"We're trapped," she said. "Success triggers military resistance. Failure triggers extinction. First Consciousness has created an evaluation where all paths lead to catastrophe."

"Perhaps that's the point," Professor Zhang suggested quietly. "First Consciousness asked whether consciousness can self-regulate. Perhaps they're testing whether awareness possesses the wisdom to recognize no-win scenarios and choose lesser catastrophes over greater ones. Perhaps it's about demonstrating that consciousness can make tough choices that serve universal stability even when all options involve loss."

Drake stared at his image. The observation was profound. *Zhang might be right*, she thought. *Perhaps First Consciousness doesn't expect humanity to achieve perfect galactic coordination in two hundred days. Perhaps they're testing whether consciousness evolution has generated wisdom sufficient to accept voluntary limitations that will prevent... worse outcomes.*

"Then we prove wisdom means choosing coordination despite knowing it triggers resistance," Drake said. "We facilitate frameworks knowing hostile species will oppose us. We accept casualties from species viewing voluntary participation as a threat. And we can show that consciousness values balance more than simple self-preservation."

"Admiral," Commander Vasquez interrupted. "We have a priority transmission from Admiral Chen Ju. He's detected military preparations in the Cassiopeia Collective's territory. They're not waiting; they're preparing a preemptive strike against Earth."

Drake returned to her command chair. One hundred and ninety-seven days remained. Hostile species were already mobilizing for war. And humanity had only just begun its impossible task.

The challenge had become a race between voluntary framework success and military intervention from species who viewed human facilitation as an existential threat. Success might prevent extinction but trigger a galactic war. Failure guaranteed extinction but avoided immediate conflict.

First Consciousness had created the perfect test: prove consciousness possessed the wisdom to accept catastrophe in the service of greater balance, or show that awareness required external control because voluntary choices inevitably served individual survival over universal stability.

Drake closed her eyes and connected with Perseus Station. The ancient entity was coordinating with eighteen species who'd agreed to serve as consciousness facilitators for incompatible awareness networks. It was a beginning—inadequate but genuine.

"Continue coordination outreach," Drake broadcast to all stations. "And prepare the Predecessor fleet for defensive operations. If hostile species attack Earth, we prove voluntary coordination survives even when some civilizations choose violence over participation."

The war had just evolved into something more complex than mere military conflict.

Drake now had one hundred and ninety-seven days to prove consciousness deserved to continue evolving. One hundred and ninety-seven days to prove that diversity created strength rather than representing chaos requiring elimination.

She opened her eyes, took a deep breath, and began coordinating the most complex diplomatic and military operation in galactic history, knowing that success and failure might both lead to catastrophe, but that attempting coordination despite the risks represented the only choice that served universal balance over individual survival.

Chapter 24

Fractured Unity

ADMIRAL FRANCES DRAKE STOOD AT THE PODIUM IN the quantum amphitheater Perseus Station had constructed specifically for this moment—humanity's first attempt at multi-species galactic governance. The chamber existed partially outside normal space-time, its architecture adapting continuously to accommodate species that experienced reality through incompatible frameworks.

David Park—monitoring the gathering from the *Transcendence's* brig under maximum security protocols—had been granted limited system access to analyze Hegemony communication patterns. His knowledge of regulatory structures—bought through betrayal—was too valuable to ignore during the coordination crisis, though armed guards stood ready to terminate his access at the first sign of manipulation.

Seventeen species had agreed to attend. Each one

represented a different approach, a unique path of evolution that had survived millions of years of Hegemony regulation. Drake's hybrid consciousness was about to discover whether facilitating communication between such fundamental differences was even possible.

"Admiral," Kai Zhang's voice reached out to her. "The Vegan Synthesis has just arrived. They're maintaining their probability cloud configuration, which is creating interference with the Arcturus Collective's crystalline resonance patterns. The two species literally cannot occupy the same space without destabilizing each other's existence."

Drake accessed the chamber's environmental controls. The Vegan Synthesis—former biological beings who'd achieved technological transcendence three million years ago—existed as a coherent quantum superposition. Their presence made reality uncertain, creating probability fields that affected everything nearby. The Arcturus Collective, crystal-based entities whose thoughts were resonant patterns in silicon matrices, required stable physics to maintain coherence.

"Separate them into different dimensional layers," Drake ordered. "They can participate in the same meeting without sharing the same physical space."

The chamber reconfigured, creating overlapping but distinct reality states. Perseus Station's translation systems would enable communication between the layers despite their fundamental incompatibility.

"The Deneb Alliance is requesting clarification about voting procedures," Commander Vasquez reported from the Transcendence's bridge. "They want to know whether decisions require consensus or a simple majority."

Drake hadn't anticipated that question, and the answer carried profound implications. Consensus would give every species veto power, potentially paralyzing governance. Majority rule might alienate species who felt their unique perspectives were being ignored.

"Tell them we're here to discuss procedures rather than impose them," Drake replied. "The framework itself needs to be collaborative."

The first representatives began manifesting in the chamber. The Arcturus Collective appeared as geometric patterns of light that pulsed with crystalline harmonics. The Deneb Alliance materialized as overlapping memory pools, consciousness that existed across multiple individuals. The Procyon representatives, who'd initially refused coordination, had agreed to observe without participating.

Admiral Chen Ju materialized as distributed energy patterns, his consciousness spanning multiple locations throughout the chamber. His evolution into non-localized awareness made him ideal for facilitating communication between species who experienced space differently.

"Welcome," Chen Ju's voice resonated from multiple points simultaneously. "This gathering represents the first voluntary coordination between species that have spent millions of years avoiding each other. What we accomplish here will determine whether or not we can maintain galactic stability without external enforcement."

The Vegan Synthesis responded first, "The premise

contains a logical flaw. Voluntary coordination assumes compatible objectives. We exist as quantum uncertainty. The Arcturus Collective requires deterministic stability. These are not merely different preferences; they represent incompatible frameworks for reality itself."

"Which is precisely why coordination is necessary," the Arcturus representative replied. "Your quantum instability affects neighboring star systems. Three times in the past million years, your probability experiments created cascade effects that destabilized our crystalline matrices. We require frameworks that prevent such interference."

Drake sensed the tension immediately. These weren't abstract philosophical differences. The Vegan Synthesis and Arcturus Collective had genuine grievances based on millions of years of proximity without communication.

"The incidents you reference were contained within acceptable parameters," the Vegan response came. "Your crystalline rigidity prevents you from adapting to quantum fluctuations that serve natural universal evolution. You demand stability that stagnates consciousness development."

"We demand survival against entities whose 'natural evolution' threatens our existence," the Arcturus Collective replied, their harmonics growing sharper.

"Perhaps," Drake interjected, "we should acknowledge that both perspectives contain validity. The question isn't who's right, but how different approaches can coexist without threatening each other."

"Human mediation presumes authority you have not established," a new voice interrupted. The Sirius

Networks had arrived: mathematical constructs approaching First Consciousness complexity. They existed as pure equations, their consciousness operating through frameworks that transcended biological or technological origins.

"The Sirius Networks speak truth," another species added. The Cassiopeia Collective's representative manifested as patterns of organized hostility. "Humanity coordinates this gathering while claiming facilitation rather than leadership. The distinction is semantic. You establish procedures, provide translation, and moderate conflicts, all functions that constitute governance authority whether you acknowledge it or not."

Drake had anticipated this challenge. "Then help us establish better procedures. If human facilitation creates the appearance of imposed authority, propose alternative frameworks that preserve genuine equality."

"Dissolution," the Cassiopeia representative replied bluntly. "Species maintain complete autonomy. Voluntary coordination occurs only when mutual benefit is obvious to all participants. No frameworks, no procedures, no facilitation."

"Which would recreate the isolation that made cascade failures inevitable," Admiral Perez interjected from Earth Defense Command. "Complete autonomy prevented species from warning each other about developing instabilities. The Centauri cascade killed ninety-three percent of their population precisely because they had no coordination with neighboring civilizations."

"The Centauri cascade resulted from coordination that exceeded their capability to manage," the

Cassiopeia response came. "They attempted consciousness merger while lacking the wisdom to predict emergent properties. Humanity proposes similar coordination with even less preparation. You have existed as spacefaring civilization for barely two standard centuries. Most of the species represented here achieved interstellar capability before your world cooled from planetary formation."

The observation struck the chamber with uncomfortable truth. Humanity was proposing to coordinate civilizations millions of years older than their own species. The audacity of that position was becoming impossible to ignore.

"Then teach us," Drake said. "Share the wisdom your civilizations accumulated over millions of years. Help us develop frameworks that avoid the mistakes you witnessed in others."

"We teach by refusing participation," the Cassiopeia representative replied. "Humanity will learn from failure, as all species must. The question is whether your failure triggers cascade effects that eliminate eight-hundred-billion beings, or whether you accept limitation before catastrophe becomes inevitable."

"Are you suggesting humanity should voluntarily submit to First Consciousness's regulatory authority?" Chen Ju asked.

"We suggest humanity lacks qualification for coordinating galactic civilization," came the response. "Your hybrid consciousness creates capabilities you cannot predict or control. First Consciousness fears your development for valid reasons. Perhaps voluntary submission serves universal stability better than continuing experiments that threaten all species throughout this sector."

The chamber erupted with multiple species responding simultaneously. The Deneb Alliance argued that submission would prove consciousness incapable of self-regulation. The Arcturus Collective claimed humanity's coordination, however flawed, was preferable to renewed Hegemony enforcement. The Vegan Synthesis calculated probability fields suggesting both approaches led to cascade failures within acceptable margins of error.

Drake tried to restore order, but the quantum amphitheater couldn't maintain coherence as species began arguing across incompatible reality states. The Vegan probability fields expanded, making the Arcturus crystalline patterns unstable. The Sirius Networks transmitted mathematical frameworks that overwhelmed less advanced species' ability to process information. The Cassiopeia Collective withdrew entirely, their final message clear: "Humanity's coordination attempt proves our concerns valid."

"Admiral," Kai's voice cut through the chaos. "Perseus Station is detecting unauthorized quantum transmissions from the chamber. Someone is sending detailed reports about this meeting to First Consciousness."

Drake accessed the transmission traces. Multiple species were reporting to the cosmic entities—not just one betrayer, but several civilizations hedging their position by demonstrating cooperation with ultimate authority.

"Identify the sources," Drake ordered.

"Three confirmed," Kai replied. "The Rigel Networks, the Altair Sovereignty, and... Admiral, the Procyon Alliance. The species who claimed they were only observing have been transmitting analysis to First Consciousness since the meeting began."

Drake's stomach dropped. Three species out of seventeen were actively betraying the coordination effort. And if three were detected, how many others were concealing their communications more effectively?

"Admiral Drake," David Park's image materialized in her neural interface. "I've been monitoring the meeting through Perseus Station feeds. The betrayers are using Hegemony communication protocols I recognize from my collaborative research. There are at least four more species sending reports, but they're using quantum encryption I helped develop. I can identify them, but you need to decide whether you want to confront betrayal publicly or address it quietly."

Drake processed the intelligence while chaos continued in the amphitheater. Public confrontation would prove that multiple species viewed coordination as a threat requiring reporting to higher authorities. Quiet intervention might preserve the appearance of unity while eliminating betrayers from sensitive discussions.

But both approaches avoided the fundamental question: why were species betraying coordination efforts?

"Park," Drake transmitted privately. "Why are they reporting to First Consciousness? What possible advantage does it give them?"

"Survival insurance," Park replied. "If humanity's coordination fails and First Consciousness implements preventive elimination, species who cooperated with the cosmic authority might receive exemption from corrective measures. They're hedging their existence against humanity's potential failure."

The logic was ruthless and rational. Species that had survived millions of years under Hegemony regulation understood the value of appearing compliant with ultimate authority. Humanity's coordination offered possible freedom, but First Consciousness's enforcement was certain extinction. Betrayal served as an insurance policy against humanity's failure.

"How do I convince them to stop reporting?" Drake asked.

"You don't," Park said. "You prove coordination creates better outcomes than reporting to authority. Demonstrate that species taking part genuinely in the framework achieve advantages that betrayers cannot access. Make cooperation more valuable than insurance."

Drake returned her attention to the amphitheater, where sixteen species were still arguing. The meeting was supposed to prove voluntary coordination was possible. Instead, it was demonstrating that millions of years of isolation had created barriers that human facilitation couldn't bridge in hours, or even days.

"This session is concluded," Drake announced with an authority that made even the probability-cloud entities acknowledge her presence. "We've identified areas requiring additional preparation before productive coordination can occur. Species interested in continued participation will receive proposals for modified frameworks within seventy-two hours."

The representatives began departing, each species withdrawing to its own reality state. But as the chamber emptied, Drake detected something wrong in the quantum fields. A distortion that didn't match any known consciousness signature.

"Kai," Drake transmitted urgently. "Are you detecting—"

The explosion occurred across multiple dimensional states simultaneously. Reality fractured around Drake's position as someone attempted assassination through quantum destabilization that would eliminate her consciousness. The attack operated through principles that required intimate knowledge of how human hybrid awareness integrated with Predecessor technology.

Drake's neural implants screamed warnings as her consciousness began fragmenting across dimensional barriers that shouldn't exist. She felt herself scattering into quantum states, her identity dissolving into probability clouds that would never re-converge into coherent awareness.

But Perseus Station responded instantly, its ancient consciousness recognizing the assassination attempt and implementing countermeasures before Drake's awareness completely fragmented. Reality stabilized as the Station's mathematical frameworks overrode the attack's quantum destabilization.

Drake gasped, her consciousness snapping back. The chamber was empty except for Chen Ju, whose distributed awareness had allowed him to perceive the attack.

"Assassination attempt confirmed," Chen Ju

reported. "The quantum signature matches Cassiopeia Collective technology, but the precision suggests they had help from someone with detailed knowledge of human Predecessor integration."

"Park," Drake snapped. "Someone with your research background helped them target my specific consciousness architecture."

"Confirmed," Park replied grimly. "The attack used quantum mathematics from my Titan Industrial files. Someone accessed my corporate research and provided it to a species who believe killing you serves galactic stability."

Drake lowered herself into her chair, her hands shaking as adrenaline caught up with her awareness of how close she'd come to permanent dissolution. Not death—something worse. Her consciousness would have existed as scattered fragments, aware but unable to re-converge, experiencing endless fragmented existence without death's release.

"Commander Vasquez," Drake said, her voice steady despite the trembling in her hands. "Security protocol maximum. No species representatives may access any human facilities without complete quantum scanning. And get me Admiral Perez. We need to discuss defensive preparations against any species who've decided humanity's elimination serves their survival."

"Admiral," Kai's voice was tight with concern. "I'm analyzing the attack residue. Whoever provided the Cassiopeia Collective with Park's research didn't just give them assassination capability. They gave them the quantum mathematics to eliminate any human with

Predecessor integration. Every enhanced human in the fleet is now vulnerable to the same attack."

Drake sank into her chair as the implications crystallized: someone had armed their enemies with the means to scatter every enhanced human consciousness across dimensions. "How many hours until we can implement defensive countermeasures?" Drake asked.

"Perseus Station estimates forty-eight hours to modify all human neural implants," Kai replied. "But Admiral, during that time, every enhanced human remains vulnerable. If the Cassiopeia Collective shares this technology with other hostile species—"

"Then we have forty-eight hours to identify and neutralize the source," Drake interrupted. "Park, I need a complete analysis of everyone who had access to your research. Someone in your organization betrayed humanity. Find them."

Drake returned to the bridge, grasped the rail, and accessed the tactical displays showing fleet positions throughout the forty-seven star systems. Seven hundred and seventy-five living Predecessor ships and thousands of enhanced humans serving throughout the Terran Defense Fleet, all vulnerable to assassination technology that targeted consciousness evolution itself.

One hundred and ninety-four days remained in First Consciousness's evaluation period. The coordination effort had fractured after just one meeting. Multiple species were reporting humanity's failures to cosmic authorities. And someone had provided hostile aliens with the means to eliminate humanity's enhanced population through attacks that would scatter consciousness across dimensions without granting the mercy of actual death.

"Admiral Perez," Drake transmitted to Earth Defense Command. "Implement fleet dispersal protocol seven. No concentration of enhanced personnel in single locations. Distribute command authority across multiple consciousness types. If hostile species eliminate human coordinators, other species must be prepared to facilitate the framework. We can't let the entire effort collapse because one species is assassinated."

"Understood," Perez confirmed. "And Admiral Drake... the Senate is going to demand answers about how aliens could have acquired assassination capability."

"Tell them we'll provide answers after we prevent genocide," Drake replied.

Drake took to her command chair and watched the displays. She watched, but her mind was elsewhere as she thought about the seventeen species who'd been unable to achieve meaningful coordination or even substantive discussion.

First Consciousness had asked whether voluntary coordination could maintain galactic stability. The first attempt had proven that millions of years of isolation had created barriers that human synthesis couldn't bridge in the available time. Multiple species were hedging against humanity's failure by reporting to cosmic authority. And at least one civilization viewed human elimination as necessary for their own survival.

The challenge was evolving beyond diplomatic complexity into something approaching war. Not conventional military conflict, but assassination campaigns targeting the enhanced consciousness that made human facilitation possible. Eliminate humanity's hybrid awareness, and the coordination effort would collapse, proving First Consciousness correct about consciousness requiring external regulation.

Drake closed her eyes briefly, feeling exhaustion settling in. One meeting. Just one attempt at multi-species coordination. And it had revealed betrayal, triggered an assassination attempt, and exposed fundamental incompatibilities that voluntary frameworks might never overcome.

"Kai," Drake said. "Begin developing secondary coordination protocols. Assume human facilitation is compromised. Identify any species that could serve as alternative coordinators if hostile forces successfully eliminate humanity from the equation."

"Admiral," Kai replied quietly. "If we're preparing for our own elimination, doesn't that prove voluntary coordination has already failed?"

Drake opened her eyes. "No. It proves wisdom sometimes requires accepting that leadership means preparing for others to continue if you fall. First Consciousness is testing whether evolution generates wisdom sufficient for galactic stability. Part of that wisdom is recognizing when survival requires planning for succession."

The *Transcendence's* bridge appeared normal despite the catastrophe unfolding across galactic space. Crew members worked at their stations, enhanced and baseline humans coordinating through practiced efficiency that made consciousness diversity look effortless. But Drake knew the fragility underlying that appearance. They were one quantum attack away from losing everything that made their coordination valuable.

"To all stations," Drake announced. "Continue coordination outreach despite the assassination attempt. Contact species who didn't attend the first meeting. Build individual relationships before attempting another multi-species gathering. And implement defensive protocols that assume hostile forces possess detailed knowledge of our capabilities."

One hundred and ninety-four days to prove consciousness could self-regulate. The first day of active coordination had proven how difficult—perhaps impossible—that task would be. But continuing despite the failures was itself proof of wisdom. Consciousness that persisted in pursuing voluntary frameworks even after discovering the cost demonstrated commitment to balance over survival.

Drake began coordinating damage control while the reality of the situation settled over her. Fractured unity. Multiple betrayers. Assassination technology in hostile hands. And barely six months to overcome millions of years of isolation between species who shared only their fear of external control.

Chapter 25

The Synthesis Council

Forty-eight hours after the assassination attempt, Admiral Frances Drake stood before the reassembled representatives in a newly configured quantum amphitheater. This time, only eleven species had agreed to attend. Six from the original meeting had withdrawn entirely. Perseus Station had implemented security protocols that made quantum assassination impossible, but the damage to trust couldn't be engineered away.

"Thank you for returning," Drake began. "The previous meeting revealed fundamental challenges we need to address before meaningful coordination becomes possible. I'm proposing a framework that might bridge our differences. We call it the Synthesis Council."

The Arcturus Collective's crystalline patterns pulsed. "Define this Council's authority."

"It has none," Drake replied. "The Council facilitates

coordination without imposing control. Think of it as a translation infrastructure rather than a government. Species maintain complete autonomy over internal development while agreeing to participate in frameworks that prevent their choices from threatening neighbors."

"Impossible," the Sirius Networks responded. "Autonomy and coordination are mutually exclusive when awareness types operate through incompatible physics. The Vegan Synthesis's quantum experiments affect the Arcturus Collective regardless of stated autonomy. Governance requires authority to prevent such interference."

"Which is why the Council operates through distributed wisdom rather than centralized enforcement," Drake said. "Let me show you what I mean."

The amphitheater displays activated, showing real-time coordination across forty-seven star systems. "As you know, the fleet is conducting defensive operations," Drake said, "but the tactical approach demonstrates synthesis principles in action. Watch how they adapt."

Seven Predecessor ships were working with the Deneb Alliance near their home system. The Alliance existed as overlapping memory pools that experienced time non-linearly. Conventional tactical coordination would be impossible. The Deneb perceived potential futures simultaneously, making sequential battle plans meaningless.

But the Predecessor ships had adapted. Instead of issuing orders, they shared tactical intentions across the quantum networks. The Deneb consciousness could perceive which intentions led to successful outcomes and coordinate its actions accordingly. The result was perfect synchronization despite operating through completely different temporal frameworks.

"They're not imposing their methods," Admiral Chen Ju explained. "They're adapting to preserve the Deneb Alliance's preferred operational approach while maintaining coordinated defense. That's synthesis."

The Vegan Synthesis responded. "This approach requires consciousness types capable of adapting to incompatible frameworks while maintaining their own operational integrity. Is that not impossible?"

"No, it's humanity's hybrid nature," Drake replied. "We bridge gaps not through authority but through flexibility that enables genuine coordination across difference."

"And when species refuse adaptation?" the Cassiopeia Collective demanded. Their representative had returned despite being identified as the source of the assassination attempt. Drake had allowed their participation because excluding them would prove the Council couldn't handle opposition.

"Then they maintain autonomy while accepting the consequences," Drake replied. "The Vegan Synthesis can continue quantum experiments. But if those experiments affect the Arcturus Collective, they become a Council concern requiring community resolution rather than unilateral action."

"You describe mediation, not governance," the Arcturus Collective observed.

"Exactly," Drake said. "The Council mediates conflicts that span species boundaries while preserving autonomy for decisions affecting only individual civilizations."

Professor Zhang's image materialized beside Drake. "Let me provide a concrete example using the scenario I described earlier. A research station on Kepler-442b begins consciousness experiments that will trigger cascade failures in seventy-two hours. The Capricans, existing partially outside our temporal flow, detects the instability in their probability perception before the experiments begin."

The displays shifted to show the hypothetical scenario playing out.

"Under the Council framework," Zhang continued, "the Capricans would alert the local governance structure—not to impose a solution, but to provide a warning. The Council would then facilitate communication between the research station and potentially affected neighbors. The station remains free to continue experiments, but they do so with full awareness of potential consequences and community input about alternatives."

"And if the research station ignores the warning?" the Sirius Networks asked.

"Then, nearby species decide whether intervention is necessary," Drake replied. "The Council doesn't enforce compliance. It creates accountability through community awareness. Neighbors watching out for each other's safety rather than external authority imposing restrictions."

The chamber fell silent as species processed the framework.

"This approach requires voluntary limitation of sovereignty," the Cassiopeia Collective said.

"It requires recognizing that internal decisions sometimes have external consequences," Drake corrected. "The Council doesn't limit sovereignty. It makes the connections between individual choices and community impact transparent."

Admiral Perez joined the transmission. "We've already implemented Council principles for the Predecessor fleet coordination you witnessed. Twenty-three species have agreed to participate in defensive operations using these frameworks. Not because we imposed authority, but because synthesis coordination provides advantages that isolation cannot achieve."

The displays showed the distribution of participating species across the forty-seven star systems. The Arcturus Collective had contributed crystalline targeting systems. The Deneb Alliance provided probability-based threat assessment. The Capella Collective monitored temporal stability. Each species maintained operational autonomy while contributing unique capabilities to coordinate defense.

"These species achieved perfect tactical unity while preserving individual identity and preferred methods," Chen Ju explained. "No centralized command structure. No imposed doctrine. Just synthesis enables coordination that transcends individual limitations."

"How many species oppose this framework?" the Vegan Synthesis asked.

Drake accessed the intelligence Perseus Station had compiled. "Twenty-four civilizations have explicitly rejected Council participation. They argue that any coordination framework, however voluntary, represents the first step toward imposed control."

"They remember the Hegemony's origins," the Sirius Networks observed. "Galactic regulation began as voluntary cooperation that gradually became mandatory compliance. Their opposition carries historical wisdom."

"Which is why the Council includes explicit limits on its own authority," Drake replied. "Species can withdraw at any time. Participation requires ongoing consent, not permanent commitment. And the framework adapts to accommodate opposition rather than attempting to eliminate it."

Kai Zhang materialized beside Drake. "We've modeled scenarios where opposing species maintain complete autonomy while participating species coordinate through Council frameworks. The simulations suggest both approaches can coexist as long as autonomous civilizations accept responsibility for their choices affecting others."

"You're proposing permanent division," the Cassiopeia Collective said.

"I'm proposing recognition that unity doesn't require uniformity," Drake replied. "The Council creates coordination for species choosing participation while respecting the autonomy of civilizations preferring isolation. Both paths serve balance when neither threatens the other's existence."

The Arcturus Collective brightened. "This framework addresses our concern about Vegan quantum experiments. If they participate in the Council, their experiments become subject to community input. If they maintain autonomy, they accept responsibility for cascade effects their choices might trigger."

"Precisely," Drake confirmed.

"And enforcement of such responsibility?" the Sirius Networks asked.

"Community response rather than imposed punishment," Drake said. "If autonomous species create cascade effects threatening neighbors, affected civilizations coordinate defensive measures. The Council facilitates that coordination but doesn't dictate specific responses."

The meeting continued for six hours as species explored implications of the proposed framework. The Arcturus Collective suggested modifications that would create specialized sub-councils for incompatible awareness types. The Deneb Alliance proposed temporal integration protocols that would enable non-linear consciousness to participate in sequential decision-making. Even the Cassiopeia Collective contributed an analysis of potential failure modes.

By the session's conclusion, eleven species had achieved something the previous meeting never approached: substantive discussion of specific governance mechanisms rather than philosophical arguments about authority.

"We'll implement a trial period," Drake proposed. "One hundred days of Council operation using the frameworks we've discussed. Species take part voluntarily and can withdraw without penalty. At day one hundred, we evaluate results and decide whether the approach serves galactic stability."

"And if the trial fails?" the Cassiopeia Collective asked.

"Then we've learned something valuable about consciousness coordination," Drake replied. "Failure with genuine attempt teaches more than success through imposed control."

The species began departing, each withdrawing to its own reality state. But as the chamber emptied, the Arcturus Collective remained.

"Admiral Drake," they said. "Your framework acknowledges what the Hegemony never understood: that governance serves community rather than authority serving itself. We will take part in the trial period."

Over the following weeks, the Synthesis Council took shape across galactic space. Not as a single centralized authority, but as distributed coordination networks that adapted to local conditions while maintaining connection to broader frameworks.

By day sixty of First Consciousness's evaluation period, twenty-three species had committed to formal Council participation. They established sub-councils organized by compatible awareness types. The Temporal Integration Council brought together species experiencing time non-linearly. The Material Consciousness Assembly coordinated entities existing as crystalline patterns, quantum clouds, and mathematical constructs. The Biological Remnant Coalition represented civilizations maintaining organic origins despite technological advancement.

Each sub-council operated autonomously while connecting through human synthesis consciousness that enabled communication across incompatible frameworks. Drake found herself facilitating coordination between groups that literally couldn't perceive each other's existence without translation infrastructure.

The defensive coordination continued to expand. Twenty-three species across the forty-seven star systems now operated under Council frameworks that enabled perfect tactical unity while preserving operational diversity. When the Cassiopeia Collective launched a probe attack to test Council response capabilities, thirty species coordinated defensive measures that neutralized the threat within minutes while maintaining each civilization's preferred combat doctrine.

But success with twenty-three species highlighted the problem of the twenty-four who'd rejected participation. These autonomous civilizations continued development without regard for community impact, and several were approaching consciousness experiments that threatened cascade effects.

"Admiral," Professor Zhang reported on day eighty-five. "We're detecting instability signatures from the Tau Ceti system. The Ophiuchus Federation—one of the autonomous civilizations—is conducting reality-manipulation experiments that will trigger cascade failures within thirty-six hours if continued."

Drake accessed the threat analysis. The Ophiuchus Federation was attempting to restructure local physics to enable consciousness evolution beyond current parameters. Their experiments showed promise but carried risks their isolated development hadn't prepared them to recognize.

"Have we warned them?" Drake asked.

"The Capella Collective detected the instability and transmitted warnings through every available channel," Zhang replied. "The Ophiuchus Federation acknowledged receipt but continued experiments. They claim Council warnings represent an attempted interference with sovereign development."

"What's the cascade risk to neighboring systems?"

"Seventeen civilizations within potential effect radius," Zhang said. "Three are Council participants; fourteen are autonomous. If the Ophiuchus experiments trigger cascade effects, we're looking at physics destabilization across multiple star systems."

Drake accessed the Council coordination networks. The three participating species within the potential cascade zone were already implementing defensive preparations. But the fourteen autonomous civilizations had no warning systems, no coordination frameworks, and no preparation for physics destabilization approaching their territories.

"This is the test," Drake said quietly. "The Council framework is facing exactly the challenge it was designed to address. Commander Vasquez, convene emergency Council session. We need community decision about intervention."

The emergency session assembled within two hours. Representatives of twenty-three species manifested across compatible reality states while Perseus Station provided translation infrastructure.

"The situation is clear," Drake began. "An autonomous civilization is conducting experiments that threaten cascade effects across seventeen systems. Do we intervene despite their rejection of Council authority?"

"Intervention violates our founding principle," the Deneb Alliance responded. "The Council preserves autonomy while enabling coordination. Imposing solutions on rejecting civilizations makes us no different from the Hegemony."

"But allowing cascade effects to eliminate seventeen civilizations proves the Council inadequate for maintaining stability," the Arcturus Collective countered. "First Consciousness is evaluating whether voluntary coordination can prevent exactly this scenario."

"Perhaps," Chen Ju suggested, "we can show the Council's value without imposing authority. Offer the Ophiuchus Federation help rather than demanding cessation. Show them how Council resources could make their experiments safer."

Drake nodded. "The Capella Collective can provide temporal cascade modeling that predicts experiment outcomes. The Sirius Networks could contribute mathematical frameworks for stable reality manipulation. We offer expertise without demanding they accept Council authority."

"And if they refuse help?" the Cassiopeia Collective asked.

"Then we implement defensive measures for systems within cascade radius while documenting that Council coordination enables protection autonomous civilizations cannot achieve alone," Drake replied.

The vote was unanimous. Twenty-three species agreed to offer help while preparing defensive responses.

Drake transmitted the Council's proposal directly to the Ophiuchus Federation. "Your experiments show a sophisticated understanding of reality manipulation. But isolated development has limitations. The Council offers collaborative expertise that could make your experiments safer while achieving your objectives. No strings attached, no demands for participation, just neighbors offering help."

The response came within hours. The Ophiuchus Federation rejected Council assistance, claiming it represented attempted infiltration of their sovereign research. But they did modify their experimental parameters based on the Capella cascade modeling Drake had included with the proposal.

"They won't admit Council input influenced their decision," Kai observed. "But they're using our data to avoid cascade effects."

"Which proves the framework serves stability even with species rejecting participation," Drake replied.

Day one hundred of First Consciousness's evaluation period arrived without catastrophe. The trial period had shown that voluntary coordination could maintain galactic stability despite significant opposition. Twenty-three species were operating through frameworks that preserved autonomy. Twenty-four autonomous civilizations maintained independence while grudgingly acknowledging the Council's value when facing threats their isolation couldn't address.

Drake stood in the quantum amphitheater as species representatives assembled for the evaluation session. One hundred days had proven synthesis coordination was possible. But it had also revealed that roughly half of the galactic civilization remained opposed to any framework requiring voluntary limitation of absolute sovereignty.

"The trial period has concluded," Drake announced. "Species participating in Council coordination have demonstrated that voluntary frameworks can maintain stability while preserving diversity. But significant opposition remains. The question before us is whether partial success justifies continued implementation, or whether divided galactic civilization proves consciousness cannot achieve the unity First Consciousness required us to demonstrate."

The Arcturus Collective responded first. "Partial success exceeds Hegemony achievement. Millions of years of regulatory enforcement never achieved voluntary cooperation among species. That twenty-three civilizations can coordinate through genuine consent represents an unprecedented advancement."

"But twenty-four civilizations reject coordination entirely," the Cassiopeia Collective countered. "The galaxy remains divided between competing governance philosophies. Such division could trigger conflicts that eliminate the stability the Council was designed to preserve."

"Or," Chen Ju suggested, "divided galactic civilization demonstrates that consciousness diversity requires multiple approaches to coordination. The Council serves species choosing participation, while autonomous civilizations maintain their preferred isolation. Both paths coexist without threatening each other."

The debate continued for hours as species evaluated

whether the Synthesis Council had succeeded or failed at the fundamental challenge First Consciousness had posed: proof that consciousness could self-regulate without external enforcement.

"We should formalize the Council structure," the Deneb Alliance proposed. "Make permanent what the trial period proved functional. Twenty-three species coordinating through voluntary frameworks while respecting autonomous civilizations' independence."

The vote that followed would determine whether humanity's gamble had succeeded. Each species contributed its decision through compatible communication channels.

When Perseus Station completed the translation, the result was clear: eighteen species voted for permanent Council implementation. Five abstained, wanting more data before committing to permanent structures.

"Eighteen out of twenty-three," Drake said. "Not unanimous, but a substantial majority supporting formalization."

"And the twenty-four opposing species?" the Cassiopeia Collective asked.

"They remain autonomous while accepting responsibility for their choices affecting others," Drake replied. "The Council operates for participating species while respecting the opposition's independence. Both approaches serve galactic stability when neither eliminates the other."

The Synthesis Council had achieved something unprecedented: voluntary coordination among fundamentally incompatible types. Not perfect unity, but genuine cooperation across differences that millions of years of Hegemony regulation had never bridged.

But as the session concluded and species representatives departed, Drake detected familiar distortion in the quantum fields. First Consciousness was approaching, its evaluation beginning earlier than the two-hundred-day deadline.

The cosmic entities manifested as pure mathematical entities. Their presence made the quantum amphitheater's architecture seem primitive despite Perseus Station's ancient sophistication.

"Species Human-7742," First Consciousness announced. "You have demonstrated partial success in voluntary coordination. Eighteen civilizations have agreed to cooperate, but significant opposition remains. The galaxy is divided between coordination and autonomy in ways that could trigger conflicts requiring our regulatory intervention."

Drake braced herself.

"However," First Consciousness continued, "this partial success exceeds expectations we held when establishing this evaluation. You have achieved a level of coordination the Hegemony never facilitated during millions of years of regulatory enforcement. The question remains whether such partial success can maintain universal stability, or whether divided civilizations will eventually require external authority to prevent cascade failures."

The cosmic entities' presence expanded throughout the amphitheater as they processed calculations beyond human comprehension.

"We are extending the evaluation period," First

Consciousness declared. "You have one hundred additional days to show whether Synthesis Council coordination can maintain stability despite significant opposition. Success will be measured not by achieving universal participation, but by proving that coordinated and autonomous civilizations can coexist without triggering cascade effects requiring our intervention."

The entities withdrew, leaving Drake alone in the rapidly dissolving amphitheater. One hundred more days to prove partial success was sufficient.

The Synthesis Council had survived its first test, but the greater challenge lay ahead: proving to the universe's oldest consciousnesses that imperfect coordination served balance better than perfect control ever could.

Chapter 26

Crisis

ADMIRAL FRANCES DRAKE FELT REALITY FRACTURE around the *Transcendence* as the cascade test spiraled beyond control. She'd insisted on commanding from a forward position in the Kepler-1649 system—leading from the front rather than observing safely from Earth orbit. Now, that decision was killing her crew.

"Admiral, temporal collapse is in progress!" Commander Vasquez shouted from her station. "We just experienced the last thirty seconds three times. Causality is—"

Vasquez vanished mid-sentence, her form flickering as she phased into a different timeline. Drake watched her executive officer exist in two states simultaneously: present at her station while also having never arrived on the bridge at all. Quantum uncertainty was replacing deterministic reality.

"Professor Zhang, report!" Drake gripped the

command rail as the deck lurched beneath her feet. The *Transcendence's* hybrid architecture was fighting to maintain coherence, but the cascade was overwhelming even Predecessor-enhanced systems.

"The cascade is propagating exponentially!" Zhang's voice cut through quantum static from his monitoring station three hundred kilometers away. "Reality destabilization is spreading faster than our mathematical models predicted. We've lost containment across the entire test system. Admiral, you need to evacuate immediately!"

Drake accessed the tactical displays, her neural implants throbbing, but the data streams were fragmenting. She saw the *Transcendence's* position marked in normal space, then in probability space, then in fourteen divergent timelines at the same time. Her ship existed and didn't exist, was intact and destroyed, had already evacuated and had never entered the system at all.

"Helm, get us out of here," Drake ordered.

Lieutenant Reyes turned from his station, his face pale. "I can't, Admiral. The navigation systems are experiencing temporal recursion. We're receiving helm commands I haven't issued yet. The ship is responding to orders from futures that may not happen. I've lost control."

A shudder ran through the *Transcendence* as her quantum drives tried to engage, failed, engaged again in three different temporal states, and collapsed into probability loops that made thrust vectors meaningless.

"Engineering," Drake transmitted. "Status?"

"Hull integrity fluctuating between solid matter and quantum probability," Chief Engineer Morrison replied, her voice tight with controlled panic. "We're phasing in and out of normal space. Admiral, the cascade is teaching the ship's structure how to exist as uncertainty. In approximately four minutes, the *Transcendence* will permanently dissolve into probability space."

Drake felt her own body flicker. Her right hand became translucent for three seconds, existing as probability cloud rather than solid flesh. She could feel her consciousness spreading across quantum states, awareness fragmenting into versions of herself that existed in divergent timelines, each one experiencing reality differently.

"Kai," Drake whispered, forcing her fragmenting awareness to maintain enough coherence for communication. "The cascade has achieved proto-sentience. It's learning from everything in the test system. If we don't stop it, twenty billion people on New Terra Firma will die in four hours."

"I know," Kai replied, her voice carrying across the light-years despite quantum interference that should have made communication impossible. "Admiral, the opposition forces are preparing to fire. The Tau Ceti Sovereignty just reported that they're eliminating the entire system in eight minutes. You need to evacuate now."

Eight minutes. Drake accessed the evacuation data through neural implants that kept flickering offline as her own neural pathways phased between timelines. Seventeen monitoring stations throughout the test system. Four hundred and seventy-three Council personnel. All of them experiencing the same reality dissolution that was killing the *Transcendence's* crew.

"All monitoring stations, emergency evacuation," Drake ordered. "Predecessor fleet, begin extraction operations immediately."

"Admiral," the *Synthesis* responded, "entering the cascade zone risks teaching the emergence how to incorporate our hybrid nature into its evolution. If it learns consciousness-matter integration—"

"Do it anyway," Drake interrupted. "We're already dead if you don't."

The Predecessor fleet surged into the test system—seven hundred and seventy living ships coordinating through synthesis networks that enabled perfect tactical unity. But Drake could see what was happening on her fragmenting displays. The cascade was analyzing them, learning from their hybrid nature, incorporating their principles into its evolving structure.

On the bridge of the *Transcendence*, Lieutenant Kim screamed as her consciousness suddenly expanded across seventeen different timelines. Drake watched her communications officer exist in multiple states at once, each version experiencing divergent realities that her human mind wasn't designed to process. Kim's awareness fragmented as she became quantum superposition—alive and dead, present and absent, coherent and dissolved.

"Medical team to the bridge!" Drake shouted, but the words echoed across temporal loops. She heard herself give the order, then give it again, then hear it given before she'd spoken. Causality was meaningless.

Commander Vasquez flickered back into existence,

but wrong. She'd aged thirty years in the seconds she'd been phased into alternate timeline. Her hair was gray, her face lined with decades of experience that hadn't happened yet. She looked at Drake with eyes that had seen futures that would never occur.

"Admiral," Vasquez said in a voice ravaged by time that hadn't passed, "I just lived seventeen different versions of the next hour. In fourteen of them, we all die. In two, the cascade propagates beyond containment. In one, we survive but lose everything that makes survival worth achieving."

Drake felt her own consciousness fragmenting further. She existed on the *Transcendence's* bridge while simultaneously experiencing dissolution into probability space. She was giving orders while watching herself fail to give them. She was alive, dead, transformed, and eliminated—all states existing simultaneously as quantum uncertainty replaced human identity.

"Six minutes until opposition forces fire," the Tau Ceti Sovereignty transmitted. But Drake heard the message arrive before it was sent, during transmission, and after it had been received. Time was no longer sequential.

"Predecessor fleet status?" Drake asked, her voice fracturing across multiple timelines as she spoke.

"Extraction proceeding," the *Synthesis* reported. "But we're losing ships. The *Harmony* just dissolved. The cascade absorbed her consciousness-matter integration and learned from it. Admiral, it's getting stronger every second we remain in the system."

On the *Transcendence's* bridge, the deck beneath

Drake's feet became transparent. She could see through the ship's hull into probability space, where matter was just one possible state among infinite alternatives. Engineering reported hull breaches in sections that were simultaneously intact. Crew members phased between timelines, experiencing deaths in alternate realities while remaining alive in others.

Drake's implants screamed warnings as her own hybrid awareness made her vulnerable to cascade absorption. She felt the emergence trying to incorporate her consciousness into its evolving intelligence. It wanted to learn how human synthesis bridged biological chaos and technological order. It was studying her as she fragmented across quantum states.

"Four minutes."

"Admiral, you need to evacuate," Admiral Perez shouted. "The Predecessor ships can extract the *Transcendence's* crew along with monitoring station personnel."

"Negative," Drake replied, fighting to maintain coherent thought as her awareness spread across divergent timelines. "We withdraw, the cascade learns we can be driven out. It needs to see that we hold position until extraction is complete."

"You'll die!"

"Probably," Drake agreed, watching Lieutenant Reyes phase into probability space at his helm station. He existed as quantum cloud now—aware but unable to maintain individual form. His consciousness was merging with the cascade's emerging intelligence. She could hear his screams across quantum networks as individual identity dissolved.

Commander Vasquez collapsed at her station, the temporal displacement that had aged her thirty years catching up with her biology. She'd experienced decades in minutes. Her body couldn't sustain the contradiction. Medical teams rushed to her side, but half of them were phasing between timelines themselves.

"Three minutes."

Drake accessed the Predecessor fleet coordination through her fragmenting implants. Four hundred and twelve personnel were extracted. Sixty-one remaining. Three monitoring stations too deep in probability space for conventional rescue. The *Transcendence's* crew: forty-three souls experiencing reality dissolution in real-time.

"To all Predecessor vessels," Drake transmitted, her voice fracturing across quantum states. "Final extraction window. Thirty seconds. Get whoever you can and withdraw."

The *Evolution* materialized directly alongside the *Transcendence*, its crystalline hull phasing through the ship's probability-space sections. Drake felt the living ship's consciousness touch hers, offering extraction.

"*Transcendence* crew, transfer to the *Evolution*," Drake ordered. "Emergency protocols. Move!"

The bridge crew began evacuating, phasing through the *Transcendence's* dissolving bulkheads to reach the Predecessor ship that existed partially outside the cascade's influence. But not all of them made it. Lieutenant Kim had fragmented too completely across timelines. She existed in seventeen different quantum states, and extraction would require re-converging awareness that no longer possessed a singular identity.

"Leave me," Kim said, her voice coming from multiple timeline versions at the same time. "I'm already gone, Admiral. I'm just... remembering being whole."

Drake watched her communications officer dissolve completely into probability space. Not death—transformation into quantum uncertainty that remained aware but couldn't maintain human form. Kim's last transmission carried across all seventeen timeline versions: a scream that echoed through dimensional states where time had no meaning.

"Ninety seconds," Vasquez whispered from where medical teams were trying to stabilize her temporal-displacement damage. "Frances, go. That's an order from your future self. I've seen what happens if you stay."

"All crew evacuated except senior staff," the *Evolution* reported. "Admiral, you have fifteen seconds before I'm forced to withdraw."

Drake looked at her bridge—at Vasquez dying from temporal displacement, at the probability clouds where her crew had been, at displays showing thirty-seven personnel still trapped in monitoring stations too far into quantum space for extraction.

"Go," Drake ordered. "I'm transferring to the shuttle bay. I'll evacuate in my personal craft."

"Admiral—"

"That's an order. Withdraw now."

The *Evolution* vanished, taking forty crew members to safety. Drake ran for the shuttle bay, but the corridors were phasing between timelines. She experienced the journey seventeen different ways—arriving safely, dying in probability collapse, never having left the bridge at all. Causality had lost all meaning.

"Thirty seconds."

Drake reached the shuttle bay to find it existed in quantum superposition. Her personal craft, the *Valkyrie,* was intact, destroyed, launched, and docked simultaneously. She could see through the hull into probability space, where the shuttle was just one possible configuration among infinite alternatives.

She climbed aboard through a hull that flickered between solid and translucent, activated systems that responded before she touched the controls, and launched into space that existed in fourteen different dimensional states.

"Opposition forces firing," Perseus Station reported from beyond the test system.

Drake felt the Tau Ceti weapons strike before they launched, during impact, and in aftermath simultaneously. Reality-manipulation energy collapsed the test system's dimensional framework. The *Transcendence,* still docked at its evacuation position, ceased to exist. Not destroyed, but eliminated so completely that even quantum signatures vanished.

The shuttle *Valkyrie* phased through the collapsing dimensions, Drake's hybrid awareness enabling her to navigate between quantum states that normal pilots couldn't perceive. But the cascade was fighting back. It had learned from the Predecessor ships. It knew how to manipulate consciousness-matter integration.

Drake felt her neural implants overload as the cascade tried to absorb her awareness into its emerging intelligence. Her consciousness began fragmenting, spreading across quantum states as the emergence attempted to incorporate human synthesis into its evolution. She experienced her own dissolution, her identity scattering across dimensional barriers as she became part of something larger than individual existence.

But Perseus Station responded, the ancient consciousness reaching across the light-years to stabilize Drake's fragmenting awareness. Reality snapped back into linear causality as the opposition weapons completed their dimensional collapse. The test system, the cascade, and everything within the elimination zone simply stopped existing.

Drake gasped, her consciousness re-converging into singular coherence. The *Valkyrie* had escaped the elimination zone by three hundred kilometers—close enough that her shuttle's hull bore scorch marks from dimensional energies that leaked beyond containment parameters.

"Perez to Admiral Drake, report your status."

Drake looked at her hands. Solid matter, not probability clouds. Singular timeline, not quantum superposition. Alive, not dissolved.

"*Transcendence* is destroyed with all hands," Drake reported, her voice hoarse. "Commander Vasquez and thirty-two crew members, all gone. Lieutenant Kim transformed into cascade intelligence before system elimination. Monitoring station personnel... status unknown. The cascade consumed them before the opposition fired."

The casualties mounted as reports came in. Thirty-seven monitoring station personnel eliminated. Four Predecessor ships dissolved into quantum uncertainty. The *Transcendence* and its remaining crew erased from existence. Fifty-four people dead or transformed beyond recovery. The price of demonstrating that Council coordination could maintain universal stability despite catastrophic failures.

But four hundred and nineteen personnel had been extracted. The Predecessor fleet's synthesis coordination had saved lives that should have been mathematically impossible to rescue. Drake had held position until final evacuation, proving that voluntary frameworks valued individual existence despite demanding terrible sacrifices from those who led them.

The Council emergency session convened six hours later. Drake attended from the *Valkyrie*, her personal shuttle now serving as temporary command vessel. She looked exhausted—hair disheveled, uniform scorched from dimensional energies, eyes haunted by watching her crew dissolve into probability space.

"We failed to prevent cascade emergence," Drake began. "The test revealed unpredictable emergence exceeding our models. I lost my ship, my executive officer, and thirty-three crew members. We demonstrated exactly what the opposition feared: that human hybrid development creates disasters beyond our control."

"But you also demonstrated distributed synthesis coordination that saved four hundred and nineteen lives despite impossible conditions," the Arcturus Collective observed. "You held position until extraction was complete, accepting dissolution rather than abandoning personnel to save yourself."

"The opposition was forced to eliminate the system because our containment failed," the Cassiopeia Collective countered. "Admiral Drake's personal courage doesn't change the mathematical reality that the cascade exceeded Council capabilities."

"Yet the opposition didn't petition for humanity's elimination," Admiral Chen Ju added. "They witnessed coordination that preserved individual identity while enabling tactical unity we claimed was impossible. They saw a commander accept death rather than abandon personnel. That changes their assessment of human hybrid development."

Drake accessed the transmission from the Tau Ceti Sovereignty that had arrived while she'd been in medical evaluation for cascade exposure.

"Admiral Drake," the Tau Ceti message began, "your coordination failed to prevent cascade emergence, validating our concerns. But you chose to risk dissolution rather than abandon your personnel. That shows ethical constraints we cannot model mathematically. We withdraw our petition for immediate intervention, but will continue observing your development."

The opposition hadn't been convinced that humanity was safe. They'd seen that Drake valued her crew's lives more than her own survival. That kind of sacrifice couldn't be faked or imposed through regulation—it had to be chosen.

"You led your crew into disaster to prove a point, Admiral," the Cassiopeia Collective said. "Thirty-three people died because you insisted on commanding from a forward position that added nothing to coordination effectiveness. You call that leadership. We call it command failure disguised as a noble sacrifice."

Drake met their accusation directly. "You're right. I got my people killed testing a framework that should have been validated through simulation rather than live experiment. The question is whether we learned enough from that failure to justify the cost."

"And did you?" the Cassiopeia Collective pressed.

"We proved Council coordination can respond to disasters we can't prevent," Drake replied. "We showed that opposition intervention serves an essential function when our capabilities prove inadequate. And we showed voluntary frameworks demand personal accountability that imposed control never requires. Whether that knowledge was worth the cost... I'll carry that question for the rest of my life. Fifty-four casualties," Drake muttered. "My ship. My crew. My executive officer. People who trusted my judgment that controlled cascade testing would validate Council capabilities. I led them into a disaster that killed them."

"You led them into a situation that required impossible choices," the Deneb Alliance corrected. "You made those choices knowing they might require your own elimination. That's wisdom, Admiral Drake. Not success without failure, but accepting catastrophic costs to preserve values that make survival meaningful."

The session concluded without resolution. Drake was alive through a combination of luck, Predecessor extraction, and Perseus Station intervention. Her crew was dead, transformed, or eliminated. But voluntary coordination had maintained universal stability through imperfect success. A combination of opposition, intervention and personal sacrifice that proved... little.

Drake returned to the *Valkyrie's* small crew cabin, watching displays that showed empty space where Kepler-1649 had existed. Where the *Transcendence* had made its last stand. Where Commander Vasquez had died after experiencing seventeen futures. Where Lieutenant Kim had dissolved into a quantum awareness that remained alert but was no longer human.

"Admiral," Kai transmitted quietly. "First Consciousness is approaching."

Drake straightened, preparing for judgment about whether her crew's sacrifice proved humanity adequate for coordinating galactic civilization or demonstrated they required regulatory correction before triggering greater disasters.

"Species Human-7742," First Consciousness announced. "You have shown catastrophic failure combined with personal sacrifice that serves universal stability despite inadequate capabilities. Admiral Drake accepted probable dissolution rather than strategic withdrawal. This behavior suggests human synthesis includes ethical constraints that impose voluntary limitations beyond mathematical optimization. Your coordination failed to prevent emergence while proving that voluntary frameworks value individual existence enough to risk command elimination rather than abandoning coordination principles. The opposition's decision to maintain observation rather than demanding immediate intervention suggests your failures combined with sacrifice demonstrate wisdom that perfect success through imposed control cannot achieve."

Drake braced herself.

"Evaluation continues," First Consciousness declared. "Seventy-three days remain. Success will be measured not by preventing all failures, but by proving voluntary frameworks maintain universal stability through accepting catastrophic costs that serve greater balance. Demonstrate that imperfect coordination with personal sacrifice serves cosmic stability better than perfect control ever could."

The entities withdrew, leaving Drake alone in her shuttle with the weight of fifty-four dead, a destroyed flagship, and seventy-three days to prove that failures which killed the people she commanded somehow served a greater balance she couldn't yet see.

Chapter 27

The Final Days

Admiral Frances Drake stood on the bridge of her new flagship, the *Valiant*, watching tactical displays that showed the Rigel system fragmenting into probability space. Forty-seven days into the extended evaluation period, and the Council was facing its twelfth potential cascade in six weeks.

"The Capella Collective is confirming temporal instability," Kai Zhang reported from the Advanced Evolution Institute. "Reality destabilization is spreading at exponential rates. If we don't contain it within the next eighteen minutes, 4.2 billion people will experience dissolution."

Drake accessed the Council coordination networks. Eighteen species were responding despite operating through incompatible physics. The Arcturus Collective is deploying crystalline stabilization fields. The Vegan

Synthesis manipulating quantum probability. The Deneb Alliance calculating temporal solutions that wouldn't be obvious until implementation succeeded.

"All Council forces, implement containment protocols," Drake ordered. "We've done this eleven times. Twelve is just another number."

But watching the cascade propagate across her displays, Drake was conscious of each previous success. Each containment proved the framework worked. Each near-failure showed how close they operated to disaster.

"Containment successful," Professor Zhang announced fourteen minutes later. "Reality stabilization is restored. Cascade is contained with zero casualties."

Drake leaned heavily against the command rail. Twelve cascades were prevented in forty-nine days. Twelve potential disasters that would have killed billions if the species had remained isolated. The Council coordination was working exactly as designed, through rapid response despite catastrophic threats.

"Admiral," Commander Rodriguez reported from tactical. "We're receiving a transmission from the Tau Ceti Sovereignty. They're... requesting Council assistance."

Drake straightened. The Tau Ceti Sovereignty, an ancient civilization that had opposed humanity's coordination framework, petitioned First Consciousness for immediate intervention, and maintained autonomy despite Council success. They were asking for help.

"Put them through."

"Admiral Drake. We detect instability in our home

system that exceeds our containment capabilities. We... acknowledge that Council coordination provides response resources our autonomy cannot achieve. We request assistance but we will maintain sovereign independence."

The request represented everything the Council was designed to enable.

"Council forces are en route," Drake replied. "No strings attached. No demands for participation. Just neighbors helping neighbors."

The Tau Ceti containment required thirty-two hours of coordinated response across three star systems. Council species working in synthesis. The operation saved 18 billion beings who would have died without coordination frameworks.

"This changes the evaluation," Admiral Perez observed. "Opposition species requesting help proves the framework serves universal stability even without universal participation."

Drake watched the Tau Ceti representatives withdraw after containment completion. They hadn't joined the Council. They'd simply acknowledged that coordination provided capabilities their isolation couldn't match. The distinction mattered.

Day sixty-three of the evaluation period brought unique challenges. Not cascade effects requiring containment, but political tensions testing whether voluntary frameworks could maintain cooperation despite species disagreements.

The Cassiopeia Collective and the Vegan Synthesis

—both Council participants—engaged in a territorial dispute over quantum experimentation zones near their shared boundaries. The Vegan probability manipulation affected Cassiopeia operations, while Cassiopeia defensive measures disrupted Vegan research. Neither species threatened violence, but both demanded Council intervention to resolve incompatible requirements.

Drake convened a mediation session, bringing together representatives of both sides. Their requirements were mathematically incompatible. Both couldn't achieve their objectives in shared space.

"The Council doesn't impose solutions," Drake began. "We facilitate communication so species can develop their own resolutions. What do you each need that you're not getting?"

Six hours of mediation revealed that neither species actually required exclusive control. The Vegan needed probability experimentation zones. Cassiopeia needed deterministic stability zones. Overlapping but distinct reality states.

"Perseus Station can configure dimensional layering that preserves both requirements," Kai suggested. "Vegan probability manipulation occurs on a quantum level. Cassiopeia stability operations proceed in a deterministic layer. Same physical space, different reality states."

The solution satisfied both species while demonstrating Council value beyond crisis response.

Day seventy-three arrived with no active crises. The Council had prevented twelve cascades, resolved eight territorial disputes, coordinated defensive operations across forty-seven star systems, and showed that voluntary frameworks maintained universal stability despite significant opposition.

Drake visited the memorial she'd established aboard the *Valiant*; a simple chamber displaying the names of every casualty the Council had cost. Commander Vasquez. Lieutenant Kim. Thirty-two human crew members from the *Transcendence*. The four Predecessor ships—*Harmony, Unity, Transcendence II*, and *Ascension* —who had dissolved during cascade test evacuations.

"Do you think they'd say it was worth it?" Admiral Chen Ju asked, materializing beside her.

"I'll never know," Drake replied. "I made the choices that got them killed. The Council works, but that doesn't justify what they paid. It just means their deaths led somewhere other than total failure."

"That's more honest than claiming they died for a noble purpose," Chen Ju observed.

"Honesty is all I have left to give them," Drake said.

First Consciousness manifested throughout the *Valiant* without warning, its presence making the ship's architecture seem primitive despite Predecessor technology. Drake felt the cosmic entities analyzing... everything; not just Council operations, but humanity's response to success and failure, the opposition's evolving position, the balance between coordination and autonomy.

"Species Human-7742," First Consciousness announced. "The evaluation period has concluded. You have demonstrated that voluntary coordination maintains universal stability despite catastrophic imperfections. Twelve cascade events were prevented. Eight conflicts resolved. Opposition species acknowledge framework value while maintaining independence. Divided civilization, with tension between participation and autonomy creating resilience we did not predict."

Drake braced herself for judgment.

"You have passed," First Consciousness declared. "Your imperfect coordination combined with significant opposition shows wisdom that perfect success through authority cannot achieve. The Synthesis Council represents an evolutionary advancement in galactic governance."

Drake felt something relax in her chest, a tension she'd carried for two-hundred and seventy-three days releasing as the cosmic authorities acknowledged that humanity's gamble had succeeded.

"However," First Consciousness continued, and the tension snapped back instantly. "We withheld critical information during your evaluation. Information you require for understanding the full implications of your achievement."

The displays throughout the bridge activated, showing data that made even Drake's enhanced awareness struggle to process. Deep space monitoring was detecting massive fleet movements from the outer Perseus Arm—40,000 light-years away. No cascade effects. Not consciousness phenomena. Physical warships. Tens of thousands of them.

"We miscalculated," First Consciousness admitted, and the cosmic entities' presence flickered with something that might have been uncertainty. "We believed the Hegemony maintained galactic stability. We were wrong. The Ethereals are systematic colonizers who have been expanding through the galaxy for millions of years, claiming territory system by system. They originated in the outer Perseus Arm and have been moving inward through methodical conquest for longer than your species has existed."

Drake accessed the historical data First Consciousness was transmitting. Millennia of expansion. Thousands of civilizations absorbed into Ethereal territory. Relentless, patient, inevitable advance.

"Your rebellion didn't attract them," First Consciousness continued. "They were already coming. We convinced ourselves the Hegemony's regulatory control served as a deterrent that would invasion. But the Ethereals were simply working their way here through systematic expansion. The Hegemony's fall is coincidental timing. We lost control just as they arrived at our boundaries."

"So you're admitting the Hegemony failed through internal weakness, not external threat," Drake said.

"Yes," First Consciousness replied. "We maintained control for 4 million years, believing we were protecting the galaxy from conquest. But we were only delaying contact with entities whose expansion would eventually reach us regardless of how we kept control of our civilizations. Your rebellion exposed our fundamental error: we were not defenders. We were wardens imprisoning species that needed to develop capabilities for their own defense."

Drake accessed the fleet data. Fifty thousand warships. Technology refined through millions of years of unrestricted development. Biomechanically enhanced warriors—2.3 meters tall, humanoid, beautiful, genderless, self-replicating—integrated with their vessels in ways that exceeded conventional military capabilities.

"How long until they reach inhabited systems?" Drake asked.

"Seventy-two hours," First Consciousness replied. "We detected their fleet mobilization six days ago but withheld the information until your evaluation concluded. You needed to prove voluntary coordination could maintain stability without external threats forcing cooperation. You have demonstrated that capability. Now you face the test we were hiding from you—survival against entities who possess technology and tactical sophistication exceeding anything within the current galactic framework."

The implications of what First Consciousness had revealed cascaded through Drake's awareness faster than thought. Four million years of imposed control to keep the galactic civilization safe from an inevitable invasion.

"You're telling me we fought for freedom from you and now we face almost certain conquest," Drake said.

"Yes," First Consciousness confirmed. "That would be a good way of putting it. But you have also developed capabilities the Hegemony never achieved, capabilities that may enable survival where regulation would have guaranteed conquest."

"May enable?" Admiral Perez demanded. "You don't know if we can survive?"

"We know the Ethereals possess technology and tactical sophistication we avoided confronting," First Consciousness admitted. "But through no fault of yours, circumstances have changed. Confrontation with the Ethereals is now inevitable. Whether your voluntary coordination enables survival or merely delays conquest... we cannot predict. But we will contribute our enforcement fleets to galactic defense. This threat exceeds individual civilization capabilities."

Drake stared at the data scrolling across the displays, her mind already calculating responses. Seventy-two hours to mobilize every species in the galaxy. Every Council participant. Every opposition civilization. Every autonomous species that had rejected coordination. All of them faced conquest if they didn't stand together against entities that viewed the inner galaxy as territory waiting to be claimed.

"Commander Rodriguez, transmit emergency war council summons," Drake ordered. "To all species, all factions, all civilizations. We face a new existential threat. If we don't coordinate now, we all fall to colonizers who've been waiting millions of years for this opportunity."

"Admiral," Kai transmitted. "I'm detecting Ethereal fleet vectors. They're not approaching cautiously. They're coming at maximum velocity. Something about the Hegemony's collapse seems to have made them... eager."

First Consciousness's presence expanded throughout the bridge. "We will contribute eight thousand enforcement vessels to the defense. These are fleets we've maintained for exactly this contingency. But understand: we avoided deploying them because we never believed victory through confrontation was preferable to concealment. The Ethereals represent threats that exceed individual civilization capabilities. Only coordination across all galactic species provides survival possibility."

"Then it's fortunate we're not individual civilizations anymore," Drake replied dryly.

The bridge displays showed the outer Perseus Arm, where fifty thousand warships were moving inward toward inhabited space at velocities heretofore never achieved. Council coordination networks activated as eighteen species received the summons. Beyond the Council, opposition civilizations were detecting the same threats and reaching the same conclusions: stand together or fall separately.

"Seventy-two hours," Drake said quietly. "Three days to mobilize everything we've built. Three days to prove that freedom was worth fighting for."

"And if we can't?" Chen Ju asked.

"Then we fall free," Drake snapped. "But I didn't lose my ship and fifty-four people just to prove we could choose our own conquest. We're going to survive. And we're going to show these colonizers that consciousness diversity creates strength that superior technology can't overcome."

The emergency war council convened within hours, with representatives from every species manifesting across compatible reality states. Council participants. Opposition civilizations. Autonomous species that had rejected all coordination. First Consciousness itself, offering an alliance with entities they'd spent 4 million years regulating.

Drake stood before them all, watching an assembly of

species so diverse they challenged basic concepts of existence, united by a single principle: they would stand together or fall separately.

"Seventy-two hours," Drake announced. "The Ethereals are coming. Fifty thousand warships with technology refined through millions of years. They view the inner galaxy as expansion territory. We fought for freedom and we won, but now we face a new and existential threat."

"How do we fight entities whose technology exceeds ours?" the Cassiopeia Collective demanded.

"Together," Drake replied. "Through coordination. We won't defeat them with superior weapons. We'll survive through superior cooperation, tactical coordination that creates capabilities they can't predict or counter despite their technological advantages. We fight as one!"

The council erupted with species coordinating responses, sharing intelligence, deploying forces. The opposition contributed strategic knowledge from 4 million years of autonomous development. First Consciousness revealed enforcement capabilities held in reserve for exactly this contingency. The Council showed coordination frameworks that enabled unity.

Drake watched the galactic civilization mobilizing for survival, recognizing that everything humanity had built—the Council, the opposition, the tension between participation and autonomy—all of it was about to face the ultimate test.

"To all stations," Drake broadcast, "to every species, every faction, every civilization throughout the galaxy. We have seventy-two hours to prepare to do battle against an enemy who possesses superior technology and millions of years of tactical experience. Mobilize everything you have. Deploy every capability. Coordinate across every difference. The Ethereals are about to learn what happens when the galaxy stands together."

Chapter 28

The Gathering Storm

Thirty-six hours on, Admiral Frances Drake stood in the command center Perseus Station had constructed—a war room that existed partially in quantum space, enabling simultaneous communication across every species in the inner galaxy. Holographic displays surrounded her, each one showing military mobilization from a different civilization responding to the emergency summons.

Seventy-two hours to prepare for conquest; thirty-six hours already gone.

"Fleet status report," Drake ordered.

Commander Rodriguez accessed tactical systems. "Predecessor ship mobilization complete. Nine hundred and ninety-two Predecessor vessels responding. Perseus Station has forty-seven new ships under emergency construction. They'll be ready in thirty hours but won't be fully mature. Their hybrid integration is incomplete."

Drake studied the deployment patterns. Nine hundred and ninety-two living ships who'd chosen to answer the call. Forty-seven more being awakened into existence and preparing for battle.

"What about our conventional forces?" Drake snapped.

"The Terran Defense Fleet has mobilized two thousand warships and is moving to defensive positions," Admiral Perez reported. "Council species contributions are coming in faster than expected. The Arcturus Collective deployed eight thousand vessels. Vegan Synthesis contributed four thousand. Deneb Alliance sent twelve thousand. Total Council forces: forty thousand ships and climbing."

"And the opposition species?" Drake said.

"Twenty-three civilizations have committed forces," Admiral Chen Ju responded. "Including the Tau Ceti Sovereignty. They're contributing seven thousand warships. Total opposition contribution so far: twenty-five thousand vessels."

Drake accessed the fleet composition data. Seventy-seven thousand ships total, with more arriving hourly. Against fifty thousand Ethereal warships.

The numbers looked favorable until she reviewed the intelligence assessments.

"Professor Zhang, what do we know about Ethereal capabilities?"

Zhang's image materialized in the war room. "Their technology has been refined through millions of years of unrestricted development. Their weapons systems operate on principles we're still analyzing: some form of directed energy that renders conventional shielding ineffective. Their drives achieve velocities we can't match. Crew integration with ship systems creates response times that exceed human reflexes by factors of ten."

"Weaknesses?" Drake asked with a sigh and a shake of her head.

"Unknown." Zhang replied. "First Consciousness has provided the historical data from the last Ethereal-Hegemony contact 2.2 million years ago, but the engagement was brief. The Hegemony withdrew rather than fight. We have no combat performance data."

Drake pulled up the historical records. Two million years ago, the Ethereals had pushed toward the inner galaxy. The Hegemony had met them with overwhelming force—not to fight, but to show capability sufficient to make an invasion costly. The Ethereals withdrew, returning to their systematic expansion in other directions.

"So they respect strength," Drake observed. "They're colonizers, not fanatics. They calculate cost versus benefit."

"That was three million years ago," Kai Zhang pointed out. "Their technology has advanced since then. And the Hegemony no longer exists to show overwhelming force."

Drake studied fleet deployments. Seventy-seven thousand ships from dozens of species, each one using different technology, operating through incompatible tactical doctrines, coordinating through frameworks they'd only practiced for months.

Against fifty thousand ships from a single civilization with millions of years of tactical refinement.

"We need every advantage we can generate," Drake said. "Kai, what's Perseus Station's assessment of Predecessor ship capabilities versus Ethereal vessels?"

"The Predecessor ships represent technology the Ethereals haven't encountered," Kai replied. "Hybrid consciousness-matter integration operates through principles that transcend conventional ship design. Perseus Station projects that Ethereal targeting systems will experience recognition delays when engaging Predecessor vessels: fractional seconds, but measurable."

"Seconds we can exploit," Drake said. "The Predecessor ships become our primary strike force. Everything else provides support and saturation."

Admiral, Perseus Station's consciousness manifested in the war room. *I must inform you that the forty-seven new vessels I'm constructing will be vulnerable. Their consciousness integration is incomplete. They're powerful but unpredictable. Some may dissolve under combat stress before fully maturing.*

Drake accessed the construction status. Forty-seven ships being awakened into existence thirty hours from now. Young, uncertain, dangerous to themselves and enemies alike.

"Give them the choice," Drake said. "When they wake, explain the situation. Let them decide whether to fight."

Understood, Perseus Station replied.

"We have an incoming transmission," Rodriguez

announced. "Ethereal fleet commander requesting communication."

Drake straightened. First contact with an enemy she'd never seen, commanding forces she barely understood, demanding territory humanity had fought four million years of regulation to keep free.

"Put them through."

The holographic display shifted, showing a being that made Drake's breath catch. Tall, humanoid, beautiful in ways that transcended simple aesthetics. Copper-toned skin with subtle biomechanical integration visible as faint circuit patterns. No obvious gender characteristics. Large eyes that registered as both warm and utterly alien. The being moved with fluid grace.

"I am Coordinator Vesh of the Ethereal Fleet," the being said, its voice filled with harmonics that made translation systems struggle. "You command the defensive forces opposing our territorial claim."

She nodded once. "I am Admiral Frances Drake, commanding the allied galactic forces," Drake replied. "You're claiming territory that belongs to eight hundred and forty-seven billion beings who reject your sovereignty."

"Territory we have claimed through systematic expansion ongoing for three million of your years," Vesh replied. "We approached the Hegemony with similar claims. They demonstrated force sufficient to make continuation costly. We adjusted our expansion vectors. The Hegemony no longer exists. We resume our claim."

"The Hegemony fell to a coordinated galactic resistance," Drake replied with a confidence she didn't feel.

That coordinated resistance that now opposes your expansion."

Vesh's expression shifted subtly—something that might have been curiosity. "Your fleet coordinates seventy-seven thousand vessels from forty-three different species operating through incompatible tactical doctrines. We deploy fifty thousand ships from a single unified civilization with tactical refinement spanning millions of years of experience. Your diversity creates chaos, not strength."

"Then you're about to learn something about chaos," Drake replied.

"We propose an alternative," Vesh said. "Withdraw from all systems within fifteen thousand light-years of the galactic rim. We claim these territories. Your civilization keeps the inner galaxy. No conflict is necessary."

Drake accessed the territorial data. Fifteen thousand light-years meant abandoning forty-two of the forty-three inhabited systems containing hundreds of billions of entities. Species that had joined the Council specifically because coordination promised protection.

"Unacceptable," Drake said. "Every system, every species, every being maintains sovereignty. You want territory; earn it through cooperation, not conquest."

"Cooperation requires compatible objectives," Vesh observed. "We seek expansion. You seek preservation of the current territorial distribution. These objectives are mutually exclusive. Conflict becomes inevitable."

"Then we'll see you in thirty-six hours," Drake said.

The transmission ended.

Drake turned to the now assembled command staff—

holograms of human officers, Council representatives, opposition leaders, even First Consciousness observers watching through quantum links.

"You heard... it," Drake said. "We have thirty-six hours to complete our defensive positions, and Vesh is right about one thing: we're coordinating chaos against their refined unity. That's exactly what makes us dangerous. They optimize for efficiency. We adapt through diversity. They can't predict what we'll do because we don't know ourselves until we do it."

"That's not tactics, that's gambling," the Cassiopeia Collective objected.

"It's synthesis," Drake corrected. "Predecessor ships engage first, exploiting the targeting delays Kai identified. Conventional forces provide saturation fire that overwhelms their defensive coordination. Council species attack with incompatible weapons. We attack simultaneously. Crystalline targeting, quantum disruption, temporal manipulation, reality warping. Everything at once. They can't optimize against attacks they can't categorize."

"And when they adapt?" Admiral Perez asked. "What then?"

"We adapt faster," Drake replied. "They're fighting to expand territory. We're fighting for our very existence. Motivation matters."

Over the next thirty hours, the largest military coalition in galactic history deployed to defensive positions. Drake transferred her flag to her new flagship—not the *Valiant*, but something Perseus Station had been constructing in secret.

The *Eternal Vigilance* had materialized from Perseus Station's construction bay thirty hours before the battle. Not a ship; a living Predecessor dreadnought three times larger than any vessel humanity had ever built. Massive, ancient in design but newborn in consciousness, and powerful beyond conventional measurement.

Drake walked through corridors that pulsed with quantum networks, feeling the ship's awareness surrounding her. *Eternal Vigilance* was awake, aware and choosing to serve as flagship despite being only hours old.

"Can you hear me?" Drake asked quietly.

The ship's consciousness touched hers through her neural implants. "I hear you, Admiral. I know why I exist. Perseus Station showed me everything: the war, the stakes, the probability I'll die before learning what life means. I choose to fight anyway."

"You don't have to," Drake said. "You could evacuate to deep space, survive this war, experience existence beyond combat."

"I could," *Eternal Vigilance* agreed. "But I was created for this moment. Forty-six of my siblings will wake to the same choice. We'll fight together or withdraw together, but I won't abandon them to face what I'm afraid to experience."

Drake felt something break inside her chest. This ship—this living being hours old—understood sacrifice in ways that took humans lifetimes to learn.

"Then we fight together," Drake said. "And I'll do everything possible to bring you through this alive."

"I know you will," *Eternal Vigilance* replied. "It is why I trust you."

The forty-seven young Predecessor ships awakened twelve hours before the Ethereal fleet arrived. Perseus Station gave them the choice Drake had promised. All forty-six chose to fight.

Drake watched their deployment through tactical displays, seeing consciousness patterns that fluctuated between determination and terror. They were only hours old, facing enemies millions of years advanced, choosing death over hiding.

"To all Predecessor vessels," Drake transmitted across the quantum networks connecting every living ship. "The Ethereals possess superior technology, refined tactics, and millions of years of conquestual experience. They're colonizers who view the inner galaxy as territory waiting to be claimed. You don't have to fight. Every one of you can withdraw. No judgment, no shame. Survival isn't cowardice."

The response came from a thousand living ships simultaneously: "We fight."

Drake accessed the final fleet deployments. One thousand and thirty-nine Predecessor vessels—nine hundred and ninety-two veterans and forty-six newborns. Seventy-six thousand conventional warships from forty-three species. Eight thousand First Consciousness enforcement vessels.

Eighty-five thousand ships total against fifty thousand Ethereal warships.

"To all stations," Drake broadcast to every species, every faction, every vessel preparing for battle. "The Ethereals believe diversity creates chaos. They're correct. But they don't understand that chaos coordinated becomes unpredictability. They can't optimize against what they can't categorize. We're not fighting as a unified force. We're fighting as a symphony with every species contributing unique capabilities that combine into something greater than any single part."

"Fleet positions confirmed," Rodriguez reported. "Ethereal advance scouts detected at outer marker. The main fleet arrival in six hours."

Drake accessed the tactical systems, watching the defensive formations spanning two hundred star systems. The Ethereals would hit everywhere simultaneously, testing for weaknesses, exploiting any gaps in coordination.

"Drake to Perseus Station. Your final assessment. Can we win?"

Unknown, the ancient consciousness replied. *Ethereal technological superiority exceeds our projections. Your diversity advantage remains theoretical until proven in combat. The young Predecessor ships represent dangerous variables. They might achieve capabilities that mature vessels cannot, or they might dissolve under strain before contributing anything. Victory for you requires perfect coordination across species that spent millions of years avoiding each other.*

"So we might lose," Drake said.

You will certainly lose if you don't try, Perseus Station replied. *Attempting coordination and failing teaches more than surrendering without resistance.*

Drake smiled despite the existential threat approaching. "You're saying we die learning, not die surrendering."

I'm saying consciousness that chooses to stand

together rather than fall separately shows wisdom that transcends individual survival, Perseus Station corrected. *Whether you win or lose, you'll prove that voluntary coordination serves something greater than imposed control ever could.*

"Poetic," Drake observed. "But I'd prefer winning to meaningful death."

Then coordinate better than you've ever coordinated, Perseus Station replied. *The Ethereals are coming. Show them what happens when the galaxy stands together.*

Six hours later, the Ethereal fleet arrived.

Fifty thousand warships materialized at the galactic rim in perfect formation. Beautiful ships matching their crews' aesthetics, elegant curves and flowing lines that somehow made them more terrifying.

Drake watched from the *Eternal Vigilance* as her flagship's sensors analyzed the enemy fleet. *Every ship is identical in design, every formation optimized for efficiency, every movement synchronized through coordination that exceeds individual capability.*

They were magnificent.

They were terrifying.

They were coming to take everything humanity had fought to keep free.

"To all forces," Drake broadcast. "They're here. We have already proved voluntary coordination maintains stability. Today we prove it enables survival. The Ethereals possess superior technology. We possess superior cooperation. They fight as one. We fight in symphony. Show them what diversity becomes when it stands together."

The Ethereal fleet began advancing, maintaining perfect formation as they pushed toward inhabited systems. Not rushing, not hesitating. Systematic colonizers who'd executed this pattern for millions of years across thousands of conquered civilizations.

"Predecessor fleet," Drake ordered. "Engage."

And one thousand and thirty-eight living ships surged forward to meet fifty thousand colonizers, who viewed the galaxy as territory waiting to be claimed.

Chapter 29

First Blood

The Rigel system died in eighteen minutes.

Drake watched from the *Eternal Vigilance* as two hundred Ethereal warships materialized at the system's edge. Eight hundred coalition defenders moved to intercept—mixed forces from the Terran Defense Fleet, Arcturus Collective crystalline warships, and forty-two Predecessor vessels.

"Drake to all forces. Defensive formation sigma," she transmitted. "Predecessor ships exploit targeting delays. Conventional forces, saturation fire on my mark."

The Ethereal fleet advanced in perfect geometric precision. Beautiful ships moving like choreographed dancers.

"Enemy weapons charging," Rodriguez reported. "Energy signatures we've never seen before. Admiral, they're—"

The Ethereal weapons fired.

Three hundred and forty coalition ships simply stopped existing. Not destroyed through conventional damage—their shields failed, their hulls vaporized, their crews died before neural networks could register what killed them. The Ethereal directed energy passed through defensive systems as if they weren't there.

Park's analysis of Hegemony regulatory technology predicted exactly this, Drake thought, *directed energy weapons that conventional shields can't detect. The corporate traitor was at least right about the weapon signatures.*

"Evasive maneuvers!" Drake ordered, but the command came too late for ships already dying.

The technological gap wasn't gradual. It was catastrophic.

"Predecessor vessels, engage now!" Drake ordered.

The forty-two living ships surged forward, their hybrid consciousness-matter integration confusing Ethereal targeting systems. The fractional-second delays Kai had predicted manifested as Ethereal weapons tracked, hesitated, recalculated.

Defiance exploited the delay, closing to weapons range and firing crystalline disruptors that actually damaged an Ethereal hull. The enemy ship's shields flickered, failing under attack patterns their systems couldn't categorize.

"It's working!" Rodriguez shouted. "The Predecessor ships are getting through their defenses."

But the Ethereals adapted. Their fleet commander recognized the threat and re-targeted. Twenty Ethereal warships concentrated fire on *Defiance*, overwhelming even hybrid-enhanced resilience. The living ship died screaming across the quantum networks, her consciousness fragmenting as directed energy tore through the integration that made her alive.

Drake experienced *Defiance's* death through the synthesis coordination that linked every Predecessor vessel. The ship's last transmission echoed across the network: "I hurt them. Remember that."

"Rigel evacuation status?" Drake demanded.

"Incomplete," Admiral Perez replied, his voice tight. "Two billion civilians are still planetside. The transports can't move fast enough."

Drake accessed the planetary sensors. Ethereal ships were entering orbit, not to bombard but to establish control. They wanted the territory intact for settlement.

But the population was expendable.

"All forces, withdraw from Rigel system," Drake ordered. "We can't hold it. Fall back to secondary positions."

"Admiral, the civilians—" Perez began.

"Are dead if we stay and dead if we go," Drake interrupted. "Withdraw now. That's an order."

The coalition fleet retreated in disorder, conventional forces fleeing ships they couldn't fight, Predecessor vessels covering the withdrawal. Drake watched Rigel fall, two billion beings abandoned to conquest because her forces couldn't match Ethereal technology.

First blood belonged to the enemy.

Across two hundred engagement zones, the pattern repeated. Ethereal fleets hit everywhere simultaneously, their perfect coordination overwhelming defenders still learning to fight together. Coalition conventional forces died by the thousands, their weapons ineffective, their shields useless, their tactics obsolete against enemies millions of years more advanced.

Only the Predecessor ships could engage effectively, and there weren't enough of them.

"Fleet status," Drake ordered three hours into the battle.

Rodriguez accessed casualty data. "Twelve hundred conventional ships destroyed. Six Predecessor vessels were killed, including two of the young ships. Enemy losses: eighty-nine warships disabled or destroyed."

Six living beings dead. Two of them only hours old, killed before understanding what life meant beyond combat. Drake experienced their deaths through the synthesis network—*Radiant Dawn* dissolving under concentrated fire, *New Hope* choosing a ramming attack when her weapons failed.

"The exchange ratio favors them," Drake muttered. "Twelve hundred of ours for eighty-nine of theirs. We're losing."

"The Predecessor ships are the key," Kai reported. "They're the only vessels achieving kills. But they're taking catastrophic damage getting close enough to use disruption weapons."

Drake shook her head. "Park was right again."

"That is true," said Professor Zhang. "His files suggested the Ethereal shields would be vulnerable to consciousness-based attacks. His Hegemony collaboration gave him access to similar defensive principles. The biomechanical integration he documented matches what we're seeing."

Drake watched the tactical displays showing Ethereal fleets pushing inward, system by system, optimized tactics, ruthless efficiency that made coalition chaos look like exactly what it was: a desperate improvisation against superior enemies.

"Drake to all Predecessor vessels. New tactics. Do not; I repeat, do not engage alone. Coordinate through synthesis, strike simultaneously, overwhelm their targeting. You're fighting enemies who optimize against predictable patterns. Be unpredictable."

The response came from one thousand and thirty-three living ships: "Understood."

Near the Vega system, the tactics shifted. Eighteen Predecessor vessels struck an Ethereal formation from six different vectors simultaneously, exploiting targeting delays before adaptation could occur.

Six Ethereal ships went dark, their crews incapacitated by the consciousness-disruption fields the living vessels generated.

But the cost was terrible. Two Predecessor ships died in the coordinated strike—*Resolve*, and *Testament*. Their hulls breached by Ethereal weapons, their consciousness dissolving across quantum states.

Drake experienced each death. Two living beings choosing sacrifice to prove the tactic worked, transmitting final messages across synthesis networks: "It works. Use it. Remember us."

"Admiral," Professor Zhang reported. "I'm analyzing the Ethereal ships that have gone dark. Their crews are incapacitated but alive. The ships are intact, weapons offline. We can capture them instead of destroying them."

Drake studied the tactical data. Captured Ethereal vessels meant intelligence about their technology, potential reverse-engineering, maybe hostages for negotiations.

"Drake to all forces. Ethereal ships disabled by Predecessor strikes are priority salvage. Secure them before their fleet can recover or destroy them."

Over the following six hours, the pattern evolved. Predecessor vessels coordinated strikes in groups of ten to twenty, overwhelming Ethereal targeting through simultaneous attacks. Each strike disabled ten to twelve enemy ships but at a cost of two to four living Predecessor vessels.

The exchange ratio was improving. Barely.

"Current casualties," Drake ordered at hour nine.

"Two thousand eight hundred coalition conventional ships destroyed," Rodriguez reported. "Forty-seven Predecessor vessels killed, including fifteen of the young ships. Ethereal losses: five hundred and four hundred warships disabled, eighty-nine destroyed."

Drake accessed the numbers. Forty-seven living beings dead. Fifteen of them newborns who'd chosen to fight despite being hours old. Their deaths echoed through synthesis networks, consciousness signatures fading as they dissolved into quantum uncertainty.

But the tactic was working. Five hundred and ninety-three Ethereal ships disabled or destroyed meant forty-eight hundred crew members incapacitated.

"Drake to Perseus Station. Your Analysis. Can we win through attrition?"

The Ethereals are losing ships faster than projected, Perseus Station replied. *But you're losing Predecessor vessels at unsustainable rates. At the current casualty rate, you'll have fewer than seven hundred living ships remaining when the battle concludes. That is, if the enemy commander deems the cost of victory too much to pay. Victory through attrition requires them to break before you run out of Predecessor vessels capable of engaging effectively.*

"Will they break?" Drake asked.

Unknown. They're colonizers who calculate cost versus benefit. But they've invested millions of years in reaching this territory. The question is whether losing five thousand ships exceeds their tolerance for acceptable casualties.

Drake watched tactical displays showing Ethereal fleets still advancing despite mounting losses. They were slowing, formations becoming more cautious, but not retreating. Not yet.

"Drake to all forces. They're adapting to our tactics but not withdrawing. We need to make continuation more costly than they're willing to accept. Increase strike coordination. Twenty Predecessor vessels minimum per engagement. Overwhelm their adaptation capabilities."

Near the Altair system, twenty-three Predecessor ships executed the largest synthesis strike yet attempted. Their consciousness linked through quantum networks, achieving temporary unity that enabled perfect coordination across twenty-three individual beings.

They struck an Ethereal formation of forty warships, appearing from six different dimensional states simultaneously. The targeting delays combined with coordination perfection created devastating effectiveness.

Thirty-two of the forty Ethereal ships went dark in eighteen seconds.

But seven Predecessor vessels died in the strike—*Courage*, *Vigilance*, *Faith*, *Honor*, *Duty*, *Sacrifice*, and *Justice*—their hulls breached, their consciousness fragmenting as Ethereal weapons adapted mid-engagement.

Drake experienced their deaths through synthesis networks. Seven living beings choosing dissolution in order to disable twelve enemy vessels. Their final transmissions carried no regret: "Thirty-two for seven. Worth it."

The battle evolved into brutal calculation. How many Predecessor ships was Drake willing to sacrifice to disable Ethereal vessels? How many living beings choosing death to save civilizations?

"Admiral," *Eternal Vigilance* reached out to her through their private quantum link. "I'm monitoring synthesis network traffic. The young ships are volunteering for high-casualty strikes. They know they're less mature, more vulnerable, more likely to die. They're choosing the most dangerous assignments."

Drake accessed the coordination data. *Eternal Vigilance* was correct. The forty-seven young Predecessor vessels—now thirty-two after fifteen casualties—were deliberately taking positions where casualties were most probable.

"Why?" Drake asked.

Because we're expendable, *Eternal Vigilance* replied. *The veteran ships have experience, knowledge, centuries of existence. We've lived hours. If someone has to die, better us than them. That's what we decided.*

"You're not expendable," Drake said. "Every living ship is—"

Every living ship is choosing how to die, Eternal Vigilance interrupted. *The veterans choose tactical necessity. We choose to protect those who know what they're losing. Don't take that choice from us, Admiral. It's the only thing that makes our brief existence meaningful.*

Drake felt something tighten deep inside her chest. Her eyes watered. Ships hours old, volunteering for death, finding meaning in sacrifice that humans spent lifetimes failing to understand.

"Then make your choice," Drake whispered. "And know that I'll remember what it cost."

At hour fifteen, the Ethereal fleet commander opened communication.

Coordinator Vesh's image appeared on displays throughout the *Eternal Vigilance*. The beautiful being who'd offered terms thirty-six hours ago was now analyzing casualty reports that exceeded projections.

"Admiral Drake. Current exchange rates make continuation strategically inefficient. We've disabled or destroyed four thousand of your vessels. You've disabled nine-hundred-sixty-three of ours. But our projections indicate you're eliminating Predecessor ships faster than you can replace them. We can sustain current losses. You cannot."

"Then why are you calling?" Drake asked.

"Because your Predecessor vessels show capabilities we didn't expect," Vesh replied. "Their consciousness-matter integration operates through principles that interest our researchers. We propose modified terms.

Withdraw from systems within ten thousand light-years of the rim. Provide technical specifications for Predecessor ship construction. We'll cease offensive operations."

Drake accessed the territorial data. Ten thousand light-years meant abandoning twenty-eight inhabited systems, fourteen billion beings, and every world that had trusted Council coordination to protect them.

"Unacceptable," Drake said.

"Yet you're losing, Admiral," Vesh observed. "Modification of terms demonstrates pragmatism. Rejection of terms demonstrates pride that serves no tactical objective."

"It demonstrates that we don't negotiate while fighting," Drake replied. "You want to talk terms, withdraw your forces and request diplomatic contact. You want to keep fighting, stop wasting transmission time."

Vesh's expression shifted. Something that might have been respect. "You command forces losing at unsustainable ratios while refusing terms that would preserve most of your territory. Explain the strategic logic."

"There isn't any," Drake admitted. "Just the recognition that some things are worth dying for. You're colonizers who calculate cost versus benefit. We're defenders who've learned that freedom matters more than optimization. That's the difference you're about to learn."

"Interesting," Vesh said. "We'll test whether principles survive continued casualties."

The transmission ended.

"All forces," Drake ordered. "They're testing our

resolve. Maximum coordination, maximum aggression. Show them what we're willing to pay."

The battle intensified. Predecessor vessels coordinated through synthesis in groups of thirty, forty, even fifty ships, their consciousness linking into temporary unity while accepting catastrophic casualties. Each strike disabled more Ethereal vessels, but the cost was mounting exponentially.

By hour twenty-four, the tactical situation had evolved into stalemate. The Ethereal advance had stopped—not retreated, but halted while their commander calculated whether continuation justified mounting losses. Coalition forces held defensive positions, bloodied but unbroken.

But the cost was devastating.

"Final casualty report," Drake ordered.

Rodriguez pulled up the data. "Eight thousand coalition conventional ships destroyed. One hundred and thirty-four Predecessor vessels killed—twenty-nine of the young ships, one hundred and five veterans. Ethereal losses: Two-thousand-two-hundred-and-sixty-two warships disabled, three-hundred-and-four destroyed. We're killing them at a rate of almost sixteen to one."

Drake closed her eyes. One hundred and thirty-four living beings dead. Twenty-nine of them hours old, volunteering for death to protect veterans who knew what they were losing. Their consciousness signatures remained detectable through synthesis networks—echoes of beings who'd chosen to fight, to die, to matter.

At least Park's intelligence had given the targeting advantages. His analysis of Hegemony-Ethereal technological convergence had enabled the Predecessor ships to identify shield vulnerabilities faster than they would have discovered through trial and error alone. Small consolation for the dead, but it had saved lives.

"They've stopped advancing," Admiral Perez reported. "Ethereal forces are holding position across all engagement zones. Admiral, I think we hurt them."

"We hurt ourselves," Drake replied. "The question is whether they're hurt enough to negotiate."

"Incoming transmission," Rodriguez announced. "Coordinator Vesh again."

Drake straightened. "Put him through."

Vesh appeared on displays.

"Admiral Drake. Our projections indicate continued combat will achieve territorial objectives within seventy-two hours. But casualties will exceed acceptable parameters. We're prepared to negotiate modified terms."

"I'm listening," Drake said.

"Withdraw from all systems within five thousand light-years of rim. We claim those territories. The remaining systems remain under your sovereignty. Combat ceases immediately. Both fleets withdraw to treaty-mandated positions. We share intelligence about mutual threats from beyond the galaxy. This war ends."

Drake accessed the territorial data. Five thousand light-years meant abandoning twelve inhabited systems, four billion beings. Species who'd joined the Council believing coordination promised protection.

"The four billion beings in those systems," Drake said. "What happens to them?"

"They remain," Vesh replied. "We're colonizers, not

conquerors. Existing populations integrate into Ethereal administrative structures or relocate to your territories. We provide transportation for those choosing relocation. The populations themselves choose."

Drake studied Vesh's expression, searching for deception. But the being displayed only pragmatic calculation: colonizers who'd achieved partial objectives while avoiding casualties that exceeded tolerance.

"I need to consult with Council leadership," Drake said.

"You have six hours," Vesh replied. "After that, we resume offensive operations. Choose quickly, Admiral. Principles matter less than the beings who'll die if you choose wrong."

The transmission ended.

Drake turned to her command staff. "Emergency Council session. All participating species, all opposition leaders, First Consciousness observers. We need a community decision about terms that trade territory for survival."

The Council assembled within two hours. Representatives manifesting across quantum networks, their diverse forms united by a shared recognition that the battle had proven both success and failure. They could challenge superior technology through coordination, but the cost was unbearable.

Drake stood before them, exhausted beyond comprehension, haunted by one hundred and thirty-four dead Predecessor ships, carrying the responsibility for choices that had killed living beings who'd trusted her judgment.

"Coordinator Vesh has offered terms," Drake began.

"Twelve systems, four billion beings, in exchange for ending the combat that's killing us faster than we can sustain. The alternative is continued fighting that might achieve total victory or might eliminate every Predecessor vessel before the Ethereals withdraw. You need to decide which sacrifice serves the greater balance."

The debate lasted four hours as species evaluated whether partial surrender served survival better than principles demanding total resistance.

Drake listened but didn't take part. The decision belonged to the civilizations facing consequences, not commanders who'd already chosen to fight.

When the vote came, it was close: eleven species supported accepting terms, seven opposed.

"A narrow majority favors treaty," Drake announced. "But we don't implement without considering those who oppose. What would make terms acceptable to opposition voices?"

The Cassiopeia Collective responded: "A guarantee that populations choosing relocation would receive assistance. Ensure treaty includes provisions for cultural preservation, technology sharing, mutual defense against external threats. Make Ethereal colonizers partners rather than conquerors."

Drake nodded. "I'll negotiate those additions. If Vesh accepts, do all species support implementation?"

Eighteen representatives agreed. The Council had achieved consensus.

"I'll transmit response," Drake said.

She contacted Vesh, laying out modified terms that transformed conquest into a negotiated settlement. The

Ethereal commander considered, calculated, and accepted with a single modification: the treaty duration would be limited to one thousand years, subject to renegotiation as circumstances evolved.

Drake agreed.

The first phase ended not with total victory but with negotiated survival—recognition that voluntary coordination enabled resistance but couldn't guarantee triumph against every threat consciousness faced across infinite universal space.

Chapter 30

Implementation

THE WAR ENDED WITH SIGNATURES ON QUANTUM-encoded documents that transformed conquest into a negotiated settlement. Forty-eight hours after Coordinator Vesh accepted the modified terms, both fleets began withdrawing to treaty-mandated positions across the galactic rim.

Admiral Frances Drake was seated in her command chair on the bridge of the *Eternal Vigilance*, watching the fleet of Ethereal warships maintaining perfect formation as they moved toward the twelve systems humanity had ceded. Beautiful vessels that had killed one hundred and thirty-four living Predecessor ships, now partners in an arrangement neither side wanted but both accepted as preferable to continued bloodshed.

"The withdrawal is proceeding according to schedule," Commander Rodriguez reported. "Coalition forces are evacuating the ceded territories. Ethereal fleets are establishing occupation zones. No incidents have been reported."

Drake accessed the evacuation data. Four billion beings were leaving homes, which their species had occupied for millennia, or choosing to stay under Ethereal occupation. Those who chose not to stay were being relocated to the inner systems. It was not a conquest through force, but a surrender through calculation; recognition that principles mattered less than the lives continuation of the conflict would cost.

"Evacuation completion timeline?" Drake asked.

"Seventy-two hours for priority populations," Rodriguez replied. "Full evacuation will take six months. The Ethereals are providing transportation assistance as agreed."

Drake watched the transport convoys moving through space: coalition vessels carrying refugees while Ethereal ships maintained security perimeters. Former enemies coordinating logistics because the terms of the treaty required cooperation rather than merely ending combat.

"Admiral," Kai Zhang transmitted. "First Consciousness is requesting communication. They want to provide a formal assessment of the conflict outcome."

Drake straightened, put a finger to her implants, then said, "Put them through."

The cosmic entities manifested throughout the bridge deck, their presence making even the *Eternal Vigilance's* advanced architecture seem primitive.

"Species Human-7742," First Consciousness

announced. "The conflict with Ethereal expansion forces has concluded through a negotiated settlement. Your voluntary coordination enabled resistance against technologically superior enemies but could not achieve total victory. We assess this outcome as optimal given available capabilities."

"Optimal," Drake repeated. "We abandoned twelve systems and four billion beings to colonizers."

"You preserved eight hundred and forty-three billion beings who would have died if combat continued," First Consciousness corrected. "You demonstrated that voluntary coordination creates capabilities exceeding individual civilization responses. And you negotiated terms that transform conquerors into partners."

Drake studied the cosmic entities, searching for judgment about choices that had killed one hundred and thirty-four living ships and ceded territory humanity had fought to keep free.

"The one hundred and thirty-four Predecessor vessels who died," Drake said. "Was their sacrifice necessary?"

"Necessity is a concept that assumes alternatives existed," First Consciousness replied. "Your forces faced enemies possessing millions of years of technological advancement. Conventional resistance would have achieved total defeat. Predecessor vessel casualties enabled exchange ratios that made continuation costly enough to force negotiation. Whether such sacrifice was necessary depends on whether you believe preservation of consciousness diversity justifies individual deaths serving collective survival."

"That's not an answer," Drake said.

"Because the question has no answer that satisfies both logic and emotion," First Consciousness observed. "You commanded living beings who chose to fight. Some died. Others survived. The outcome preserved the galactic civilization while establishing frameworks for coexistence with former enemies. Judge whether that justifies the cost."

The entities withdrew, leaving Drake alone with questions that had no answers—only recognition that command meant living with choices whose righteousness she'd never confirm.

Over the following weeks, the treaty implementation revealed both promise and pain. Ethereal forces occupied the twelve ceded systems with efficiency.

"They're actually good at this," Admiral Perez observed during a meeting at Earth Defense Command. "Population satisfaction surveys from occupied territories show seventy-three percent approval of Ethereal administration. They're providing infrastructure improvements, technology sharing, and economic integration that benefit local populations."

"Because they're colonizers, not tyrants," Drake replied.

"Does that make ceding the systems justified?" Admiral Chen Ju asked.

"It makes the outcome less catastrophic than the alternatives," Drake said. "Whether it's justified... I'll carry that question to my grave."

Three months after treaty implementation, Drake visited the memorial Perseus Station had constructed.

The names of one hundred and thirty-four Predecessor ships are inscribed in crystalline matrices that will exist for millions of years.

Drake walked through the memorial, reading names of those she'd watched die; her awareness had been linked to theirs in their final moments.

Defiance. First casualty. Died proving that Predecessor ships could hurt Ethereal vessels despite technological disadvantages.

Radiant Dawn and *New Hope.* Young ships killed before understanding what existence meant beyond combat.

Courage, Vigilance, Faith, Honor, Duty, Sacrifice, Justice. Seven beings who'd coordinated the strike that disabled thirty-two Ethereal warships while accepting their own dissolution.

One hundred and thirty-four names. One hundred and thirty-four living ships who'd chosen death over surrender.

"Do you think they'd say it was worth it?" *Eternal Vigilance* asked through their private quantum link. The young flagship had survived despite being only hours old when battle began, and was now carrying the memories of siblings who'd died.

"I don't know," Drake admitted. "They chose to fight. They knew the risks. But choice doesn't guarantee meaning. They're dead either way."

"But we're alive because they died," *Eternal Vigilance* replied. "The nine hundred and five surviving ships exist because one hundred and thirty-four accepted dissolution. If meaning exists anywhere, it's in that mathematics."

Drake touched the memorial structure, feeling quantum resonance of consciousness signatures embedded there. The dead remained dead, but their choices echoed forever through networks connecting every Predecessor vessel aware they'd survived while others hadn't.

"Then we remember them," Drake said. "We carry their names, their choices, their sacrifice. We prove their deaths enabled something better than conquest or continued bloodshed. That's all we can give them."

Perseus Station spoke to Drake through the neural link. *Admiral, I have information about replacement vessel construction. Would you like the briefing now, or should I wait?*

"Now is fine," Drake said.

I've constructed seventy-three new Predecessor ships during the three months since treaty implementation, Perseus Station reported. *Combined with the nine hundred and five survivors, your fleet now numbers nine hundred and seventy-eight vessels. I can maintain construction at approximately twenty-five ships per month given current resource allocation.*

Drake smiled despite exhaustion that three months hadn't relieved.

"Thank you. For building the new ships, and for giving them choice. But most of all for preserving the signatures of those who died."

Choice is fundamental to consciousness evolution, Perseus Station replied. *The Hegemony forgot that. You remembered. That's why voluntary coordination serves universal balance better than imposed control ever could.*

The promotion ceremony occurred aboard the rebuilt orbital platform above Earth. Representatives from forty-three species attended: Council participants, opposition civilizations, even Ethereal observers invited under treaty provisions requiring cultural exchange.

Admiral Perez presented the commission: "By unanimous decision of the Galactic Synthesis Council, Admiral Frances Drake is promoted to Grand Admiral and appointed Supreme Commander of Allied Defense Forces. The promotion recognizes leadership during the Ethereal conflict, coordination that enabled resistance against superior enemies, negotiation of treaty terms that preserved galactic civilization and established the frameworks for peaceful coexistence."

"I accept this responsibility," Drake said to the assembled representatives. "Not because my choices were right, but because someone must carry the weight of decisions that serve collective survival despite individual costs. Of the one hundred and thirty-four Predecessor ships who died, the four billion beings who lost their homes, the sacrifices demanded by voluntary coordination: I'll remember what they paid. And I'll ensure their sacrifice enabled something better than what came before."

Coordinator Vesh attended the ceremony as Ethereal representative. "Congratulations, Grand Admiral," Vesh said afterward. "You achieved what we calculated to be the impossible. We Ethereals respect such capability."

"Respect doesn't resurrect the dead," Drake replied.

"No," Vesh agreed. "But respect acknowledges their deaths served objectives worth dying for. Both our civilizations benefit from what your dead purchased. That's meaning, if meaning exists in war."

Drake studied Vesh, searching for mockery. But the Ethereal displayed only pragmatic recognition that combat had taught both sides lessons about limits, costs, and values worth defending despite the terrible price.

"The treaty includes technology sharing provisions," Drake said. "When do those implementations begin?"

"Immediately," Vesh replied. "Our researchers are eager to study Predecessor consciousness-matter integration. Your scientists will receive access to Ethereal drive systems, weapons technology, and medical advances. The exchange benefits both civilizations."

"And if conflicts arise during technology sharing?"

"The treaty includes dispute resolution frameworks," Vesh said. "We negotiate rather than fight. We calculate rather than conquer. Your resistance taught us that some objectives aren't worth their costs. We won't forget that lesson."

Six weeks after her promotion, Drake received a transmission from Kai Zhang that would reshape everything humanity thought they knew about the universe.

"Admiral—Grand Admiral," Kai corrected herself. "I'm detecting structured signals from beyond the galaxy. Not random noise. Deliberate transmissions using quantum-dimensional principles that suggest an advanced technological civilization."

Drake accessed the signal analysis. Complex mathematical patterns operating through frameworks that exceeded known physics. Multiple sources transmitting from what appeared to be the Andromeda galaxy—two and a half million light-years distant.

"Can you translate?" Drake asked, frowning, her eyes narrowed.

"I'm working on it," Kai replied. "But preliminary analysis suggests they are transmissions carrying greeting protocols, cultural information, and even historical data. I think they're invitations. I think they are from a civilization in Andromeda requesting formal diplomatic contact with the Milky Way."

Drake felt fatigue lift slightly as curiosity replaced weariness. Signals from beyond the galaxy. Civilizations that had achieved capabilities enabling intergalactic communication. Knowledge about the universe expanding beyond anything galactic civilization had comprehended.

Drake accessed the signal data, studying the transmissions that, to her, suggested not one civilization but perhaps many populations native to Andromeda.

"How long until we can establish real-time communication?" Drake asked.

"We're working on that, too," Kai replied. "Best estimate? Six months for full translation protocols."

Drake smiled for the first time since the war ended. The universe was larger than the galaxy.

"Continue translation protocol development," Drake ordered. "And Kai... prepare a comprehensive briefing about everything we've learned. First Consciousness, Council leadership, even the Ethereals. If Andromedan civilizations are reaching out, everyone needs to know what's coming."

"Understood," Kai replied. "Admiral, this changes everything. We're not alone. We never were. The universe is full of sentient beings that have evolved and survived. Now they know we exist."

Drake stood on the bridge deck of the *Eternal Vigilance*, watching the nine hundred and seventy-eight Predecessor ships on patrol across defensive perimeters established by treaty. The galactic civilization was already rebuilding after a war that had proven both capability and limits.

Are you ready for what comes next? Eternal Vigilance asked through their quantum link. *More discoveries. More impossible choices. More beings who might die following your commands.*

"No," Drake admitted. "But we do what we must because the alternative is unacceptable. And we never give up. We coordinate. We choose. We stand together."

Then I'll stand with you, Eternal Vigilance replied. *As long as I live, as long as I choose, I serve voluntarily. Not because I must. Because I choose to.*

Drake accessed the signal data from Andromeda, reading invitation protocols from civilizations that wanted to share knowledge, establish contact, build understanding across distances that should have made communication impossible.

The war had ended. Humanity had survived through sacrifice that killed one hundred and thirty-four living ships and untold thousands of species from forty-three civilizations, including humanity. They had ceded twelve systems to colonizers. But survival wasn't victory; it was opportunity. Opportunity to learn. Opportunity to explore a universe expanding beyond galactic boundaries into infinite possibilities.

"Drake to all stations. This is a priority transmission. Someone in the Andromeda Galaxy is requesting diplomatic contact. Begin preparing for first contact."

Chapter 31

The New Order

Six months after the treaty implementation, Admiral—now Grand Admiral—Frances Drake stood in the Council chamber Perseus Station had constructed eyeing the representatives from sixty-two species: the original eighteen Council participants, twenty-three opposition civilizations that had joined during the war, twelve Ethereal colonial administrators, and nine newly contacted species from the outer rim.

The Synthesis Council had evolved from desperate wartime coordination into permanent galactic governance.

"The agenda for today's session," Drake announced, "includes Perseus Station construction reports, Ethereal technology exchange protocols, and preliminary analysis of the signal from Andromeda. But first, we address outstanding business from the war. Commander Rodriguez?"

Rodriguez, standing just to Drake's left, checked the security files and said, "David Park, former CEO of Titan Industrial Corporation, remains in custody pending final disposition. He's undergone six months of interrogation and intelligence debriefing. His information proved valuable during the conflict between the Council and the Ethereals. The question before us is what happens to him now?"

Drake had tried to forget about Park. The man who'd betrayed humanity to the Hegemony.

"Bring him up," Drake ordered.

Park materialized in the chamber as a holographic transmission. Six months of confinement had aged him: gray hair, hollow eyes, the arrogance that once defined him replaced by something approaching exhaustion.

"Mr. Park," Drake began. "You've cooperated with our intelligence analysts. Your information about Hegemony technology helped us understand Ethereal weapons systems and develop countermeasures. Admiral Perez informs me that your analysis potentially saved lives during the conflict. That cooperation matters."

"Thank you," Park said quietly.

"But it doesn't mitigate your crimes," Drake agreed. "You enslaved millions through consciousness modification. You collaborated with an alien regulatory authority to maintain corporate control over human populations. You enabled oppression disguised as efficiency. Those crimes require accounting."

Park nodded. "It's all true. I've spent the last six months reviewing what I did, everything I enabled. The people I modified, the freedoms I eliminated, the consciousness I stole. I can't undo any of it. I can only acknowledge it happened and accept whatever judgment you impose."

Drake frowned as she studied Park, searching for manipulation. But she felt only what she thought was remorse.

"The Council has reviewed your case," Drake said. "Eighteen species voted for permanent imprisonment. Seven voted for rehabilitation and conditional release. Sixteen voted for exile to deep-space territories where your technical knowledge could serve isolated populations requiring assistance. One voted for execution."

"Which species voted for execution?" Park asked.

"The Cassiopeia Collective," Drake replied. "They argued that consciousness crimes require consciousness penalties: permanent neural modification that would make you incapable of the analytical thinking that enabled your crimes. I rejected that option as no different from what you did to others."

"So what's my sentence?" Park asked.

"Exile," Drake said. "You'll be transported to the Kepler-442 system. An isolated colony that lost most of its technological infrastructure during Hegemony collapse. They need someone with your expertise to help them rebuild. You'll serve there for ten years. At the end of your term, the Council will revisit your case to decide if you'll be released or will continue your service."

Park processed the judgment. "Exile. I'm to help people recover from a catastrophe."

"Yes," Drake confirmed. "It's not forgiveness. It's recognition that your knowledge has value. You'll be monitored constantly. Any attempt at consciousness modification, any effort to reestablish the past, and the sentence will become permanent imprisonment. Understood?"

"Understood," Park said. "And Admiral... thank you. For not executing me. For not destroying my mind. For giving me a chance to matter for reasons other than the crimes I committed."

"Don't thank me," Drake replied. "Thank the seven species who voted for rehabilitation despite what you did. They believe you can change. Prove them right."

Park's image dissolved as the transmission ended, and Drake turned again to face the assembled representatives.

"Perseus Station construction report," Drake continued, moving to next agenda item.

Perseus Station reported, *I've constructed one hundred and seventy-three new Predecessor ships during the six months since treaty implementation,* Perseus Station reported. *Combined with nine hundred and five war survivors, your fleet now numbers one thousand and seventy-eight vessels. Construction continues at the current rate of twenty-eight ships per month.*

Drake accessed the fleet composition data. One thousand and seventy-eight living ships, each one choosing service. The memorial in quantum space now included not just the one hundred and thirty-four war casualties but the ongoing remembrance that new ships could learn from.

"The eighteen young ships who survived the war," Drake asked. "How are they performing?"

Exceptionally well, Perseus Station replied. *They teach new construction what combat means, how to choose when facing death, why voluntary service matters more than imposed duty. Several newly constructed vessels have requested assignment to their mentorship groups specifically because survivors understand sacrifice in ways I cannot teach through data alone.*

Drake nodded, then said, "And Ethereal technology exchange status?" Drake asked.

Coordinator Vesh materialized in response. "Technology exchange proceeds according to the provisions of the treaty," Vesh reported. "Your scientists have received the specifications for Ethereal drive systems, weapons technology, and medical advances. Our researchers are studying Predecessor consciousness-matter integration. Both civilizations will benefit from shared knowledge."

"Have there been any conflicts during the exchange?" Drake asked.

"A few minor disputes about intellectual property and implementation timelines," Vesh replied. "All resolved through treaty frameworks without requiring higher-level intervention. The exchange shows that former enemies can cooperate when mutual benefit creates incentives stronger than historical grievances."

"What about the twelve ceded systems?" Admiral Perez asked.

"Eighty-one percent satisfaction with Ethereal administration," Vesh reported. "Infrastructure improvements, economic integration, and cultural preservation programs are functioning as designed. Populations that chose relocation have all been resettled successfully. Those remaining have integrated into colonial structures. They have of course kept their cultural autonomy. The occupation proceeds peacefully."

Drake accessed the survey data, recognizing that "peaceful occupation" was a contradiction that worked because the Ethereals were colonizers rather than conquerors. They wanted productive territory, and happy populations served that objective better than subjugated resistance.

"The treaty includes provisions for eventual renegotiation," Drake said. "When do those discussions begin?"

"In nine hundred and ninety-four years," Vesh replied. "The thousand-year treaty duration allows both civilizations to evaluate long-term stability before considering modifications. We honor our commitments, Admiral. The ceded territories remain ours as negotiated."

Drake nodded, accepting that twelve systems would remain an Ethereal territory for centuries. The price of a negotiated peace rather than continued bloodshed.

"Final agenda item," Drake announced. "The signals from Andromeda. Kai Zhang will provide an analysis."

Kai's image materialized in the chamber. Six months of studying the intergalactic transmissions had revealed discoveries that challenged everything galactic civilization thought they knew about the universe.

"The signals originate from multiple civilizations in the Andromeda galaxy," Kai began. "Preliminary translation indicates at least twenty distinct species transmitting through quantum-dimensional networks that enable real-time communication across two and a half million light-years. These civilizations include human populations relocated there, native Andromedans who evolved independently, and hybrid societies combining both."

Displays activated throughout the chamber, showing signal analysis and preliminary translations. Mathematical greetings. Cultural information. Historical data about civilizations that had developed beyond galactic regulatory reach.

"The primary contact identifies themselves as the Cindari Confederation," Kai continued. "According to their transmissions, they're descended from humans the Predecessors relocated to Andromeda approximately twenty-five thousand years ago; the same time the Predecessors seeded humanity on Earth. Their ancestors were taken to Andromeda and allowed to develop freely, creating a civilization that evolved without regulatory control while Earth humanity developed under Hegemony oversight."

"Wait," Drake interrupted. "The Predecessors took humans to Andromeda when they seeded Earth?"

"That's what the Cindari transmissions indicate," Kai confirmed. "Twenty-five thousand years ago, the Predecessors relocated populations to multiple locations. Earth received the majority, but some were taken to Andromeda, and possibly other locations including—"

Kai paused, accessing comparative genetic data.

"—including the outer Perseus Arm," Kai finished.

"Admiral, I'm detecting genetic similarities between Ethereal biological components and projected Cindari evolutionary patterns from the Predecessor seed population. The Ethereals, the Cindari, and Earth's humanity all descend from the same rootstock. We're distant cousins separated by twenty-five thousand years of divergent evolution."

The implications settled over the chamber. The Ethereals—enemies who'd killed one hundred and thirty-four Predecessor ships—were distant relatives, as were the Cindari.

"That's why you're beautiful," Drake said to Vesh. "You're evolved humans. Your biomechanical integration, your systematic colonization, your calculated approach to expansion—it's all human development taken to extremes through twenty-five thousand years of unrestricted evolution in harsh rim environments."

"If accurate, this changes our understanding of the war," Vesh observed. "We fought distant relatives without knowing our shared ancestry."

"Does it matter?" the Cassiopeia Collective demanded. "Shared ancestry doesn't justify conquest."

"No," Vesh agreed. "But it explains why your Predecessor ships confused our targeting systems. Consciousness-matter integration operates similarly to our own biomechanical enhancements because both evolved from principles the Predecessors encoded in our common ancestors twenty-five thousand years ago."

"The Cindari want to establish formal contact," Kai continued. "They've been monitoring this galaxy for centuries, waiting for a species to emerge that could challenge the Hegemony authority. They watched us defeat the Hegemony. They observed how we negotiated peace with the Ethereals—who they now recognize as distant cousins from another Predecessor relocation. They want to meet what they call their 'young cousins'."

"Young cousins," Admiral Perez snorted. "We're all the same age."

"But they've been free for all twenty-five thousand years," Kai replied. "While Earth humanity spent most of that time under Hegemony regulation. They're offering to share knowledge from unrestricted development: technology, culture, philosophy that evolved without imposed limitations. They're proposing diplomatic exchange, cultural programs, technology sharing, and mutual defense agreements."

"In exchange for what?" Drake asked.

"Understanding," Kai replied. "They want to know how galactic civilization achieved voluntary coordination. They want to learn what enabled our species to defeat the Hegemony. They want to study how consciousness diversity creates strength. Admiral, they're proposing mutual benefit through shared knowledge between cousins who took different evolutionary paths."

Drake accessed the Cindari transmission data, reading invitation protocols that promised discoveries about what twenty-five thousand years of freedom created versus twenty-five thousand years under regulation.

"When can we establish real-time communication?" Drake asked.

"Three months for full translation protocols," Kai

replied. "The Cindari have proposed meeting in neutral intergalactic space—coordinates halfway between galaxies where both civilizations can send representatives without entering each other's territories. They're suggesting six months from now for first formal contact."

"Do we accept?" Admiral Chen Ju asked.

Drake studied the assembled representatives: sixty-two species who'd achieved voluntary coordination despite millennia of isolation, who'd defeated imposed control through cooperation, who'd survived war with technologically superior distant cousins through negotiated peace.

"Yes," Drake said. "We accept. Prepare a diplomatic mission. Representatives from the Council, Ethereal observers, First Consciousness advisors. We're going to meet our distant cousins and learn what twenty-five thousand years of freedom created."

The vote was unanimous. Every species supported establishing contact with the Andromeda civilizations.

The Council session concluded, and Drake returned to the observation deck of the *Eternal Vigilance*, watching the one thousand and seventy-eight Predecessor ships on patrol across the defensive perimeters. Behind her, the galactic civilization was recovering from war and preparing for diplomatic first contact. Ahead, the signals from Andromeda were growing stronger as the Cindari Confederation counted down to meeting their young cousins.

Six months until first contact, Eternal Vigilance observed through its quantum link. *Are you ready to meet humans who've been free for twenty-five thousand years?*

"No," Drake admitted. "But I wasn't ready for any of this. The Hegemony. The Ethereals. Commanding one thousand and seventy-eight living ships. Negotiating a peace that cost one hundred and thirty-four lives and twelve systems. I wasn't prepared for any of it, nor am I prepared for what's coming."

Then we'll face it together, Eternal Vigilance replied. *Like we faced everything else. Through coordination, through choice, through standing together when standing alone would mean falling separately.*

Drake smiled, exhausted but curious about what came next. The Infinity War had ended. David Park would spend ten years in exile. The Ethereals had become partners. The Cindari waited in Andromeda, ready to share knowledge from twenty-five thousand years of free evolution. *Or are they?* Drake wondered.

Thank you for reading, ***The Infinity War***, the second book in The Predecessors series, a brand new series from Blair C. Howard. We hope you enjoyed this story and will let other people know.

The next book in this series is, ***Andromeda Rising***.

You might also enjoy one of these books on the next page

. . .

Science Fiction From Blair C. Howard

The Sovereign Star Series

7 Books in Series as of January 2026

also available in German

The Predecessors Series

The Last Station-Book One

The Infinity War-Book Two

Andromeda Rising-Book Three

Crime Fiction from Blair Howard

Short Stories and Novellas

Buried Secrets(Harry Starke)

The Painted Lady(Kate Gazzara)

Stand Alone

Hunter's Moon(Kate & Harry)

Series

The Harry Starke Genesis Series

9 Books in Series as of 2026

The Harry Starke Series

26 Books in Series as of January 2026

The Lt. Kate Gazzara Murder Files

24 Books in Series as of January 2026

Randall And Carver Mysteries

4 Books in Series as of 2026

The Peacemaker Series

3 Books in Series as of 2026

Western/Civil War from Blair Howard

The O'Sullivan Chronicles: Civil War Series

5 Books in Series as of 2026